DEATH NOTICE II

FATE

ZHOU HAOHUI

**TRANSLATED FROM THE CHINESE
BY ZAC HALUZA**

HEAD
of ZEUS

First published in the UK by Head of Zeus Ltd in 2020
Originally published in China as *Si wang tong zhi dan: su ming* by Beijing
Times Chinese Press, Beijing, in 2014

Copyright © Zhou Haohui, 2014
English Translation Rights © China Educational Publications Import and
Export Corp., Ltd, 2020

9 7 5 3 1 2 4 6 8

A catalogue record for this book is available from
the British Library.

ISBN (HB): 9781838930806
ISBN (XTPB): 9781838930813
ISBN (E): 9781838930790

Typeset by Siliconchips Services Ltd UK

Printed and bound in Great Britain by
CPI Group (UK) Ltd, Croydon CR0 4YY

Head of Zeus Ltd
5–8 Hardwick Street
London EC1R 4RG
WWW.HEADOFZEUS.COM

DEATH NOTICE II

FATE

Also by Zhou Haohui

Death Notice

CONTENTS

DEATH NOTICE I: THE STORY SO FAR

When Sergeant Zheng Haoming, a well-liked officer in the Chengdu criminal police force, was murdered in his digs on the twenty-first of October 2002, a 'death notice' was found at the scene. The news made ripples across the city and beyond.

Captain Pei Tao of the regional Longzhou police received a mysterious request to attend. He learnt that the late sergeant had been a member of the April 18th Task Force, set up eighteen years prior after a series of murders linked to the Sichuan Police Academy. Captain Han Hao of the Chengdu police ordered the task force reinstated and the investigation into those distant events of the eighteenth of April 1984 began anew. Pei Tao was joined by Captain Han's assistant, Lieutenant Yin, psychologist Ms Mu and Technical Surveillance Officer Zeng. Team member Captain Xiong of Chengdu's special police unit was subsequently killed in the line of duty; he was replaced by SPU Captain Liu.

When prominent businesswoman Ye Shaohong was also murdered, the team discovered that a vigilante called Eumenides (named after the Greek goddess of vengeance) was behind the serving of death notices on her and other figures deemed guilty of unpunished crimes. It seemed Eumenides could not be stopped. In the final showdown on the twenty-fifth of October 2002, the task force was unable to prevent the killing of the powerful Chengdu figure 'Mayor' Deng, despite the best efforts of his bodyguard Brother Hua; Captain Han was even blackmailed into unwittingly murdering the mayor himself.

In the end it was revealed that Pei Tao's former police academy classmate and best friend Yuan Zhibang – long thought dead but actually hiding behind a new identity – had been secretly training a new Eumenides, creating a dark force for administering justice outside the law.

With former police captain Han Hao now on the run and Yuan Zhibang dead by his own hand, the April 18th Task Force needs to quickly find a replacement captain and unmask the new Eumenides before more lives are lost...

CHENGDU POLICE:
CURRENT AND FORMER OFFICERS

Captain Ding Ke – retired captain of the Chengdu criminal police

Captain Han Hao – disgraced former captain of the Chengdu criminal police

Captain Pei Tao – co-opted from Longzhou to serve on the April 18th Task Force for the Chengdu criminal police

Captain Xiong Yuan – former captain of the special police unit (SPU); killed in the line of duty on 24 October 2002

Commissioner Song – commissioner in charge of Chengdu criminal police

Huang Jieyuan – retired former lieutenant in the Chengdu criminal police

Lieutenant Yin Jian – officer of the Chengdu criminal police and member of the April 18th Task Force

Ms Mu Jianyun – psychologist and lecturer at the Sichuan Police Academy

Sergeant Zheng Haoming – former sergeant in the Chengdu criminal police and member of the original April 18th Task Force; murdered on 21 October 2002

SPU Captain Liu Song – captain of Chengdu's special police unit

TSO Zeng Rihua – chief technical surveillance officer for Chengdu criminal police

Vice Commissioner Xue Dalin – former vice commissioner of Chengdu criminal police; murdered on 18 April 1984

CHENGDU POLICE CASES

January 30th, 1984 – the hostage case involving Wen Hongbing and Chen Tianqiao

March 16th, 1984 – the huge drugs bust led by Vice Commissioner Xue Dalin

April 7th, 1984 – the robbery at former hostage Chen Tianqiao's home

April 18th, 1984 – the murder of Vice Commissioner Xue Dalin, and the warehouse explosion that left police academy student Meng Yun dead

January 12th, 1992 – the Bagman Killing

PROLOGUE

24 October 2002, midnight
Outskirts of Chengdu, Sichuan Province

Two men stood in the shadows beside a fetid pool of stinking river water on the outskirts of Chengdu. Heaps of rotting, months-old rubbish gave off a hideous stench. It was usually only the most desperate beggars that ventured out here, but the two men – one considerably younger than the other – had chosen this spot on purpose. They'd been meeting in godforsaken places like this for more than a decade. It ensured they didn't get disturbed. This particular rendezvous, however, felt very different from their previous encounters.

The young man's eyes glittered with excitement, but the older man appeared to be anything but eager. 'You should get going,' he rasped. 'I've already said everything I need to.' The moonlight shimmered dimly as it reflected off the river, illuminating the scars on his disfigured face.

The young man stayed silent for a while, then blurted out, 'Where will we meet next time?'

His question was met with a grating laugh as gruesome as the man's damaged face. 'Why do you ask these unnecessary questions? You know there won't be a next time.'

The young man glanced away. He'd known that this day

would come eventually, but knowing it and confronting it were two very different things.

'Pei Tao's already got wind of my whereabouts. I need to settle things with him once and for all,' the scarred man said. He looked directly into the younger man's eyes. 'You have nothing to fear. You're already more than strong enough to shoulder this responsibility on your own.'

'The path ahead isn't very clear to me,' the young man said softly.

'I understand how you feel. But it's a path you have to take.' His cracked lips parted to reveal a set of bone-white teeth. 'It's your fate – it was set in motion eighteen years ago.'

'But—'

'I'm aware of the urges you have, how much you long to experience those sides of life that I have kept from you. Once I'm gone, you should act on these urges. They'll teach you things that I never could.' The older man turned away swiftly, hiding the tears that welled in his misshapen eyes, and with a pained grunt he hobbled off down the track beside the river.

The young man gazed fixedly at the retreating figure of his mentor. He wanted to rush after him, but he knew that nothing he could say would change his mind. So he stood there watching the scarred man limp away, his mind plagued by the same old thoughts:

Who is he? And who am I?

Why am I here?

The past eighteen years had brought him no closer to resolving these questions. But his mentor's last words had planted a seed of hope. Perhaps it was finally time for him to go and find his answers.

I

THE NEW CAPTAIN

26 October 2002, 9:25 a.m.
The remains of the Jade Garden restaurant

It was already nearly twenty-four hours since the explosion had ripped apart the Jade Garden restaurant, but the air was still thick with the smell of smoke and death.

More than twenty firefighters were combing through the debris, raking over the brick and concrete rubble with their heavy-duty equipment. A handful of white-clothed men flitted among the figures dressed in red. They worked in pairs and carried large black plastic bags. Every now and then they would interrupt the firefighters' work, lift something from the rubble and place it inside their plastic bags. Their stern, unsmiling expressions looked almost like masks.

Xingcheng Road was lined with row after row of towering office blocks. High up inside one of them, the young man stood staring at the ruined restaurant through a telescope. He focused on every detail of the scene unfolding below him and soon realised that the objects the men in white – forensic scientists from the provincial police department – were placing inside their black bags were human remains.

'My mentor…' he murmured to himself. He felt both sad and resentful, but above all he felt profoundly confused.

His mentor had left him. Despite all the assurances that the scarred man had given him two nights prior, it was hard to fight the feeling that his world had been torn apart, just like the restaurant outside the window. Who else but the scarred man, he thought, could answer the questions that gnawed at him?

'*It's a path you have to take,*' his mentor had told him. '*It's your fate.*'

The time had come for him to continue down that path.

28 October, 3:17 p.m.
Thousand Peaks Hotel

The luxurious Thousand Peaks Hotel was located in a busy district of Chengdu. Being a five-star hotel, every one of its thirty-six floors was practically perfect in every detail.

Teacher Wu Yinwu had never seen such opulence in all of his fifty-eight years. He couldn't help but feel overwhelmed at the sight that greeted him as he entered the suite at the top of the hotel. When he gingerly lowered himself onto the astonishingly soft leather sofa, he placed both hands on his knees and carefully sat up straight, as though worried he might damage it.

He was accompanied by three high-school students – two young men and one young woman. It was immediately apparent that these youngsters were what most parents would describe as 'juvenile delinquents'. Although they too marvelled at the plush surroundings, they exhibited none of Teacher Wu's restraint. They tore around the suite, leaping over the furniture and playing with the massive flatscreen TV on the wall.

One of the young men wore a large gold earring in his ear. When he tired of racing around the room, he flung himself onto the sofa next to his teacher. 'Shit, this feels good,' he said with a malevolent chuckle.

'Do be careful, all of you,' Teacher Wu pleaded quietly, but Gold Earring ignored him and focused instead on the other young man, who sported a curly perm and was just then opening the mini fridge on the coffee table.

Gold Earring's eyebrows shot up. 'Hey!' he hollered. 'No hogging all the food for yourself!'

When Curly pulled his head out of the fridge, he was clutching two bottles of beer. He tossed one to Gold Earring, opened the other for himself, tilted it to his lips and took a satisfied sip.

'You shouldn't be helping yourselves like that,' Teacher Wu said, his voice wispier than a strand of cotton. 'It's all got to be paid for, you know.'

'But not by us!' said the young woman, walking over from another corner of the room. 'What's there to worry about?' She had a round, chubby face and dyed red hair.

Curly handed her a beer. 'Care for a swig?'

'Half of it's probably backwash,' Red shot back. She plucked a can of cola from the fridge. As she opened it she smiled and looked over at the older man. 'Want one, Teacher Wu?'

He waved his hand at her. 'No, no, I'm fine.'

Gold Earring sat up straight, extended an arm round Teacher Wu's shoulders and with the other brought his bottle of beer up to the teacher's lips. 'Come on.' He winked. 'Have a drink.'

Teacher Wu pushed the young man's hand away. 'Stop it,' he said angrily. 'I told you, I don't want any.'

'Teacher Wu says he doesn't want any,' Curly said mockingly.

'There's no point forcing him.' He smirked and the other two burst into malicious giggles.

Teacher Wu shifted uncomfortably, feeling nothing short of humiliated, and wondered to himself again why the man hadn't arrived yet.

Once his students had done laughing at him, they too had questions.

'What's going on? Where's the guy who said he'd meet us here?' Gold Earring asked. 'He's not stood you up, has he?'

Curly shot him a nasty look. 'You think this guy would rent us a deluxe room just to stand us up? Use your brain, man.' He took another swig from his bottle.

'Still, there's no need for him to keep us waiting,' Red said with displeasure. 'I already told two friends I met online that I'd hang out with them later. Tell him to hurry up, okay?'

Curly considered this for a moment, then pulled out his mobile and dialled a number. He pressed it to his ear briefly. Then he frowned.

'What is it?' Red asked, hovering over him.

Curly lifted a finger from his bottle and pressed it to his lips. 'Shhh.' His eyes darted to the door of the suite.

The room fell silent and they all heard the faint strains of a melody. It was coming through the unlocked door.

The music stopped. Slowly, the door began to open. As everyone watched in astonishment, a peculiar man came into the suite.

He towered over all of them. His clothing was quite ordinary except for two striking details: he wore a pair of black gauze gloves, and his face was almost entirely hidden behind a ski mask, save for his eyes, which gleamed brightly.

'Who... Who are you?' Teacher Wu asked, slowly rising to his feet.

'I'm the person who asked to meet you.'

The man shut the door. He spoke in a low voice, but his enunciation was crisp and clear.

'What's up with you, bro? Just got out of plastic surgery?' Curly asked, grinning broadly.

Gold Earring and Red laughed.

The man showed no reaction but simply picked up one of the wooden chairs from beside the coffee table and dragged it over to the door, blocking the exit. He sat down on it. His gaze slowly swept across the three teenagers. There was nothing cruel in the way he looked at them, but he had such a forceful presence and his eyes were so piercing and powerful that Curly and the others were silenced straight away.

'Sit down, please,' he said.

Teacher Wu immediately sat down on the sofa. The three teenagers weren't normally inclined to obedience, but on this occasion fear flickered across their faces. None of them was sure why the man's voice had this effect on them, but something about his tone compelled them to do as he'd asked.

Gold Earring and Red hesitated and glanced over at Curly, the de facto leader of their group.

Curly considered the situation. Deciding that he was unwilling to suffer this particular indignity, he stuck his chin out and cleared his throat. 'We agreed to come here on certain conditions. You'll have to make good on those conditions before we do anything else.'

The man raised his right hand. Within it were three scarlet envelopes, the sort used for gifting money on special occasions.

'Here you are.'

His directness gave Curly pause. He waited a moment, then took several steps forward and accepted the envelopes.

'This one is for you. Give that one to the girl and the third one to your other friend,' the man instructed.

Seconds later, all three envelopes were in the hands of their intended recipients. Teacher Wu looked on blankly, struggling to work out what was happening. He had somehow become a mere spectator.

Gold Earring opened his envelope first. Inside was a flimsy piece of paper – clearly not what he'd been hoping to find. When he'd finished reading what it said, he couldn't restrain himself any longer.

'What the hell is this supposed to be?'

Curly was looking at the contents of his own envelope. Several lines of text had been written on the slip of paper inside. The calligraphy was flawless.

Death Notice
THE ACCUSED: Xie Guanlong ('Curly')
CRIME: Humiliating a teacher
DATE OF PUNISHMENT: 28 October
EXECUTIONER: Eumenides

'Is this a fucking joke?' He crumpled the paper into a ball and flung it at the man.

'It's not a joke, no,' the stranger replied icily. 'You're all guilty, as judged by your fellow citizens. My name is Eumenides and I'm your executioner.'

Curly snorted. 'Give me a fucking break. You think putting a ski mask on your head makes you some kind of superhero? Get the hell out of our suite!'

Teacher Wu sprang up from the sofa. Something was very wrong here, he thought. 'Wha... What's going on?' He rushed over to Red and peered at her sheet of paper.

The printed characters quivered in her trembling fingers. Her face was as white as snow. 'This is Eumenides! Don't you know what that means?' she said, her voice tense.

Gold Earring and Curly stared at her, frowning in confusion.

She grabbed Gold Earring by the shoulder. 'He's a murderer. A real live murderer. Last week he killed that woman who ran over a fruit seller in her BMW. It's all over the internet!'

Her panic was contagious. Both her classmates now looked equally stricken. They'd heard about the BMW woman's murder, of course. Could her killer really be the man standing before them?

'On the eleventh of last month, you humiliated your teacher, Mr Wu,' the man said, his voice building from a low murmur to a booming shout. 'Not only that, but you also filmed his humiliation and posted the footage online. Despite being widely condemned on the internet, you haven't shown any contrition. What do you have to say for yourselves?'

Gold Earring's hands were shaking so violently that the piece of paper slid through his fingers. He sidled over to Curly. 'What the hell do we do now?'

'We get out of here,' Curly answered through gritted teeth. 'Screw this guy – let's go.' But there was a flaw in this plan. The exit was still blocked by the man in the chair. If they wanted to leave the room, they'd have to deal with the stranger.

'Get out of my fucking way!' Curly snarled.

'Come here.' The man's soft, almost gentle voice sent shivers down Curly's spine. His bravado disappeared like leaves in the wind.

'No,' Teacher Wu said, planting himself between Curly and their guest. 'Don't listen to him.' He avoided looking the masked man in the eye as he spoke. 'They've already apologised to me. Don't give them any more trouble, I'm begging you.'

The man's face widened in an emotionless grin. 'They've already apologised, you say? I was watching the four of you as you arrived here. I've seen the way they treat you. Can you honestly say that their apologies have changed anything?'

Teacher Wu grimaced. The man was right, of course. The students would never respect him as their teacher. He knew that. What he did not know, however, was that the masked man was still reeling from the death of his own teacher.

The man glared at each teenager in turn. 'There will be no forgiveness for your crimes,' he hissed.

The three students shrank back in alarm.

Wincing, Wu fought his own fear and tried again to mediate. 'Actually, it's not nearly as serious as you think. They're just kids! They were only having fun when they recorded that video. Please, think about what you're doing. I'm their teacher – I'm responsible for them.'

The man shifted his gaze onto Wu. 'You honestly still consider yourself their teacher?' he said sharply. 'Why didn't you think of that when they were wreaking havoc in your classroom? Do you even know what it means to be a teacher?'

Teacher Wu's tongue hung useless in his mouth.

'A teacher should pass on wisdom, impart knowledge and resolve doubts. Look at these students of yours. What have you done for them? Have you imparted anything? Resolved any of their confusion? Your role in your own humiliation is undeniable. I invited you here today because I wanted you to see what happens when you shirk your responsibilities towards your pupils.'

Wu flinched at each rebuke and hung his head in shame. No response came to his lips.

Curly jolted into action. Propelled not by courage but rather by desperation, he pulled out the hatchet he kept stashed in his coat. It was a dead ringer for the axes carried by the gangsters in the Hong Kong action movies so popular with his generation. 'You gonna get out of my way or not?' he yelled. 'If you aren't gonna move, you better get ready for some pain!'

'What are you waiting for?' the man asked with chilling calm.

Curly clenched his jaw and charged at the intruder. He raised his right hand high and plunged the hatchet at the man's neck.

The man reached out with one hand, caught Curly's wrist in mid-air and twisted his hand. Curly doubled over in pain and the hatchet fell to the floor. Pinching his index and middle fingers together, the stranger then gently drew his hand across Curly's neck. The teenager's cries ceased as his eyes widened and his lips trembled.

There was a long, deep wound across the young student's throat. Blood poured from the cut and splattered onto the suite's luxurious carpet. Loath to let the blood stain his own clothing, the man released his left hand and Curly dropped to the floor. The teenager twitched several times and was then motionless.

Red's shriek was ear-piercingly loud, but the man didn't seem worried about being discovered. After all, he'd chosen the suite specifically for its thick, soundproof walls.

Teacher Wu stiffened. He shook himself, as though stirring from a dream. 'You killed him! How could you? Why?' The more he wailed, the frailer his voice became.

The girl retreated to the corner of the room, but Gold Earring saw an opening and sprinted towards the door. To the stranger, however, his movements were laughably slow. Quick as a flash, his left arm shot out and Gold Earring was pressed tight against his chest, as helpless as a child. Slowly, the man raised his right hand in the air.

Teacher Wu crumpled to his knees and began kowtowing on

the floor. His forehead smacked the carpet with one sickening thump after another. 'Please, I'm begging you! Don't kill anyone else!'

The man's right hand froze. 'You don't want me to punish him?'

Still on his knees, Wu crawled towards the man. His voice was choked with tears. 'Please, stop punishing my students. It's all my fault. I failed in my duty as their teacher.' Tears streamed down his face.

The man was silent for a moment. 'Are you willing to amend for your mistakes?'

'I am! I am! Just let my student go.'

The man brushed the tip of his foot across the carpet and the hatchet slid across the floor, coming to a stop a few centimetres from Teacher Wu's knees. 'Cut off your left hand,' the man said coolly.

Wu looked up. 'What?'

'Cut off your left hand,' the man repeated. 'If you do that, I'll let them go.'

'But...' Wu sputtered. A knee gave out and he dropped to the carpet.

'Your choice. I won't force you.'

Gold Earring could see all too clearly the throat-cutting blade clasped between the man's fingers. Terrified, he tried to wrench himself out of the man's grip, but his body was too traumatised to manage it. He shot his teacher a pleading look and strained to speak through the vice-like pressure on his neck.

'Please...'

'Just give me a second.' Teacher Wu raised his hand to quiet his pupil. Steeling himself with a few quick breaths, he picked the hatchet up off the floor. It looked as sharp as a butcher's knife.

The man's eyes glittered with anticipation.

The teacher let out a savage, wordless cry, raised the hatchet and held the blade over his left wrist.

His cry faded to a crackling rasp. He gasped for breath and slowly lowered the hatchet to the floor. His wrist remained untouched.

The stranger shook his head in disappointment. His right hand glided across Gold Earring's neck and the young man instantly met the same fate as Curly. His body fell to the floor, his startled eyes gaping at Wu. The teacher toppled back onto the carpet in a daze, as though someone had clubbed him over the head.

Seconds later, Red's scream tore Wu out of his nightmarish trance. He watched as the man approached the last remaining student in the room and yanked the girl up by her flame-coloured hair. She had all but lost the courage to fight back. Her voice was choked with sobs as she pleaded, 'Please, Teacher Wu, help me.'

Wu let out another wild cry. This time he was truly unhinged. The hatchet rose and came driving back down with the speed of a bullet. His strike was as precise as it was forceful: it severed his hand in one clean blow.

The man let go of the girl. He stepped aside and she rushed over to her teacher. Her tears had ceased – she was too overwhelmed by the shock to even cry.

Teacher Wu had wrapped his sleeve tightly around his stump of a wrist to try and stem the bleeding. Whimpering, he fought through the pain. His gaze was fixed on the man and his eyes glowed with steely resolve.

'Teacher Wu! Teacher Wu!' The girl began sobbing again. She picked up his severed hand from the floor and held it close to her chest.

Wu felt an emotion that was utterly unfamiliar to him, something he had never felt before. Pride.

The man nodded approvingly at him. He glanced at the hatchet, his gaze lingering on its bloody blade, inhaled deeply, then narrowed his eyes at the young woman. 'I've carried out each of your sentences,' he said. 'Even though you're still alive, you have in a sense already died once today. From now on, you'll have a quite different understanding of what it means to be alive.'

He fixed his piercing eyes on Wu. 'As for you, you've finally found the bravery and dedication required of a teacher.'

7:35 p.m.
Chengdu railway station

A newscaster's voice blared out from the TV screen at the train station. 'Following the initial investigation into the explosion on Xingcheng Road on Friday, we now have a basic understanding of what happened. This was an act of terrorism. The explosion resulted in the deaths of two people, but there were no further casualties. One of the individuals killed was Guo Meiran, the owner of the Jade Garden restaurant. The other was Yuan Zhibang, the perpetrator of the explosion. The police have revealed that Yuan was behind another fatal explosion in Chengdu eighteen years ago that killed two people. The police believe that Yuan is the serial killer known by the name Eumenides, the individual behind several murders here in Chengdu, including that of businesswoman Ye Shaohong, whose death has incited heated debate both online and in the media.'

Captain Pei Tao let out a low sigh. Shaking his head, he removed himself from the crowd surrounding the television and made his way towards the ticket-inspection gate. Just as he was reaching for his ticket, he heard a voice behind him.

'Just a moment, Captain Pei.'

When he turned around, he was surprised to see the striking figure of the psychologist Ms Mu. She was several metres away but approaching quickly, and she had two police officers with her. The one on the left, sporting glasses and a tousled mess of hair, was the Chengdu police force's top computer expert, Technical Surveillance Officer Zeng Rihua. His companion, Lieutenant Yin Jian – of average height and with a bookish air – had, until yesterday, been Captain Han Hao's assistant. Together with Pei, these three officers comprised the April 18th Task Force, which had been convened with the explicit purpose of stopping Eumenides.

'Captain Pei,' said Ms Mu, 'you can't leave Chengdu.'

'Why not?' he snapped.

'We haven't completed our assignment,' TSO Zeng said with a grimace. 'Yuan Zhibang may be dead, but his apprentice is still out there. And the new Eumenides isn't going to stop killing. I'd like to see how the news anchors explain themselves when his next murder comes to light.'

Pei hesitated momentarily then shook his head. 'I'm aware of all that, but I can't stay here. I have to get back to Longzhou. I only requested one week's leave before I came to Chengdu and there's a lot of work waiting for me back there.'

TSO Zeng snickered. 'That's already been taken care of.'

Lieutenant Yin opened his messenger bag and removed a piece of paper that had been neatly folded into quarters. With a solemn expression, he handed it to Pei, who unfolded it.

Two words were printed at the top of the paper in thick black ink: *Transfer Order*. Pei read on.

Acting upon the urgent recommendation of the leadership of the Chengdu Criminal Police and the approval of the Provincial Department of Public Security, the Longzhou Police Department has agreed to transfer Captain Pei Tao to the Chengdu Criminal Police Force, where he will assume the roles of Captain of Criminal Police and full-time Leader of the April 18th Task Force until further notice. The Sichuan Provincial Department of Public Security will select a suitable candidate to temporarily fill the post of the above-mentioned officer from within the province.

Pei's eyebrows twitched. Lieutenant Yin, meanwhile, was already saluting him.

'Captain!'

Once he had refolded the transfer order, Pei rubbed his jaw thoughtfully. 'This is... Well, it's all a little sudden, isn't it?'

'The order wouldn't have been issued so quickly if Commissioner Song hadn't pushed for it,' Lieutenant Yin explained. 'The commissioner wants to see you as soon as possible. He wants to keep the investigation moving.'

8:47 p.m.
Interrogation room, Chengdu criminal police headquarters

Lieutenant Yin's stomach churned as he entered the interrogation room. Without a doubt, this was going to be the most difficult interrogation he had ever conducted.

The officer on duty strode over to him. 'You took your time,' he whispered. 'Go ahead and take over for me. I'm not cut out for this kind of work.'

'What do you mean?' hissed Lieutenant Yin.

'He won't say anything except that he's waiting for you.'

Lieutenant Yin nodded. 'I see. Consider yourself relieved.'

The officer exhaled loudly and left. Lieutenant Yin sat down in the newly vacated chair. The man on the other side of the table watched him with bloodshot eyes.

'Captain...' Lieutenant Yin said hesitantly, at a loss as to how to begin.

'Why are you still calling me "captain"?' sneered Han Hao, disgraced former leader of the April 18th Task Force. 'Have you forgotten what I taught you? When conducting an interrogation, do everything you can to remind the suspect of your power and authority and their lack of it. Otherwise you can forget about getting any results.'

'Captain... Han...' No matter how hard he tried, Lieutenant Yin couldn't bring himself to call his erstwhile superior officer by any other name. Casting aside all pretences of authority, he began to plead. 'Stop making this so hard for us. Tell us the truth about what happened.'

Han tensed at Lieutenant Yin's sudden change in attitude. After a pause, he asked, 'What took you so long?'

'We've had some internal adjustments...' Lieutenant Yin took a breath, then decided that there would be no harm in telling the truth. 'There's been a change in personnel. Pei Tao has been made the acting captain of the criminal police and the head of the task force.'

Just days earlier, Pei Tao had been one of Han's prime suspects. Now Pei had taken his old job and it was Han himself who was behind bars. The irony was not lost on him. He gave the lieutenant a bitter smile. 'When does it become official?'

'The transfer order has already been issued. I presume he'll officially become acting captain tomorrow.'

'Excellent.' Han shut his eyes and sighed. 'Just in time for him to interrogate me. And settle a few scores, no doubt.'

'Don't drag this out until then, Captain. Just tell us what we want to know. You're still a cop, regardless of which side of the table you're on. When it comes down to it, we all want the same thing.'

They both fell silent. Finally, Han shook his head. 'Not today. I'm too exhausted. I need some time to rest.'

'All right.' Lieutenant Yin glanced at the two officers flanking him. 'Take Captain Han back to his cell.'

As the younger officer handcuffed Han, he paused. 'We still need to, um, check the items on your person.'

Han stood up and raised his arms, allowing the officer to remove his keys, ID card, wallet, mobile phone and other miscellaneous items from his pockets. But when the officer reached for the pendant around his neck, Han shook his head.

'I'd prefer it if you didn't take that. There's a photo of my son inside,' he explained.

The officer shot Lieutenant Yin an inquiring look.

'Open it,' the lieutenant said, eyeing the copper pendant.

The officer did as he was told. There was nothing unusual about the pendant's appearance or weight. When opened, it revealed a photograph framed behind a thin layer of Plexiglas. The picture showed the beaming face of a boy who appeared to be seven or eight years old. Lieutenant Yin felt a pang of sympathy for Han. It was a face that would make any father smile.

'Let him keep it,' he said.

9:03 p.m.
The Green Spring

He sat by himself, his features shielded by a cap pulled low over his face.

Every time he fulfilled one of his notices, he treated himself to a delicious meal. It was a tradition that he'd started last month and one he planned to continue. Lately he'd become rather fond of Huaiyang cooking, the famously refined cuisine of eastern China. Its emphasis on subtly sweet flavours and its avoidance of the spiciness of Sichuan cooking appealed to his sensibilities. In his view, it truly deserved its status as one of the Four Great Traditions of Chinese cuisine.

The Green Spring served the best Huaiyang food in all of Chengdu. It was an upscale restaurant, with prices that matched the quality of the artwork on its walls. Its customers came from the uppermost echelons of society and the entire dining experience was extremely elegant.

Whenever he ate there, he sat at the most out of the way table he could find, in a spot that afforded a clear view of his surroundings. No matter his environment, it was imperative that he occupy a strategic position.

Soft lighting illuminated the charming sketches of bamboo that covered the wallpaper. He glanced down at the tableware set before him and noted the sophisticated design of each piece. His lips twitched into the shadow of a smile. Here, his mind was at ease.

There was only one thing at the Green Spring that he enjoyed more than its exquisite cuisine and that was the music. In the middle of the restaurant was a circular pool six metres in diameter, surrounded by delicately painted landscapes, and in the middle of the pool there was a stage.

The young man scheduled his visits to this restaurant to coincide with the nightly violin performance at nine o'clock and a quick glance at his watch revealed that it was time.

The performer, a young woman, emerged. As she worked her instrument, her graceful features were taut with concentration. Raven hair cascaded over her shoulders and a white blouse clung to her lovely figure above a long emerald skirt. She swayed above the stage like a pale lotus over a lake.

He wasn't sure why he enjoyed her music so much, but he knew how it made him feel. It transported him far from the city, to a sea of tantalisingly unfamiliar emotions.

When the young woman had finished her first piece, he summoned a waiter. 'Give the violinist a bouquet of your best lilies and charge it to my bill.'

The waiter bowed. 'Yes, sir. Would you like to include a message?'

He shook his head. 'Give them to her anonymously.'

'Of course, sir.' With another bow, the waiter left.

When she'd finished playing her next piece, a restaurant employee approached the stage holding a bouquet of lilies. As the young woman accepted the flowers, she raised them to her nose, sniffed and gave a low bow to the audience.

As she did so, she opened her eyes. He met her gaze and, against his better judgement, found himself willing her to notice him. Even so, he knew she wouldn't spot him. Her sightless eyes could not even see the flowers clutched in her hands.

29 October, 8 a.m.
Conference room, Chengdu criminal police headquarters

The members of the April 18th Task Force had gathered in the police conference room once again. Their collective attention was currently focused on the video playing on the room's projector screen.

The video appeared to have been filmed with a handheld camcorder. The quality was poor and shaky, and it was rather brief at only four minutes and fifty-five seconds.

'Now this is what I call fucking geography,' a male student said to camera. A gold hoop hung from one of his ears.

The camera pulled back, and the task force realised they were looking at the inside of a classroom. An older teacher in a white cap was standing on the dais at the front of the room, absorbed in the lecture he was giving to his two dozen students. The students, however, were doing anything but paying attention. Some had fallen asleep on their desks, while others were chatting loudly among themselves. A few were making gestures at the camera.

Seconds later, a young man with curly platinum hair let out a whoop. 'And now,' he proclaimed, 'let's welcome Xie Guanlong to the stage!'

The student with the gold earring shot out of his seat, sprinted towards the platform and snatched the hat from his teacher's head. The teacher stared at him in silence, his face red with embarrassment. The student spun the hat twice around his index finger, then placed it back on his teacher's head. He returned to his seat, smiling and waving at the camera.

The teacher continued standing there, flushed and humiliated. A few seconds passed and he resumed his lecture, but his voice was drowned out by loud insults and horseplay from his students. The camera followed the student with the gold earring as he raced around the room. Other students rose from their seats and joined in the chaos. In a matter of seconds, a storm of laughter and expletives was pouring through the conference room's speakers.

About a minute later, the teenager with the gold earring returned to the stage at the front of the class. He attempted to flick his teacher's cheek, but this time the teacher stepped out of the way.

'Don't distract your classmates,' the teacher said in a lifeless monotone.

The camera turned and the curly-haired student now faced the lens. 'This guy's an idiot. Exhibit one.' He leant back and tossed a half-full bottle of water. It soared towards the platform and struck it with a violent thump, scattering the teacher's notes to the floor.

'Behave yourselves,' the teacher squeaked.

The camera spun around to reveal the face of a plump teenage girl. 'You see that?' she asked. 'This is *our* class. We run this place.'

The screen went dark and the members of the task force shook their heads in silence.

Despite having already viewed the recording in preparation for the meeting, Pei was fuming. He was all too familiar with that type of behaviour – he'd sat next to students just like them, year in, year out. Even though he knew what Eumenides had done to them, a disturbing thought prodded at the edge of his consciousness. *They deserved it.*

'Lieutenant Yin, fill in the rest of the team,' he said to his new assistant.

Lieutenant Yin nodded and picked up several neatly stacked

sheets of paper. 'First, let me tell you about the circumstances surrounding this video,' he began. 'It was shot on the eleventh of September, a little over a month ago, at a vocational high school. The students were all seniors. The girl who shot the video – the red-haired one who spoke to camera right at the end – uploaded it to one of her social-media accounts two days later. It soon went viral. Most people online were enraged by what they saw; they started demanding that the three students be punished for humiliating their teacher. It wasn't long before the story leaked from the internet into the real world. The media then reported that a large group of individuals had shown up at the vocational school's entrance and refused to allow those students in. Finally, the pressure got too much for the trio and they apologised to their teacher. Teacher Wu did not press charges as he wanted the scandal to blow over as soon as possible. His employers thought differently, however. Two weeks later, the school forced Teacher Wu to resign.'

Ms Mu seemed shocked. 'They punished the teacher instead of disciplining their own students?' she said.

Lieutenant Yin shrugged and shook his head. 'A lot of vocational schools are primarily concerned with how much money they can bring in. Since parents keep these schools in business, the students reign supreme. As for the teachers, they're replaceable.'

'And they call that education?' she said angrily.

Pei was surprised at her reaction and wondered why she seemed to be taking it so personally. Then he remembered that before joining the April 18th Task Force she'd been a lecturer at the Sichuan Police Academy. 'If the school doesn't respect the teachers,' he said, 'why would the students? No wonder they played up.'

Lieutenant Yin nodded in agreement. 'A lot of people were

furious about that, just like you. When Eumenides started collecting the names of potential victims online, these three students were some of the most frequent suggestions.'

Pei looked up sharply. 'If they were mentioned so often on that thread, why didn't I know about them until after two of them had been killed?'

Lieutenant Yin gulped and stared down at the table.

TSO Zeng chipped in. 'We started keeping track of the replies to Eumenides' manifesto with the intention of gathering more leads. But after he killed that hit-and-run BMW driver, the number of views and replies that post received shot through the roof. It currently has more than forty thousand replies. Even sorting that thread by the names most frequently mentioned would leave us with hundreds of people to monitor. We simply don't have the resources.'

'We all know how important Yuan Zhibang was to Eumenides,' Ms Mu interjected. 'His teacher and mentor. No matter how cold and calculating Eumenides may seem, he would have been hit hard by Yuan's death in the Jade Garden explosion. These three students would have stood out to him as top candidates for his next death notices.'

TSO Zeng nodded. 'Okay, okay. I may have overlooked that. I appreciate your attention to detail.'

Ms Mu nodded and turned back to the screen.

'Good point, Ms Mu,' Pei said. 'Now, let's talk about what happened at the hotel.'

Lieutenant Yin stood up and fiddled with the projector, and a gory image filled the screen. Two bodies lay sprawled on the floor of a luxurious hotel room. The green carpet around them was stained with dark, matted patches that looked like ghastly shadows.

'These murders took place at the Thousand Peaks Hotel. The victims, Xie Guanlong and Yan Wang, were the same two male students who featured so prominently in the recording we just watched. They were killed in an identical manner to the BMW driver – their throats were slashed. Three death notices were found at the scene. The format and writing were exactly the same as the ones previously left by Eumenides.'

'Three death notices?' TSO Zeng said. 'But weren't there only two victims?'

'The young woman also received a death notice, but she survived. The murderer forced Teacher Wu to chop off one of his own hands in exchange for her life.'

TSO Zeng raked his fingers through his dishevelled hair. 'That doesn't sound like Eumenides at all.'

'Exactly. We're trying to work out why he made that decision. Unfortunately, the two surviving witnesses from that day are currently in no condition to undergo police questioning. Mentally, the girl is in a fragile state. Understandable, considering the trauma she suffered in the hotel. As for Wu, he had surgery last night, but he's still under observation.'

'Tell the team everything we know about how Eumenides carried out these murders,' Pei prompted.

Lieutenant Yin continued. 'Posing as a reporter, Eumenides contacted the three students and Teacher Wu, pretending that he wanted to do a joint interview with all four of them. As an incentive, he offered each of them a sizeable fee, and he also promised to use his connections to get Teacher Wu his job back. Needless to say, all four agreed to the conditions.

'After depositing two thousand yuan in Teacher Wu's bank account, Eumenides asked him to reserve a suite at the Thousand Peaks Hotel for the twenty-eighth of October. Teacher Wu complied and he and his three students duly arrived at the hotel at the appointed time. Not long after, Eumenides knocked on their door.'

'Sounds like a watertight operation,' TSO Zeng said with a shrug. 'I have to give him credit for one thing: he's a good planner. Did he leave any trace evidence at the hotel?'

'Nothing,' Lieutenant Yin said, his frustration obvious. 'We searched the room but found no fingerprints, footprints, hair or anything else. The hotel staff couldn't even provide us with a description. He entered the room wearing gloves, plastic covers over his shoes, and a ski mask. He also managed to evade the hotel's surveillance cameras – his back is all that's visible in the security footage.'

TSO Zeng threw up his hands. 'Isn't that just great!'

Ms Mu looked around the table, surprised at all the pessimistic expressions. 'But we have two witnesses who saw the murders with their own eyes,' she said. 'They were looking right at Eumenides.'

Pei's face brightened. 'That's exactly what we should be focusing on. Ms Mu, we need you to follow up on this lead.'

'That young woman, you mean?'

'I want you to evaluate her psychological condition,' Pei said, nodding. 'If she's stable enough, ask her to describe exactly what she witnessed. You're the expert, so I'll leave the details to your discretion. Just give me your report once you're done.'

'Of course, sir.'

Pei turned to Lieutenant Yin. 'I want you to get in touch with the hospital regarding Teacher Wu. If his physical condition permits it, arrange a time for me to meet him as soon as possible.'

'Yes, sir.'

TSO Zeng stretched lazily in his seat. 'And I'll just stay here twiddling my thumbs, shall I?'

'Of course not,' Pei said, shaking his head. 'I have an important task for you. I want you to search all available databases for records of lost, orphaned or homeless children aged seven to thirteen between the years 1985 and 1992. I don't care how you find them, I just want to see your report. Do I make myself understood?'

TSO Zeng suddenly looked fully alert. 'You want me to search for Eumenides,' he said.

'That's right. When Yuan Zhibang chose his successor, he would have looked for a child that society had long since forgotten about. A child young enough for Yuan to mould but old enough to survive without him having to be constantly at the boy's side. So somewhere between seven and thirteen, I'd say.' Pei grimaced. 'It took more than six months of hospital treatment after the April 18th explosion until Yuan was deemed fit enough to be released from hospital – scars and disfigurements notwithstanding. He came out in January 1985. We'll assume that he began searching for a successor immediately after that. And judging by what we've seen of the young Eumenides' skills thus far, he's got to have been in training for at least a decade. All of which means that Yuan couldn't have found his new apprentice any later than 1992.'

TSO Zeng clapped his hands. 'Sound logic, Captain. But it's going to take a bit of effort to cover a timespan like that. You're asking me to sift through almost a decade's worth of records. I mean, I might actually break a sweat.'

'I need results, TSO Zeng, not excuses. Now, does anyone else have any questions?' Pei glanced around the room. None of the others spoke up, so he got to his feet. 'That concludes this meeting then. You all have your instructions.'

Lieutenant Yin stood up as well. 'Captain, about Han…'

'I wanted to talk to you about that,' Pei said. He glanced at his watch. 'We'll interview him together, at ten o'clock.'

2

UNDERCURRENTS

8:30 a.m.
The Longyu Building

A meeting was taking place inside the headquarters of the Longyu Corporation. All twelve participants were in mourning attire and their faces were even more sombre than their outfits.

The middle-aged woman in the centre seat kept her head low as she wiped away tears. A young boy was nestled against her, his eyes large with terror and incomprehension.

Mayor Deng was dead, but his spirit loomed large.

The late businessman's bodyguards were standing beside the widow and her son. Two middle-aged men sat across from her. One was overweight, the other thin. The plumper of the two was attempting to comfort Mayor Deng's widow with kindly, optimistic comments. His cheeks sagged with excess skin, giving him the appearance of a chronically depressed basset hound.

Mrs Deng soon stopped sobbing and looked up at the plump man. 'That's enough, Vice President Lin. I understand what you're saying. No matter what happens, things will eventually get better. If you have anything significant to say, I'd like to hear it now.'

'Well...' Vice President Lin stammered uncertainly.

The thin man, his voice as cold as the expression on his face, interjected. 'Allow me, Vice President Lin. Following Mayor Deng's untimely demise, you, Mrs Deng, have become the Longyu Corporation's majority shareholder. We've invited the board of directors here for a very important reason. We need to decide on potential candidates for the position of president of the company.'

'But, Vice President Meng,' Mrs Deng murmured, 'isn't this... a little soon?'

Vice President Lin shook his flabby jowls and sighed. 'We haven't even held Mayor Deng's funeral procession yet. I must confess that it does feel rather improper to be bringing this up at this time. But the Longyu Corporation simply cannot continue operating without someone at the helm. Not least given that bidding for the Songhua property is to begin shortly.'

'If only my husband were still here,' Mrs Deng said, sniffing back her sobs.

'Indeed,' Vice President Lin agreed. 'If Mayor Deng were still in charge, a successful bid would be a foregone conclusion. We cannot let an opportunity like this slip through our fingers. Unless a capable individual takes charge of the company now, I'm afraid the outlook may not be so rosy.'

'So you agree, Lin?' Meng turned his gaze on the woman. 'Mrs Deng, is there anything you would like to say regarding this matter?'

'I...' She turned towards Brother Hua, her late husband's bodyguard, and gave him a pleading look. But Brother Hua kept his features emotionless and said nothing. Left with no other option, she forced a smile. 'I'm not a businessperson. I simply married one. What advice could I possibly have to offer?'

'Very well, then.' Vice President Meng finally allowed himself a smile; his tightly stretched skin wrinkled around the edges of his face. He picked up a file and placed it in the centre of the table. 'We've already drawn up the documents that will confirm the appointment of our new president. This will officially come into effect once the shareholders have signed it.'

Sheng, the bodyguard standing on the other side of Mrs Deng, scowled at him. 'You don't fool me, Vice President Meng. It's obvious you all conspired together to draft this document. Don't sign it, Mrs Deng!'

Vice President Meng glared at Sheng, who licked his lips and visibly recoiled.

'Remember your position, Sheng,' said Brother Hua, the senior bodyguard. 'You think you have any say in this matter?'

Like a reprimanded dog, Sheng obediently lowered his head.

Vice President Lin looked at Brother Hua and chuckled. 'After all the years you spent at Mayor Deng's side, you have a stake in the company too. By all means, speak your mind!'

'I have no interest in this,' Brother Hua said quietly. 'All I care about is finding that man.'

The room fell quiet.

'Regardless of what happens today,' Brother Hua went on, 'I don't want to see the Longyu Corporation tear itself apart from the inside. This is no occasion for schemes and power grabs. If we can't stand united at a time like this, I can assure you this company will be finished a year from now.'

Vice President Lin and Vice President Meng both shivered.

9:30 a.m.
Criminal police headquarters

Lieutenant Yin was standing outside Captain Han's holding cell. 'Bring him out,' he said to the officer on duty.

The officer opened the thick iron door and walked over to Han's camp bed. 'Han...' he began, but before he could say another word, Han had sprung up and hurried over to Lieutenant Yin, stony-faced and silent. He practically led the way to the interrogation room himself. After all, in his time as police captain, he'd walked countless criminals down that same route.

Once they'd reached the main office area, he stopped and turned to Lieutenant Yin. 'My stomach's acting up. I need to use the bathroom.'

Lieutenant Yin frowned. 'Why didn't you use the toilet in your cell?'

'You expect me to go like a common criminal? I've had enough humiliation for one day, Lieutenant Yin.' He glared at him, and the young officer buckled.

Lieutenant Yin and another officer accompanied Han to the bathroom. Once Han was inside a cubicle, the officer unlocked the cuff from his own right hand and relocked it over a nearby pipe. Then he and Lieutenant Yin waited outside the bathroom.

Han knew the building like the back of his hand. Naturally, he was aware of the eighty-square-centimetre opening in the ceiling above him, which was used for inspecting the pipes. He also knew that this opening led directly to the sewer behind the building's southern wall.

He pinged open his pendant and retrieved the length of wire from behind his son's photograph. Within seconds, he'd snapped open the cuff around his left hand.

Several minutes later

Lieutenant Yin knocked on the cubicle door. 'Captain? Captain Han?'

There was no answer.

Lieutenant Yin's brow creased. He lowered himself to the

floor and peeked under the cubicle door. There was nothing there except the base of the toilet.

He jumped up and kicked the door open. The cubicle was empty save for the pair of handcuffs still swaying gently from the pipe.

Captain Pei was there within minutes. He stared in disbelief at the cubicle, then spun round to face Lieutenant Yin, eyes blazing.

'How were these cuffs opened?'

'I… I don't know,' Lieutenant Yin stammered.

'Did he have something on his person? Did you even search him?'

'Just a pendant,' Lieutenant Yin said, forcing each word out from the pit of his stomach. 'There was a photo of his son inside.'

Pei shook his head and muttered under his breath. He crouched down and picked up something off the floor of the adjacent cubicle.

'This one?' He held the object in his fingers out to Lieutenant Yin. It was a small photograph of Han's smiling son.

Lieutenant Yin's face went pale. He nodded.

Rather than rebuke him, Pei immediately began barking out orders. 'We need to move as fast as possible. Alert all transport stations and ports within a ten-kilometre radius and monitor his friends and family members. Han has no money on him and no phone – he can't have got far.'

Lieutenant Yin stared blankly at the captain.

'Lieutenant Yin!' Pei bellowed, thumping him on the shoulder.

The lieutenant gave a start. 'You mean me?' he asked, stirring to attention.

'Who else would I be talking to?' Pei said incredulously.

'Yes, sir!' Lieutenant Yin exclaimed, his face flushing red. He snapped Pei a crisp salute and marched away.

2:26 p.m.

When Ms Mu returned to police headquarters, she headed straight to Captain Pei's office to submit her report.

'The girl's mental state has already stabilised quite a bit,' she told him. 'But her recollection of the details of the murders is rather fuzzy. That's not unusual for someone who's been through such a traumatic experience.'

Pei detected something in Ms Mu's voice. 'Give it to me straight,' he said. 'What have you learnt?'

Ms Mu smirked. 'During the meeting earlier, there was some confusion as to why the young woman survived despite having received a death notice. Well, now I know why Eumenides spared her. Before leaving the hotel room, he told her that in a sense she had already died.'

'A metaphor, I take it?'

'Think about what she'd just witnessed, Captain. Two of her close friends were murdered in front of her. Her teacher cut off his own hand to save her. In Eumenides' mind, this was her punishment, just meted out in a different way.'

Pei considered this. 'It doesn't sound like his usual style,' he said finally.

'It's also the first time he's acted entirely alone. We can presume that this change in methodology is just one example of how the master and apprentice versions of Eumenides differ. Given the right circumstances, this new Eumenides seems capable of one thing his predecessor lacked – forgiveness.'

'An excellent analysis.' Pei stroked the stubble on his cheek. 'Go and take a break – you've earned one. And then meet me at five; it's about time we paid Teacher Wu a visit.'

'You think he's ready to see us?'

'According to the doctors, the operation to reattach his

hand was successful. And considering his age, as well as the fact that Eumenides never directly threatened his life, his mental state should be more stable than the girl's. With a bit of luck we'll be able to pick up a new lead or two.'

'Are you sure about that? It may not go the way you hope.'

'What do you mean?' Pei asked, surprised.

'Firstly, let's not forget that the man was forced to chop off his own hand,' Ms Mu began. 'Secondly, Teacher Wu is far from what you'd call the epitome of bravery. His co-workers have generally described him as quite timid. Remember how he acted in the video? So, in my view, him saving the girl's life could have produced one of two outcomes. Either he's had a personal breakthrough and shed his former cowardice or he's become even more down on himself for having failed to protect the lives of two of his own students.' She shook her head. 'If it turns out to be the latter, we really will have our work cut out for us.'

'Let's hope it's the former then.'

'What about Lieutenant Yin? Isn't he responsible for getting in touch with Teacher Wu?'

'You haven't heard? Captain Han escaped!'

'What?' The blood drained from Ms Mu's face.

'Lieutenant Yin's currently in charge of the search for him. I've been helping him coordinate it when I've had the time.'

'Have we located him yet?'

Pei massaged his temples. Fatigue was finally catching up with him. 'We haven't made any progress yet. It's all taking far too long – I'm worried that Han might have already made it out of the city.'

Surprisingly, Ms Mu smiled. 'Han won't leave Chengdu.'

Pei's eyebrows shot up. 'Why not?'

'Because Eumenides is still here. Captain Han's not the kind of person to give up on a grudge. And after what Eumenides did to him, do you think Han would let him go that easily?'

Pei nodded and silently berated himself for having failed to realise this earlier.

'I recommend you keep an eye on Han's family,' she continued. 'Han's not very good at controlling his emotions, as I'm sure you've experienced firsthand.'

Pei thought back to the photo he'd found in the bathroom. 'Yes, and I know who he's going to make contact with first.'

4:09 p.m.
Chengdu PSB archives

Without a doubt, it was the loneliest office in the whole city. The archives of Chengdu's public security bureau were not housed within the actual PSB building but were instead tucked into the northeast corner of the building that contained the municipal archives. The entire staff consisted of just one employee. The lone receptionist sat at the desk at the end of the room.

Due to a recent reduction in funding, the PSB had been forced to hire a temp as a receptionist. It was Ms Zhu's second week in the job and at this particular moment she was filing her nails in what seemed to be a futile effort to keep herself from falling asleep with boredom.

Something was blocking her light. Ms Zhu looked up and saw a man standing on the other side of her desk. She gasped. 'You scared me half to death! I didn't even hear you come in.'

The man's forehead was furrowed as though he was in pain. He covered his mouth with a handkerchief and coughed twice. 'The sign says that visitors are supposed to stay quiet,' he rasped.

'You've got a cold, huh? I've only just got rid of one myself.'

She extended her right hand and the man passed her a PSB identity card. When she ran it through the reader, a police officer's face appeared on the screen, along with several lines of biographical information. *Xu Zhankun, Dongcheng Substation*, the screen read.

As she looked up to compare the man's features to those in the image, he sneezed. Despite the handkerchief he held in front of his mouth, Ms Zhu still felt flecks of saliva spatter against her face. She recoiled in disgust.

'Sorry!' he said. Turning to one side, he sneezed a second time.

Ms Zhu tossed the card back at him and gestured hurriedly towards the door. 'Go ahead,' she said, wiping her face with the sleeve of her other arm. She had no desire to catch another cold, especially not so soon after her last one.

Ten minutes later, Officer Xu emerged from the archive room with a stack of folders in his hands. 'It would be great if you could make copies of these for me,' he said, still holding the handkerchief over his mouth.

As Ms Zhu took his paperwork, she experienced a newfound loathing for the archive's policy prohibiting the removal of any original documents from the building. This man had picked out a dozen or so folders. Altogether she would have to copy several hundred pages.

Nearly twenty minutes later, Ms Zhu placed the still warm stack of papers onto the desk, along with a printed list of the copied materials.

'Seventy-nine yuan for the copies. Sign at the bottom, please.'

The man handed her several crisp bills and signed his name. She studied his signature curiously. If she hadn't seen him physically sign it, she would have sworn that the characters had been printed by machine.

She glanced up to get a better look at the man, but he was already striding out through the exit.

7:02 p.m.

After receiving a high-level report from the PSB archives centre, Captain Pei was forced to alter his original plan to accompany Ms Mu to the hospital.

At around three o'clock that afternoon, a police officer from the Dongcheng substation named Xu Zhankun had been ambushed in the street by an unidentified individual while conducting a plainclothes investigation. Subsequent analysis revealed that Officer Xu had been injected with triazolam, a sedative typically used to treat severe insomnia. Xu reported the ambush to his superiors immediately upon awakening and initially believed it to be related to another investigation. When he returned to his station's cafeteria at approximately six o'clock that evening, he discovered that his ID card was missing. Only then did he begin to suspect his attacker's true motive.

Armed with this information, TSO Zeng had tracked down the card's recent activity and discovered that someone had used it to retrieve a large number of documents from the PSB archives that afternoon. But it was the card-bearer's signature that really shocked TSO Zeng. Those perfectly defined characters... They were uncannily similar to the handwriting on the death notices.

Captain Pei and TSO Zeng immediately rushed over to the archives, where they met with Officer Xu and with Ms Zhu, the receptionist who'd been on duty in the afternoon.

Since Officer Xu had been ambushed from behind in an out-of-the-way area, he was unable to be of much help. Ms Zhu, on the other hand, could at least report that the man in question had been rather tall. She was unable to describe the rest of his physical appearance, due to the large handkerchief that he had used to cover most of his face.

Pei held up the files that Eumenides had copied and eyeballed TSO Zeng. 'Tell the team to meet me back at headquarters in an hour!'

8:46 p.m.
Conference room, criminal police headquarters

Each member of the task force took turns flipping through the files that Captain Pei and TSO Zeng had brought back to headquarters.

Lieutenant Yin was the last team member to arrive. There were bags under his eyes and his fingers were twitching.

'How's the search for Han progressing?' Pei asked him.

'There was a mugging by the river around noon today. A young couple called it in. Judging from the descriptions they gave, Captain Han was the perp.'

'How much money did he steal?'

'A little over six hundred. He also stole the male victim's jacket, presumably in order to change his appearance. I've already added the jacket's details to the bulletin.'

'Take that out immediately,' Pei snapped. 'He'll have already ditched the stolen jacket by now.'

Cupping the phone to his ear, Lieutenant Yin hurriedly relayed the captain's instructions to the officer on the other end.

'Right, let's get started here,' Pei ordered, and the team began studying the documents on the table.

Eumenides had selected a total of thirteen files from the PSB archives that afternoon. Pei gave the team ten minutes to read through them, then asked for their thoughts.

'I can't see any connection,' TSO Zeng said. 'There are literally no links between these crimes.'

The others all agreed. The thirteen files related to thirteen different cases. Most of them were murder cases; a few were robberies. The oldest dated back several decades, while the most recent had happened within the past year. None of the team members could see any link between the suspects, who were of different ages and genders. Some of the perpetrators were still in prison, while a few had already been executed for their crimes. The investigations had been carried out by completely different police stations or departments.

The task force was stumped.

Liu Song, the new captain of the city's special police unit, spoke up in frustration. 'So what was he trying to do? Each of these cases has already been investigated. The perpetrators have all been punished. Why would he risk so much for these documents?'

The others remained silent.

'These files are so disparate,' TSO Zeng finally said, 'it's almost as if he picked them at random, isn't it? What if he was looking for one file in particular and the other twelve were simply meant to throw us off the scent?'

Pei nodded approvingly.

'But how can we tell which of the thirteen was the one he was interested in?' SPU Captain Liu asked, frowning.

Pei clasped his hands together so that the tips of his thumbs were touching. 'Right, team, we're going back to the archives.'

9:40 p.m.
Chengdu PSB archives

The room's walls were lined with neatly filed documents that had been arranged in perfect chronological order. A thick layer of dust covered the spine of each folder, testament to the months – or even years – that they had lain untouched.

Captain Pei quickly scanned the piles of folders. The slots formerly occupied by the thirteen files stood out to him. Using a pen, he drew several circles around the edges of the folders adjacent to each of the slots.

'Turn the lights off,' he told TSO Zeng.

Zeng flipped the switch and a single beam of light cut through the darkness from the torch in Pei's hand. Pei directed it at the circles he had just drawn, tilting his head to study the markings from different angles. After observing them for a full three minutes, he let out a long sigh of satisfaction.

'Feeling confident, Captain?' TSO Zeng asked, relieved by the change of mood.

'Come and have a look at this,' Pei said, shining the torch onto one of the lower circles.

Zeng squatted down and studied the illuminated files. They looked somehow different from the others, but he wasn't sure why.

'The dust has fallen off quite a few of the folders here. Which means that someone went through them recently. Just picture it: Eumenides flipped through each of these folders one at a time until he finally found what he was looking for. Then he plucked a single file from the stack.'

TSO Zeng grunted in agreement.

'Now look at these other circles,' Pei said, redirecting his torch beam. 'The dust around the missing file is essentially undisturbed. Eumenides wasn't searching for anything at all in these instances; he simply plucked a file at random. Since he couldn't stay in the archives for too long, he moved quickly. In fact, he was rushing.'

Zeng snapped his fingers. 'So he was trying to distract us

with these random files, just like I thought. The one on the bottom left was his real objective.'

Pei grinned at the TSO. 'Now let's see what Eumenides was really looking for.'

TSO Zeng flipped the lights back on and rummaged through the stack of folders that he'd placed on a nearby table. He carefully checked the date on each label, comparing it against the date on the shelf from where it had been removed. He soon found the file he was looking for.

It was from 1984. A line of text was written below the year: *January 30th Hostage Case.*

10:13 p.m.
Surgical ward, Chengdu People's Hospital

Teacher Wu had been transferred to a private intensive-care room after his surgery. The doctors expected him to make a full recovery. With the help of some physiotherapy, they declared, he should be able to use his reattached left hand with little difficulty.

Word of the hotel murders had spread like wildfire since the morning. Endless waves of reporters swarmed into the hospital, representing various media outlets both local and national. Anyone who tried to get into the intensive-care unit, however, was promptly turned away by the hospital staff. The patient had just come out of surgery, they explained, and could not be disturbed.

Moments after the head nurse had turned away yet another couple of reporters, a third individual strode up to her. He appeared to be no older than twenty-five and his casual attire instantly set him apart from the well-dressed journalists.

His jacket hung open, revealing a cotton shirt that clung to his well-defined chest and abdomen. His aviator sunglasses further enhanced his confident air.

'Which room is Teacher Wu's?' he asked calmly and matter-of-factly.

The head nurse, a woman in her late thirties, gave him a steely glare. 'Are you a relative?'

'No.' He shook his head and held out a badge. 'Police.'

The nurse's expression softened immediately. 'My apologies, sir. I didn't know.'

'Don't worry about it,' the man said, flashing a congenial smile.

'Those journalists are a pain in the neck. I thought you were one of—'

He cut her off with a wave of his hand. 'I understand. You're simply doing your job, and that's very admirable. In fact, you've all gone above and beyond the call of duty today. I'll talk to my team later and have them send a couple of officers to assist your staff.'

The head nurse beamed.

'Would it be all right if I went into Teacher Wu's room?' the man asked.

'Of course.' The nurse turned and pointed down the hall. 'It's the third on the left, Room 707.'

After thanking her with a nod, he headed into the intensive-care unit. *All beauty and no brains*, he thought as a sly smile crept across his lips.

10:40 p.m.
Bahamas Bar

The bar was packed. It was impossible to take a step in any direction without elbowing at least three people. Which was exactly why Captain Han had chosen to hide out there.

He'd been forced to mug a young couple at noon and their expressions haunted him, their eyes full of shock, terror and disgust. *One more for the list*, he thought. *Murder, escaping from police custody, and now petty theft.*

A newly opened bottle of beer came sliding across in front of him. He looked up. A woman with bleached hair and heavy make-up was sitting on the stool next to him. She leant in close. 'Free of charge, Mr Han,' she whispered into his ear.

Every muscle in Han's body tensed.

The woman chuckled and her thick make-up began to crack. 'This comes courtesy of that fellow over there. I'm just the messenger.'

She pointed to a distant, dimly lit corner of the bar, where a man was sitting alone at a small table. The tip of a cigarette flared red, lighting up the man's eyes.

'Him?'

Captain Han's heart beat faster in his chest. His hands hovered as he considered his next move.

'I don't know about you,' the woman said, 'but I tend not to ask too many questions when a free drink is involved.'

With beer in hand, Han stood up and strode towards the man.

Earlier that night: 9:30 p.m.
The Green Spring

He sat in the same booth as last time. Until recently, he'd always avoided making repeat appearances at public locations. But he'd been unable to stop himself from returning to this place.

The past two days had been harder than he'd expected. He needed to sort through his emotions, and this restaurant was the perfect spot to wind down and think.

His mentor, he reflected, was not the first father figure he had lost. It was the third.

First he had lost his real father.

In truth, the years he'd spent with his real father had not been happy ones. His father had been weighed down with too many worries, too much pain. Even now, his memories of the affection his father had shown him were still steeped in sadness.

The urge to try and relieve his father of his pain had sprouted when he was very young and grown stronger with time, but in the end it had amounted to nothing. His father had vanished from his life without warning. He didn't remember how or why. It was a long time ago.

On the day his father disappeared, his second father figure entered his life. He remembered it very clearly – it was his sixth birthday. The second man was known simply as 'Uncle' and brought so much joy. In his memory, Uncle was young and dashing and never without a smile. The two of them became fast friends from their very first meeting.

Once upon a time he'd loved jumping into his father's arms. Uncle was different though. Simply looking at Uncle's face used to make him feel at peace, as if nothing bad would ever happen to him again. He still remembered that face, like a photograph that he could turn to at any time.

Uncle knew plenty of ways to make him happy. A snack here, a joke there, and lots of funny faces. Uncle also took good care of his mother. She was bedridden and would often urge him to listen to Uncle. The three of them always smiled when they were together.

When Uncle was around, he forgot the pain of his father's absence. These were the happiest memories of his life.

Then Uncle was gone. His mother succumbed to her illness not long after. For the first time in his life, he was truly alone.

The orphanage became his new home. He didn't like the place and the people there didn't like him. His memories of his years there contained not a single shred of happiness. He kept to himself. None of the other children ever knew what he was thinking and nor did they want to. It was a suffocating environment. He wanted to struggle, to fight, but he felt so weak. That was how he began his adolescence.

Then, one day, *he* appeared. A man far stranger than anyone he had ever encountered. Despite the man's grotesque features, there was an irresistible charisma about him that he could only describe as magical.

His fear of the strange man turned into curiosity, curiosity turned into infatuation and eventually awe. He drew closer to the man, absorbing his wisdom and strength like a shrivelled plant greedily sucking nutrients from the soil. With this man, sunlight had finally returned to his life.

He was shown the world as it truly was. He saw how many innocent people continued to suffer and how many evil people were able to execute their sadistic acts unchecked. For the first time in his life he had a purpose. He knew that taking this path would not be easy, but it could change the world. The man showed him the way forward and he followed it. He now had a new name for this man, a title that filled him with reverence. *Mentor.*

Just when he thought he was finally strong enough to repay the enormous debt to his mentor, his mentor left. Now there was no one who knew about his past. He'd become completely invisible. But all that had changed last night.

Even as his own memories seemed to be drifting away, the truth began to creep into view. On the news reports about the explosion last night he'd seen some familiar old photographs. Photos of Uncle. Except the reporters called him Yuan Zhibang.

So many of his questions were answered in that instant. He realised why Uncle had vanished so suddenly. And why his mentor had chosen him. But there were still questions – his head felt swollen with them.

Where had his father gone? Just how had Yuan Zhibang come into his life?

If he was to unravel the answers, he would need to begin his search from deep inside his own memory.

His father had left him and Uncle had taken his father's place. He remembered the date very clearly. It was his birthday: the thirtieth of January 1984.

Whenever he recalled that period of his childhood, he always pictured a white hospital room, his mother lying on the bed, her face pale and drawn, her gaze weak and pleading. But on the thirtieth of January 1984 he was happy. His father had promised to buy him a cake for his birthday. He was practically trembling with excitement. A golden cake slathered with icing – how delicious that would be.

Inside the hospital, he and his mother waited for his father. But his father was nowhere to be seen. After a long while, three strange men turned up. The one in charge wore a sombre expression that seemed to suck the air from the room. Even though he didn't know why they had come, he began to sob.

But then he was immediately pulled into a warm embrace.

He looked up to see a pair of kind, nice eyes. That was his first memory of Uncle. In mere seconds, Uncle turned his tears into laughter. The cold room turned warm. The man gave him things that his father never had. A lollipop. A toy drum. Uncle even sat him inside a big car. He asked him where they were going.

'To look for your daddy,' Uncle said.

He became even happier. 'Today's my birthday,' he bragged. 'My daddy's going to get me a birthday cake with lots and lots of icing.'

Before he got out of the car, the man handed him a pair of headphones. 'Twinkle, Twinkle, Little Star' blared out from the tape player and he was transfixed. He listened eagerly as he licked his fresh lollipop, singing along with the recording.

As promised, the man took him to see his father. His father was standing next to a stranger, but it wasn't clear what they were doing.

The man held him, and his thoughts returned to his birthday cake. But by the time they left, his father had still not given him the cake he'd promised. He would have to wait until that evening before he would see the birthday cake. The smiling uncle was holding it; he said that his father had entrusted him to deliver the cake to the birthday boy.

The cake tasted as sweet as it looked. In the years that followed, the night of his sixth birthday would become one of his most treasured memories. After that day, however, he never saw his father again.

Where did his father go? Who was the smiling man and who was the stranger with his father? These questions haunted him for years. No matter how hard he searched for the truth, he was never able to put the pieces together. But last night's broadcast had shed new light on everything. His mentor and uncle were one and the same. Yuan Zhibang.

He had been a police officer. The car that he had sat him in was a police car.

Yuan must have had some reason for coming into his life. Could it be that his father was... a criminal?

At great risk to himself, he gained access to the city's police archives and finally learnt of his father's fate. The answers within that folder filled him with sadness and left him with even more questions. He had always suspected that the truth would reopen the deep psychological wounds that had long since scarred over. Still, he had no choice but to continue his search.

There was something, he realised, that had drawn him to the Green Spring. It wasn't the restaurant's elegant Huaiyang cuisine, nor its sweet, house-brewed wine. It was the young woman. Like himself, she had also lost her father.

He had a lot to think about and he needed the serenity that the restaurant afforded. But there were several diners there tonight who were lowering the tone of the place.

Three men sat at the table closest to the stage. He recognised their faces. The overweight one was Lin Henggan and the thin one was Meng Fangliang. They were both vice presidents of the Longyu Corporation. Following the recent death of Mayor Deng, they were now the company's most senior associates. The third was a younger man, Sheng, who'd been one of Mayor Deng's most capable bodyguards. He was drunk, his thick neck just a few shades short of crimson.

Vice President Meng was patting Sheng on the shoulder with his free hand. Sheng listened intently to what was being said, nodded, swallowed the last of his 100-per-cent-proof rice wine and banged his glass down on the table.

Vice President Lin now leant towards Sheng and shook his

hand. The older man looked both solemn and expectant. Sheng gripped his fleshy hand and seemed overcome with pride.

The two vice presidents got up from their table and made their leisurely way to the restaurant's exit. Neither noticed that they were being watched from a nearby corner.

The bodyguard poured himself another glass of *baijiu*, revelling in what Vice President Meng had just promised him. Mayor Deng was gone. Why should he work himself to the bone for a dead man's estate? If he chose to follow a different master now, he could rise far above Brother Hua, who remained sickeningly loyal to the Deng family.

The final strains of the Bach sonata dissipated and the young woman on the stage in the middle of the pool set her violin back on its stand.

Sheng whirled around. 'What do you think you're doing?' he yelled. 'Don't stop! Keep playing! Keep playing!'

Sheng may have been a philistine when it came to the arts, but tonight was one of the most important nights of his life and he was damn well going to celebrate.

A waiter hurried over. 'I'm sorry, sir, but the performance is over.'

'Fuck that! You think I don't have the money?' Sheng brandished a handful of hundred-yuan bills at the waiter and slammed them onto the table. 'Keep the music coming!'

The young woman stood stationary on the stage, blinking through sightless eyes. Her thin frame reminded the man in the corner of a dandelion stem. A waitress rushed over, took her by the arm and led her down the steps and off the stage.

Sheng leapt up from his seat and staggered after the violinist. 'Are you trying to insult me? I have connections all over this

city. I can get you fired and make sure you never work again!'
But by the time he reached the stage, she'd already vanished
through a back door.

'Go ahead and run, damn it!' he roared. 'If you ever come
back here, I'll fucking smash your head in! Don't you know
who I am?'

The restaurant's entire staff watched in shock as Sheng
burst out of the exit. He stumbled across the car park and leant
against a car door to catch his breath.

Suddenly, a handkerchief was pressed against his mouth. It
only took half a second to register the sharp smell coming from
the cloth, and before he knew it, the drunken bodyguard felt his
arms and legs slipping from under him. He lost consciousness.

30 October, 1:12 a.m.

Sheng gradually came to. His head seemed to be filled with wet
cement and it hurt like hell.

He was sitting up in the driver's seat of his new car. The
seatbelt was strapped across his chest and the car was at a
standstill though its engine was purring. He squinted at the
glowing dashboard and wrinkled his nose. The car reeked of
alcohol.

'Shit,' he hissed. *Must have blacked out again.*

He searched for his last memory. He remembered flying into
a drunken rage inside the restaurant and then chasing after
the violinist. But after that, nothing. Judging from the
evidence around him, he must have left the restaurant and
passed out while driving.

At least my car's still in one piece. But where the hell am I?

He peered through the windows. Although the streetlights

around him were dim, they illuminated enough of the wide road for him to see the crash barriers to either side. But there was a conspicuous absence of other headlights or taillights. He was certain that he'd never been there before. *Never mind. I'll just drive. If I see someone, I'll ask them where the hell this is.*

Sheng shifted the car into gear and pressed the accelerator. The engine growled and the vehicle set off along the wide road.

He thought back to his earlier conversation with the two vice presidents and grinned. He was going places. Unconsciously, he pressed harder on the accelerator.

By the time he saw the roadworks signs blocking the road in front of him, the needle on the speedometer was edging past the 100 km/h mark. An LCD sign spelt out a curt message in red: *No Road Ahead!*

The alcohol had dulled Sheng's reactions, but he still managed to slam his foot on the brake in time. Even so, his speed didn't change. He continued hurtling towards the sign at the same rate.

He stomped on the brake pedal but felt no resistance. The car rocketed towards the warning signs as if it had a mind of its own. A sober realisation prodded at him. *This is not going to end well.*

The rows of red X signs drew closer. Gritting his teeth, Sheng wrenched the steering wheel to the right. The car began to turn, but it was too late. Lights smashed against the windscreen with a deafening crack. He shut his eyes and waited for the next impact.

But none came. A strange sensation filled his stomach. Anxiety butterflies. Was he... floating?

He stared through the windscreen and saw only darkness. Then, suddenly, the headlights illuminated something in the near distance. It was rushing closer and closer.

Pavement.

★

After falling twenty metres from the unfinished flyover, the car smashed into the ground, bonnet first, and crumpled like an accordion.

The sole witness to Sheng's death watched the carnage through a pair of binoculars. He lingered on the wrecked luxury vehicle, spotlighted by a single intact headlight. Allowing himself a wry smirk, he slunk back into the night.

3

UNMASKING EUMENIDES

8 a.m.
Commissioner Song's office

Captain Pei passed a folder to the commissioner.
'An unidentified man gained access to our PSB archives yesterday afternoon while masquerading as an officer. He made copies of thirteen files, but this was the one he wanted. From his behaviour and his signature, I'm confident that this man is Eumenides.'

Commissioner Song's eyebrows quivered at the mention of Eumenides.

'My team spent the whole of last night combing through these documents,' Pei continued, 'but we still haven't found any direct links between the hostage case and the April 18th murders.'

'I see,' the commissioner said, rubbing his bony chin. 'This case was a few years before my time. Tell me what you know about it.'

'To put it simply, it was a hostage situation that went wrong. The victim, a forty-five-year-old male named Chen Tianqiao, had borrowed ten thousand yuan from a thirty-two-year-old man named Wen Hongbing. Wen requested on multiple occasions that Chen pay him back, but to no avail.

On the thirtieth of January 1984, three days before the New Year Festival, Wen knocked on Chen's door and demanded his money. This time, when Chen wouldn't cough up, Wen refused to take no for an answer. He was younger and stronger than Chen and was able to overpower him and take him hostage, whereupon he revealed that he was wearing an improvised explosive device around his waist.

'Wen threatened to detonate the bomb and kill both of them unless Chen repaid him by the end of the day. Chen finally agreed. He wrote his wife, now ex-wife, a note instructing her to borrow the money off friends, but when he passed her the note he gave her hand a deliberate squeeze. This was a signal the two of them had established in case he was ever forced to speak to her under duress. She immediately called the police.

'Wen took Chen back to his apartment. Thanks to the wife, the police quickly arrived on the scene. It became a hostage situation, but Wen wouldn't release Chen. In order to prevent Wen from detonating the bomb and killing everyone else in the building, an SPU marksman shot him through one of the apartment windows.'

Commissioner Song had listened to Pei's concise summary in silence. Now he shook his head in confusion. 'Why would Eumenides be interested in this case? Is he looking to punish Chen?'

'We can't rule that out. But it's from eighteen years ago. It's ancient history. Why focus on it now?'

The commissioner had nothing to contribute.

'Whatever his reasons,' Pei said, 'we can't let this lead go unexplored, no matter how tenuous. I've already ordered my people to look into Chen Tianqiao.'

'And...?'

'He was born in 1939. He's registered as a Chengdu resident

and as far as we can tell he hasn't done an honest day's work in his life. He's knee deep in debt, but it's seemingly very hard to pin a legal case on him. Whenever he defaults on a loan, his creditors come to us, but often there's little the police can do because it's generally a civil rather than a criminal matter. Most of his creditors give up, although occasionally someone pushes back. Like Wen Hongbing.

'Eventually, Chen got sloppy. In 1991 he was arrested and locked up for seven years. Prison didn't change him one bit and he went back to his old racket as soon as he got out. As far as we know, he's spent the last two years outside the country, dodging creditors. He's rumoured to be in Thailand or Vietnam.'

'Carry on searching for him. We can't afford to ignore this lead.'

'Yes, sir. But there's another lead that might be more worthy of our attention right now.'

'And what's that?'

'Yuan Zhibang's name is in the files for the January 30th case.'

'Oh?' The commissioner flipped to the last page, which listed the officers involved in the investigation. Yuan's name was indeed there. 'How is that possible?' he asked, perplexed. 'Yuan hadn't even graduated from the police academy at that point. He wasn't qualified to take part in any investigation.'

Pei nodded. 'That's exactly what I've been trying to get my head around. I want to know what role Yuan played. It may help us find a connection to the April 18th murders. But the official account of the showdown at Wen's apartment is unusually brief, and it doesn't mention what Yuan was doing there either. Which makes me wonder whether the department was deliberately trying to hide something.'

Commissioner Song rummaged through the documents in the folder. The account was indeed brief – just a single paragraph, in fact:

Officers arrived outside the building and began negotiating with Wen Hongbing through his window. Wen grew increasingly agitated. He demanded that Chen Tianqiao pay him back immediately. When Chen indicated that he lacked the wherewithal to do so, Wen threatened to detonate the bomb on his person. In order to prevent the loss of life, the lead investigating officer ordered that Wen be shot. Wen was shot in the head by an SPU marksman's bullet. He died immediately. Officers then rushed into Wen's apartment, neutralised the explosive and secured Chen Tianqiao.

Song banged his fist down on the page. 'How the hell was this report able to pass evaluation?'

Pei's response was halfway between a wince and a grin. 'Wasn't Xue Dalin vice commissioner back then?'

Commissioner Song tensed. Pei was right. The hostage case happened just a few weeks before the notorious drugs bust that came to be known as the March 16th Narcotics Case.

'My theory,' Pei continued, 'is that Vice Commissioner Xue and the rest of the department were so preoccupied with the events leading up to the March 16th bust that none of them bothered to read this report very closely.'

Commissioner Song nodded and gently closed the folder. 'What do you plan to do now?' he asked.

'I can't help wondering if there's some secret behind this case. And if there's one person who could enlighten us and tell us what role Yuan played in all this, it would have to be the lead investigating officer. The same person who typed up this report—'

'You want to talk to *Captain Ding Ke*?' the commissioner interrupted, gaping at the last page in the file. 'Tell me you're joking.'

Captain Ding Ke was a legend in law-enforcement circles. Not just within the province of Sichuan but right across the country.

'I know he won't give up this information easily, but I have to try.'

The commissioner shrugged. 'You don't know, do you?'

'Know what?'

'Captain Ding has been missing for years. None of our attempts to locate him have succeeded.'

Pei's face fell. 'And I thought I was so close to finding out the truth behind this case,' he said, shaking his head.

'I'm curious – did you know Captain Ding Ke personally?' the commissioner asked.

'He taught a few classes at the academy. He was also the captain of the criminal police at the time, with two decades of experience already under his belt. But in April 1984, just weeks before I graduated, he stopped teaching. I later heard that he'd fallen ill due to overwork. And then he retired, before he'd even had the chance to recover.'

The commissioner nodded. 'Captain Ding Ke was a legend for one key reason: he successfully closed every investigation he took on. That's a 100-per-cent success rate – something no other officer ever achieved. He fell ill right before the April 18th murders, Eumenides' debut appearance' – Song sighed – 'and I can't help but think that if he hadn't retired, the Eumenides case would have been solved a long time ago.'

Pei leant forward, his curiosity piqued. 'Where did Captain Ding go after he left?'

'He moved out to the countryside. But even though he was retired, he was still in touch with the force. Whenever an investigation hit an impasse, one of his former subordinates would look him up. We usually had to push him to get any assistance, but over the next few years he helped us crack quite a few cases.

'Whenever we thanked him, he'd always say the same thing: "If you come back here again, I'll go somewhere nobody can find me." Everyone assumed he was joking.' The commissioner shook his head ruefully. 'That was back in 1992. A decade ago, come to think of it. A particularly brutal crime shook Chengdu that year. I'm sure you know the one I'm talking about.'

Pei lit up. 'The Bag— I mean, the January 12th case?'

'There's no need to censor yourself,' Song said. 'You can call it by the same name everyone else uses. The Bagman Killing.'

The captain forced a nod. He still remembered the pictures that had circulated around the province after the first body parts were discovered.

'The details of that case were so brutal, they proved too much for some members of the team,' Commissioner Song said, dropping his voice. 'Two officers asked to be taken off the case. I had only just been transferred to Chengdu from out at Guangyuan. The entire Chengdu police force was mobilised for that investigation. We scoured the whole city, but we couldn't find a single trace of the suspect. When we'd exhausted all other options, we tried to contact Captain Ding. This time he was nowhere to be found. Both his wife and son told us that he'd vanished as soon as news of the crime had gone public. Naturally, he'd anticipated that we'd come looking for him. Not even the man's own family knew where he'd gone.'

'So he just disappeared? You've not seen him since?'

'As I said, it's been a decade. We've put feelers out across the city, left messages on online forums – we've tried everything. But all to no end. Either Captain Ding Ke is dead or he doesn't want to be found. Trust me on that.'

'But, sir, why would he do that? Just because he was sick?'

'His illness wasn't physical, Pei. He was tired of police work. Tired of the relentless stress, the never-ending stream of cases, one after the other. Most of us find ways of dealing with it, but I suppose it was different for him. After all, he had the pressure of a perfect record to live up to.'

'So finding him won't be easy. But presumably it won't be quite so hard to track down the others.' Pei thumbed through the file as he spoke, coming to a stop at the last page with the full list of officers.

The commissioner grunted. 'I'll have my people give you more information on them. A lot of men have come and gone over the past decade and many of those officers aren't in our main database any more. I'll send you our findings as soon as they're ready.'

'Excellent. Thank you, sir.' Pei stood up and saluted, and Commissioner Song reciprocated.

Pei raced down the hallway at speed and nearly collided with TSO Zeng.

'Captain Pei!' the TSO shouted.

'What's the situation, Zeng?'

'I've found out why Eumenides is so interested in this case. And I know who he is!'

Pei's eyes widened. Before TSO Zeng could utter another word, Pei gripped him by the shoulder. 'Notify the rest of the team. Tell them to meet me in the conference room immediately!'

A low-resolution image of a black-and-white photograph was projected above them. The photograph, blurry and yellowed around the edges, showed a group of young boys and girls who appeared to be between about four and thirteen years old.

'This picture was taken in 1986, at an orphanage here in Chengdu,' TSO Zeng explained. 'Why am I showing you this particular photo, you might ask? Well, one of these children disappeared a year after it was taken.'

His face broke into a wide grin.

'Get on with it,' said Ms Mu.

'Thanks to the records I accessed, as well as the subsequent visit I paid to the orphanage, I've confirmed the identity of the orphan who went missing. His name was Wen Chengyu. His father was Wen Hongbing, the man killed in the standoff with the police in the January 30th hostage case in 1984.

'And here we are eighteen years on from the death of Wen Hongbing and just days after the death of Yuan Zhibang. Yuan's protégé, Eumenides, pulled the files from the archive. This is no coincidence.'

The room was so quiet that the only thing each person could hear was their own heartbeat. Everyone was thinking the exact same thing: somewhere in that picture was a young Eumenides.

'Wen Chengyu...' Pei said, slowly sounding out each syllable. 'Which of these children is him?'

TSO Zeng aimed his laser pointer at the screen and the red dot rested on a boy at the far left end of the front row. He was one of the younger children in the group, probably about eight years old. His features were not especially striking, but there was something odd about the way he held himself. Whereas the other children were smiling or yawning, he was standing very straight and to attention, with an unusually serious expression on his face for someone of that age.

Ms Mu's training kicked in. She began to imagine how different things might have been if the boy had grown up in better circumstances. He might have become a fine young man, perhaps the head of his class, or the sort of older brother who looked out for his siblings.

But the other members of the team were looking at the boy through the tainted lens of what fate had in store for him – a future as a cruel murderer who would give them the biggest challenge they had ever faced.

The room went still and the officers' hearts grew heavier.

Ms Mu broke the silence. 'In order to bring down a killer,' she said, 'one needs to understand what they were like before they turned into a murderous monster. It's a person's experiences that determine what they become. Perhaps you can tell us more about what kind of person Wen Chengyu became, Captain Pei.'

'Me?' said Pei, taken aback. 'What would I know?'

'If Wen Chengyu is Eumenides, when he first met Yuan Zhibang he would have been a highly impressionable child, a blank slate. His eventual psychological, moral and social character would have been formed entirely under Yuan's conscious manipulation. You knew Yuan better than any of us, Captain, so you may also have an insight into how he would have educated and trained this boy. I've read your personal file. Out of everyone here, you are the most experienced in investigating violent criminals. You are best placed to provide us with the most accurate description of the kind of monster Yuan created.'

Pei rubbed his cheek thoughtfully. 'I suppose you're right. If I were in Yuan's place, I would create a killer. Someone to work in the shadows, someone with a razor-sharp intellect, a cool head and a thirst for continual improvement. Stimulation and challenge would excite him. He would have to be strong and persistent. He'd have to adhere to a strict code of behaviour, no questions asked. And most important of all, once given an objective, he would stop at nothing to achieve it.'

'Good,' Ms Mu said.

'Fat lot of help that is,' TSO Zeng said. 'It's all theoretical BS.'

'Actually,' Ms Mu said, unperturbed, 'the captain's description will enable me to work backwards and draw up a personality profile of Eumenides. Let's start with his social life. We can infer from Captain Pei's insights that Eumenides has lived a solitary existence, but that doesn't mean he lacks social skills. When approaching strangers, including his victims, he would have to be charismatic. He may well have multiple legal identities, but if Yuan did establish a code of behaviour for him, as Captain Pei suggests, that would certainly have prohibited luxuries like friendships or romantic attachments. To compensate, Eumenides may have fostered a love of music, the arts or perhaps fine cuisine. And notwithstanding his mentor's edicts, he may still have developed feelings for someone – feelings that he cannot express openly.' She glanced around the room and noted the sceptical looks. 'Any questions?'

'A few,' SPU Captain Liu said. 'First off, how did you get all that from what Captain Pei said?'

'The captain described Eumenides as being intelligent, sensitive and hungry for knowledge. That sort of personality tends to be fascinated by perfection, particularly with regards to beauty. There's clearly no place for that in his day-to-day activities, so he'll only be able to indulge this fascination in private and intermittently. His life is stressful and lonely, but as a human being he needs some way of relaxing, and in my view he may well find that through food or music. I would even go so far as to say that if I'd been in Yuan's place, I would have consciously cultivated Eumenides' interest in such things in order to provide him with a safe way of relieving his stress.'

'You also said that he might develop feelings for someone,' Pei pointed out.

'All human beings have emotional needs. Not even someone like Eumenides can fully repress everything. In fact, he'll get more and more desperate to meet those needs as time goes on. You can imagine how strong the emotional bond between Eumenides and Yuan was after all those years. Essentially, Yuan assumed the role of Eumenides' father. But now Yuan is dead and he has no one. This is very new to him and not necessarily something he's ready for. We can be all but certain that he's going to look for someone else to fulfil those roles in his life.'

'But Yuan would have warned him against getting attached to anyone,' Pei said.

'Emotions embody our most primitive instincts. You can't simply force them to disappear just because someone commands it.'

'What kind of person would he choose then?'

'Well, there's a very high probability that it's a woman.'

'How can you be sure?'

'It's simple statistics. Firstly, an estimated 90 per cent of the population is heterosexual. Secondly, he's propelled by another subconscious motivation – the need for a mother. His father figure may have just died, but Eumenides hasn't had a female figure in his life for almost twenty years. Wen Chengyu's records state that his mother succumbed to a terminal illness about six months after his father was killed. Eumenides might look for a woman in a similarly frail state, subconsciously hoping that he will somehow be able to heal her. He may also be looking for someone who, like him, has just been bereaved. Someone he can empathise with.'

Pei folded his arms across his chest. 'Excellent work, Ms Mu,' he said.

The psychologist responded with a reserved smile.

Pei turned to TSO Zeng. 'Tell us what else you've found.'

Zeng pulled a sheet of paper from his stack of documents. First, he noted Wen Chengyu's date of birth: the thirtieth of January 1978. 'I've got everything here, including his medical records. These show that after his mother died in June 1984, young Wen was sent to live at the Bright Moon Orphanage in Shuangliu, on the southern outskirts of Chengdu. Oddly enough, Wen Chengyu never thought of himself as an orphan. The records state that he repeatedly insisted that his father was not dead, just missing. This created a rift between him and the other children at the orphanage. On the thirtieth of January 1987, the now nine-year-old Wen Chengyu vanished during a group outing and was never seen again.'

Pei raised an eyebrow. 'His disappearance and his father's death both happened on his birthday.'

'I don't believe that's a coincidence either,' TSO Zeng said, setting down the documents. 'As I've already said, Wen Chengyu was born in 1978, which would make him twenty-four years old right now. His father was killed on the day of his sixth birthday. Unbeknown to him, Yuan took part in the police operation that resulted in his father's death. Several months later, Yuan was hospitalised on account of the injuries he sustained in the warehouse explosion. As we all know, he spent the next three years recovering from his wounds on the police department's budget. Then on the thirtieth of January 1987, Yuan abducted Wen Chengyu and began training the boy to be his successor. He clearly chose that day because it was the anniversary of Wen Hongbing's death.'

Zeng paused to glance around the room, relishing the attention. 'Now, this is my own analysis. One: Wen had no idea that the police had shot and killed his father. Instead, he remembered only that his father vanished on the thirtieth of January that year. It was his birthday; he wouldn't have forgotten that. Two: I also believe that Yuan never revealed his true identity to Wen. And three: this *has* now been revealed to Wen, thanks to recent reports in the media. Something about Yuan's former life as a police officer triggered Eumenides' memory and made him think about his father. He then realised that his father's last known movements would be contained somewhere in our files. All he had to do was search for case files marked the thirtieth of January 1984.'

The others pondered TSO Zeng's words in silence. Then Lieutenant Yin's phone rang and he hurried out into the hallway to answer it.

Captain Pei was the first to speak up. 'So, now that Wen knows his father is dead, how will he have reacted to that?'

'With great sadness,' Ms Mu said, 'and intense disappointment. He'll want to find out everything he can about his father's death, beyond the sparse details of the report. And having seen Yuan's name in the file, he'll be anxious to learn what role his mentor played on that day. But most important of all, he'll want revenge.'

'Against who?' Pei asked. 'The hostage – Chen Tianqiao? Captain Ding Ke? The marksman?'

Ms Mu frowned. 'That's hard to say. But I'd recommend that we try and locate each of those three as soon as possible.'

'The commissioner is collecting information on all of the officers involved in the January 30th case. As soon as we have those details, we'll track them down. In the meantime, Captain Ding Ke and Chen Tianqiao are our main focus. Their whereabouts are currently unknown, but I'm hoping that the other officers will help bring us closer to both individuals.'

Lieutenant Yin ran back into the room, his face as pale as a bedsheet. His eyes locked onto Captain Pei's.

'We need to go to the hospital!'

9:40 a.m.
Chengdu People's Hospital

The police had already cordoned off a wide area in front of the hospital building. In the centre lay a man in a hospital gown. There was a thick bandage around one arm and his face was planted nose down in the ground. Two young police officers stood next to the body, glaring at the crowd that had gathered around the cordon.

Captain Pei and Lieutenant Yin ducked under the tape and approached the officers.

'Teacher Wu didn't make it then?' Pei asked, although he already knew the answer.

'Dead as soon as he hit the ground, sir,' answered one of the officers with a shrug. 'One advantage of being called to a hospital, I guess. There was no shortage of doctors to check the body.'

'He jumped from the seventh floor,' the other officer added. 'The grass might have cushioned the landing, but for a frail guy pushing seventy that would have been like using a piece of paper to shield yourself from a grenade.'

Pei crouched beside the corpse. He put on a pair of gloves and gently lifted the head of the deceased off the ground, revealing the mud-covered face.

The fall hadn't done the man's looks any favours. Deep creases radiated from the corners of his closed eyes and his lips were contorted in pain. Blood oozed from his mouth and nostrils, staining the surrounding mud dark purple.

Pei turned away from the body and took a deep breath. 'Do you know the specifics of what happened here?' he asked

'Of course,' the second officer said, nodding. 'He jumped. He died.'

'It was suicide?' Pei said, surprised. 'Are you sure?'

'Absolutely. His family visited him earlier and said that he was acting abnormally and seemed depressed. He wouldn't speak and he refused to eat any breakfast. He was just staring into space. At around eight fifty he told them that he needed to be alone for a bit, so they left his room and waited out in the hall. Twenty minutes later, Teacher Wu fell to the ground. A few members of the public witnessed the whole thing. He just climbed out the seventh-storey window and jumped.'

'Why would he want to kill himself?' Pei asked.

'Well...' The officer faltered. Swallowing, he tried again. 'According to his family, he killed himself because of the police.'

'Meaning...?' Pei cocked his head.

'His wife and son said that he started acting strangely after an officer barged into his room last night and interrogated him. I got an earful when I asked for their statements earlier.'

'Was it one of our officers who interrogated him?' Pei asked, looking over at Lieutenant Yin.

'No,' Yin said. 'You, me and Ms Mu are the only people from the criminal police who've been here.'

'Contact every local station immediately and find out if any of them sent an officer here.' Turning to the other two officers, Pei said, 'I want one of you to take me to see Teacher Wu's family.'

Teacher Wu Yinwu's adult son, Wu Jiaming, was in the reception area talking to some of the hospital staff. When the police stepped into the room, he stopped what he was saying and frowned.

'Hello, sir. I'm Captain Pei from the criminal police.' Pei tried to keep his tone as sympathetic as possible.

Wu Jiaming snorted and shot him a derisive look.

Pei ignored the slight. There was no time to waste. 'I need to ask you a few questions. Firstly, did a police officer visit your father last night?'

'Why are you asking me?' he spat. 'Can't you keep track of your own people?'

Blood rushed to Pei's cheeks.

'Yes, an officer did come here yesterday,' interjected a woman in a white uniform. 'It was me who directed him to the patient's room. I'm the head nurse.'

'What did he say to the patient?'

'I wouldn't be able to tell you that.'

Before Pei could ask the nurse another question, Wu Jiaming pointed an accusing finger at him. 'How the hell could she know what he said? He barged in, told us to leave the room and then locked the door!'

Pei frowned. No officer would behave like that. Not unless they were willing to risk suspension. An uncomfortable lump began to form in his throat.

'Did you see this officer's credentials?' he asked the head nurse.

'I did. In fact, he showed them to me before I even asked.'

'How closely did you look at them?'

Her voice wobbled. 'Not very closely.'

Pei's phone rang and he excused himself.

'Captain Pei, it's Lieutenant Yin.'

'Talk to me, Lieutenant.'

'I have some bad news about that officer.'

10:02 a.m.
The Longyu Building

Vice President Lin and Vice President Meng did not look happy.

'At three o'clock this morning I received word that Sheng had been involved in a car accident,' Brother Hua said, lowering his head to avoid the two men's eyes. 'I reached out to my contacts in the traffic police to find out more.'

'What did they say?' Vice President Lin asked.

'They called it a drink-driving accident. His car plummeted off the edge of an unfinished flyover. It was a twenty-metre drop, equivalent to driving off a six-storey building. The first responders had to rip the car apart to find what was left of him.'

Vice President Meng grimaced. 'Sheng had a habit of mixing fast cars and alcohol, didn't he? I seem to remember Mayor Deng reprimanding him for that before. And now he's paid for it with his life.'

But Vice President Lin still had questions. 'Where exactly was this unfinished flyover?'

'At the Douzi Zhuang exit on the southern highway. The flyover will connect to the expressway outside the city once it's completed.'

'I thought Sheng lived downtown? What was he doing all the way out in the suburbs?'

Brother Hua nodded. 'The location of Sheng's death isn't the only suspicious detail.'

Both men looked startled. They watched Brother Hua with hungry anticipation.

'When they tested Sheng's blood, they found that his blood alcohol concentration was over 0.2 per cent. He shouldn't even have been able to drive at that point. But for the sake of argument, let's assume his tolerance for drink was such that it allowed him to drive all the way to the edge of the city. Why would he drive onto an unfamiliar road that was blocked off? The initial investigation has concluded that his car smashed through the barrier at the entrance to the unfinished flyover, stopped and then carried on again. A kilometre further on, his car plummeted off the end of the flyover.'

Brother Hua paused at the memory of his late colleague. 'Now, does that strike either of you as logical behaviour for an intoxicated driver?'

Vice President Meng nodded and Vice President Lin scratched his fleshy chin.

'According to the trace analysis done at the scene,' Brother Hua continued, 'Sheng didn't brake when he got to the end of the road but tried to swerve away instead. Even if we ignore all the other suspicious things about his death, why would he try to avoid the edge of the flyover by turning away from it instead of simply slamming on the brakes?'

'Could his brakes have failed?' Meng ventured.

'That's exactly what I wondered. What if someone brought his car onto the flyover, tampered with the brakes and let him drive off? Unfortunately, as Sheng's vehicle was totally destroyed, we've no way of verifying that.'

Vice President Lin gazed down at his feet. 'There are a lot of unexplained things about this crash,' he said softly. 'It's not good.'

'I believe he was murdered,' Brother Hua said.

Vice President Meng coughed in shock. 'But who would want to murder Sheng?'

Brother Hua tossed something onto the table. 'This was found in one of Sheng's pockets. It was probably the only thing in the car that was left intact.'

They all stared at the scratched plastic lighter. Meng's brow creased as he recognised the insignia.

'"Courtesy of the Green Spring",' Brother Hua read. 'Sheng had a habit of pocketing a complimentary lighter whenever he went out to dinner. When I found this, I was very curious as to who he was drinking with last night. I paid a visit to the Green Spring earlier today and had a look at their security footage.'

Lin picked up the lighter and twirled it around in his hand. With a soft click, he lit himself a cigarette. After several puffs, he said, 'I underestimated you, Brother Hua. You're wasted as a bodyguard – you should have become a cop.'

'Sheng worked under me. An attack on him is an attack on the Deng estate,' Brother Hua said calmly and without emotion. 'I'm simply doing my job.'

'Sheng did have dinner with us last night,' Vice President Meng said, 'as you'll have seen. And he did seem quite drunk when we left him. But Lin and I had nothing to do with what happened after that.'

Vice President Lin took a long drag on his cigarette, reducing a large segment of it to grey ash. 'We don't even have the skills to pull off what you're implying.'

'Don't worry, I believe you. The footage from the security cameras made the purpose of your dinner abundantly clear. Sheng was drunk in your presence, which means that he was no longer resisting your overtures. With an operative of the Deng estate in your pockets, why would you want to touch him?'

Vice President Lin met this accusation with a jovial grin. 'Brother Hua, we're all on the same side here. We might disagree on certain things, but there's no reason for any of this cloak-and-dagger stuff you're implying. You know that Mayor Deng kept Sheng in a highly visible position these past few years and Sheng had no shortage of enemies. Now that Mayor Deng is gone, a lot of these enemies are bound to be feeling a little more courageous.' He drummed his fingers on the table. 'But then again, perhaps we're simply making too much of this. For all we know, Sheng simply got drunk and drove off the flyover all by himself.'

'Sheng was murdered, believe me. And I know who killed him,' Brother Hua said, his expression stony.

'Who?'

'The killer who sent Mayor Deng his death notice. Eumenides.' Brother Hua's voice was dripping with hatred – and laced with a tinge of ice-cold fear.

'You're saying that he killed Sheng too?' Lin said. 'Why?'

Brother Hua fixed both men with a cool stare. 'The crimes listed on Mayor Deng's death notice could apply to any one of us.'

The two vice presidents stiffened. *Premeditated murder, racketeering, drug dealing, extortion.* Despite the company's legitimate facade, no one in the top tier of the Longyu Corporation was innocent of the accusations enumerated in the death notice.

Brother Hua watched the two men closely. Beads of sweat had already formed on Vice President Meng's forehead. He knew that they were asking themselves the same question. *What if the murder of Mayor Deng had not sated Eumenides' thirst for blood?*

'Perhaps I should personally see to your security for the time being. I suggest we set aside internal matters regarding the Deng estate for the moment, given that we're dealing with such a formidable enemy. I'm sure Mayor Deng would say the same if he were still here.'

'We would very much appreciate that.' Vice President Lin nodded. 'You're an indispensable member of the Longyu security team.'

'Absolutely,' Vice President Meng agreed.

'I'm just doing my job,' Brother Hua said.

12:51 p.m.
Criminal police headquarters

After lunch, Pei shut himself inside his office to review his notes. He needed a quiet environment and a clear head.

At ten past ten the previous night, a man claiming to be a police officer entered the intensive-care unit where Teacher Wu was being treated. His conversation with Teacher Wu lasted about thirty minutes and during that time he specifically requested that no one else be allowed into the ward. He was wearing sunglasses that obscured much of his face and he left the unit at around ten forty-five. When questioned as to the man's features, the staff were only able to provide the vaguest of descriptions.

The nurses stated that the man's departure left Teacher Wu in a strange mood. He appeared to be suffering from depression and a lot of stress. Teacher Wu did not sleep well that night, and his mood the next morning was even worse. He refused to see his wife and son when they came to visit. Twenty minutes after their arrival, he jumped out of the window in his room.

Lieutenant Yin's calls to Chengdu's local police stations had confirmed that none of them had dispatched an officer to the hospital. Not a single law-enforcement agency in the city could explain what that man had been doing in Teacher Wu's room.

The task force had initially suspected Eumenides. In fact, Lieutenant Yin was still convinced it was him. Ms Mu, however, thought differently.

'There are several reasons why that theory doesn't hold water,' she'd explained. 'As far as we know, Eumenides never issued Teacher Wu with a death notice. And if he'd come back for Wu, he would have gone after the girl as well. Also, this "interrogation" achieved the exact opposite of what Eumenides intended for Wu. He wanted Wu to rediscover his dignity and sense of duty, qualities patently lacking in Wu's decision to commit suicide. Which makes me think that the person we're looking for is most likely not Eumenides.'

Pei was inclined to agree with her. 'Teacher Wu may not have seen Eumenides' face in the hotel,' he said, 'but he heard his voice. Wu's wife and son both stated that Wu reacted normally when he heard the man's voice outside his hospital room and again when he entered it. Which would imply that it wasn't the same individual as the man from the hotel.'

Fatigue was creeping over Pei like an approaching fog.

He tried to focus on his computer screen and began blinking repeatedly until the blurry blotches sharpened into individual characters.

He was shaken out of his doziness by several soft but urgent knocks on his door.

Lieutenant Yin entered the room. 'We have some news!' he said excitedly. 'About Captain… about Han.'

'Well, what is it?' Pei said impatiently.

'We've had Han's friends and family members under surveillance for the past few days. His wife and son in particular. This morning, Han's wife received a call on her mobile that lasted nearly twenty minutes. We traced the number and it was registered only this morning. She left her workplace immediately afterwards and went to pick up her son from school. After that, her phone received multiple short calls from the same number.'

'So Han's planning to meet up with his wife. When exactly?'

'We think it'll be within the next few hours. We're awaiting your orders.'

'Where's Han's wife right now?'

'She and her son went into a KFC near the school an hour ago. They're still there.'

Pei stood up. 'Then that's where we'll go. Get hold of SPU Captain Liu and tell him to bring ten officers from the special police unit. Make sure they're all new recruits. They mustn't be people Han recognises.'

'Yes, sir!'

4

SUBWAY CHASE

1:45 p.m.
KFC, Tianying Shopping Centre

Mrs Han and her son had been sitting at the same empty table in the KFC for more than an hour. The restaurant was packed. Customers kept bringing their trays over and hovering, waiting for them to get up and leave, but still they stayed put.

An anxious-looking man in his twenties now carried his meal over, but Mrs Han barely noticed. Having waited beside the table for several seconds, he turned around and promptly collided with another customer. A cup of drink tumbled off his tray. Crying out in surprise, he reached for the cup but succeeded only in knocking the lid off. Dark-brown cola splashed onto the table between Mrs Han and her child.

As the boy backed into the window, Mrs Han stood up and frantically checked her clothes for stains. Mumbling a hurried apology, the man set down his tray and waved at the nearest member of staff. 'I spilt my drink. Could you come and clean this up?'

Mrs Han was visibly relieved to see that her clothes were dry. But her handbag was on the table and had got drenched in cola.

'Let me take care of that.' The man picked up her bag and

wiped the bottom with a handful of napkins. 'I'm really, really sorry.'

It took him only a moment to clean the handbag as the cola all but slid off the high-quality leather.

'It's okay,' she said, taking it back and sitting down again.

The man retreated to a table behind her. He took several bites from his sandwich, then wiped his mouth with a napkin. Using the napkin as cover, he slipped his thumb underneath his collar and whispered into the device concealed there.

'Bravo One, Bravo One, do you copy? Bravo Three reporting.'

Radio waves carried his voice to a jade-green van in the car park outside. Inside the van were Captain Pei and the other core members of the task force.

'This is Bravo One,' Pei replied into his radio.

'The package has been delivered, over.'

'Excellent. Continue your surveillance, over.'

Pei set down his radio and flipped a switch on a machine at his side. Muffled voices began to issue from the speaker:

'Sit up straight. Did any of it get on your clothes?'

'No. I'm okay. Why isn't Daddy here yet?'

'Don't worry, Dongdong. Daddy's busy right now. If you're good, you'll get to see him, all right?'

'Okay.'

The voices belonged to Captain Han's wife and their son. Their recorded conversation had now provided the task force with the first concrete evidence that Han was indeed planning to meet his family.

Apprehending a veteran of the police force would not be easy. But the pebble-sized listening device and GPS tracker that Bravo Three had attached to the bottom of Mrs Han's handbag would help.

Hours passed. The KFC slowly emptied, but the mother and

son showed no signs of leaving. Pei and the others listened intently to the speaker inside the van, but the only sounds they heard were the beeping of Dongdong's game console.

Lunch was long since over. The SPU officers stationed inside and outside the restaurant were already on their sixth shift.

TSO Zeng yawned. 'What are they still doing in there – pitching a tent for the night?'

A mobile ringtone chimed through the speakers. Zeng jolted and nearly fell onto the audio monitor.

'Hello?'

Pei and the others leant in close, straining to make out the faint words coming through the speaker.

'Okay, I understand.' There was a rustling sound as Mrs Han placed her phone back inside her handbag. *'It's time to go, Dongdong,'* she said.

'Yay! Is Daddy coming?'

'Come with Mummy and you'll find out.'

'This is Bravo One,' Pei said. 'They're on the move. Someone give us a visual update.'

'Mrs Han and her son are heading for the door.'

'Follow them. I want everyone to spread out and stay near the targets. Be sure to keep your distance. I repeat, keep your distance!'

'Understood.'

The next report came moments later.

'The targets are getting into a taxi. Please advise.'

Mrs Han's voice issued from the speaker: *'Take us to the Guangyuan Temple metro.'*

'They're going to the Guangyuan Temple subway station!' Pei yelled into his radio. 'I repeat: Guangyuan Temple. Bravos Two, Three, Four and Five, follow the taxi. Everyone else, take up positions near the station.'

The radio squawked as each officer confirmed Pei's orders.

Lieutenant Yin, in the driver's seat, didn't wait for the captain's command. The van lurched ahead like a horse bursting out of a stable.

Taking a deep breath, Pei peered through the van's window. His heart pounded as he realised why Han had kept them waiting so long.

Cars were flooding onto the streets. Rush hour had begun.

5:56 p.m.
Guangyuan Temple subway station

Even though the trains were now running at four-minute intervals, Guangyuan Temple station was still drowning beneath a roiling sea of commuters. It was the peak of the rush hour. Mrs Han pushed her son through a seemingly endless crowd until finally they reached the platform.

The police surveillance team had already fanned out and assumed their positions and several plainclothes SPU officers stood guard at both entrances to the platform. The only variable in this scenario was the steady stream of arriving and departing trains. It was quite possible that Han had already boarded one of those trains and was waiting for his wife to do the same. That would be very risky, however, for once the police had got on the train with Mrs Han, he could be caught like a rat in a trap.

Pei was taking no chances. In case Mrs Han and Dongdong slipped onto a train just before the doors shut, he'd ordered that one plainclothes officer should board every single train out of the station regardless. If the targets hadn't got on, the officer would then disembark at the next stop and return to Guangyuan Temple. This would ensure an efficient cycle of officers boarding each departing train.

Wary of being spotted, neither Pei nor any of the other team members set foot on the platform. Lieutenant Yin parked their van near the station's main entrance and they oversaw the operation remotely from there.

Mrs Han clutched her phone in one hand and her son in the other. Her stomach churned with anxious anticipation. After waiting for what felt like hours, a ringing sounded from her handbag.

The phone was at her ear in an instant. Her heart thumped as she listened to her husband's voice.

'Board the next train.'

'The next train? Which direction?'

'It doesn't matter. Whichever comes first. Call me as soon as you see it pulling in.'

A low rumble came from the northbound tunnel. Mrs Han moved to the centre of the platform and walked her son over to the automatic doors. When the train's headlights lit the tunnel, she picked up her phone and made the call.

'A train's coming into the station.' Her throat tightened, turning her words into a husky whisper.

'Once you're on it, stay by the door. Don't hang up.'

The voice coming through the phone's speaker was too quiet for Pei to hear, but Mrs Han's side of the conversation had given him all the information he needed.

'Everyone, focus all your attention on the next incoming train!'

'Yes, sir. It looks like the targets are about to board the train. Please advise.'

Pei bit his lip as he considered his options. 'Bravo Two, Three, Four and Five, remain on the platform. Everyone else, follow your targets.'

Four plainclothes officers remained near the benches at the centre of the platform. Several other officers moved to wait behind the platform's automatic doors and two of them queued up right behind Mrs Han and Dongdong.

The incoming train lurched to a halt. A signal beeped and the platform doors slid open. Mrs Han got onto the train. Most of the other passengers pressed further inside, but she and her son remained by the train door.

As the plainclothes officers boarded, the one nearest Mrs Han leant into her concealed microphone and began reporting what she was seeing. 'No suspect in sight within the train. Mrs Han is holding her phone to her ear. She must still be in contact with him.'

Scowling, Pei amended his previous command. 'Bravo Six and Seven, get off the train and regroup with the officers on the platform. Everyone else, stay on your targets.'

Mrs Han put her phone back in her bag. There was no hint of tension in her face as her gaze swept the carriage and the many passengers elbowing their way down the train.

A series of low beeps signalled the train's imminent departure. Mrs Han gripped her son's hand and the two sprinted out through the closing doors just in time.

The doors slammed shut.

Inside, two conspicuous passengers could only look at each other in shock.

★

'The targets jumped off the train! The doors shut before we could follow. Please advise.'

Pei took a deep breath. He had expected something like this, which was why he'd ordered Bravo Six and Seven off the train. Still, he couldn't help but shiver as he pondered Han's plan.

The subway tunnels formed a massive and labyrinthine chessboard. Pei was more than up to the challenge, but the situation unnerved him. Just as he was using his officers as pawns for the task force's own ends, Han was doing the same with his wife and son.

'All officers on that train, get off at the next stop and come back,' Pei said, focusing on the GPS monitor. The targets' position blinked red amid a mass of longitude and latitude lines. 'Everyone still on the platform, keep your eyes on the targets.'

Mrs Han called her husband after getting off the train. It was a short conversation, lasting ten seconds at most, and Pei could only pick up her side of the exchange.

'Should I get off the train like before?'

That single sentence made his forehead clammy. Han was going to pull his trick a second time. He'd already diverted more than half of Pei's team. How was Pei supposed to respond?

The southbound train was already pulling into the station. Mrs Han and her son boarded it and again remained standing right beside the doors.

'The targets are on board. Please advise!'

Pei heard the tension in Bravo Three's voice. Every officer was on tenterhooks.

The officers that had boarded the last train were already on their way back. With that in mind, Pei decided to risk putting as many people on this departing train as possible. 'Bravo Two, stay put. Bravos Three through Seven, get on that train!'

This time Mrs Han did not jump off. The doors closed. There was a lurch and the train set off.

SPU Captain Liu leant into his microphone. 'Bravos Three, Four, Five, Six and Seven, I want one of you to get off at each station in sequential order. Everyone remaining will stay with the targets.'

Pei was nervous. There were only five officers on that train. Liu's plan would only be good for the next five stops. If Mrs Han and her son disembarked at the last stop, the team would have to rely on a single officer to apprehend Captain Han. He thumped the back of the driver's seat in frustration. 'Let's go! Follow the route of the subway tracks!' he yelled.

Lieutenant Yin stamped on the accelerator and the van rumbled down the road.

Pei spoke into the radio again. 'I want you all to pay close attention. The targets are leaving Guangyuan Temple station on a southbound train. All officers who have lost sight of the targets are to board a train heading in that direction asap.'

'Yes, sir.'

'Boarding a train now, sir.'

'Affirm—'

'Ca— Got a bad sig—'

There were no other responses.

'Damn it!' TSO Zeng muttered. 'There's no radio signal in the tunnel.'

At that instant, the red dot vanished from Pei's monitor.

'Damn you, Han.'

Pei repeated his order into the radio several times. Two minutes passed before the red dot reappeared. The train carrying Mrs Han and her son had reached the next station.

Bravo Three disembarked to stand guard on the platform,

as per Liu's orders. Mrs Han and her son, however, did not alight. Now only four officers remained on board.

When the doors opened at the next stop, Mrs Han sprinted out with her son. She called her husband, as instructed.

As soon as the SPU officers updated him, Pei ordered Bravo Four to disembark. Bravos Five, Six and Seven were to remain on board in case Mrs Han doubled back.

His radio crackled as three other officers reported in from the train directly behind, having just left the previous stop.

Again, Mrs Han waited for the train to start beeping, then leapt back aboard with her son. The doors slid shut.

Bravo Four was left stranded on the platform. It would be at least two minutes before the other officers arrived. The surveillance team on the targets' train had been whittled down to three.

Above ground, the situation wasn't much better. Rush hour had clogged all of the city's main arteries. Even though Lieutenant Yin had switched on the sirens, they were still moving at a crawl. In the time it had taken Mrs Han's train to pass through two stops, they had barely advanced thirty metres.

The train was already nearing the third station. Bravo Five's voice came through the radio.

'The targets are getting off the train. Please advise!'

'Bravo Five, get off and follow them. Bravo Six and Seven, stay on the train.' Pei was not about to deviate from the original plan. He needed people on that train. There was every chance that the targets would repeat their trick.

The red dot on his GPS map remained static.

'The train's pulled out, but the targets are still here on the platform. Please advise,' Bravo Five radioed in.

Pei allowed himself a moment to breathe. Reinforcements would step onto the platform in moments.

The red dot was moving.

'Stay with them! Are the targets leaving the station?'

'No. They're heading for the interchange with Line C.'

'They're changing lines?' Pei asked dejectedly.

'Guangyuan Temple... Zhenghan Street... Shita Temple...' Lieutenant Yin rattled off stops from memory. 'They're at Yangkou Road now. Line C runs east–west from there.'

The downtown area was served by three subway lines. Line A ran in a continuous loop, Line B ran north–south and Line C ran east–west. Mrs Han and Dongdong had entered the metro at Guangyuan Temple, at the northwest corner of Line A. From there they went southwest. Taking Line C east would buy them more time if they were taking a quick route to Line B. Driving there, however, would be hell.

Bravo Five followed Mrs Han and her son down the stairs as an eastbound train pulled into the platform. She boarded the train with them but was fully aware that her targets might jump back onto the platform at the last second. Bravo Five was the only member of the surveillance team to have made it this far and she was determined not to slip up now.

Mrs Han hung up her phone and casually glanced around the carriage. Her gaze came to rest on Bravo Five and she smiled.

Bravo Five glanced away, her cheeks burning with humiliation. How could she have been spotted?

Pei's voice came through her earpiece. 'Bravo Five. Bravo Five, this is Bravo One. Please respond.'

She coughed into her hand and turned away from Mrs Han. Leaning into her concealed microphone, she whispered, 'Bravo Five here.'

'What is the status of the targets?'

She whirled around to see Mrs Han and her son standing on the platform. 'They're off the train,' Bravo Five said, her voice betraying her disappointment. 'I don't know how, but she spotted me. I'll have to double-back at the next stop.'

Pei clenched his teeth until his whole skull hurt. The red dot began moving west, only to vanish seconds later. 'They're on a train!' he yelled.

Seconds later a new message came through over the radio. The rest of the surveillance team had reached Yangkou Road station. Pei ordered them to board the next eastbound train and continue the pursuit.

The van was still crawling along. Pei tapped the back of Lieutenant Yin's seat.

'We're wasting time. Use the hard shoulder or go down a cycle lane if you have to. I don't care if you break the law or go against the traffic flow, you need to speed things up!'

'That's not going to make any difference if we're still going from stop to stop. Just tell me the final destination and I'll get you there,' Lieutenant Yin shot back.

Where was Han leading them?

Pei looked down at a map of Chengdu and mentally traced Mrs Han's path through the city. There was no logic to it. Unless… 'Where's the next interchange station?' he asked.

'Central Gate,' Yin said instantly. 'It's the busiest in the city. All the lines run through it.'

'If I were Han, that's exactly where I'd go to meet my wife and son. Get us to Central Gate!' Pei said.

Keeping an iron grip on the steering wheel, Lieutenant

Yin manoeuvred the van out of the dense lines of traffic and roared into the cycle lane with the siren blaring. Cyclists and pedestrians scrambled to get out of the way.

Pei exhaled loudly, relieved that they were finally moving.

They were now travelling in the same direction as the flickering red dot, which gave them all a much-needed boost. Yin continued to race the van down the narrow cycle lane at breakneck speed, driving flawlessly.

TSO Zeng pumped his fist. 'We're almost on top of them!'

The dot stood still for a moment, then began inching away from them. Pei and the other team members looked at one another. Mrs Han and her son were on the platform!

The excited voice of a young boy came through the radio.

'Daddy—' Dongdong cried.

His voice was suddenly cut off, as if someone had clapped a hand over his mouth. The sounds coming through the radio degenerated into whispery static. Seconds later, there was a click and the speaker went silent.

'He found the bug,' Pei said.

The team fell quiet. Lieutenant Yin guided the van back into the main lane. 'We're at the station,' he said.

Pei wrenched the side door open and the others poured out after him and sprinted towards the entrance. Commuters yelled out in confusion as they rushed past.

At the sound of heavy footsteps pounding through the station, Han froze. Without saying a word, he turned away from his wife and child and ran.

'Daddy!' cried Dongdong.

The boy took a few steps towards his father, but his mother quickly grabbed him and held on tight.

A line of uniformed officers streamed past them and the boy began to sob.

Using every last bit of energy, Han sprinted back onto the platform for Line A. He ran through the security check and leapt over the ticket turnstile. Ignoring the angry yells from behind, he peered down over the escalator barrier. The lights of an approaching train flooded the tunnel below. It was a five-metre drop to the platform.

The rapping of boots against the linoleum floor drew nearer. He needed to move.

Han vaulted the barrier and hurled himself down through the gap beside the escalator. His body twisted mid-air and when he landed his right ankle hit the floor with a grim crunch.

SPU Captain Liu was the first to reach the turnstile. He glanced over the barrier and spotted Han hobbling below. He was about to follow him and vault over the barrier himself when a hand grabbed his wrist.

'Forgot to buy a ticket, huh?'

Liu's head whipped around to see a middle-aged metro employee. She had an iron grip on his wrist and was holding on tight.

'Let me go!' he yelled as he pulled away from her. 'I'm a police officer!'

Captain Pei and Lieutenant Yin rushed over.

'Police!' shouted Pei, holding out his badge.

The employee's eyes widened and she released him. 'I had no idea,' she murmured, backing away.

Liu ignored her. 'Han's already on the platform,' he shouted. 'We have to get down there now!'

All three officers vaulted the gate and sprinted down the

escalator. When they reached the platform, they spotted Han limping into the train to their left. They raced towards him – and the train's doors shut right in front of them.

Han stood on the other side of the doors, panting. He leant against the handrail and leered at them through his gasps of pain.

SPU Captain Liu let out a strangled yell. He raced to the door and banged on the glass.

Captain Pei watched helplessly as his disgraced predecessor shook his head and grinned sourly. He wondered what emotions were going through Han's head. Concern for his family, embarrassment at his former colleagues seeing him like this or pride at his successful escape? One thing was certain – he was no longer the man that Pei had first met less than a fortnight ago, at the start of this investigation, when they'd both turned up at the apartment of their murdered fellow officer, Sergeant Zheng Haoming.

'Call off the chase,' Pei said as the train pulled out of the station. He turned back and headed for the platform exit.

SPU Captain Liu punched the fibreglass barrier for good measure then followed him and Lieutenant Yin.

TSO Zeng and Ms Mu were waiting for them upstairs, on the other side of the security gate. Standing next to them were Han's wife and child, both of whom looked completely petrified

TSO Zeng hurried over to Captain Pei. 'What happened?'

'He got away,' Pei said, shaking his head glumly. 'We missed him by seconds.'

'Damn,' muttered Zeng.

Mrs Han, her cheeks still wet with tears, let out an audible sigh of relief. Her son gripped her hand. 'Are you going to arrest me for harbouring a fugitive?' she asked, watching Pei through reddened eyes. There was a mocking tone to her voice and it made Pei uncomfortable.

'Your name is Han Dongdong, isn't it?' Pei asked the boy with a friendly smile.

The boy's face froze.

'I have a picture of you.' Pei opened his right hand to reveal the photo he'd retrieved from the bathroom at police headquarters.

The boy tilted his head in surprise.

'Do you know where your daddy went, Dongdong?'

'Sure. He just told me.'

Pei tried to keep his expression neutral. They might have lost Han this time, but there was still hope. 'Oh?' He smiled again, almost carelessly. 'Where'd he go?'

'He's going to catch a bad guy,' the boy answered, his voice swelling with pride. 'A real bad guy. And he told me to pay attention in school. When I grow up, I'm going to be a police officer too.' He puffed out his chest.

Pei ruffled the boy's hair. 'I'm sure you'll become a great police officer one day.'

He heard a muffled sob and he looked up. Tears were rolling down Mrs Han's cheeks. Pei felt sorry for the woman, but at the same time he was glad to see her tears because it meant that her son had told the truth.

'Take the two of them home,' he said to Lieutenant Yin. 'There's no need to bring them in for questioning.'

Nodding, Lieutenant Yin crouched down and scooped Dongdong up into his arms. He knew exactly where to take them, being familiar with their home. As Han's former assistant, he knew the disgraced captain's family better than anyone.

Mrs Han scowled at Pei. Swiping at her tears with one hand, she followed Lieutenant Yin and her son out of the station.

The remaining team members watched the retreating figures until they disappeared into the twilight.

'Did Han really put us through all that just to say a few words to his son?' Pei said, to no one in particular.

'If you were a father, you'd understand,' Ms Mu replied.

TSO Zeng snorted. 'At the very least, we should have taken the two of them in for questioning.' He raised an eyebrow at the captain. 'Why'd you let them go?'

'Two reasons. For one thing, they don't know anything beyond what they've already said. But more importantly, Han's son has told me everything I need to know.'

9:07 p.m.
The Green Spring

The woman's pale fingers danced across the strings. Gentle music flowed from her violin like rivulets washing over the customers as they dined.

As she set down her violin, an immaculately dressed waitress tiptoed up onto the stage and handed her a bouquet of fresh flowers. 'From a customer,' the waitress said in a hushed voice. 'There's no message or name.'

'Wait a moment, please,' the violinist replied. She reached out and selected a different bunch of flowers, which she passed to the waitress. 'Please send these lilies back as a gift,' she said in a near whisper. 'Make sure to thank the customer for their generosity.'

'Of course,' the waitress said. She stepped swiftly off the stage and walked over to a two-person table tucked into a quiet corner. The customer seated there looked up at her in confusion.

'Sir, our violinist thanks you for your patronage,' the waitress said, presenting the customer with the lilies.

He gazed at the flowers as though committing the aroma

and shape of every petal to memory. When the opening strains of Beethoven's 'Romance in F major' reached his ears, he looked up at the young woman on the stage. His eyes betrayed a slight glimmer of happiness.

An hour later, the violinist stood at the restaurant's entrance. The black band on her left arm made a striking contrast to her white clothing. A single character was traced upon it in white: '*xiao*', meaning 'filial'. The garment was a *xiao gu*, worn to honour the memory of a recently deceased parent.

The colleague standing next to her was a decade her senior. 'Are you sure you don't want me to take you home?' he said.

'I'm sure,' she said, her voice gentle but firm. 'Someone's coming for me. But I appreciate your offer.'

He shook his head. The woman had just lost her father and she'd never mentioned any other relatives or friends. Who could possibly be coming for her?

The friendship between the Green Spring's head chef and the blind violinist had caused a few tongues to wag, but he didn't care. Besides, they finished their shifts around the same time so it made sense for him to drive her home.

Her unexpected refusal had given him an uneasy feeling in the pit of his stomach.

'You don't need to worry about me,' she said. 'I have Niuniu to keep me company.'

He glanced down at the pedigree Labrador sitting obediently at her feet. The guide dog had been a gift from her father before his death. Well trained, intelligent and loyal, Niuniu spent most of her evenings napping in the back of the restaurant while her owner performed.

'Well, all right,' he said, his resolve finally weakening. After saying goodbye, he set off towards the car park.

She listened to his retreating footsteps and when she was sure he was gone, she tugged on Niuniu's lead. The dog leapt up and began guiding her forward. When they reached a flight of steps, Niuniu turned to touch both her legs, indicating that they were about to descend. Once her owner had cleared the steps, Niuniu resumed her quicker, lighter pace.

The two of them were soon out of the restaurant's courtyard and on a quiet side street. The young woman's right ear twitched as she registered the sound of tyres on the road. She stopped walking and waited. There was a gentle hissing of brakes and then the whirr of an automatic window being lowered.

'Do you need help? I can take you wherever you need to go.'

It was the voice of a young man. She turned towards him and leant forward slightly. A faint but sweet fragrance reached her nose. Lilies.

'I've been waiting for you,' she said calmly. 'Have you been following me?'

He didn't answer. 'Get in the car first,' he said. 'It's cold outside.'

She took a cautious step back and shook her head. 'No. I'm not getting into your car.'

'I understand. In that case, why don't we find somewhere to sit down and have a chat. There's a café nearby. We could go there.'

She knew the place he was talking about. Despite her initial reservations, she nodded. But she had one condition. 'I'll walk there myself.'

'Okay. I'll wait for you inside.'

★

He instinctively chose the café's most secluded table. Then he signalled to a nearby waiter.

'A young woman in a white dress is on her way here. She's blind. Could you go out and help her find her way in?'

The waiter was surprised but agreed to do as he'd been asked. He soon returned, accompanied by the young woman, whom he guided across to the table.

'Please take a seat,' the man said softly, unsure of what to say next. He'd not planned this meeting. In fact, he wasn't even sure why he'd suggested it in the first place.

The young woman slid onto her seat with practised dexterity. Her dog sniffed at the air then lay down at her feet, maintaining a watchful eye on the two of them.

'Why have you been following me?' she asked bluntly.

'I haven't been following you. I was simply eating at the restaurant earlier, and I saw you as I was driving away, so I wanted to be of assistance,' he said, neglecting to mention that he'd spent an hour waiting for her in the car park after his meal.

'No, you've been following me. Don't lie to me.' She frowned. 'I might be blind, but sometimes being blind means you can see things that others can't.'

'That's true,' the man said, smiling to himself. 'Like with those lilies earlier.'

'Today wasn't the first time you sent me flowers.'

He didn't say anything. He couldn't deny it and nor did he wish to.

'You've come to the restaurant every day for the past week. Each time you've stayed until I've left. I can still sense what's happening, even if I can't see you. You've been following me. Don't lie about it.'

He sucked the air through his teeth. 'All right. I've been following you. But not out of any malicious intent. I just wanted to make sure you got away safely. Because...' He hesitated, shocked at the words that were coming. 'I recently lost someone who was very close to me.'

'What do you mean?' the young woman asked, her voice softening.

He bit his lip. It was the first time he'd ever spoken to anyone about his personal feelings. Yuan would have called him weak, but it felt so liberating.

'I know you've lost your father,' he said quietly.

She coughed and her eyes began to water.

'My own father recently passed away as well,' he continued. 'I understand what you're going through. To suddenly lose the person who takes care of you. It feels like the foundations of your life have been torn from under you.'

'Your father, you mean?' Tears streaked her face. All hostility had evaporated.

'Yes, my father,' he repeated.

She blinked away her tears. 'That's why you've been giving me flowers? And following me?'

'No,' he said, shaking his head. 'I gave you flowers because I liked your music.'

She looked surprised. 'Do you enjoy classical music?'

'I'm not very familiar with the genre, but I like the pieces you play. Especially the one you open with every night. It always makes me think of the family that I've lost.'

'It's by a Czech composer named František Drdla. It's called "*Sehnsucht*", which means "Longing". It's meant to evoke those who have already left us.' She sighed quietly to herself. 'I don't believe that you're lying to me about your father.'

The sounds of the café grew quiet and muddled and he could hear her gentle, peaceful melodies echoing in his ears once again. But at the same time the faces of the dead flashed before his eyes, alternately murky and crystal clear, merging and overlapping with one another in macabre fluidity. A stabbing pain flared between his temples. He shuddered.

'Is something wrong?' she asked, genuinely concerned.

'It's nothing.' Taking a deep breath, he massaged his forehead. 'I also enjoy the third piece you play,' he said in an attempt to change the subject.

'The third one?' She rested a hand against her left cheek. 'How does it make you feel?'

'It makes me feel at peace.'

'Do you have a lot on your mind? Are there things that make you feel confused and uncertain? Worries from the past or concerns about the future?' She paused. 'Maybe even something right in front of you?'

He looked away from her, even though he understood how meaningless that gesture was.

She smiled. 'The piece you're talking about is "Méditation" by the French composer Massenet. It's a famous reverie. I've found that it has a way of speaking to the audience if there's something troubling them.'

Her smile infused her features with a lovely glow. It was, in fact, the first time he had ever seen her smiling. The sight stirred something inside him.

'You have a beautiful smile.'

She lowered her head in apparent embarrassment, but her smile remained.

'You're not a bad person,' she said a moment later.

'Oh? And why do you say that?'

'Because you understand my music.'

'What did you think of me before you came in here? Did you think I was dangerous?'

'No, not exactly,' she said, almost apologetically. 'I'm just trying to keep my life as quiet as possible, in light of recent events.'

'What do you mean? Are you in some kind of trouble?'

'There was a customer last night. He was drunk and he ran after me. You were there, weren't you?'

'I was. I was about to chase after him, but the waiters got to him first. I was worried about you. It's why I followed you today – because I was concerned something similar might happen again.'

'If it does, it won't be because of him. He's dead.'

'He is?' he asked, feigning shock.

'It happened after he left the restaurant last night. They say it was a car accident, but I've also heard there may be more to it. A few of his friends came looking for me this afternoon. They suspected that his accident was some sort of retaliation for his outburst towards me. I told them I didn't know anyone who was even remotely capable of doing something like that. But then you showed up again today, and, well, I started thinking.'

She paused again and adopted a more diplomatic approach. 'I'm not saying I suspect you of any wrongdoing. It's just that I thought we should talk face to face.'

An invisible hand tightened around his chest, but he kept himself in check. He knew which 'friends' she was referring to.

'Don't dwell on it. You know it had nothing to do with you,' he said soothingly. 'Some people don't realise how many enemies they've made. And even if there was foul play, there's no reason that anyone would link it to you.'

'You're right. Maybe I'm being paranoid. I suppose it's just in my blood. My father was a police officer, you know.' When she said that, her face darkened.

'Is something wrong?' It took all his effort to control his surging emotions and maintain a natural tone of voice. 'It's late. You should be getting home.'

She fidgeted in her seat and he had to remind himself that regardless of how long he'd been watching her, she was still a stranger.

'Yes, it's late,' she said, tugging at a dangling lock of hair. 'Can you still take me home?'

'Of course,' he said. Even though it was their first actual meeting, he felt a deep connection that he couldn't explain. Somehow he knew without question that he was responsible for her safety.

'Thank you.' She smiled again. 'By the way, my name is Zheng Jia.'

9:30 p.m.
Criminal police headquarters

The doorbell rang. When Captain Pei opened the door, TSO Zeng was standing outside. He produced a scrap of paper from his pocket and handed it to Pei.

Huang Jieyuan
Male, 48
Current owner of the Black Magic Bar
Mobile number: 13020011590

'Huang Jieyuan was Captain Ding Ke's assistant during the January 30th hostage case. He understands the case better than anyone, after Captain Ding himself.'

'Excellent work,' Pei said. 'What a relief.'

'Unfortunately, he's the only person we were able to track down,' Zeng said. 'I'm not very hopeful that we'll succeed in finding Captain Ding. Like the commissioner told you, they've been looking for him for a decade already. As for the other names in the report, a few of them have actually passed away in the meantime. And then there's Zhong Yun, the SPU marksman that took out Wen Hongbing. For some reason, we can't find any information on him either.'

'You mean he's missing too?'

'What I mean is that "Zhong Yun" doesn't exist. I can't find a single record on anyone with that name. It must be an alias.'

'Interesting. Let's focus on Huang Jieyuan first and see where that gets us. Maybe he'll bring us closer to this "Zhong Yun".'

'Why don't I give him a call right now?'

'It's late,' Pei said, brushing TSO Zeng's suggestion away with a wave. 'Let's wait until tomorrow.'

'Tomorrow?' Zeng repeated in disbelief. 'Chief, we're up against Eumenides here.'

'I'm very aware of that. Trust me.' Pei stared pointedly at TSO Zeng.

The younger officer eventually nodded. 'You're the captain, Captain.'

5

SETTING THE TRAP

31 October, 8:33 a.m.
Back office, Black Magic Bar

'Phone call for you, Mr Huang,' the bar's manager said softly.

'Who is it?' Huang Jieyuan mumbled, rubbing the sleep from his eyes.

'He says he's with the public security bureau.'

'What?' The words sent a familiar jolt of adrenaline through his system. Now completely awake, he sat up and picked up the receiver. 'This is Huang Jieyuan.'

'Hello, I'm calling on behalf of the archives centre at the public security bureau,' a male voice stated.

'The PSB archives, huh?' Huang said, trying to figure out what interest the bureau could possibly have in him.

'That's right. We have a few questions regarding a case from 1984. The January 30th hostage case, to be specific. Am I correct in saying that you were Captain Ding's assistant at the time and that you were directly involved with this investigation?'

'Er, yes. But why the sudden interest in the January 30th case?'

'Oh, it's nothing too serious. We've started doing spot-checks on old investigations and our last check revealed that the January 30th case files aren't quite up to department standards. My superiors have asked me to fill in the gaps by interviewing the individuals involved and submitting a supplementary report.'

Huang chuckled. 'I think your superiors are being rather optimistic. It's been almost two decades. How much do you expect us to remember? Besides, I've been retired for years. I no longer report to any of you.'

'I take your point,' the caller said. 'All we're asking is that you assist us by giving us a little of your time. Nothing more.'

'I don't have a whole lot of time to give,' Huang replied lazily. 'I've got enough on my plate as it is.'

The line was silent for several seconds. When the caller spoke again, it was with a more amiable tone.

'Actually, I think we can both help each other out here. What if I provided you with some newly uncovered files regarding a certain investigation. The Bagman Killing, for instance.'

Huang's mouth fell open. 'Now that is an interesting proposal.'

'Does that mean you're willing to tell me about the January 30th case?'

'Fine. I'll track down my old logbooks. You should find them useful.'

'Oh? What logbooks?'

'I used to keep personal records of every case I was involved in. I'd write down every detail, including some that didn't make it into the official reports. I'd even go so far as to say that those logbooks are worth more than the records you have on file.'

'How soon could you get us these logbooks?'

Huang detected a hint of desperation in the man's voice.

'That depends on when I start looking,' he said with deliberate vagueness. 'I keep all my logbooks in my garage. They're mixed in with a lot of old papers, bills, random junk. It's been years since I looked at them.' He went quiet for a moment. 'It's actually been a decade since I was last in uniform. I didn't expect to ever touch those logbooks again.'

'Well, I hope to hear back from you as soon as possible.'

'Don't get too excited. I assume you'll need some time to prepare the Bagman files.'

'Yes, of course.' A gruff laugh came from the other end. 'You are a true businessman, Huang.'

Huang responded with a sly laugh of his own. 'As long as we understand each other, then I think this could be the start of a long and fruitful friendship.' They exchanged numbers and he hung up.

At that, Huang's smile faded like sunlight on a cloudy day. He beckoned to the bar's floor manager.

'Yes, Mr Huang?'

'I need to use your mobile.'

10:47 a.m.
Huang's residence

A woman walked through the main gate of the Lai Yin Yuan housing development. She exchanged a wave and a nod with the guard at the entrance. In her right hand she held a plastic bag bulging with groceries.

A younger man followed behind, pedalling a three-wheeled pedicab. His sturdy physique and swarthy complexion identified him as one of the millions of migrant workers who moved to the cities to earn their living as manual labourers. In the back of his small vehicle was a hefty basket of ruby-red apples.

'Those apples look delicious,' the guard said, beaming.

'That's right,' the woman said cheerfully. 'Cheap, too. He

offered to deliver them right to my door if I bought a few more. I'll bring you some later.'

'Only if it's no trouble.' The guard walked over to help the young fruit vendor.

'Thank you, thank you,' the vendor said hoarsely.

The woman led the vendor to her building's garage, fished out her key and pointed to a gap between two bicycles near the door. The young man hoisted up the basket of apples and shuffled over with it, trying to maintain his balance. He set it down on the cement floor with a thud.

'Thank you so much!' She handed him a note from her purse.

He accepted it, but rather than leave immediately, he scanned the garage and let his gaze settle on a large stack of old magazines and newspapers in the corner.

'Do you still want all that paper, ma'am? I can take it off your hands and give you thirty yuan for it.'

The woman stared at the stack of papers in surprise. She'd never seen it before. Nor the two massive cardboard boxes to either side of it.

When a pair of men burst out of the cardboard boxes, she was even more surprised. One of the men rushed forward and shut the garage door. The other pounced on the fruit vendor and pinned him to the ground.

This all happened in seconds. The woman screamed in shock as the garage door slammed shut. One of the men was yelling something at her, but it took time for her to register what he was actually saying.

'Don't be afraid. We're police officers!'

Still frozen in shock, Huang's wife gaped at the man facing her. 'Captain Pei…' she said, reading aloud the name on his badge.

★

With Commissioner Song's approval, Captain Pei had got in touch with Huang the previous evening, right after TSO Zeng had given him his contact details. Since it was possible that Eumenides was monitoring the other members of the task force, Pei and Commissioner Song decided to keep the rest of the team in the dark.

Huang had phoned Pei again that morning, after which Pei and SPU Captain Liu had immediately gone to Huang's home, taking a considerable amount of old paper and cardboard with them. Once they'd finished setting up, they waited inside the boxes.

The identity of the person who'd called Huang claiming to work for the PSB archives was clear enough. Eumenides was trying to track down information on the January 30th case, just as Pei had expected.

Pei and Liu had waited inside the garage for more than an hour before the door opened. The captain almost blew his cover when Huang's wife entered, but that was before he noticed the young man who'd followed her inside. His appearance suggested that he was simply a migrant worker selling fruit, but Pei was well aware of Eumenides' talent for disguise. He snapped into high-alert mode and when the vendor offered to buy the scrap paper for the outrageously high price of thirty yuan, his suspicions were confirmed. He sprang into action and Liu followed suit.

Once she realised that the two men were police officers, Huang's wife began to recover her equilibrium. But she was still extremely confused. 'What are you doing here?' she asked.

'Who is he?' Pei said, pointing at the young man who was being held down by SPU Captain Liu.

'What did I do?' the man cried, his eyes huge with terror. 'Please, I'm not a criminal!'

Mrs Huang blinked in bewilderment. 'He's just a fruit vendor! What's going on here?'

Pei crossed his arms. 'How much did you pay for those apples?'

'Fifty yuan.'

'Why were they so cheap?'

'I don't know. They were on sale, I suppose.'

'Did you approach him first or did he approach you?'

'He approached me. I was at the market and he ran over, saying that he wanted to give me a bargain on some apples. And he offered to deliver them straight to my home. That's why I decided to buy them.' She glared at the young man. 'Hey, what sort of scam were you trying to pull?' she asked.

Liu pressed on the young man's wrists. 'Come on, spit it out!' he growled.

The vendor's face contorted in pain and he let out a choked yell. 'Okay, I'll talk! I'll talk!' he said, panting for breath. 'Someone told me to sell her those apples cheap. He paid me a lot of money. Two hundred yuan! How could I say no?'

Liu caught Pei's eye and Pei nodded. Liu tightened his grip on the man's wrists. 'Who was it?' he barked. 'Where is he?'

The vendor's words came out in guttural spurts punctuated by yelps of pain. 'I don't know, honest! I never saw him before today. I just assumed he was the woman's husband or maybe a relative.'

'Like we can believe a word he's saying!' Huang's wife snapped.

'The guy was pretty tall, but I can't say for sure what he looked like. He was wearing a big hat, and he had a scarf around his face. He told me to deliver the apples to her garage and that there might be a stack of waste paper in there. If I collected the paper, he'd pay me five yuan per kilogram. I wasn't going to turn down an offer like that.'

The young man looked over towards the stack of paper as he spoke.

'That's not ours,' Huang's wife said.

'Where's the man now?' Pei asked. 'How were you supposed to give him the scrap paper once you'd picked it up?'

'He told me to wait outside the main gate. He said I'd able to find him right away.'

'What do we do, Captain?' Liu hissed. 'This could be our chance to track Eumenides. Why don't we let this guy take the scrap paper and we'll follow him.'

'It's already too late,' Pei said with a grimace. 'Eumenides is most likely watching the house. It's been a few minutes since we shut the door. He'll know something's up.'

'Then what should we do?'

Pei squeezed his sweaty palms into a fist. He couldn't afford to hesitate now.

A low thumping came from outside. Footsteps.

Pei looked over at Liu. 'Open the door,' he mouthed. He gave a signal with his hand, and the two of them wrenched the garage door open.

They recognised the man standing outside. It was the guard from the front gate. He did a double-take at the sight of two additional strangers inside the garage. Dazed, he held out an envelope to no one in particular.

'Someone asked me to give you this letter.'

'And where is that person now?' Pei asked, taking the envelope.

'He ran off after he gave it to me. All he said was to come to this garage and hand it to whoever was inside.'

'Was he tall? Wearing a hat and with a scarf covering most of his face?'

'As a matter of fact, yes.'

Pei glanced at Liu, who nodded. 'He saw us.'

Captain Pei removed two items from the envelope: a slip of paper and a jade pendant of Guan Yin, the Buddhist Bodhisattva of Mercy. A short note was written on the paper in immaculate print.

2 p.m., Mad World internet café

Huang's wife let out a sudden cry.

'What's wrong?' Pei asked.

'That looks like the Guan Yin pendant my son wears.' She took the jade image and held it in her hands. 'Yes, it's definitely his! But what's it doing here?'

Pei didn't answer. He had a sinking feeling in the pit of his stomach.

11:23 a.m.
Conference room, criminal police headquarters

All the members of the task force were present in the conference room. They'd been joined by a plump middle-aged man with a resolute but anxious air about him.

Pei introduced him. 'This is Huang Jieyuan, former lieutenant in the Chengdu criminal police. Ten years ago, a certain incident caused him to leave the world of law enforcement and try his hand at business. He currently owns the Black Magic Bar.'

'That's all well and good,' TSO Zeng said, 'but how's it going to help our investigation?'

Pei scowled at him. 'Huang was Captain Ding Ke's assistant on the January 30th hostage case. He was there when Eumenides' biological father was killed and that's why I've asked him to sit in on the task force's operations as an external consultant.'

'There's also the matter of my son,' Huang said impatiently.

Pei nodded and briefed the others.

'Huang Deyang is fourteen years old and in his second year at Chengdu Number 3 Junior High School. An athletics meet was scheduled to take place there today. According to his fellow students, Deyang left the track just after 9 a.m. to buy a drink but did not return. Our attempted ambush at Huang's garage took place two hours after the boy went missing.'

TSO Zeng turned to Captain Pei. 'Last night, you told me to wait before getting in touch with him,' he said, nodding at Huang. 'Looks like you and Liu had other plans.'

'It wasn't that I didn't trust you. We were concerned that Eumenides might be monitoring the team.'

'But you trusted Liu,' Ms Mu interjected. 'The real reason, Captain Pei, is your need for control.'

Pei did not reply.

'His need to control what?' Zeng asked. 'Us?'

'Everything. The captain doesn't want a single thing to be outside his control. But, Captain Pei,' Ms Mu said, her tone now one of gentle reprimand, 'you're the head of this task force. It's your job to trust us.'

'You're right,' Pei said. 'And I should have coordinated with the team to ensure that we had eyes on Huang's entire family. You have my sincere apologies for that, Huang.'

Huang shook his head. 'As it happens, I think you were right to try and keep this under wraps. It's precisely because someone didn't keep this operation secret that my son's life is now in danger.'

Pei inhaled sharply. 'What do you mean?'

'There's a reason why Eumenides is being so brazen. To begin with, he was trying to be low key, hence his attempt to masquerade as an employee of the PSB archives centre. But when he realised that I'd seen through him and had alerted Captain Pei, he resorted to more extreme measures.'

'Eumenides called you at eight thirty,' Lieutenant Yin said. 'He got to your son a little after nine o'clock. It was almost eleven when Captain Pei and SPU Captain Liu received that envelope in your garage. Does that mean he saw through your bluff when he was talking to you?'

Huang let out a long breath. 'I suppose it does,' he said, hanging his head. 'But what I still can't figure out is how he knew. I was extremely cautious about how I communicated with Captain Pei. I didn't even use my own phone to call him.'

This was precisely what Pei had been puzzling over since he'd received Eumenides' note. 'Let's focus, people. We don't have time to sort out all the answers right now. We've only got two hours until Eumenides' deadline. What's our next step?'

'To decide that, we need to know what our opponent is planning,' Ms Mu replied.

'Isn't it obvious?' TSO Zeng asked, glancing around the room.

He was met with a series of blank faces.

'Go on,' Pei said.

'If I were Eumenides, I'd be compelled to seek out the truth behind my father's death. Huang, you may be the last remaining link to that event, but you're also being watched by the police. So how can Eumenides get round that? In many ways, getting that information out of you could be even trickier than committing a murder. If I were him, I'd want as much control as possible over my dealings with you. And what's the best way to achieve that?'

Zeng came to a deliberate pause and waited. No one said anything.

'By video chat, of course! That way, he can observe Huang without having to be physically in his presence. He can monitor your facial expressions and tone of voice, Huang, to determine whether you're telling the truth. And he can use your son as leverage – and actually show him to you – without revealing his location. Think about it – it's pretty obvious, no?'

Pei nodded. 'I agree with you, Zeng. So now we need to ask ourselves two questions: what does Eumenides want to know and what should we let him know?'

The room grew tense as the team pondered this question. After about thirty seconds, SPU Captain Liu broke the silence. 'Let's make Eumenides focus on the special police unit. We know he wants to get to the truth behind his father's death, and the man who shot and killed Wen Hongbing was an SPU marksman. I recommend that we select the name of a retired SPU officer, someone older but still very capable, and leak that to Eumenides.'

'That would be extremely dangerous,' Pei said.

'When is dealing with Eumenides ever safe? Besides, I can't think of a single member of the SPU, retired or not, who wouldn't risk his life to avenge Captain Xiong's death,' Liu said, swallowing uncomfortably at the mention of his fallen captain's name. 'If I wasn't too young to have been the marksman in 1984, I'd volunteer myself.'

'Fine,' Pei said, fixing Liu with a grim stare and trying hard not to show how furious he was. 'Choose someone as soon as possible and tell them to report to me right away.'

'Understood!' Liu got up and strode out of the conference room.

'Coming up with a name will be easy enough,' Huang said. 'The hard part will be making Eumenides believe us.'

'We need to be clever about how Eumenides gets the name. We can't be too obvious.' Pei looked at Ms Mu. 'Do you think you could coach Huang through this?'

'Certainly,' she said. 'Give us an hour to go through it. With a few corroborating details and some psychological tricks, we'll reel Eumenides in and eliminate his doubts one by one.'

'Excellent. Make the conversation with Eumenides last as long as possible, to give TSO Zeng enough time to track his location.'

TSO Zeng snickered. 'I thought you'd forgotten about me, Captain.'

'Online tracking is your expertise,' Pei said with an easy smile. 'This is your chance to shine.'

Raising his eyebrows, Zeng said, 'You can rest assured that I've been ready for this day for a long time.'

Pei checked his watch. 'It's currently seven minutes after twelve. Lieutenant Yin and TSO Zeng, you'll come with me to the internet café right now. Huang, you and Ms Mu will discuss your plans in greater detail and then meet us there at one thirty.'

Ten minutes later, Captain Pei, Lieutenant Yin and TSO Zeng jumped into a police car and headed to the Mad World internet café. Lieutenant Yin drove.

'Captain, I know that now might not be the best time to talk about this, but there's something you should be aware of,' TSO Zeng said, looking Pei right in the eye. 'It's about Teacher Wu's death.'

'Do you have a lead?' Pei asked, visibly interested.

'I wouldn't call it a lead,' Zeng said, shrugging. 'It's basically public knowledge now.'

Pei sighed. Zeng wasn't making this easy. 'Out with it! What happened?'

'The fake cop who talked to Teacher Wu in the hospital – turns out he's an online journalist. Teacher Wu committed suicide as a result of that interview.'

'How do you know that? Is the interview online already?'

'It's gone viral! The headline is "Serial Killer Eumenides Kills Again – Shamed Teacher's Career Comes to a Bloody End".' That juicy enough for you?'

Lieutenant Yin half-turned towards them from the driver's seat. 'What kind of shameless reporter would write something like that? It's pure sensationalism, not journalism!'

'That's not all.' Zeng smiled grimly. 'The reporter also posted the audio recording of the interview. Half a dozen news sites have shared it already. A single listen of this "final interview", as people are calling it, tells you everything you need to know about why Teacher Wu killed himself.'

Pei shook his head. 'Did the interviewer go too far?'

'Let me play a bit of it for you.' Zeng pulled out an MP3 player. 'Have a listen,' he said, turning on the external speaker.

A low, wishy-washy voice issued from the device.

'*According to your account,*' the disguised voice began, '*the killer let the girl go because you agreed to cut off your own hand. You finally found your inner courage and realised what it meant to truly assume the responsibilities of a teacher. Is that correct?*'

'*Well... Uh...*'

'*Okay, let me put it more simply. Do you consider yourself a heroic person? Are you a responsible teacher?*'

'*I... I suppose I wasn't before. But after this experience, I believe that... that I can be that kind of person.*'

'*So you think you acquitted yourself well in this scenario? What about the deaths of those two young men? They were just seventeen years old, not even adults.*'

Pei heard a strained, gasping noise. Several seconds passed before the interviewer spoke again.

'*Did you go to the Thousand Peaks Hotel because the killer promised to give you back your teaching job?*'

'Yes,' Teacher Wu answered despondently.

'*After everything that's happened, do you still believe you're fit to work as a teacher?*'

Teacher Wu said nothing.

'*It sounds to me as if you're not even fit to step inside a school. So why did you go to the hotel? Is it because teaching is nothing more than a job to you? Because you care more about earning a salary than honouring the responsibility that goes with the job?*'

'*I… I don't want to answer that,*' Teacher Wu said, his voice trembling.

'*Why not? Have you not found your courage? Have you considered that had you not gone to the hotel that day – or had you never become a teacher in the first place – then those students would still be alive? In which case, does that not make you responsible for their deaths?*'

Teacher Wu's stammering attempts to form words gave way to pained sobs.

'The bastard,' Pei hissed, his forehead furrowing. 'Asking those questions to an old man who had just been seriously injured. He was deliberately trying to provoke him.'

TSO Zeng paused the recording. 'You're right. But from the reporter's perspective, a measured and amicable interview wouldn't have got nearly as many clicks. Maybe he was hoping that Wu would buckle under the stress and, you know, it would make his interview a little more interesting…'

'It's despicable!' Pei spat, his features contorting with anger. 'What do we know about this reporter?'

Zeng shook his head. 'Not much. These kinds of online journalists all write under pseudonyms. And you heard how he disguised his voice in the recording? He isn't an idiot; he's taken plenty of precautions to make sure we can't track him down.'

'Leave this with me for now,' Pei said, taking the MP3 player from Zeng. 'I don't believe that this person will be as impossible to trace as you suggest.'

Zeng spread his hands. 'Okay, let's assume we track him down. Then what? He won't bring us any closer to Eumenides.'

Lieutenant Yin smashed a fist against the steering wheel. 'He broke the law, damn it! This so-called journalist posed as a police officer. Let's bring him in first and then decide what to do with him.'

'Easy, Lieutenant Yin. Now's not the time.' Pei patted his overzealous assistant on the shoulder. 'Let's stay focused on our real objectives.'

Lieutenant Yin clenched his jaw and stayed silent.

'You know, we're sweating blood here, going after Eumenides,' Zeng said. 'But then something like this happens. Something that makes you so angry, you almost wish someone like Eumenides would take care of such people.'

Pei looked over at TSO Zeng, shocked at his comment. And yet, loath though he was to admit it, he understood exactly what his officer meant.

6

FACE TO FACE

12:32 p.m.
Mad World internet café

The Mad World café had about a dozen computers, half of which were occupied when Captain Pei arrived. With the manager's cooperation, Pei and TSO Zeng checked each customer's ID. Once they'd confirmed that everyone was who they claimed to be, Lieutenant Yin ushered them out of the building.

'Eumenides chose this place for a reason. Do you think he's installed a virus on one of the computers, ready for Huang?' Pei asked Zeng.

'All he wants to do is talk to Huang. What good would a virus do?'

'Even so, I think we should check every terminal. Do we have time?'

'Fine.' Zeng glanced at his watch. 'I should have enough time to do some quick security scans if I hurry. You and Lieutenant Yin take care of the other prep work. I've got this.' He pulled up a chair to the nearest computer and began typing away at two different keyboards.

Pei walked over to Lieutenant Yin. 'Zeng's checking the computers, but for all we know the real threat could come from somewhere else. We need to ask ourselves why Eumenides chose this location.'

'Do you think he intends to harm Huang?' Yin asked, sucking in his cheeks. He stepped towards the exit and surveyed the locale. 'There's a three-storey furniture shop, a four-storey electronics centre and a bank,' he said, pointing at each of the buildings in turn. 'Someone on the roof of the bank would have a perfect view of everything going on inside this café.'

Pei nodded. 'We need people at each of those locations. You take care of that, Lieutenant Yin. I want everyone in position within half an hour.'

As Yin radioed for reinforcements, Pei pulled out his phone and called SPU Captain Liu.

'How's the situation over there?'

'We've already chosen someone. Should I bring him over to meet you?'

'No. It's imperative that he stays away from the internet café. But I want you to give me a detailed bio. Send me all the files you can on this person.'

'Yes, sir. I can be there in approximately forty minutes to brief you, Ms Mu and Huang in person.'

At precisely 1:30 p.m., SPU Captain Liu, Ms Mu and Huang arrived at the Mad World internet café. They convened in the management lounge, which Pei had converted into a temporary command centre.

'How'd the prep work go?' he asked Ms Mu.

'We've agreed on a psychological strategy,' she said with a curt nod. 'Huang knows the steps and how to guide Eumenides between each one. But to be honest, sir, everything hinges on Eumenides.'

Pei grunted in approval. 'Liu, let me see the files on the former SPU officer you've chosen.'

Liu passed him a chunky manila folder. 'Everything's inside this.'

'Excellent,' Pei said, flipping through it. He handed it on to Huang. 'As you know, Huang, your task is to convince Eumenides that this man is the marksman that the January 30th files refer to as "Zhong Yun". We have less than half an hour. Memorise as much of it as you can.'

Huang weighed the thick stack of files in his hands. He shook his head. 'Sorry, but there's no way I'm going to remember this much.'

'You won't need to,' Ms Mu said. 'He's just an old comrade-in-arms who worked with you a couple of decades ago. Of course you won't know everything about him. In fact, it'll be suspicious if you *do* answer all of Eumenides' questions about him.'

'I want you to look at the files as well, Ms Mu,' Pei said. 'Help us decide which details we should reveal to Eumenides and which we should keep secret.'

Ms Mu nodded and immediately began studying the documents with Huang.

Pei walked over to TSO Zeng, who was checking the café's final few terminals. 'How's everything?' he asked. 'Any results?'

'I found a few viruses here and there but none I could trace back to Eumenides,' Zeng said, his fingers a blur as they sped across the keyboard. 'Though if I were Eumenides, I'd make absolutely sure that I left no trace.'

'So where does that leave us?'

'If I were him, I'd note the IP addresses of the computers I intended to target. This would allow him to set a trap and then to trigger it only when he's ready to do so.'

'And what can we do about that?'

'Well, we did the right thing by coming here early and checking. But what we do after two o'clock will be even more crucial. I'll monitor the servers here. No matter which computer

Eumenides attacks, I'll be able to keep an eye on everything that's going on. While Ms Mu and Huang are keeping Eumenides occupied, I'll trace him through the network.'

Pei nodded. 'Let SPU Captain Liu know when you need his people at a specific location.'

'You may as well tell him to get them ready now then.' Zeng smirked. 'I'm not leaving here empty-handed.'

2 p.m.

SPU Captain Liu stood watch at the entrance to the internet café, raking the surroundings with vigilant eyes. A bunch of officers under Lieutenant Yin's command had formed a tight circle around the building.

Huang was sitting in the management lounge. His heart was racing at a mile a minute.

'There's nothing to worry about,' Ms Mu said. 'Just do what we practised and you'll have your son back with you in no time.'

TSO Zeng had taken up position behind the main server. At precisely 2 p.m. a window flashed on his monitor. 'Terminal 33! He's uploading a piece of software onto it.'

'What kind of software?' Pei asked.

'I've never seen it before. It looks like some kind of control program. We won't know what it actually does until it activates though. Should I block it from the server?'

'No, let him upload it to the network. I have a feeling it's the only way Eumenides will let us talk to him. Hurry up and trace his IP address.'

'He's begun installing the software,' Zeng said, typing at lightning speed. 'Focus your attention on Computer 33. I'm making a copy of the software so I can analyse it. He's hidden his IP address, but I'll crack it in a few seconds.'

Pei scanned the internet café. Seconds later, his eyes locked onto the most isolated terminal in the building. The placard on the black divider read: 33.

A chat window flashed onto the monitor just as Huang, Ms Mu and Pei reached it. A couple of words appeared inside it:

I'm here.

The black font was unmistakeably familiar. So familiar that, for a brief instant, Pei expected to see the words *Death Notice* appear next.

Huang sat down in front of the computer and typed his response into the window.

So am I.

Eumenides' reply came fast.

I see you.

A green light appeared on the computer's external camera and another window popped up on the screen, relaying the camera's live feed. The feed from Eumenides' end, however, did not appear.

Three names came up in the chat window, one after the other.

Huang
Captain Pei
Ms Mu

Huang's mouth twitched uncertainly, while Pei stared daggers at the camera. He stepped forward, as if to show Eumenides that he wasn't afraid of being seen.

Ms Mu was taken aback. The thought of being watched by an unseen man didn't sit well with her. She reached out and turned the camera away.

Seconds later, another message appeared.

Don't turn the camera off and don't move it. Let me see you.

Pei shook his head disapprovingly at Ms Mu and returned the camera to its original position. Reluctantly, the psychologist stepped out of the camera's field of vision. She gave Huang a pointed look. He began typing again, more frantically this time.

Where is my son?

Eumenides responded swiftly.

Put on a pair of headphones. I want to hear your voice.

Huang hesitated.

Every computer in the Mad World internet café was equipped with a bulky set of headphones with a built-in microphone. Huang slowly donned the ones at his terminal.

'Where's my son?' he asked.

'Your son is with me,' a robotic voice answered.

'Is he okay?'

'For now.'

'I want to see him. Turn on your camera.'

'It wouldn't make any difference,' the voice said coldly.

'Don't hurt him!' Huang roared. 'For your own good, you better not hurt him.'

For a moment, Eumenides was silent. Then Huang heard a soft sigh rustling through his headphones.

'Understand this: should any harm befall your son, you'll have only yourself to blame. If you hadn't pulled that idiotic trick this morning, your son would be playing with his classmates right now.'

Huang took a deep breath. It required all his willpower to keep his anger under control. 'What are you trying to achieve with this?' he growled.

Pei saw that TSO Zeng was waving him over, so he left the terminal and went to speak with him in private.

'I've already traced an IP address,' Zeng said, handing him a scrap of paper with a series of numbers scrawled on it. 'This belongs to the Blue Star internet café, about ten kilometres from here.'

'Another café?' Pei said suspiciously. Would Eumenides really be so brazen as to conduct this conversation from a public place?

'There's a 99 per cent chance it's a Trojan horse,' Zeng said hastily. 'A Trojan horse is—'

'I'm not that much of a Luddite, TSO Zeng,' Pei interrupted.

'Great.' Zeng nodded. 'So, to sum up, Eumenides is communicating with us through a series of computers under his control. All we have to do is uncover the links all the way to the other end of the chain.'

'How long is that going to take?'

'That's the problem. There's no way of telling how many links there are until I've found the last one. I'll need to check each IP address one at a time – and I'll have to go to each one in person.'

Pei resisted the urge to punch the nearest monitor. 'I see. Go and find SPU Captain Liu and tell him where you need to go. Don't waste a single second. I don't care how many computers it takes, I want you to go through all of them until you find him.'

Zeng shifted uncomfortably from foot to foot. 'There's one more thing.'

'What is it?' Pei snapped.

'The program that Eumenides uploaded onto Huang's computer is still running, but I haven't figured out what it is.'

'Didn't you just say you were able to copy it?'

'Yes, but I can't run it. The control interface has already been deleted, so I can't tell what it's actually supposed to do. I've just started going through the program's back end. A few modules are clearly performing some kind of external monitoring and giving feedback in real time.'

'What exactly is he monitoring?'

'I'm not sure. Could be audio, picture, temperature, light, vibration. There are too many possibilities. There's also some kind of special hardware that's doing the monitoring.'

'You mean there's something installed on that specific computer?'

'That's right. When I run that program on the server, it doesn't produce any values. But when it's running on Computer 33, it sends out a continual stream of feedback in the form of a wave graph. There has to be some kind of device hidden in that computer. Maybe inside the CPU. Let me check it one more time. I'll find it eventually, I promise.'

Pei dismissed his suggestion with a wave of his hand. 'That's not a priority right now. Whatever it is, let him keep monitoring us. Let him think he's in control.'

Zeng nodded.

'Find SPU Captain Liu and head out immediately,' Pei repeated.

'Yes, sir.' Despite his earlier disappointment, there was a spring in TSO Zeng's step as he hurried off in search of the SPU captain.

Pei quickly headed back to the corner of the café. Huang was still deep in conversation with Eumenides. Ms Mu gave him a thumbs-up and he took a deep breath. If he listened closely, he could dimly make out the audio through Huang's headphones.

'Tell me about the January 30th case.'

The voice put Huang in mind of an ice-cold blade. It gave him the chills. 'You've already stolen the case files,' he replied. 'You have records and photographs. What else could I possibly contribute?'

'I want the details that weren't in the report. The ones that were intentionally left out.'

Again, Huang pictured a knife. It was digging into his flesh, driven by a forceful hand. He needed to say something, but he knew he mustn't offer up too much without being prompted by Eumenides first.

'Okay,' he said, allowing himself a sigh. 'Ask me whatever you want. I'll answer to the best of my ability.'

The city's spidery web of telecommunications cables propelled Huang's words from one computer to the next until finally they reached the end of the line.

The young man on the other end of the transmission clenched his fists. He had been plagued with doubts for too long. With the opportunity to find out the truth now in his grasp, a shadow of paralysing fear hung over him.

He swallowed. 'Why was Yuan Zhibang involved in this case?'

'Yuan was about to graduate from the police academy. He

had been assigned to the criminal police as an officer in training. Captain Ding Ke, the officer in charge, was his adviser.'

'Would a trainee officer be qualified to take part in such a dangerous case?'

'Unlikely. But Captain Ding ordered Yuan and me to find the suspect's family. He wanted us to bring them to the scene because he thought that having his family there would make the suspect see reason.'

Huang paused.

'But that's not what happened.'

'No. Something occurred after we got in touch with his family and we had no time. Yuan went straight to the apartment building.'

The young man's breath felt tight in his chest. Shadows stirred in the deepest recesses of his memory. 'What happened?' he asked, holding on to his emotions as firmly as he could.

'We located the suspect's wife and child at the hospital. His wife was bedridden with a serious illness and wasn't physically able to travel to where the suspect was. Since we were trying to reach the suspect on an emotional level through his family, our hopes now rested with his son. The boy was only six years old. We assumed that he'd be very shy around strangers, but for some reason he took quite a shine to Yuan.'

The young man knew this to be the truth: he had liked Yuan from the moment they'd met. But why? He searched his memory for the reason, but nothing stood out save for a warm and cheerful smile. Yuan Zhibang... Was that really the same man who eventually became his cold, unsmiling mentor?

'Since Yuan got along so well with the boy, Captain Ding made the last-minute decision to have Yuan bring him to the apartment building in the hope of using him to get through to the suspect.'

One by one, the blanks in the young man's memories were

being filled in. 'You bought a toy for the boy,' he said. 'And you gave him a pair of headphones and played him a tape of children's music. Am I right?'

'Yes,' Huang said, almost hesitantly. 'That was all Yuan's idea. Despite only just having met one another, the boy trusted him completely. I still remember watching as Yuan strode towards that building with the kid in his arms. The boy was singing and he looked absolutely delighted. That was precisely the effect we were hoping to achieve. How could any father continue down such a self-destructive path while his loving son was watching?'

'Tell me what happened after that,' the young man said. A lump was forming in his throat and it almost hurt to speak. 'Tell me what happened after Yuan arrived.'

'I... I'm not exactly sure what happened.'

'How can you not know?' the man said angrily.

'Before he went up the stairs, Yuan put on a wire in order to keep everyone apprised as to what was going on inside. There was only one earpiece tuned to that frequency and Captain Ding was wearing it. Only he and Yuan knew what was going on inside that apartment.'

'Was there a recording?'

'Yes, a recording should exist. I've never listened to it, though. Captain Ding didn't allow it.'

'What about the other officers?'

'I was Captain Ding's assistant. If he was going to let anyone listen to that recording, it would have been me.'

'That's not standard protocol,' the young man said, suspicion creeping into his voice.

'You're right. It isn't. To be honest with you, there was a lot about that case that didn't follow standard procedure. Yuan going inside the apartment, for one. That's why so many details weren't included in the official file.'

'So something went wrong inside the apartment? And the details would be on that recording, wouldn't they?'

'Probably.'

'What do you think happened?' the young man pressed.

'I've already told you that I don't know.'

'I want to hear your best theory. You used to be a cop, after all. And you worked with Captain Ding Ke.'

Huang exhaled, muttered 'All right,' then paused again. Finally, he said, 'I believe someone made a mistake.'

'What kind of a mistake?' Without realising it, the young man whispered his next question. 'Was it Yuan?'

'No. It was the marksman's mistake.'

His breath hissed through his teeth. 'The marksman? What did he do?'

'I believe that Yuan had made headway with the suspect. But the marksman's firearm went off before he could finish.'

Blood froze in his veins. 'You mean that my father was… that he was killed by the marksman after he had stopped resisting?' His voice dropped to a low snarl. 'Why did that happen?'

'So, you are him,' Huang said evenly.

The young man ignored this. 'Why did the marksman's gun go off? I want an answer!'

'I don't know,' Huang said. 'I can't even be sure that the marksman was the one who screwed up. It's just a guess.'

The younger man took several slow, controlled breaths. 'What led you into making that guess?'

'Based on what I saw, it seems more likely than anything else. Like I said, we were outside waiting for Captain Ding Ke's orders. After Yuan went in, the captain listened to the situation in the apartment. I saw his expression relax. The situation must have been improving. And then he gave us the signal to get ready to storm the room, which was crucial. That would have meant that—'

'I know what it means,' the young man muttered. 'Unless you want to risk serious consequences, you don't rush in until the situation has cooled down.'

'We assumed that the crisis had passed. But just as we were about to move in, we heard a gunshot.'

'Did Captain Ding order it?'

'He looked just as surprised as the rest of us when the shot rang out. We ran into the apartment as soon as we heard it.'

'What did you see?' His lower lip trembled. He knew what Huang would likely describe, but he still needed to hear it.

'The suspect had a bullet in his forehead. He was on the ground, motionless. The hostage, however, was safe and sound. Yuan held the boy close, cradling the child's head against his chest. He didn't let him see the bloody scene at all.'

Fragments of memory flashed through the young man's head.

The man holding him tight, hugging his head against his chest. A sense of warmth. Comfort. He was focused on the lullaby in his ears, but in the distance he heard a cracking sound, like a paper bag being popped. In the time capsule of his memories, that moment felt peaceful and beautiful. But when he superimposed his newfound knowledge, it was suffocating.

He curled his hands into fists. Suddenly, a small window appeared in the corner of his monitor, momentarily distracting him from his pain.

Warning: this system is under an attack originating from 211.132.81.252.

They were fast, he had to admit that. The young man glanced

at the clock in the bottom right corner of his screen. It seemed it was time to go.

'Captain, I'm at the Blue Star internet café,' TSO Zeng said into his phone. 'I've already tracked down the next link in the chain, inside an office in the south part of town. This guy is making us run circles around the whole damn city.'

Pei looked calmly at his watch. It was 2:23 p.m. 'How long will it take you to reach the office?'

'Probably about twenty minutes if I floor it. You have to stall him, Captain.'

'Understood. Get there as soon as you can.' Pei hung up and hurried back to Huang's computer.

'Tell me the marksman's name.'

Pei held his breath when he heard that question come rustling through Huang's headset. This was it – time for Huang to turn the tables on Eumenides.

Huang had given sincere answers to each of Eumenides' other questions, keeping Ms Mu's advice in mind. *'The best place to hide a lie is between two truths.'*

He had already told the truth. Now it was time to lie.

'I don't know his name,' he said after a few seconds of deliberate hesitation.

'Right,' Eumenides said, his voice dripping with sarcasm.

'He signed the records with an alias—'

'Don't play dumb,' Eumenides cut in. 'Do you expect me to believe that he used an alias during the operation?'

Huang had no intention of giving a longer explanation. 'I honestly have no idea what the marksman's name was.'

After a long pause, Eumenides spoke again. His voice was icy. 'You're saying that we can end our conversation now. Is that correct?'

'No!' Huang said, this time with genuine panic. 'You haven't told me where my son is.'

'Tell me the marksman's name.'

'I don't know it.'

'I've already asked you twice. I won't ask you a third time,' Eumenides said menacingly. 'You have five seconds to remember.'

Huang recoiled at the shift in tone. He exhaled. 'If I tell you his name, what will happen to my son?'

'Your son is quite hungry right now,' Eumenides said. 'If you hurry, you just might be quick enough to have dinner with him.'

'All right. I'll tell you. I do know the marksman's name.'

'Then say it.'

'His name is Chen. Chen Hao.'

'Where is he now?' Eumenides asked evenly.

'He's still working for the police. He's been promoted and he's now captain of a force in the eastern district.'

'Chen Hao. Captain of the eastern district's criminal police...'

Huang heard the clacking of keys through his headphones. Seconds later an image appeared on his screen. It was a personnel file with a photo of a man wearing a buzz cut and an intense stare.

'Is this him?'

'Yes,' Huang answered, suppressing his surprise. 'How come you have his file?'

'The Chengdu police intranet isn't nearly as secure as you might think.' Eumenides made a scuffing noise that sounded vaguely like laughter. Then his tone became more serious. 'He's thirty-eight years old now.'

Huang glanced at Chen Hao's date of birth. Some quick

mental arithmetic confirmed Eumenides' statement. 'Yes, that's right,' he said, unsure where Eumenides was going with this.

'Eighteen years ago, he would have been twenty-one,' Eumenides said. 'That's younger than Yuan. And you expect me to believe that he was an SPU marksman?'

'Actually,' Huang said, desperately searching for something to say, 'he might have lied about his age when he joined the force.'

'Enough!' Eumenides barked. 'I have the names of all SPU officers active in Chengdu eighteen years ago. None of them are called Chen Hao. The police selected this man as bait, nothing more. And am I correct in guessing that this Chen Hao has already been secretly co-opted into the task force?'

Huang felt sweat beading on his brow. He shot a panicky glance over at Captain Pei and Ms Mu, who were both right next to him.

A snort of contempt came through his headphones. Huang nearly blushed as he remembered that Eumenides was still watching him. 'If you still want to see your son, Huang,' the man said in a voice bristling with rage, 'you'll stop playing these childish games with me. My patience is running out. I'll give you another chance, but only one.'

Huang inwardly shook his head. The urge to resist Eumenides had all but evaporated. 'No,' he murmured a moment later. 'I can't betray another police officer for the sake of my son.'

'I understand your plight,' Eumenides said, a little gentler now. 'Let's try this a different way. I won't force you to tell me his name. Your self-respect wouldn't permit you to do that anyway. Let's find a happy medium.'

Huang gazed into the camera with anxious expectation.

Eumenides went on. 'I'm going to show you the photographs of every SPU officer that was active eighteen years ago, one at a time. I'll ask you only one question. All you'll have to do is tell me "yes" or "no".'

Huang remained silent.

TSO Zeng, SPU Captain Liu and the handful of SPU officers accompanying them were now inside the offices of a marketing company. After producing his credentials, Zeng sat down at the computer terminal in question and began tracing the next link in the chain.

Mad World internet café

A large image appeared on the monitor of Computer 33.

'Is this him?' Eumenides asked.

His voice sounded far away, as if it was being carried to Huang's ears from across a distant valley. The photograph showed a muscled, swarthy man. The answer was on Huang's lips as soon as he saw the image, but something prevented him from speaking.

'If you don't say anything, I'll take it as a silent "yes",' Eumenides said.

The hair on the back of Huang's neck stood up. 'No. That isn't him.'

'Great. The more you cooperate, the sooner you'll see your son.' A different image popped up on the screen and Eumenides repeated his question. 'Is this him?'

'No.' A second later, he was looking at a new photograph.

'Is this him?'

'No.'

After almost a hundred faces had flashed across his screen, Huang's vision was swimming.

'Is this him?' Eumenides asked, his intonation unchanging with each question. A picture of a large, square-jawed man appeared on Huang's monitor.

Huang blinked. His pulse thumped in his temples.

'Is this him?' Eumenides repeated, slower this time.

Huang licked his dry lips. He glanced over at Ms Mu.

'She can't help you, Huang. Give me an answer. Yes or no?'

Huang drew a deep breath. Through his teeth he hissed, 'I want to see my son.'

'And you will. As long as you answer my questions.'

'No. I want to see him now!' Huang barked. The veins in his forehead bulged.

Ms Mu took a step back. She had never seen Huang like this. He was acting like a cornered beast. Pent-up rage flared in his eyes, ready to explode at any second.

Eumenides said nothing.

'I need to see my son first. I'm not saying anything until I'm sure that he's safe.' Despite the anger in Huang's face, his tone was pleading. 'Otherwise I won't answer any more questions.'

'Fine,' Eumenides said curtly.

Seconds later, a video feed appeared on Huang's monitor. It showed a bed standing a couple of metres from the camera. Sitting on the bed was a boy. He was blindfolded and gagged and his hands were bound, but he didn't seem to have been physically harmed. As the boy struggled against his restraints, Huang's heart crashed to the floor.

He leant closer to the screen and called out, 'Deyang, it's your dad!'

★

Pei immediately stepped away from the terminal. He took out his phone and dialled SPU Captain Liu's number.

'Liu, where are you now?'

'We just left an internet café and we're on our way to the fifth link in the chain, which is apparently located inside a men's dorm at the Chengdu University of Technology.'

'I caught a glimpse of the video feed from Eumenides' end. The ultimate destination you're looking for is most likely a cheap business hotel. If you find any leads pointing to a place like that, tell me right away.'

'Understood! Has Eumenides asked about Chen Hao yet?'

'He has. He saw through the age anomaly right away, just like we planned.'

'Great. Now he thinks he has the upper hand.' There was a muffled shout from somewhere in the background behind Liu. 'TSO Zeng wants to talk to you.'

'Put him on.'

'Hey, Captain,' Zeng said, sounding slightly out of breath. 'While I was tracking the next connection, I intercepted a signal from that unknown program we saw at the café. It's monitoring a series of pulses that seem to indicate a constant output from Huang's end. I've already sent the intercepted signals to the server at the café. You can print out the results and see for yourself.'

'Good work,' Pei said and ended the call.

He called over the café's owner and asked him to print out the document, then went back to Computer 33. The video-feed window had disappeared and Huang no longer appeared to be on the verge of throttling his keyboard. Pei could still hear Eumenides' voice issuing from Huang's headphones.

'All right. I've already held up my end. Now it's your turn. Is this him?'

Huang nodded silently.

★

'Yang Lin. Forty years old. Twenty years with the SPU. Currently an instructor in hand-to-hand combat. Are you positive this is him?'

'Yes,' Huang said, his voice catching in his throat.

'Excellent,' Eumenides said. 'But I'd still like you to look at the rest of the pictures.'

'Why?' Huang asked, genuinely curious.

'I'm worried you might have made a mistake. It's been almost two decades, after all. You need to see all the photos before you give me a final answer.'

'Fine,' Huang said, trying not to appear too eager. After all, one of his objectives was to keep Eumenides occupied for as long as possible.

A new series of photos appeared on his monitor. The question-and-answer routine continued.

'Is this him?'

'No.'

It took more than half an hour for them to cycle through the remainder of the photographs. Huang's answer was always the same: a resolute 'No'.

'You'll be reunited with your son very soon,' Eumenides finally said.

Huang let out a deeply relieved sigh. 'Where should I go to meet him?'

'Not so fast, Huang. I'm not quite finished. I'd like to have a little chat with the man standing beside you.'

Huang looked over in surprise. 'You mean—'

'There's no need to act coy, Huang. I know Captain Pei is right next to you.'

Huang took off his headphones and handed them to the captain.

Pei hesitated before accepting them. Something wasn't right. Was Eumenides... stalling?

He donned the headphones and switched places with Huang.

As Huang stepped away from the computer, he made eye contact with Ms Mu. She gave him an encouraging thumbs-up.

The café owner approached with a folded piece of printer paper. Ms Mu flashed him a questioning look.

'Captain Pei asked me to print this out for him,' he said, shaking the piece of paper.

'Captain Pei, first I'd like to express my thanks.'

'For what, exactly?' Pei asked, keeping his face as immobile as possible.

'For helping me kill Mayor Deng.'

'Your memory of that day seems to differ from mine,' Pei replied. 'I've never given you any help.'

'I can hear that you're angry. But let's be clear about one thing. You realised that I was using Han Hao as my pawn, but you still let me proceed with my plan. If you had truly wanted to stop me, I wouldn't have been able to kill Mayor Deng. Which means you allowed me to do it. In that regard, I have already lost to you once.'

Pei chuckled. 'Don't patronise me, Eumenides. Mayor Deng is dead. I don't need to hear your twisted logic about who "won".'

'The truth is, Mayor Deng's death could never have truly been *my* victory anyway. It was my mentor's meticulous planning that made it happen. Not me. '

A shiver ran down Pei's spine. 'And now that you're fully in control, I'm supposed to understand what? That you want to make this personal – a battle between you and me?'

'Exactly. I'm sure you feel the same way. I imagine you're aching to get your revenge on me. Am I right?'

Pei stayed silent.

'It's rare that one gets the opportunity to take on such an evenly matched opponent. I've actually been enjoying myself today.'

'You saw through my trap at Huang's house. You've already got the better of me once today.'

'We're even,' Eumenides said. 'You know, I thought it would take you much longer to realise who my target was. I plucked all those random files from the archives, but you had your sights on Huang almost right away. You even figured out my identity. How did you do it?'

'Why should I tell you?' An uncomfortable thought prickled at the back of Pei's mind. Why was Eumenides drawing out the conversation like this?

'Tell me what the flaw in my plan was and I'll return the favour,' Eumenides said. 'After all, that's the only way we'll become better opponents.'

Pei had to admit, he was tempted. He thought back to what Yuan Zhibang had said about the 'catfish effect' during their final meeting inside the Jade Garden.

Yuan had told him how Norwegian fishing ships would place a single catfish in each tank of sardines when they were bringing their catch back home. The sardines used to die long before they reached harbour, but with the catfish in their tank, they made every effort to escape the predator, which built their strength and endurance and kept them alive during the long trip to shore.

It was clear that Eumenides saw Pei as his own personal catfish. As Eumenides had said, the two of them had one thing in common: they both relished the challenge of doing battle with someone of similar calibre.

Pei made his decision. If there were any weaknesses in his

strategy, he wanted to know what they were. So he made the first move and told Eumenides how he'd come to work out his identity first by analysing the dust trails in the archives then by checking the records of children who'd been reported missing between 1985 and 1992.

'Hmmm.' Eumenides let out a long exhale. 'I suppose my visit to the archives was a little rash. But then again, would anyone in my situation have been able to keep a clear head?'

Pei figured it was now his turn to ask questions. 'How did you know that we were planning an ambush this morning? I didn't tell anyone that I was talking to Huang and I'm confident there were no leaks.'

'There's a scrap-purchasing depot at the entrance to Huang's housing development. I had a chat with the fellow who runs it. He told me that Huang's wife is a bit of a neat freak. They collect the rubbish from her garage every Monday – junk mail, packaging, the previous week's magazines and newspapers. When I asked him if he'd ever noticed any piles of old papers in the garage, he laughed and told me the place was virtually spotless.'

Pei snorted to himself. Eumenides had seen the cracks in their plan before he had even set foot in Huang's garage.

'What will you do now?' he asked. 'Go after that SPU marksman – Yang Lin?'

'It's a matter of principle,' Eumenides said softly.

'Coming from you, that's a dangerous statement indeed.'

'Some things need to be seen through to the end,' he said with pride. 'For my mentor, it was the killings of Sergeant Zheng and Mayor Deng. For me, I need to find the truth behind my father's death. I'll do it my own way, no matter how dangerous.'

A silhouette entered Pei's peripheral vision. He blinked to clear his head and saw that Ms Mu was holding up a piece of paper out of range of the camera. It looked like an ECG graph.

But instead of a fairly uniform pattern of waves there were long, even lines and then sudden fluctuations. Something about it looked familiar.

He froze. It couldn't be.

'Something on your mind, Captain?' Eumenides asked.

Recovering quickly, Pei feigned a chuckle. 'Do you know what I'm thinking?'

'You're nervous. I can sense that much.'

'I'm just feeling a little claustrophobic with these headphones on.' He removed the bulky headset and set it down on the desk. As he rubbed his temples in mock exhaustion with one hand, he carefully prodded the headphones with the other. A small curved piece of metal was set into the cloth around each of its speakers. Sensors.

Eumenides had turned the headphones into a makeshift polygraph. A lie-detector.

Trying to mask his humiliation while simultaneously attempting to work out what this new development meant for Huang, Pei slowly put the headphones back on.

'I was thinking,' he said, 'that you might be able to get what you want through other means.'

'Meaning...?'

'Through normal channels. Let the police look into the truth behind the January 30th case.'

'The police? You're the ones who covered up the truth in the first place. You honestly expect me to trust you? The only way I'm going to get to the heart of this is by using my own methods. Just like before.'

'Your own methods?' Pei said, his anger building. 'Are you actually proud of your "methods"? Your criminal methods?'

'I punish evil. There's more justice in the world because of what I do.'

'No. You've merely created another kind of evil. True justice isn't anything like this twisted version of yours. Besides, you've already lost control of what you started.'

'What do you mean?'

'The punishment you inflicted on that poor teacher. You thought you were only giving Teacher Wu a shock, that you were somehow helping him regain his dignity and sense of duty, but now he's dead, and all because of you.'

'That's impossible!' Eumenides cried in apparent disbelief. 'All he did was cut off his own hand. The ambulance came in time. Besides, the personal breakthrough he achieved as a result of my actions was far more significant than any physical pain he endured.'

'You haven't heard the news, have you?' Pei asked gravely. 'Teacher Wu is dead. He killed himself.'

Several seconds passed.

'Suicide? But why?'

'You broke him. What happened in the hospital simply pushed him over the edge. Listen to the recording that's circulating online and everything will become clear.'

Pei pulled the MP3 player out of his pocket, positioned its speaker in front of his headset's microphone and hit the play button.

While the disturbing interview was being aired, he glanced up at Ms Mu. She looked furious and Pei realised it was the first time she'd heard it.

'Who was that interviewer?' Eumenides asked after listening to the entire recording. His voice was void of emotion.

'That's not important. The reporter didn't kill Teacher Wu. It was you who sent him to his doom.' Pei sneered at the camera. 'And you actually thought you were helping him.'

He heard Eumenides' breathing quicken. This was exactly

the result he'd been aiming for. But before he could land another blow, Eumenides came back with a calm response.

'You're wrong. I wasn't the one who hurt him. That was another evil act. Since you aren't able to punish that reporter, you've decided to pin the responsibility for Teacher Wu's death on me.'

'At the very least, you've lost control. That's why there are rules in society, rules that you have failed to follow. When you set yourself apart and convince yourself that you're still in charge, this is what happens'

'I thought this was going to be a friendly chat,' Eumenides said. 'I don't appreciate these petty accusations. Frankly, I'm a bit disappointed. I can't see any point in continuing this.'

'Tell me where the boy is,' Pei said, steering their exchange back on course. 'He's innocent. You already have the information you wanted. There's nothing more to be gained from keeping him captive.'

'I will let him go. But I'm not leaving just yet.' Eumenides snickered. 'I wouldn't want to disappoint Ms Mu.'

'You want to talk to Ms Mu?'

'Yes. Give her the headphones, please.'

Pei was stunned. Instead of ending the conversation now that it was obvious that Pei had nothing else of worth to offer, Eumenides was actually prolonging it. He had to know that he was giving the police more time to trace his location. What did he have up his sleeve?

He got up from the chair and gestured to Ms Mu.

Once he was out of the camera's field of vision, he whispered to her, 'Do everything you can to stall him. If he asks you something, play along. Don't lie, though. You saw the printout.'

Ms Mu nodded solemnly at the captain. Keeping Pei's orders firmly in mind, she sat down in front of the camera.

Pei glanced at his watch. It was now 3:51 p.m. They had been talking to Eumenides for nearly two hours.

His phone rang. It was TSO Zeng.

'Captain,' Zeng said. 'We've just confirmed the next point in the network. It's at the Jinhua Hotel on Shunde Street. When I phoned them, the receptionist told me that at ten o'clock this morning a youngish man and a boy checked into the room that corresponds to the IP address we have. The boy appeared dazed. The man claimed to be his uncle and said that he'd brought the boy to Chengdu to get him looked at in the nearby hospital. I ran a search on the ID card he used to check in. It belongs to a migrant worker who reported his wallet stolen yesterday.'

'It's definitely him!' Pei hissed. 'Hold on a minute.'

He glanced anxiously at Ms Mu, who was still talking to Eumenides. *Shunde Street...* The captain tried to call up a mental image of the area but kept drawing a blank. He was still not very familiar with the city.

Huang noticed the change in Pei's mood and came over to him. 'Anything I need to know?' he asked.

'How far is Shunde Street from here?' Pei asked.

'Twenty minutes.' Huang scrutinised Pei's face. 'Is something happening there?'

'That's where Eumenides is. Do you know the way?'

Huang's face lit up. 'Of course! I've lived in this city for decades. I'll drive.' Without even waiting for Pei to give the order, he raced out onto the street.

As Pei followed him, he clamped his phone back to his ear. 'Still there, TSO Zeng? When you get to the hotel, I want you to secure all the entrances and exits. Don't go into the room. I'll be there in about twenty minutes.'

'Roger that!' Zeng said. 'As long as someone continues to stall him, Eumenides won't get away this time.'

Pei glanced behind him. Ms Mu was still fully absorbed in her conversation with Eumenides, but he was sure she'd registered the change in atmosphere. Going back to update her would only waste time and it would also risk alerting the killer on the other end.

Seconds later, Huang drew up to the entrance in the patrol car and Pei hopped in. As the car lurched back into motion, Pei called Lieutenant Yin.

'We've already traced Eumenides to his current location and we're on our way over. Tell your people stationed around the café to stand down,' he ordered. 'Ms Mu's still talking to Eumenides. I want you to monitor her and report any activity to me.'

'Understood, sir.'

4:13 p.m.
Jinhua Hotel

As Pei and Huang emerged from the patrol car, SPU Captain Liu raced over to them.

'We've secured all entrances and exits to the hotel, including the windows at the rear of the building. We got here at two minutes after four and I can guarantee that no one's left the hotel since. We've also shown young Deyang's picture to the front-desk staff. They're positive that he's the boy in Room 212. Although the man with him is most likely wearing some sort of disguise, his general appearance and physique is a match for the description of businesswoman Ye Shaohong's killer.'

'Excellent,' Pei said. 'Ms Mu should still be talking to Eumenides and she just needs to keep that going for a little longer.'

'How are we going to take him down?' Liu asked.

'We'll do it the easy way,' Pei said. 'I'll take care of the electric lock, but we'll assume that the door will also have been bolted from the inside. When the moment comes, wait for my signal.'

Everyone got into position. Pei squatted by the room door with key card in hand. Liu and an SPU officer stood within striking distance of the door. Four other SPU officers hugged the walls to either side and Huang hovered nearby.

Pei raised his left hand, held it there for a moment, then lowered it slightly. Liu and another SPU officer sprinted forward and kicked repeatedly at the door as Pei slipped the card into the slot.

The beep of the door lock was followed by the deafening crash of splintering wood. Pei, Liu, Huang and the five other officers swarmed inside, firearms drawn, and swept the room.

But there was no target.

The room was exactly as seen through the monitor of Computer 33. The boy was sitting bound and gagged on the queen-sized bed. His eyes were glassy, as if he was drugged.

'Deyang!' Huang shouted, his joy tempered with anxiety. He ran to the bed and swept his boy into his arms. 'My son,' he whispered as tears welled in his eyes.

There was a desktop computer across from the bed. It was running a chat program and Ms Mu's face was visible in the chat window. The seat in front of the computer, however, was empty.

With lightning speed, the SPU officers searched the bathroom, wardrobe and even the space under the bed, but they came up empty-handed. SPU Captain Liu shot Captain Pei a defeated look.

TSO Zeng arrived. He briefly scanned the room, then shook his head in disappointment. 'Looks like we're still one step behind,' he said.

Pei's phone vibrated. It was Lieutenant Yin. 'Eumenides has

terminated his call with Ms Mu,' the officer exclaimed. 'He might be on the move.'

Pei made a concerted effort to contain the anger raging inside him. 'I know that,' he barked. 'We're inside the room now. Huang's son is here, but Eumenides is not. Why the hell didn't you alert us earlier?'

'But... but he ended the conversation barely ten seconds ago,' Yin said.

'What?' Pei glanced at the computer again. The chat window was still open. It was almost as if Ms Mu had carried on talking to Eumenides after they'd entered the room.

'I called as soon as the audio cut off on Ms Mu's computer. He must have torn off his headset and bolted – he didn't even close the call.'

'I'll phone you back in a minute.' Pei approached the desk, his heart sinking further with every step. 'He's gone. And has been gone for a while,' he said to the others.

There was a mobile phone on the desk, resting against a pair of headphones. Pei pulled on a pair of nitrile gloves and picked it up. He scrolled through its recent call log. The last call had ended a minute earlier and had been fifty-two minutes long.

'Eumenides hasn't been in this room for some time,' he said, showing the call log to the others. 'Not for the last hour or so. He's been using this phone to talk to us and he only hung up when he heard us kick the door open.'

'An hour ago?' Huang said as he untied the restraints around his son's arms and legs. 'You mean he left after his conversation with me?'

Pei nodded.

TSO Zeng slumped down disconsolately in the corner of the room. A wild adrenaline buzz had powered him from the café to each of the nodes along the trail, but now he was spent.

'If he'd already escaped, why bother pretending to talk to us? What was his goal?'

'The same as ours,' SPU Captain Liu said. 'To buy time. And we've given him plenty. Enough to get to the marksman perhaps?'

'To Yang Lin? Is he safe?' Pei asked.

'I gave him a very thorough briefing and he's being watched by two of my best officers. I'd say Yang's more than ready.' Liu pulled out his phone. 'I'll update him.'

'I have a bad feeling about this,' Pei said. 'Can you bring up any information about the program he was monitoring?' he asked TSO Zeng.

Zeng turned on his laptop and got to work. 'I've got it,' he soon said. 'The entire polygraph chart.'

Pei leant down to scrutinise the screen. 'Eumenides showed Huang the photos of every SPU officer employed by the city eighteen years ago. He made him go through them one by one. He must have still been in this room when he did that. I want you to find the pictures that he opened at these precise times.' He pointed to several peaks in the polygraph data. Each uptick was marked with a time stamp.

'Yes, sir.' Zeng opened a folder of images and began checking the times that they had last been opened.

One of them caught Pei's attention. 'Stop!' he said. 'Huang, come here.' He singled out a picture of a thin man with strikingly radiant eyes. 'Is that him?' he asked. 'Is he the marksman?'

'Yes,' Huang said, his mouth gaping in surprise. 'But how did you know? Only the officers at that crime scene knew that.'

'That's not important,' Pei said. 'What's important is that if I know, so does Eumenides.'

'It's the polygraph!' blurted out TSO Zeng.

'Precisely. Eumenides installed sensors in the headphones

for that computer,' Pei said grimly. 'There's no way you could have tricked him, Huang. Even if you had perfect control over your facial expressions, body language and tone of voice, the most miniscule fluctuations in your biometrics would have given you away.'

Huang hung his head. 'No wonder he was so adamant about the location for our conversation. It all makes sense now.'

'He must have swapped the headphones for an identical set he'd prepared beforehand,' Zeng said.

Pei stabbed a finger at the image on the screen. 'Get me this man's information,' he said to Zeng. 'I want to know where he is right now.'

7

DEATH OF THE FATHER

4:31 p.m.
Chengdu shooting range

Shooting instructor Zhong Jimin possessed a rare talent: he could discern a person's shooting ability just from the way they carried themselves. As unbelievable as it sounded to most people, he had never been proven wrong.

'A gifted marksman has much in common with a rifle,' he liked to say. 'He must be cold, unforgiving and powerful.'

The shooting range's newest customer, he thought, was a perfect example. Tall and well built, the man wore a shooter's uniform and a cap over a pair of large sunglasses. Zhong's eyes were glued to him as he approached. He emitted a forceful energy with every step – exactly the kind of shooter Zhong liked to train. A walking weapon.

Their eyes met and Zhong shivered involuntarily. Despite the dark glasses, his gaze was chilly.

The man turned and said something to one of the attendants. The young employee immediately ran over to Zhong. 'That guy wants you to train him today,' he said. 'He asked specifically for you.'

Zhong's heart raced. He briefly wondered what the man was up to, but a customer was a customer... Without another thought, he got up from his desk and hurried over.

The man stood motionless, his mouth set in a hard line.

'Good afternoon, sir,' Zhong said.

'Hello,' the man replied. He sounded relatively young.

'What kind of instruction do you need?'

'I bought a voucher for ten clay pigeons. I'd like you to accompany me as I shoot.'

'Certainly. The skeet shooting room is empty. Please follow me.'

They went into the training room, which was the size of a small gym. The attendant brought Zhong a shotgun and ammunition, then left and shut the door behind him.

The man glanced over one shoulder and then the other. He then began stretching his arms, wrists and fingers. This warm-up routine alone told Zhong that he was no beginner. Most people simply wanted to pick up a gun and start shooting.

'Are you ready?' Zhong asked, handing him the shotgun. 'I've already loaded the first shells. Keep the barrel pointed downrange and towards the ground before you begin shooting. Do you need any guidance before your first shot?'

The man handled the firearm with practised ease. His black gauze gloves gripped the stock and barrel, and his entire body seemed to meld with the gun. Zhong's jaw hung loose. This man knew his way around a firearm better than most of the cops he'd worked with. What was he doing coming here for a simple round of target practice?

'Launch the target,' the man said.

Zhong pushed a button and a clay pigeon shot out from the launcher. The disc arched against the dark backdrop like a firefly twirling through the night sky. When it reached the apex of its trajectory, a deafening blast erupted from the barrel, and the target shattered in a puff of white smoke.

'Beautiful,' Zhong said in awe.

Without turning his head, the man handed the shotgun back to him. 'Load the next shell for me,' he said softly. 'And launch the next target.'

Not much of a talker, Zhong thought.

The man handled his gun like a living machine. He fired one shot after another, never once tearing his gaze from the range. Zhong couldn't help but marvel at his results. He landed nine out of nine shots.

One clay pigeon remained. Zhong launched it and waited for the burst of gunpowder to light up the backdrop. But the shot didn't come. The man just stood there watching it arc and drop. He sighed and his posture relaxed.

'Is something wrong?' Zhong asked in astonishment.

The man finally looked over his shoulder. His eyes were dimly visible through his sunglasses and they locked onto Zhong's. The two men watched one another for a moment.

'This is my last shell,' the man said softly.

'That's right. But you missed your chance to shoot it.'

He gave a humourless smile. 'I'm not really interested in clay-pigeon shooting, you know.'

Zhong nodded understandingly. 'We also have an outdoor hunting programme. Would you be interested in learning more about that?'

'Shooting animals?' The man shook his head. 'A waste of ammunition.'

Zhong wasn't quite sure what the man meant by that. 'Well, what would you be interested in?'

The man rubbed his hand along the shotgun's barrel. 'There is one target that interests me. To a marksman, there's no challenge quite like it. When you pull the trigger, you can sense their fear. Their desperation. They might even resist, which makes the hunt all the more exciting. Of course, the key thing is to find a reason to kill this target. But once the chase is on… what a beautiful shot.'

Zhong stared warily at him.

'Doesn't that desire burn deep in the heart of every marksman? To pull the trigger on a living person?'

Zhong stiffened. Forcing a smile, he said, 'Please hand me the firearm, sir. You've reached the end of your session.'

'It's over already?' He mirrored Zhong's smile. 'But don't I still have one shell left?'

'Please hand me the firearm, sir,' Zhong said, his voice betraying his rising unease.

The man turned to face Zhong full on. 'Have you ever shot and killed anyone?' he asked.

'What?' Zhong's pulse was thumping now.

'I would like to know two things. Why you killed them and how you felt afterwards.'

The barrel of his gun was now pointing at Zhong's stomach.

Zhong decided to answer the man's questions honestly. Partly because of the weapon threatening to rip a hole in his gut, but also because the man had made him lose face. 'Yes, I have killed people. And every one of them was guilty in the eyes of the law. When I watched them drop to the ground, my overriding emotion was satisfaction at having accomplished my mission and justice having been served.' He puffed out his chest. 'When I was a marksman for the SPU, my job was to take out individuals who posed a serious threat to public safety.'

The young man went silent for a few seconds. 'Can you guarantee that everyone you killed deserved to die? That you never misused your deadly authority?'

'Yes, I can. I've taken down kidnappers, crazed killers and

dangerous fugitives. Every one of them deserved to die for their crimes.'

The man became very still. 'Do you remember, from eighteen years ago, a man named Wen Hongbing?'

Zhong was so shocked to hear that name, he was rendered speechless. He paused and thought carefully about how to answer. 'How do you know that name?' he finally asked.

'You used a pseudonym in the official police records. Was that because you were afraid that people would find out what you'd done?'

Zhong shook his head.

'But you sounded so proud just a moment ago when you were talking about all the people you've killed.'

'That was different,' Zhong said, trying to maintain his composure. He took a deep breath and decided to answer truthfully. 'That man shouldn't have died.'

'Why not?'

'Our negotiators had already de-escalated the situation,' Zhong said, his gaze wandering as he searched his memory.

'But you still shot him. You shot and killed someone who didn't deserve to die.'

'I didn't kill him,' Zhong said impassively.

'What do you mean?'

'I didn't kill him. Look, this information is classified. What's your interest in it?'

'If you didn't kill him, who did?'

Zhong stared at the shotgun in silence.

'If someone else killed Wen Hongbing, why are you the one who was given an alias?'

'Like I said, that information is classified.' Zhong took another deep breath. 'Please, sir, give me the gun.'

The man took a step closer.

Zhong stepped back. 'What do you think you're doing?' he said, his voice quivering with panic.

The young man jabbed the shotgun into Zhong's stomach. 'The real shooter wasn't qualified to pull the trigger, was he? He wasn't even a proper officer! If that fact had made it into the report, both the shooter and Captain Ding Ke would have been held responsible. Instead, Captain Ding told the team that you shot Wen Hongbing and gave you an alias in the official report. Captain Ding let the real killer off the hook and you never thought to question that?'

Zhong was shocked. So many years had passed, he'd thought the case would stay buried forever. 'Who the hell are you?'

'Tell me the truth!' the man roared. 'Is that what happened?'

'You already know the answer to that question.'

The man shuddered as if he'd been stabbed. 'But why?' he muttered to himself, grinding his teeth.

Zhong saw his chance. He stepped forward, reaching for the shotgun with his left hand and his adversary's throat with his right.

The man was a blur before his eyes. Zhong felt something shove his hands away and then an icy object was pressed against the side of his head, a sensation that was all too familiar.

'Why did that trainee officer pull the trigger? Tell me!' the man yelled, veins bulging. He rammed the gun harder against Zhong's head, his face contorting in wild desperation. 'Spit it out – I don't have all day!'

'I don't know.' Zhong's heart was hammering like a piston. 'I was just the marksman. I was watching everything from above. The suspect kept moving around the apartment, intentionally changing position so that I couldn't zero in on him. A cop went in to negotiate. The captain reported that everything was going smoothly and I began to think it might be over. But a few seconds later there was a gunshot.' His eyes were twitching now and his upper lip trembled. 'The negotiating officer had killed the suspect. I didn't see anything though. They were in a different area of the apartment when it happened.'

'Why weren't those details in the report?'

Zhong took a deep breath. 'It would have looked very bad if it came out that an untrained officer had shot and killed the suspect. So Captain Ding wanted to make it known that I'd shot the suspect, and then he was going to put a false name in the report. I resisted at first. But then he offered to promote me, to make me a sergeant. I got greedy and so I said yes. I took the blame. The report didn't have my name in it, but everyone assumed it was me. I have no idea what happened inside the building that day. Only the shooter and the captain knew. Captain Ding didn't tell me anything more than what I've told you. He didn't even let any of us into the apartment.'

The man squinted in understanding. The captain had covered up the truth right under the other officers' noses.

'But how was Captain Ding able to cover up what had happened?' the man asked, tightening his grip on the gun. 'He was a cop, not a god.'

'There was something very special about him. I don't know how to explain it. All I can say is that his influence in the department back then was extraordinary.'

The man was quiet for a moment. 'Where is Captain Ding now?'

'He vanished ten years ago. Some kind of self-imposed exile, I suppose.'

The man snarled.

'Don't make any sudden moves, son. Let's take this nice and easy,' a voice said from nearby.

Both men turned to see an overweight middle-aged man in a suit standing in the doorway. The shooting-range manager.

The younger man took aim at him. 'I'm not afraid to use this.'

The manager's eyes grew wider than the barrel of the gun and he quickly ducked outside again.

Zhong saw his chance. He snatched at the gun, but it disappeared before he could get a decent grip on it. *This bastard's just too fast,* he thought. It was his last thought before the stock cracked against his forehead.

The instructor slumped to the ground and the man with the gun ran to the door. It wasn't fully shut, so he peeked through the crack. An ambush awaited him.

The manager was flanked by five security guards to his left. He couldn't see the other side, but he guessed there were just as many guards to the right as well. They had boxed him in.

It was time to get out.

He kicked the door open and aimed high with the shotgun. There was a deafening bang and the chandelier exploded in a shower of glass. The guards leapt aside to dodge the falling shards.

Shooters from the pistol range began emerging from their booths, startled by the noise, and within seconds the place was swarming with panicked customers and staff. By the time the security guards were on their feet again, the man was gone.

Once the smoke had cleared and the chaos had died down, the manager whipped out his phone and dialled 110. To his amazement, three police officers appeared before he'd even put his phone back in his pocket.

'We're with the criminal police,' said the officer in charge, flashing his badge, which read *Captain Pei Tao*.

'I only just called you people,' the manager said, dabbing his forehead with a handkerchief. 'How the hell did you get here so fast?'

'Where's Zhong Jimin?' Pei asked.

The manager pointed a plump finger at the room in question. 'In there. It only happened a minute ago – I haven't even had time to go in and check on him. The shooter just left. If you hurry, you might be able to catch him.'

Pei shook his head disconsolately. Eumenides had got to the range before them and now he was gone. He could be anywhere.

Pei pushed through the crowd that had gathered outside the room and crunched his way across the broken glass. TSO Zeng and SPU Captain Liu followed him. He instantly recognised the dark, gaunt man sprawled on the floor as former SPU marksman Zhong Jimin. Several employees were standing nervously around the body, seemingly unsure whether they should try to help or simply stand and watch.

Pei noted the shotgun on the floor and feared the worst. But there was no blood visible. He knelt down beside Zhong and placed his fingers by his nose and lips. Zhong's breathing felt regular.

'Is he all right?' Liu asked.

'Hard to tell,' Pei answered. 'He may be concussed. Tell HQ to dispatch an ambulance immediately.'

He lifted Zhong into a sitting position and pressed his thumb into the pressure point at the centre of his chest. A few seconds later, Zhong's eyelids fluttered. He opened his eyes and looked curiously at Pei and the circle of people watching him.

'He's okay!' the manager said excitedly, rubbing his hands together. 'Zhong is okay!'

Pei glanced up at his two officers. 'TSO Zeng, take the manager and any witnesses somewhere quiet and find out exactly what happened here. SPU Captain Liu, I want you to move all civilians to the lobby.'

Pei refocused his attention on Zhong. The instructor rubbed the large welt on his forehead, gradually coming to his senses.

'Did you see him?' Pei asked.

'Who?' Zhong said, clearly very confused. 'And who are you?'

'I'm with the criminal police,' Pei said, showing him his badge. 'Did you see the person who injured you?'

'The guy kicked my ass. How could I have not seen him?'

'What I mean is did you get a good look at him? Enough to provide us with a description?'

'Oh, not really. He was wearing a proper shooter's uniform, like the kind you see in competitions. He had a hat, and sunglasses covered half of his face. It was hard to tell what he really looked like.'

Zhong turned away. Pei could understand his embarrassment at failing to provide a good description. The man was a former police officer, after all.

'Tell me what happened. Try to remember exactly what you saw. Don't leave anything out.'

After resting for half a minute, Zhong began recounting everything that had transpired over the past half hour.

'The trainee officer who shot Wen Hongbing,' Pei said. 'Was his name Yuan Zhibang?'

'It was,' Zhong said, visibly startled.

'And no one else knew that you weren't the real shooter, that you willingly took the blame?'

'Only Yuan Zhibang and Captain Ding Ke knew. You know who Captain Ding Ke is, right?'

Pei nodded.

'Captain Ding's methods were foolproof,' Zhong went on. 'If he wanted to conceal the truth about something that happened on his turf, he'd barely have had to lift a finger.'

Based on everything that Pei had heard about Captain Ding, he didn't doubt this. But why would Captain Ding have done something like that? Just to hide his slip-up? And why did he even send in Yuan to deal with Wen Hongbing and the bomb in the first place?

7:23 p.m.
Conference room, criminal police headquarters

It was quiet inside the conference room.

'Everyone needs to pull themselves together,' Ms Mu said. 'Things aren't nearly as bad as they seem. Even though we weren't able to catch Eumenides this time, we can at least take comfort in the knowledge that he's just as frustrated as we are.'

'What's Eumenides thinking now?' Pei asked urgently. 'That's the question we need to answer before we do anything else.'

'He'll be feeling very lost,' Ms Mu said. 'Eumenides originally hoped to avenge his father by finding out who killed him and tracking him down. But now all the evidence points to the killer having been his mentor. This turn of events is confusing enough for us, so imagine how hopelessly lost Eumenides must be right now. He needs to unravel this mystery or else his entire existence will be meaningless. Yuan shaped his life; he was like a stepfather to him, and he set the young man on his path to becoming a killer. This path has now led Eumenides to a locked gate, a gate that he needs to open on his own.'

'So now he'll be determined to find out why Yuan killed his father?'

'Exactly.' Ms Mu nodded. 'This is something he needs to do no matter how difficult and no matter the cost.'

Pei snapped his fingers. 'Which means he'll be focusing on two people: Captain Ding Ke and Chen Tianqiao.'

'It'll be a challenge to find either of them though,' TSO Zeng said. 'No one's heard from Captain Ding in a decade. And Chen is in so much debt that he hasn't shown his face in years and probably isn't even in the country. To be blunt, we have no way of knowing whether either of them is dead or alive.'

'I take it that your search hasn't turned up many results?' Pei said.

'Correction – it hasn't turned up *any* results,' Zeng said with a despondent shrug. 'I've been on the hunt ever since we found the January 30th files and so far there's been no trace of either Captain Ding or Chen.'

'Redouble your efforts, Zeng. Lieutenant Yin, I want you to put some people on this too. Do some on-the-ground investigating while Zeng focuses on police databases and online leads. We need to find these men before Eumenides does.'

Pei now turned his attention to the psychologist. 'Ms Mu, there's another question I hope you can help with. If Eumenides does find the answers he's looking for, how will that affect him?'

Ms Mu laced her fingers and tapped her thumbs together gently. 'That depends on what answer he's hoping for.'

'Could you be a little more specific?'

'What do *you* think he's hoping to find?' Ms Mu asked. 'What motive did Yuan have for killing Wen Hongbing? That's the big question. After all, both Huang and Zhong have stated that they had control of the situation at the apartment before Yuan killed Wen.'

Shaking his head, Pei said, 'I'm not quite sure about the motive yet. Not with the information we have right now.'

'Loosen up a little, Captain,' Ms Mu said with the hint of a smile. 'We're all speculating here. If you have something to say, let us hear it.'

'It's pointless to speculate,' Pei said, crossing his arms. 'But then again... Maybe Yuan simply screwed up. He was only a trainee officer, after all. It was his first time on a live operation. It's entirely possible that his nerves caused him to slip up.' Pei rubbed his chin thoughtfully. 'On the other hand... knowing what we do about Yuan, it's hard to say what he was thinking. Perhaps he *was* fully in control and fully intended to shoot Wen Hongbing.'

Ms Mu brightened at this. 'Okay. So let's try to work with the first hypothesis. If Wen Hongbing's death really was a mistake, then Eumenides – Wen Chengyu – will be absolutely devastated to find out that his mentor killed his father by accident. He won't quite hate Yuan, but the image of Yuan he's built up in his mind will crumble. It could very well shake him to his core. There's a chance that he'll even lose interest in playing the part of Eumenides and try to live an ordinary life instead.'

'We might know his real name now,' muttered Lieutenant Yin, 'but that piece of trash will always be Eumenides to me.'

'And if it wasn't accidental?' Pei asked.

'Then things might get a little complicated,' Ms Mu said. 'He'll undoubtedly develop an intense hatred for Yuan. He'll think that Yuan's earlier feelings towards him were faked. He'll see himself as a victim and he'll see Yuan as the person who destroyed his life. He'll then detest the fact that he ever called himself "Eumenides", since it was Yuan who initially created that identity.'

'Will he stop murdering people?' Pei said. 'That's the real question.'

Ms Mu shook her head. 'I can't say for certain. Such intense psychological stress could drive him to one of two extremes. He might be overwhelmed with regret, suddenly see the light and completely abandon the bloodstained mantle of Eumenides. Or he might become even more unhinged. He'll see Yuan's murder of his father as a crime that the law failed to punish, and to heal this wound in his heart, he'll simply seek out more targets. Murder could become his solace.'

Pei narrowed his eyes. 'What will determine which path he takes?'

'It'll come down in large part to deep-rooted traits in his psychology – behavioural patterns that can't be controlled and that can't be predicted either, unfortunately, given how little we really know about him. Of course, we can't ignore the influence of his external environment. If he has a close friend with whom he's able to share some of the pain and anger, he'll have a better chance of living a normal life. On the other hand, if he bottles up these feelings and has no opportunity to vent, there's a strong possibility that his killing spree will intensify.'

Pei paused to let Ms Mu's analysis sink in. 'Who could he possibly confide in?' he said.

9:45 p.m.
Outside the Green Spring

The young woman's white blouse and black skirt usually made her appear entirely unremarkable against the neon backdrop of the city. But today there was something different about her. She seemed less anxious and her face was alight with expectation. Even her eyes were full of life.

Once again she declined the head chef's offer of a lift home. This time she was much firmer. 'There's no need to wait for me after work any more. I have someone who's promised to take me home every night.'

The chef was astonished. He glanced curiously around the car park, but whoever was coming to pick her up seemed to be late. He tried several more times to convince her to come with him, but she refused to budge and finally he left.

'Let's go,' she said and tugged at the lead in her hand. Niuniu rose onto all fours, shook her coat of golden fur and expertly led her mistress down the steps towards their destination.

A polite voice soon interrupted their progress. 'Please come with me, miss. Your friend is waiting for you.'

She recognised the voice; it was the barista from the previous day. Smiling gratefully, she followed him into the café.

As she settled into a chair, she asked, 'Why do you like sitting in these kinds of places?'

'Cafés?' her companion asked.

'Corners. You sat in a corner at the restaurant too.'

He laughed. 'You may not be able to see, but you're much more perceptive than most people.'

'What's the advantage of sitting in a corner?'

'Peace and quiet,' he answered.

'You enjoy pairing delicate Huaiyang dishes with light wines. You love listening to violin pieces like "*Sehnsucht*" and sitting at tables in quiet corners,' she said matter-of-factly. Her eyes seemed to be looking straight at him. 'You must have a lot of stories.'

'What makes you think that?'

'Only those who've weathered significant challenges in life can truly appreciate the sort of tranquillity you seek out.

People with mundane lives are different. They like to dine on exciting, spicy dishes, like Sichuanese food, and to release their frustrations in noisy bars.'

'You do have a point,' he said softly. 'But what makes you so sure?'

'Being blind means that I have a lot of time to think.'

'Oh, yes, I suppose it does,' he said thoughtfully. 'And having nothing to distract your other senses would let you perceive things that the rest of us don't.'

The young woman laughed. 'Are you jealous?'

'A little.'

'Isn't it a bit odd that someone with all his senses envies a young blind woman?'

'A little,' he repeated.

'I think I know how you feel,' she said, tilting her head to one side. 'A lot of things are universal. The more you have of something, the more you desire its opposite. You're jealous of the world I inhabit. But me... you can't begin to imagine how badly I want to understand your world. Given your fondness for tranquil places, I can only guess what kind of life you've had.'

He stayed silent for a moment. 'Your eyes... Were you born blind?'

She nodded. 'I could still see a bit when I was little, but my vision got worse as I grew older. By the time I was ten, I was completely blind. When I try to picture how this world looks, I think back to the images of my childhood. Those memories truly are beautiful.' The corner of her mouth twitched slightly. 'But a lot of time has passed since then and many of those memories have already faded.'

'Is there a cure?'

'I stopped going to doctors a long time ago.'

'I've heard there's a type of gene therapy that can treat congenital blindness,' he said. 'You should look into it.'

'Really? Which hospitals offer that kind of treatment?'

'None in China. It's real cutting-edge technology. You'd have to go to America.'

'America?' she said coolly, shaking her head. 'I've never even set foot outside Chengdu. That sort of treatment must cost a fortune.'

'You don't need to worry about the cost,' he said casually. 'I'll take care of it for you.'

She froze. This was only the second time they'd met face to face and he was already offering to send her to America and pay for a medical procedure! Was he playing a trick on her? Was this all a joke?

Somehow, she didn't think so. The strangest thing of all was how he came across so sincere.

'I'm completely serious. I'll take care of everything. Once I've made the arrangements, all you'll have to do is go to America and have the treatment.'

'But why would you do that? Who on earth are you? Why do you care about me?'

'It's actually very simple – I just want to help you,' he said, totally relaxed.

'But we've only just met. I can't think why you'd want to help me. To be completely honest, it makes me uneasy, like... like you're trying to trick me.'

'You can think whatever you want. I'll take care of everything and you can go to America for the treatment. It's as simple as that.'

'You think I can't look after myself?' she said angrily, her cheeks flushing. 'That I'm helpless because I'm blind? If that's what you think, then there's no way I'll accept your so-called help.'

'That's not what I was saying at all.'

'Then give me a reason. Why do you want to help me?'

She waited.

'Because I'm the only person who would do this for you,' he said.

She shivered. Every nerve in her body tingled. She shifted awkwardly.

'I want to help you so that I can continue to hear your music,' he said. 'Isn't that reason enough? And it's not going to cause me any financial hardship. As far as I'm concerned, I'm simply doing what I can to help a friend in need.'

'But you're just a stranger to me,' she said, less confrontational now. 'If you want to help, you can start by letting me get to know you first.'

'I wish that was possible. But...' He paused for a spell, thinking carefully about what to say next. His words were tinged with regret. 'There are some things about me you might never be able to understand.'

'What do you mean?'

He didn't answer. She listened to the way he scuffed his shoes on the ground and to his fingers clenching at his clothing.

Silence swelled around them. She could feel it quite distinctly. It pressed down on her skin and seeped through her pores.

'I want to go home,' she said abruptly. Though she believed he was sincere in his desire to help her, she was starting to detect something strange about him. He was hiding something from her, something very serious. At the same time, she wanted to get closer to him.

Who was he?

'It's getting late. I'll take you home,' he said. 'But there's something I have to tell you.'

'What's that?'

Another anxious pause.

'Yesterday we made an agreement. I said that I would wait for you in this café every day and that I would take you home afterwards.'

'That's right.' She smiled, hoping to smooth over the earlier unpleasantness. 'I guess you could say we've officially started fulfilling that agreement.'

'I'm going to have to put our agreement on hold for now,' he said sombrely. 'I'm sorry.'

She stiffened and dropped her head in disappointment. 'Are you always so quick to go back on your promises?'

'No. It's not what you think. But there's something I need to finish, and I won't be able to see you until I've done it.'

'Then why did you bother making our arrangement in the first place?'

'It only came up today. I had no way of anticipating it.'

Her disappointment had abated a little, but not completely. 'Do you have to leave Chengdu?'

'No. I just can't meet you.'

'Will you still be able to come and hear me play?'

'Not until I've finished this.'

'And when will that be?'

'I don't know.'

She sighed softly. 'There's something I also need to tell you,' she said.

'What's that?'

'I've been blind for more than half my life now. You can imagine just how much I long to see again. Earlier you told me that you could help me do that, but then you told me that you couldn't even honour the agreement we made yesterday. To be honest, I'd far rather you honoured our agreement. At least that way I'd have a friend and not an empty promise. But I wonder if you're even able to understand that.'

'I do understand. Believe it or not, we have a lot in common.'

'Then will you rethink your decision?' she said, biting her lip.

He didn't say anything for a long time. And when he did, she could barely believe her ears.

'How did your father pass away?'

Unexpected as this question was, she found herself eager to answer it. 'He was a police officer.' The pain in her voice was tempered with pride. 'Before he died, he was tracking down a killer. It was a really big case. The killer found him first, there was a struggle, and the killer won.'

She heard a sharp intake of breath. Even though she couldn't see him, she felt his gaze on her.

'And you want to find the killer?' he said.

'Of course. Then I could ask him why he did it. I doubt he'd tell me, but I would do everything I could to make him. I'd be so angry, I'd make him quake with fear. He's the only person in the world who witnessed my father's last moments, so I'd have questions. And once I got my answers, I'd want him to suffer the most severe punishment possible.'

The harshness of her words made a striking contrast to her gentle demeanour. Hot tears ran down her cheeks.

'You want to find your father's killer. And if you had the chance, you'd take revenge. Am I right?'

She nodded.

'I'm really sorry,' he said, 'but I have no choice. There are things I need to do.'

8

BAIT

1 November, 7:41 a.m.
Holding cell, criminal police headquarters

The young man was alone in the room. His right hand was manacled to a chair.

He appeared to be in his twenties and was dressed from head to toe in fashionable brands, including a jacket unzipped to just below his chest. Despite the handcuffs, he seemed relaxed; he was leaning back in the chair and had his legs crossed. He looked more like someone in a café waiting for his date to arrive than a suspect in police custody.

The holding cell was sparsely furnished. Besides the chair, there was only a wooden table and a massive mirror that hung conspicuously on the western wall. The man sat facing the mirror, admiring his reflection.

Captain Pei and TSO Zeng stood on the other side, observing him through the two-way mirror.

'How did you find him?' Pei asked.

'It wasn't easy,' Zeng said. 'That's for sure. At first I thought it would simply be a question of tracking down his boss. Shows what I know. It turns out that online reporters generally don't have a boss, or not this one, anyway. He's a freelancer. I contacted the site that he uploaded the interview to, but they wouldn't budge. Not to begin with, anyway. I called them back and finally managed to get the name and number of the bank account that they had on record for him.'

'They gave you that information just like that?'

'Well, I might have said that I worked for the accounts department at their parent company. But come to think of it,' Zeng said with a wink, 'I can't really remember.'

Had this been any other case, Pei would have reprimanded him for failing to comply with proper legal procedures. But this was different.

'I looked into the bank account they gave me. Turns out he opened it using fake ID.'

Pei smirked. 'Giving you a reason to bring him in.'

'He's definitely sailing close to the wind. He goes by the name Zhen Rufeng online. That byline is linked to multiple unsavoury interviews and stories that infringe people's privacy. No wonder he uses a pseudonym. In fact, some of the people linked to those reports have tried to get revenge on him through their own illegal means. Which explains why he was so hard to find.'

'I'm having a hard time feeling sorry for him,' Pei said.

'We started keeping tabs on some of the online accounts he uses most frequently. At around four this morning he logged onto his QQ instant messaging account in a bathhouse downtown. I went there immediately with two other officers and we brought him back here.'

Pei noticed the marks on Zeng's forehead. 'Did you attack him?' he asked.

Zeng scratched his head awkwardly and then forced a smile. 'Who wouldn't want to punch that asshole in the face? I didn't do it on purpose, though. He hit me first and I just reciprocated. Don't let his height fool you – he's no match for me.'

Pei shook his head. 'Have you done a background check on him?'

'His name is Du Mingqiang. He's twenty-six years old, from Guizhou. I've got a lot of info on him, but I haven't found anything too out of the ordinary so far. You can have a look for yourself though.' Zeng handed Pei a file full of printouts.

'Take him to the interrogation room. I'll go first. And tell everyone that we'll meet in the conference room at eight thirty to discuss our newest plan in detail.'

'Yes, sir.'

When Zeng entered the interrogation room, the reporter was not in a good mood.

'On what grounds am I being held?' Du howled. 'What reason did you have to attack me? You're going to hear from my lawyer!'

'Hold still or you'll be saying that from inside a prison cell.'

Zeng shoved him down into the interrogation chair as Pei watched from the doorway. Then Zeng nodded and left the room, shutting the door behind him.

The room was small, about six paces wide and half as long. Pei slowly walked towards the table, but he didn't sit down.

He looked at Du. The reporter was handsome, no doubt about that. Long hair framed his angular cheekbones and prominent nose. Well-defined lips curled into a proud, rebellious smile. But it was Du's eyes that really caught Pei's attention. His irises looked as dark as his pupils. Pitch-black eyes stared right back at him.

'Is your name Du Mingqiang?' he asked.

'I know the law and I know my rights. You're legally required to tell me who you are.'

'Pei Tao, captain of Chengdu's criminal police,' he said. 'Would you like to see my badge?'

Du stiffened and shot Pei a look of utter confusion. 'You're the captain of the police? Are you aware that you've got the wrong person?'

Pei set a plain manila folder on the table. Without another word he took out an MP3 player and tapped the play button.

'According to your account, the killer let the girl go because you agreed to cut off your own hand. You finally found your inner courage and realised what it meant to truly assume the responsibilities of a teacher. Is that correct?'

He paused the device. 'Is that your voice?'

Du didn't answer. His dark eyes flitted around the room.

'Seeing as you're already here,' Pei said, 'there's no need for you to overthink things.'

'I have no idea what you're talking about,' Du said, shrugging haplessly.

Pei was not convinced. 'Maybe the name "Zhen Rufeng" will help jog your memory. We've already tracked down your online accounts, as well as the bank account you use to receive payments for your *freelance work*.' Pei enunciated the last two words with palpable distaste. 'We've also retrieved a laptop from your place of residence. I'm sure we'll find a few interesting files on that hard drive, won't we?'

Du's innocent expression gradually faded to a grimace. 'Fine. That was my voice. I put that recording online.'

'Good.' Pei put the MP3 player back in his pocket and stared coldly at Du.

'So what if it's me? I didn't do anything illegal. On what grounds am I being detained?'

Pei remained silent, keeping his eyes on the suspect.

Du sneered. 'Oh, I get it. I got in the way of your investigation.

Is that it, my esteemed captain? That Eumenides is a slippery bastard, isn't he? But even so, shouldn't you be focused on tracking him down instead of taking out your frustration on small fry like me?'

Anger surged through Pei, but he stayed his rage. 'There's no need for you to embarrass yourself any further. We already know the truth. You drove a man to his death.'

The cramped interrogation room seemed to shrink as Du turned pale. He shook his head and sighed. 'Teacher Wu committed suicide – how is that my fault? I'm just a reporter.'

'A reporter? Do you have the credentials to back that up? A press pass, for instance?'

To Pei's surprise, Du blushed.

'I might not have those, but that doesn't mean I'm not a good reporter,' Du said. 'I don't need to hide behind a piece of plastic, unlike some. I actually have talent and I don't need any so-called official credentials to prove it.'

'In that case, your meeting with Teacher Wu was on dubious grounds from a legal point of view.'

'All right, so it was an unlicensed interview,' Du muttered. His face had returned to its usual shade, but his voice was tense. 'Why are the criminal police so interested in a low-level offence like this? Don't you have bigger things to worry about?'

'Any illegal activity falls under our jurisdiction. You also pretended to be a police officer. And we found a veritable treasure trove of pornographic images on your hard drive. In short, we have the right to detain you for as long as the law permits.'

Du's eyes widened. 'You're keeping me in custody? For how long?' he asked, his lower lip trembling.

'Though we have the right to do so, we're not planning to detain you. Consider yourself lucky.'

Du's eyebrows shot up. 'What *are* you going to do with me?'

Pei was silent.

'This isn't a police state!' Du yelled, the words bursting out of him. 'I know my rights! Anything you do to me has to be in accordance with the law!'

Pei snorted. 'Oh, so now you're concerned about the law? You should have thought about that when you went to the hospital to interview Teacher Wu. Did you consider the consequences at all? I bet you had no idea you were entering into a deadly game when you pushed Teacher Wu into committing suicide.'

'What are you talking about?'

Pei opened the folder and removed an envelope. 'We found this in your home.'

Du picked it up, struggling awkwardly because of the handcuffs. 'It's my credit card statement. What's so strange about that?'

'Have you opened the envelope?'

'I always throw those letters out. I'm never overdue on my payments.'

'It was open when we found it,' Pei said. Then, intentionally lowering his voice, he added, 'But we know who opened it, and it wasn't you.'

'What the hell are you talking about?'

'Open the envelope and see for yourself.'

Du reached in and pulled out a piece of paper. It was unusually thin – it appeared to be writing paper, not a bank statement. When he spread it out on the table, his jaw fell open in astonishment.

Death Notice

THE ACCUSED: Zhen Rufeng

CRIMES: Malicious reporting, pushing a man into committing suicide
DATE OF PUNISHMENT: ● November
EXECUTIONER: Eumenides

The one thing that distinguished this death notice from all the others that Pei had seen was that instead of a specific date there was simply an ink blot.

Eumenides shouldn't have been so careless, Pei thought. *Something must have happened after the letter was delivered to Du's apartment.*

When Du finally got himself together again, he shook his head in disbelief. 'Wha... What the hell is this?'

'You interviewed Teacher Wu and you still don't know what this is?'

Bewilderment was written all over Du's face. 'One of Eumenides' death notices? For me? Why would he issue *me* with a death notice?'

'So you do know what it is,' Pei said, nodding. 'Good. This right here is the real reason we brought you in.'

'I understand! One hundred per cent!' Du blurted out. 'This is...' Slowly, his demeanour changed. 'I don't know how to describe it. I've never felt more excited in my life.'

Surprised, Pei wondered if he'd misheard.

Du laughed. 'Ha! You think it's strange, don't you, that I'm excited to see this note? You think I should be scared.' His right hand clenched into a fist and he was trembling. 'Yes, I am scared, but that's nothing compared to how excited I am. Anyone else would see this note as a threat. But to me it means something else entirely.'

'And what might that be?'

'It's the scoop of the decade!' If it hadn't been for his

restraints, he'd probably have leapt out of the interrogation chair. 'I don't care what you say about my credentials – I'm a damn good reporter. And now I have a starring role in this story. It's a dream come true! You can be sure I'll write one hell of an exclusive.'

Pei watched this strange performance with detachment. He wasn't sure whether he should pity Du or simply laugh at his arrogance.

'That BMW driver, Ye Shaohong – the restaurant owner who got herself blown up; and those two students who humiliated Teacher Wu; those are the victims I already know about. But there have to be more, right?'

Pei shook his head. Du was asking for confidential information. He weighed it up. While he wasn't supposed to divulge such details, doing so would help win Du's trust – exactly what the next step of his plan required.

'Many more, in fact,' he said. 'We've kept the names of the victims from the public. One of them was Mayor Deng.'

Du's eyes were on stalks now. 'Mayor Deng? Eumenides killed Mayor Deng? The news said he had a heart attack in the airport!'

'Do you believe everything you read in the news?'

Du grinned. 'Of course not. The mainstream media never tells people the truth. That's why society needs people like me.'

Pei tried not to let his disgust at Du's egotism show. 'Eumenides managed to get past our people as well as Mayor Deng's own bodyguards. He disappeared before we had a chance to catch him.'

Du was transfixed.

'There's something else you should be aware of,' Pei went on. 'Eumenides isn't one for empty threats. He's fulfilled every death notice he's ever delivered.'

'A 100-per-cent success rate, huh? That'll be a great detail to add to my story,' Du said to himself. His eyes flicked to the death notice then back to Pei. His forehead creased. 'But doesn't that mean...'

It's finally sunk in, Pei thought.

Du examined the death notice again. 'What's wrong with the date?' he asked.

'The number's smudged. Do you know how that happened?'

Du frowned and looked more closely at the piece of paper. Then he snapped his fingers. 'It must have been an accident. Like I said, I never open these kinds of letters; I just leave them lying around until I throw them out. When I was refilling my pen last night, I shoved an envelope underneath the ink bottle to catch any drips. It must have been this one.' He held up the envelope again. Several drops of jet-black ink decorated the back. 'I guess things got a bit messy.'

'The date was smudged when we found this letter. If this is your first time seeing it, Eumenides is the only one who knows what was originally written there.'

'Can't your forensics lab check the letter for, I don't know, impressions left by Eumenides' pen?' Du asked, almost pleading.

'Getting desperate now, are you?' Pei said. 'Well, our forensics people already checked. It appears that Eumenides wrote each death notice with a fine-tipped brush. An aesthetic choice, perhaps. But that means it's impossible to see what he originally wrote.'

Du stared at the paper. He held it right up to his eyes, as if trying to penetrate the layer of smudged ink.

'Was the envelope open when you put it under the ink bottle last night?' Pei asked.

Du shook his head. 'I don't remember. That detail didn't seem as important then.'

'Regardless,' Pei replied coldly, 'the one thing you should be thinking about now is how your name ended up on one of the killer's death notices.'

Taking a measured breath, Du lowered his gaze. 'I know what kind of person you think I am. You police types claim to be paragons of virtue and you judge me to be a slimy wannabe reporter. In your eyes, I deserve to get this letter from Eumenides. Maybe I even deserve the punishment. But that's not the main issue. The real question is: why am I here now?

'And the answer's quite simple, isn't it? No matter how many times you say that my interview caused Teacher Wu to commit suicide, your argument won't hold water in court. I know what I'm talking about – I've argued my way out of legal scrapes before. The law can't punish me and at the same time it won't allow someone like Eumenides to wantonly take my life. As a guardian of the law, you have no choice but to protect me. No matter how much you detest me, it's still your duty. Am I right?'

'Yes,' Pei said. 'You have a good grasp of the situation.'

'Like I said, I'm damn good at what I do. Prising out secrets, knowing what people are thinking, you name it. If I'd had the same opportunities that you've had, who knows, maybe I could have been a police captain.' Du chuckled. 'But my life followed a different track, and it left me with only one option – to become a great journalist.

'You think whatever you want.'

'You don't understand me and neither do your colleagues. But I don't care. Geniuses are rarely understood in their time.'

Pei was getting used to Du's narcissism, but as he observed him he felt a mix of emotions. All of his instincts told him that he was looking at a dead man.

Du grinned at him. 'But there's no need to waste our time on useless chitchat. There's only one thing I want to know: how do the police intend to respond to this death threat from Eumenides?'

'We're going to protect you.'

'Well of course you'll protect me. The question is *how*?'

'We'll have officers watching you around the clock.'

'Will you restrict my freedom of movement?'

'No. As long as you stay within sight, you can go about your day as usual.'

'Huh. I figured you'd lock me up inside a windowless room. Kind of like, well, right now.'

'That could be one solution, but we don't have the legal right to do that.' Pei paused and glanced at the two-way mirror on the far wall. 'Unless you consent to it?'

Du chuckled. 'Ridiculous. Why do something that makes everyone involved miserable?'

Pei scowled, which only made the reporter more gleeful.

'If you restrict my freedom of movement and keep me locked up,' Du said, 'it'll be much harder for Eumenides to get to me and he might even have to quit. But that's not what you want, because that would mean giving up this opportunity to catch Eumenides. As for myself, a true reporter wouldn't hide from the most notorious killer in recent history. Give me back my freedom and you'll create the right conditions for an encounter with Eumenides. That way everyone's happy, right?'

'Does that mean you're willing to accept the conditions I outlined earlier?'

Du shook his head. 'It doesn't sound as enticing when you put it like that. I think "cooperation" would be a more accurate description of our new relationship.'

Pei rolled his eyes. 'Really? This is a partnership to you?'

'Exactly! Specifically, you want to use me to lure Eumenides out into the open, and I'm willing to go along with it. This arrangement comes with a considerable risk to my wellbeing. So it's only right that I be properly compensated.'

'What precisely do you want?'

'All the dirt you have on Eumenides.'

'That's out of the question. You're talking about top-secret information. We can't make anything public.'

While Du looked disappointed at Pei's refusal, he was not disheartened. 'In that case, I can't promise that I'll act entirely in accordance with your plans. Maybe I'll hide. Or maybe I'll go looking for dirt on Eumenides by myself.'

'And you're free to do that,' Pei said coolly. 'But keep one thing in mind: if you give the police the slip, the next time we come for you, we'll bring a body bag.'

Du stiffened. 'I demand—'

'I have no interest in continuing this conversation,' Pei said. 'I've explained as much as I can. That's it. I will now dispatch a group of officers to act as your personal escort.'

8:30 a.m.
Conference room, criminal police headquarters

A scanned image of Du's death notice appeared on the room's projector screen. TSO Zeng circled the table as he summarised the details he'd amassed so far about Du Mingqiang.

'So this guy interviewed Teacher Wu, drove the man to suicide and caught Eumenides' attention as a result,' Lieutenant Yin mused.

'Have you not wondered,' Ms Mu said, 'how Eumenides

found out about this interview so quickly?'

'I'm guessing he saw it online,' Zeng said.

Ms Mu shook her head. 'Eumenides is so focused on discovering the truth about his father's death, I doubt he'd have had time to follow up on Teacher Wu's condition. Not right away, at least. The reason Eumenides knows about this reporter is because Captain Pei played him the recording at the internet café yesterday afternoon.'

'Really? Captain Pei played him the recording?' Zeng turned to Pei in surprise. 'You were planning to use the reporter as bait all along!'

Pei nodded gently. 'It never hurts to have multiple options. When I found the polygraph device inside the headphones yesterday, I began to suspect that our marksman plan might not fool him. So I improvised. I played the recording for Eumenides and intentionally provoked him. That way, though we'd lost one opportunity, we gained another.'

'What's going on with the date?' SPU Captain Liu said, squinting at the screen.

'Eumenides placed this death notice inside an envelope for a credit card statement. Du accidentally spilt some ink on it last night, which blotted out the date.'

'It's the first of November today,' Liu said. 'Are you telling us that Eumenides could make his move on Du anytime this month? Setting a trap is hard enough as it is, but sustaining it for an entire month...?'

Everyone in the room had taken part in the operation at Citizens' Square – the failed mission to protect the BMW-driving businesswoman Ye Shaohong. They were fully aware of how many people and how much effort it had taken to try and trap the killer. The prospect of maintaining this effort for up to a month was all but inconceivable.

'We can't divert too much of our energy into this,' Pei said. 'We have more important challenges ahead.'

Ms Mu looked up at him. 'I don't think the smudged date is an accident.'

'What do you mean?'

'Well, we know that this death notice was found inside an envelope for a credit card statement, but nobody knows for sure when it was put there. The envelope could have been ink-stained before the death notice was put inside it. Eumenides could have noticed that and smudged the date in order to make us think it was an accident. In other words, perhaps he obscured the date on purpose.'

TSO Zeng nodded enthusiastically. 'That's definitely a possibility. That drop of ink just happening to blot out that tiny spot on the paper is quite a coincidence, no?'

SPU Captain Liu smirked. 'Eumenides wants to keep us guessing, but he also wants to save face. That sneaky little—'

'I'm afraid it isn't that simple,' Ms Mu interrupted. 'He saw right through us.'

'Huh?'

'Eumenides already knew that we were trying to bait him, so he decided to beat us at our own game. He only needs to pick one day to kill Du. We have to be on the alert for the entire month. With that advantage, he can devote the rest of this time to his search for the truth behind his father's death.'

Liu sighed. 'You have a point. We've been so focused on the January 30th investigation that Eumenides hasn't been able to follow up on a single lead without running into us. If I were Eumenides, I'd do whatever I could to divert our attention. This Du punk is going to distract us for an entire month! I almost have to commend Eumenides for thinking this out so well.'

'So what's our next move?' Lieutenant Yin asked Captain Pei.

'No matter what, we mustn't do what Eumenides expects us to do,' Pei said. 'Therefore, regardless of Du's situation, we can't make any changes to our original plan. Our priority is still to go after all leads related to the January 30th investigation. Ms Mu and I will concentrate on Captain Ding Ke, and TSO Zeng and Lieutenant Yin will look for Chen Tianqiao. SPU Captain Liu will protect Du: assemble a team, put them on shifts and maintain round-the-clock surveillance on him. I don't care if he's shitting or sleeping – he is *not* to leave your team's sight.'

'Got it,' Liu said. 'My first time babysitting,' he added with a light chuckle.

'Hold on – are we not going to restrict Du's movements then?' Ms Mu asked. 'He's broken multiple laws – we have the right to keep him in custody.'

Pei took a deep breath. *Of course she would be the one to bring this up*, he thought. 'You're right, Ms Mu. He has broken several laws, and once this operation is over, I fully intend to turn him over to the courts. But right now, Du is our best chance to capture Eumenides.' He kept his expression stern. He couldn't afford to look weak in front of the team.

'I don't like this,' Ms Mu said, shaking her head. 'This isn't the first time we've used someone as bait. I don't have to remind you how successful our last attempts were.'

It took all of Pei's self-control not to slam his fist against the table. 'Captain Han was in charge of those operations,' he said. 'Things are different now.'

Ms Mu looked at the other team members as if to gauge their reactions and rally their support. But Zeng, Yin and Liu all stayed silent.

'You do realise that this is exactly what Eumenides wants?'

she said. There was a pained look in her eyes, concerned rather than resentful. 'His MO has always been to punish those that the law can't touch. By refusing to prosecute Du, you're playing right into Eumenides' hands. Don't you see? You're turning Du into a justifiable target for Eumenides.'

Pei glanced around the table and saw only expectant faces. They were waiting for him to make a decision. 'This is my operation,' he said, 'and we're going to carry it out as I say.'

Ms Mu met his gaze, chilly but professional. 'But how can we guarantee Du's safety?' She turned to her colleague. 'Liu, it's not that I doubt your abilities, but... If we don't restrict Du's movements, can you honestly guarantee that a handful of your officers will be able to protect him?'

'We can continue periodically interrogating him about Teacher Wu's death, and that way we can justifiably keep him from leaving Chengdu,' Pei said. 'Lieutenant Yin, you're in charge of that. Make it happen as soon as possible.'

'Understood, sir.'

But Ms Mu still wasn't satisfied. 'That won't be enough. It would be best to keep him here, at HQ, or at the very least in one specific location until the end of the month.'

'We don't have the authority to do that,' Pei said. 'Not without officially charging Du first.'

Ms Mu frowned. 'Is Du really so oblivious to how much danger he's in? If he knows what's good for him, he should be bending over backwards to cooperate with us.'

'You're thinking like a normal person,' Pei said, 'and Du is anything but. He can't wait to meet Eumenides. He's completely set on writing a story about his encounter with the killer. He'll never agree to stay put, no matter how hard we try to convince him that it's the smart choice.'

Ms Mu was taken aback. A man that could disregard the

sensibilities of others for the sake of getting a story; a man that was willing to disregard a serious threat against his own life? 'I want to talk to him,' she said.

Pei studied her quietly. 'Of course. You and Liu can go to the holding cell shortly. If you can convince him to see things your way, we'll alter our plan. If not, we let him go. But unless we actually arrest him, we can only detain him for twenty-four hours.'

9:27 a.m.
Holding cell

Du Mingqiang may have been physically restrained, but in his imagination he was running wild. He was about to face the greatest challenge of his life. It was like walking along a cliff edge: a single false step would mean death.

A thrill-seeker by nature, he loved this feeling. The more insurmountable the challenge, the stronger the adrenaline rush. It was almost time to pit his wits against his new adversary.

The door opened, interrupting his thoughts. Two people entered the room, a man and a woman.

'When are you going to release me?' Du complained, straining against his handcuffs. 'I don't appreciate being treated like a criminal.'

'We'll let you go soon, but you need to understand a few things first,' the woman said.

'Who are you?'

'I'm a member of the April 18th Task Force. My name is Ms Mu.'

'I had no idea that the criminal police force was so gifted in the looks department,' Du said with a wide smile.

'I am a lecturer in psychology at the Sichuan Police Academy,' Ms Mu said. She motioned to the tough-looking man at her side. 'And this is Captain Liu Song of the special police unit.'

They both sat down across from Du. 'You have the right to express your opinion, but this is neither the time nor the place to do so,' Ms Mu continued.

'You're a lecturer in psychology?' Du said meekly. He rolled the words around on his tongue. 'That would explain the piercing gaze. I hear that people like you can tell what I'm thinking just by looking into my eyes. You're practically psychic, huh?' With that, he shut his eyes and waggled his head from side to side. 'How's that? What am I thinking now?'

Ms Mu was lost for words. SPU Captain Liu, on the other hand, had no difficulty expressing his emotions. He smacked his knuckles against the table.

'That's enough! We don't have time to joke around.'

Du opened his eyes and winked at Ms Mu. An instant later, his mischievous face became as impassive as stone. 'You're right, we don't have time to joke around,' he said. 'But both sides have to make a proper effort. If you continue to treat me like a criminal, then we won't be able to have a proper discussion.'

A brief silence fell over the interrogation room. Du toyed with the restraints on his wrists.

'What are you waiting for?' Ms Mu called out, turning towards the two-way mirror. 'Uncuff him.'

A uniformed officer came in with a big bunch of keys and unlocked the cuffs. Du rubbed his wrists and stretched lazily in his chair. As the officer turned towards the door, Du shouted after him, 'My personal effects, please.'

The officer looked confused, but Ms Mu nodded her approval and he soon returned with a plastic container.

'Now that we're on a level playing field,' Ms Mu said as she watched Du sort through his belongings, 'may we continue our conversation?'

Du rolled his eyes and picked up his mobile. 'Yeah, I'm listening. What do you want to talk about?'

'Eumenides sent you a death notice. Do you realise what that means – how much danger you're in?'

'I do,' Du said softly. 'From what I've heard, he's carried out every single one of these notices.'

'You need to be extremely cautious over the next month. You'll be under constant police surveillance, but I strongly advise that you refrain from going outdoors. We can arrange for you to stay here at police headquarters.'

'Is that the opinion of the task force?'

Ms Mu nodded.

Du laughed dryly. 'Lady, you people need to get your stories straight. When I spoke to Captain Pei a few moments ago, he said that I'll be able to go wherever I want.' He prodded his phone but the screen stayed black. 'Shit,' he said. 'No battery.'

'You want to make a call? Use mine.' Ms Mu pulled out her phone. 'If we're going to be working together over the next month, we may as well get used to it.'

Du accepted her phone wordlessly. 'Mind if I swap my SIM card with yours? The number I need is stored on mine.'

He snapped the casing off the back of Ms Mu's phone without waiting for a response and replaced her SIM card with his.

Ignoring his presumptuousness, Ms Mu returned to the topic in hand. 'I'm aware that you spoke to Captain Pei, but I wanted to try and persuade you myself.'

ZHOU HAOHUI

Du reclined in his chair. 'You're wasting your time,' he said, waving a hand dismissively at her before dialling a number on her phone.

He set the phone on the table as the ringing went unanswered. 'Still asleep – at this hour?' he grumbled to himself.

'Your girlfriend?' Ms Mu asked.

'Someone who understands me.'

'There aren't many people who understand you, are there?'

'You must think I'm a despicable person. Immoral, even.' He began swapping the SIM cards back again.

Ms Mu nodded. 'In light of what I've been told, I'd probably agree with that.'

Du snickered. 'You're like most people. No one gets me.'

Ms Mu looked into his eyes and her voice softened. 'I'm not "like most people" – I'm genuinely interested in what goes on inside your head. From what I've surmised, your life centres around a dream, a particular pursuit that you value above all else, and you would do anything to see that dream realised.'

Du stretched his feet out, as if he was just waking up, avoided her gaze and continued fiddling with her phone. 'You're going about this the wrong way,' he said. 'You need to stop trying to get into my head in search of my weak points.'

'Everyone has weak points,' Ms Mu said. 'Don't worry. You have some too.'

'If you say so. But even if you do find mine, it'll be a waste of time.'

'And why is that?'

Du tossed her phone back to her. With a hint of a smile, he said, 'I don't think you're that great a psychologist. After all, there's at least one person whose head you can't get inside.'

'And who's that?'

'Pei Tao.'

190

She held his gaze but gave no reaction.

'The captain won't agree to what you're suggesting,' he continued. 'Letting me roam free as bait for Eumenides isn't something that's up for debate. It's central to his plan. That's why this conversation is a waste of time. Even if you did convince me, your tough-guy captain won't change his mind.'

Ms Mu's head was spinning. He was quite right. It was obvious that Pei was just humouring her.

'If that's true,' SPU Captain Liu interjected, 'why did Pei allow us to speak to you?'

Du shrugged. 'Because he knew you'd never be able to convince me. I learnt a lot about the captain during our earlier conversation, and he learnt a lot about me. I can't wait to meet Eumenides and Pei is itching to use me to find the killer.'

'You think you have it all figured out?' Liu snapped.

'Don't I?' Du paused. 'Of course, there is something else that he wants. Even though he didn't say it, I could feel it.'

'What does he want?' Ms Mu asked.

'He wants me to die at Eumenides' hands.' Du's face appeared to be displaying two conflicting emotions – his eyebrows were slanted in fear, but he was also smiling.

'Pei would never want that,' Liu insisted with a vigorous shake of his head.

'But he does. He's already set it in motion. And he's the head of the task force, isn't he?'

Frustrated, Ms Mu finally decided that this was enough. She leapt up, snatched her phone from the table and walked out of the holding cell.

'You two arrived together,' Du said to Liu coldly. 'Aren't you supposed to leave together?'

SPU Captain Liu had barely spoken since entering the room,

choosing instead to glare disgustedly at Du from his side of the table and let Ms Mu do the talking. 'I've been tasked with your protection,' he said simply.

'Oh?' Du stood up and eagerly thrust out his right hand. 'He speaks! Sorry, I forgot your name.'

SPU Captain Liu reluctantly shook Du's hand, as warm and firm as a dead fish. 'One more time: Captain Liu Song, special police unit.'

'I appall you, don't I?' Du asked with a catty grin. 'I have that effect on a lot of people, but I don't mind. They're outnumbered by the people who appreciate my journalism. As far as I'm concerned, that's all that matters.'

Liu grunted. 'Do you think I care? I'm supposed to protect you, not write your biography.'

'I'm not a fan of small talk, especially not with someone like you. Still, if we're going to be working together, we should learn a little bit about one another.'

'"Working together"? Cut the crap, Du. The situation's extremely simple: Eumenides wants to kill you and it's my job to protect you. You'll be free to go soon, but you'll have to get my permission first.'

Du raised his eyebrows. 'Like I told the woman, get your stories straight before you start laying down conditions. If I have to get your permission to do anything, that doesn't sound much like freedom to me.'

'You can choose to ignore my advice,' Liu said frostily, 'but be clear about one thing: my worst-case scenario is mission failure; yours is death.'

Du froze for a moment. Then with a resigned shake of his head he said, 'Fine. I'll do what you tell me.'

'That would be ideal.'

'We have an understanding then. Despite making some

concessions, I'm not too cut up about it. I won't even press charges for the bruises that other cop gave me or for entering my home without a warrant. After all, the best stories always begin with conflict.' Du stood up and headed to the door. 'I'd like to go home and catch up on my rest. Do I have your permission to do that?'

'You do. I'll drive you there.'

Liu escorted him to the car park.

'Shengde Gardens,' Du instructed once he'd climbed into the police car. He leant back in the passenger seat and began flipping through a copy of the morning paper that he had snatched from the lobby.

Liu drove carefully and without uttering a word, aware that anything could happen if Eumenides was involved.

'"The body of a young man was discovered floating in the Jin River early this morning",' Du read. '"Forensic tests confirmed that the individual drowned. His blood alcohol level was 213 milligrams per litre, indicating that he was intoxicated at the time of his death. The police suspect that the man slipped and accidentally fell into the river while attempting to urinate sometime after midnight." The article ends with a friendly reminder from the police to drink responsibly or else...' He trailed off. 'Or else end up drowning in a river, I guess.'

Liu was focused on the road. The traffic was light and he was making good time.

'What do you think of this story, Captain Liu?' Du asked, setting the newspaper down on his lap.

'Accidents happen every day,' Liu answered nonchalantly, although his interest had been piqued. 'If you worked in law enforcement, you wouldn't give a second thought to a story like that.'

'What if the unlucky bastard was murdered?'

'Murdered? The paper says he was piss-drunk when he fell in.'

'They can confirm that he was drunk and that he drowned. But where's the evidence that he slipped and fell in? If he was pushed in when he was drunk, wouldn't that constitute murder? By going for the most obvious conclusion, the police might be letting a killer off the hook.'

'Even if things did happen as you suggest, the police wouldn't be able to prove anything without a witness.'

'Are you saying that the police couldn't do anything?'

Liu nodded. 'You want to learn about me and my job? Fine. Then let me tell you about a mission that the SPU was given last summer: to find and rescue a lost explorer in the mountains outside Chengdu. We used ropes to climb down into a remote gully and we searched non-stop for three days and nights. We never did find the individual we were looking for, but we did find multiple badly decayed corpses. Did those people meet their deaths accidentally, while exploring, or were they the victims of something more sinister? I asked our late captain, Xiong Yuan, and you know what he said? "That's not why we came out here, Liu." His answer was frustrating, but it was the hard truth.' Liu exhaled slowly. 'Your hypothesis could be true,' he added, 'but what then?'

'There are a lot of dark corners in this world that law enforcement can't touch,' Du said quietly. 'I suppose there really is a place for Eumenides in a society like ours.'

Liu swivelled round and glared at his passenger. Du had a strange glint in his eyes. Even though Eumenides had singled him out as a future victim, did he actually admire the killer? Liu turned back to the road and shook his head. He didn't need to concern himself with that right now.

9:56 a.m.
Captain Pei's office

Captain Pei was standing at his office window, studying the industrial-concrete slab of a building across the street. It was home to the forensics division, but it looked identical to the other buildings scattered around the campus that comprised the police headquarters. He had been captain of Chengdu's criminal police for three days, but only now did it truly feel like the new job had changed him.

The door opened with a whisper and he heard soft footsteps behind him. He turned to see Ms Mu standing there.

'How did it go?' he asked.

'You already know the answer to that question, Captain,' she said crossly.

'You weren't able to convince him, huh? Well, you're right, I was expecting that.'

'So why did you let me waste my time?'

'You wanted to talk to him. I didn't have a reason to not allow you to try.'

'Stop beating around the bush. I have another question.'

'You do? Out with it then.'

'If you'd thought I might be able to persuade Du to see my point of view, would you still have let me talk to him?'

Pei had no response. He simply forced an awkward smile.

'In your eyes, Du is just bait,' she continued. 'Nothing more, nothing less. You don't care about his safety. In fact, you're hoping that Eumenides does carry out his threat, because you believe that Du should pay for his crimes. Am I correct?'

Pei avoided her gaze. 'I can't deny that I might have been thinking along those lines, even subconsciously. But so what? That doesn't change anything.

'At least you're being honest now.'

'There's no need for me to deceive you, much less myself.'

Ms Mu took a deep breath before continuing. 'I know where Eumenides is,' she said quietly.

Pei sucked in a short gasp and snapped to attention. 'Where?'

'He's inside you,' Ms Mu answered, looking him straight in the eye.

Pei went back to the window. As he gazed at the forensics building, his left hand clenched into a fist.

'That's the way it's always been,' Ms Mu went on. 'After all, you and your late girlfriend, Meng Yun, created that character. Even nearly two decades on, that role is still forcing you to reap the bitter fruits of your past. And you still can't resist the temptation.'

That last remark left Pei confused. He recalled the night that he and Meng had come up with the concept of Eumenides. He'd thought they were creating a character for a short story, but had his inspiration come from somewhere deeper? He cast his mind back to his last conversation with Yuan Zhibang, just a week ago at the Jade Garden restaurant, before Yuan blew himself up. The words still lingered in his memory:

'You and Meng were the ones who created Eumenides in the first place. You are Eumenides. As was she. You could say that there's a Eumenides inside many of us. People need Eumenides to exist.'

That rasping voice still made his heart race, even when echoing from the dark edges of his memory.

He took several long breaths then turned back to face Ms Mu again. 'You can rest assured that I won't lose sight of my duties as both police captain and the head of this task force. No matter what, I am obligated to uphold the law. Know that my desire for the April 18th Task Force to complete our investigation is greater than any emotional bias I may or may not have.'

'That's best for everyone,' Ms Mu said, seemingly happy to take him at his word.

Still, Pei was sure that she would keep a close eye on him throughout the operation. 'Let's get back to work. What should we be doing now?'

'Trying to trace Captain Ding Ke. We need to make a trip to Sichuan University. Captain Ding's son is there.'

Pei walked over to his desk and picked up a computer printout. It was a faculty registration form. In the upper right corner was a headshot of a middle-aged man. Some lines of text were printed below the photograph:

Professor Ding Zhen
Male; born 21/07/1960
Current place of employment: Sichuan University
Position: Vice dean of the College of Environmental Engineering; professor

9

LIKE FATHER...

11:03 a.m.
College of Environmental Engineering, Sichuan University

Professor Ding's personal office was on the eighth floor of the college, not far from the lift. Captain Pei, followed by Ms Mu, almost walked past the nondescript room. He knocked politely.

'Come in,' a soft, feminine voice said.

A woman in her late twenties was sitting at a small oak desk piled with textbooks and loose paper. There was a single door behind the desk.

'We're with the police,' Pei said, showing her his badge. 'We'd like to ask Professor Ding some questions regarding an ongoing investigation.'

'The professor's in a meeting right now. You'll have to wait.' Wearing a polite smile, she said, 'I'm his secretary, Gao Qiong.'

'Approximately how long will we have to wait?' Ms Mu asked as she surveyed the room.

'Hard to say,' Gao said apologetically. 'Professor Ding is a very busy man. Most people have to make an appointment to see him. However, since this is a special situation, I'm sure he'll be able to see you during his lunch hour.'

'That won't be too much of an inconvenience for the professor, will it?'

'Not at all. He usually gets his lunch delivered, so you can talk to him while he eats. If you don't mind doing that, there won't be any problem.'

'I don't mind,' Ms Mu said.

'That's fine,' added Pei.

They waited patiently. Professor Ding returned half an hour later.

'You're back, Professor,' Gao chirped. 'There are two visitors waiting for you.'

'Visitors?' the professor repeated. His brow wrinkled in displeasure as he glanced at Ms Mu and Captain Pei. 'I didn't arrange to meet anyone today.'

'They're from the police.'

'Oh.' Professor Ding paused for a moment. He was smartly dressed in a well-cut suit, with his hair immaculately parted to the side.

Pei and Ms Mu both quickly stood up.

'Hello, Professor,' Pei said.

The professor sized them up with a bright, studious expression. 'Police, huh?'

'This is Pei Tao, the new captain of the criminal police unit,' Ms Mu said. 'I'm Mu Jianyun, lecturer at the Sichuan Police Academy.'

Professor Ding shook their hands briskly. 'Pleased to make your acquaintance.'

'We do apologise for turning up unannounced,' Pei said.

'No need. Come in and have a seat.'

The professor's office was as neat as the man himself. Densely packed bookshelves lined the far wall and brick-like stacks of essays and term papers covered the oak desk.

Professor Ding took a seat in the wide chair behind his desk. 'Would you like to join me for lunch?' he asked.

'No, but thanks for the offer,' Pei said.

'Life is short, which is why one should plan one's time as efficiently as possible. For instance, I don't have to devote my entire lunchtime to eating – I can also listen to the news or participate in an unplanned chat. Are you sure I can't order lunch for both of you?'

The professor spoke with an authoritative, pedagogical tone. *Occupational hazard*, Pei thought. If he'd come here for any other reason, he might have taken the professor up on his offer. But it wasn't easy to maintain one's authority with a mouth full of food. 'No thanks,' he repeated. 'We're not hungry.'

Nodding, Professor Ding picked up the phone on his desk. 'Order my usual,' he said. Then he turned to Pei. 'You're looking for my father, aren't you?'

He'd wasted no time in getting to the point.

'That's the only thing the police ever want from me,' he said in a mocking tone. 'You've run into some trouble on an investigation – am I right? And you want my father's help.'

Pei nodded. 'That's about it. Word has it that your father got tired of the job a long time ago. But this is an extremely important case. I sincerely hope that you'll be able to help us find him.'

'A big case?' Professor Ding flashed a broad, emotionless grin. 'Any case is a big case as far as the criminal police are concerned. I know that quite well. As soon as you start working on an investigation, everything else pales in comparison, does it not? Even your own family.'

'You seem to have a bit of a bias against our line of work, Professor,' Pei said.

Professor Ding gave him an indifferent look. 'Are you married?'

'No.'

'You're better off that way. Better to be a bachelor your entire life than to become a husband and father who shirks his responsibilities.'

Pei stared awkwardly at the professor, unsure how to respond. Ms Mu wrinkled her nose in displeasure. 'Professor,' she said, 'do you have some grievance against your father? Do you believe that he failed to fulfil his rightful role in your household?'

Professor Ding narrowed his eyes at her, as if seeing her for the first time. Ms Mu looked right back at him without flinching. The atmosphere in the office was thick enough to choke on.

There was a knock at the door.

Professor Ding glanced over and visibly relaxed. 'Come in,' he said.

The secretary stepped inside. She set a takeaway container on the desk. 'Your lunch, sir.'

'That will be all, Gao,' he said.

She retreated to the door but paused and turned to Pei and Ms Mu. 'Take your time,' she said.

Her words felt like a breath of fresh air. By the time the door had closed, Ms Mu's easy smile had returned to her lips.

The professor ate quickly, gulping his meal down as if this were merely one of the many tasks he had to tick off, like marking an essay or rearranging a bookshelf. After taking several large mouthfuls, he looked up at Pei and said, 'What's this case about, exactly?'

'It's eighteen years old. Your father was in charge of it. Work on the case actually wrapped up a long time ago; we just need to ask your father some questions about a few specific details.'

'Did it involve a hostage?'

'You know about the case?' Pei asked, his surprise tempered only by his excitement.

'That one was never completely solved,' Professor Ding said with an odd chuckle.

'What do you mean?'

'My father set himself very high standards. In his twenty years as a cop, he had a 100-per-cent success rate with every case he investigated. That was the only one that he felt was never concluded satisfactorily.'

'Are you familiar with the specifics of it?'

'Not at all. I just know that there was a problem with a case involving a hostage. And the reason I know is because it was this that forced my father to retire.'

'Your father quit because of that case?' Pei asked, leaning forward.

'What did you think the reason was?'

'The official reason was health issues. Fatigue.'

'Do you really think a health problem would stop him from being a cop?' Professor Ding shook his head. 'You clearly don't understand my father. He would sacrifice everything for a case. Nothing short of keeling over at a crime scene would have stopped him.'

Pei and Ms Mu exchanged knowing glances.

'Nothing would make him abandon a case,' Professor Ding said. 'The only reason he quit was because he finally came up against a case he couldn't solve. He could never accept failure. Which was why he found an excuse to leave the criminal police, in order to preserve the flawless reputation he'd built up over his twenty-year career.'

Pei listened intently, but something didn't sound right. 'As far as I know, the January 30th case was fairly straightforward. The suspect wore an improvised explosive device and took a hostage. In the end he was shot and killed by the police. None of that's in dispute. For a man like your father, what aspect of the case could have been unsolvable? Besides, the case was already closed and archived by the time your father retired.'

'Do you really not know or are you just playing dumb?' the professor asked through a mouthful of food.

'Humour me.'

'I'd have assumed the two of you would be much more knowledgeable about the relevant details. While this case is ostensibly closed, I assure you it hasn't been completely solved. You see, about two months after the event, the police received a call about the man who was taken hostage that day. The caller said that he had been robbed by the suspect's accomplice.'

'His accomplice?' Pei asked. 'Who?'

'If there was an answer to that, my father wouldn't have quit.'

'You're saying that the identity of the accomplice, some burglar, was never found? And that's why your father resigned?'

Professor Ding nodded. 'My father's a perfectionist. He can't tolerate failure. That's why, when faced with failure, he ran away. No matter what his official excuse was, he couldn't hide the truth from me. I'm his son. No one understood him better than me.'

Pei glanced down and saw that the professor still had half his lunch to go. 'What was so tricky about that case?'

'I'm not very clear on the specifics – I've never really cared about such things. But I have a very distinct memory of my father hunching over two folders for hours. One contained the files for the closed January 30th case and the other concerned the robbery I mentioned. I'd never seen him that intense before.'

Pei massaged his forehead as he pondered what it all meant. There was something lurking behind the January 30th case. Wen Hongbing was killed in the standoff at the apartment building, so who was his accomplice and why rob Chen Tianqiao? And more importantly, how was that unidentified individual able to force Captain Ding Ke into retirement?

'I believe our discussion has come to an end,' Professor Ding said calmly, polishing off the last of his meal.

'I'm sorry?' Ms Mu said.

'My lunch break is over. Thus our conversation must suffer the same fate. I need to get back to work.'

Pei looked at his watch. Barely twenty minutes had passed.

'I'm finished, Gao,' Professor Ding said into his phone 'Please bring in those materials on the wastewater discharge from that pharmaceutical factory in Shandong.'

'Professor Ding,' Pei said impatiently, 'you still haven't told us where we can find your father.'

'He's been gone for ten years. I don't have the slightest idea where he is.'

'You don't have any way of contacting him?'

'He went into hiding. Why would he leave his contact details?'

'Why exactly did he go into hiding?'

'I believe I've already answered all your questions,' Professor Ding said irritably, tapping one finger against his temple. 'Use those analytical skills your department is so famous for.'

Gao walked in with an armful of documents.

'I'll give you thirty more seconds. Are there any more questions?' Professor Ding said as he watched his secretary set the papers down on his desk.

'All things considered, we don't have anything else to ask at the moment,' Pei said.

Nodding to himself, the professor immediately turned his attention to his work. It was as if a switch had been flipped: his entire manner changed and he ignored everyone.

Gao addressed the confused officers. 'Captain Pei, Ms Mu,

feel free to contact me if you have any more questions and I will arrange another appointment with the professor.'

Her timing was impeccable, Pei thought. 'We won't bother you any further today,' he said.

The professor did not react.

'Do you think his answers made sense?' Pei asked Ms Mu once they were in the lift.

'Which ones?'

'Firstly, his explanation as to why his father retired from the force. And secondly, his assertion that they haven't had any contact over the past decade.'

'The first point is sound. Or at least it's more probable than retiring for health reasons. Captain Ding Ke was in his fifties then, wasn't he? He was hardly frail – he was a legend and still solving every case he took on. It must be psychological. It's hard to imagine just how stressful maintaining that sort of reputation must have been. He'd have been seriously afraid of failure, so if he was faced with a case he couldn't solve, especially that far into his career, the urge to flee would have been very strong.'

Pei grunted in agreement. 'How about the second point?'

'That they've had no contact for more than ten years? That's harder to believe. It would mean that their relationship was under significant strain.'

On exiting the lift, Pei and Ms Mu stepped into a near-empty waiting room off the lobby and sat down to continue their conversation.

'What went wrong with their relationship, do you think?' Pei asked.

'Would you agree that when you're a police officer, and

especially if you're a captain with the criminal police, you'll likely have to prioritise your professional responsibilities over your familial ones?'

'It's unavoidable. Your life has to revolve around police work, so naturally you can't spend as much time with your family.' Pei nodded thoughtfully. 'One of the younger guys I worked with in Longzhou often talked about resigning. His girlfriend couldn't stand his work situation and she kept threatening to leave him.'

'What kind of a person is Captain Ding?' Ms Mu asked herself aloud. 'How did he balance his professional and his personal life?'

'Work would have been at the centre of his life,' Pei said quickly. 'I heard quite a few stories about the cases he cracked back when I was at the academy. It was said he was a workaholic and that when he was working on a case he could go for days without eating or sleeping. I remember hearing about one case in particular, which required infiltrating the inner circle of an organised-crime syndicate. To keep his new identity intact, he cut off all contact with his family for more than a month. Not even his wife knew where he was.'

'That would explain why the professor feels as he does about him. Captain Ding retired twenty-eight years ago. His son was twenty-four then. The most intense period of Captain Ding's career overlapped precisely with his son's formative years. Boys crave their father's help and guidance, but Captain Ding would have been too absorbed in his work. That undoubtedly caused a schism between them.'

'And that's why they've had no contact for more than a decade?'

'Relationships are two-way: in an estrangement, both parties bear some responsibility.'

'I was thinking the same thing. Professor Ding was already

an adult when his father went missing. He could have taken the initiative in trying to mend their relationship.'

'Yes, and therein lies the problem. We both saw how the professor views his own job. He's a workaholic just like his father. As far as he's concerned, his family may just be a fading memory. That would explain his indifference to our questions.'

Pei recalled the tone the professor had used when talking about his father. It was more than indifference; he'd detected resentment as well. Both father and son had achieved great things in their careers, but they were as distant as the two poles.

'But even given all that, some things still don't make sense,' Ms Mu went on. 'When Captain Ding went into hiding, he had already been retired for several years. People tend to rely on their families more when they get older. Even if the professor didn't have the time to seek his father out, you'd have thought his father would have made contact.' She paused. 'What if he's already passed away?'

'Unlikely,' Pei said.

'What makes you so sure?'

'He's still getting his pension.'

'His pension?' Ms Mu's eyes grew wide with disbelief.

'He's been withdrawing it from his bank account,' Pei said. 'Ten years ago, Chengdu police set up accounts for every employee so they could receive their salaries and pensions. I've checked and someone has been making regular withdrawals from Captain Ding's account. The last time was two months ago.'

'Then why haven't we been able to find him? If he's making withdrawals at banks and ATMs, can't we check security footage?'

'Headquarters has been trying to do just that, but to no avail. The money just vanishes from his account in a way they can't trace.'

'So Captain Ding is alive and mostly likely here in Chengdu. Then why hasn't anyone been able to find him?'

'I don't know. But I do know that his son has told us why the captain went into hiding.'

Ms Mu wasn't sure what Pei meant, but she was reminded of one of the last things Professor Ding had said.

'I believe I've already answered all your questions. Use those analytical skills your department is so famous for.'

'He was stuck on another case, wasn't he?' she asked.

'Exactly.'

Ms Mu shook her head. 'Sure. But when you look at it from a psychological perspective, something doesn't quite add up. Let's say that Captain Ding quit the force because he wanted to maintain his legendary 100-per-cent success rate. He'd already been retired for eight years when he vanished. Even if he couldn't solve a case, wouldn't his reputation already be secure?'

'Think about it. There was a very special case around the time he disappeared. I'm sure you've heard of it.'

'Which case was that?'

'The Bagman case.'

Ms Mu let out an involuntary gasp.

'So you do know about it.'

'Of course I do. Everyone in Chengdu does.'

'I was working at the Mount Nanming station when it happened,' Pei said. 'Even there, people were talking about it. I can imagine how terrifying the grisly details must have been to an ordinary member of the public. You must have still been in high school back then, right?'

'Yes. It was my final year. After the news of the murder, my parents insisted on coming to school every day to pick me up. The school entrance would be packed with parents waiting to take their daughters home. The killer was supposedly searching for other girls who looked just like his victim.'

Pei grimaced. 'The whole city was obsessed with that case. The citizens of Chengdu were desperate for the police to solve it and the police were under immense pressure. Seeing no other option, they turned to Captain Ding Ke for help – and presumably shifted some of the pressure onto him in the process. He might have been retired, but his connection with the force meant that the outcome would undoubtedly affect his reputation.'

'That's why he went into hiding? Out of shame?' Ms Mu rolled her eyes in disappointment. 'I wonder if this Captain Ding doesn't quite live up to his own reputation. It sounds like he's not nearly as courageous as everyone thinks.'

Pei rubbed his nose and stood up. 'I have a few ideas. Time to test them.'

'How do you intend to do that?'

'I have a theory about the relationship between Captain Ding and his son. I'll take care of this one on my own. Wait here until I get back.'

Ms Mu's jaw twitched. Pei waited for her inevitable rebuttal. 'Okay,' she said.

With no little surprise, Pei exited the waiting room and went into the lobby. After checking the building's floorplan on the wall, he got into the lift.

Meanwhile, Ms Mu shifted left and right on the hard chair. Her attention was drawn to a magazine rack: Professor Ding's face decorated the cover of one of the publications on display.

'What luck,' she muttered and began flipping through it.

She recognised the background of the cover picture – it was Professor Ding's office. The professor wore an immaculate suit and sat at the same desk where he had eaten his lunch only fifteen minutes ago. He looked straight at the camera, radiating confidence and authority.

The caption read: *Extraordinary Achievements Require Extraordinary Dedication: an Interview with Professor Ding Zhen, Water Pollution Management Expert.*

The interview spanned two pages. The first page mostly described the professor's recent academic achievements, while the second page discussed his career and personal life. Ms Mu eagerly absorbed the text of the second page.

Professor Ding, do you feel your personality has influenced your achievements in any way?
DING: Certainly. For example, I'm not the kind of person to countenance defeat. No matter what I'm doing, I always try to get the best possible results. I can't tolerate doubt, and the only way to avoid doubt is through perfect results.
How do you divide your time between work and leisure?
DING: Leisure? I have no need for that.
So you spend all your time working? You don't ever need to take a break?
DING: I do, in fact. I eat, I sleep and I work. I find relaxation in all of those things. When I tire of running experiments, I enjoy reading academic literature. When I grow tired of that, I organise a meeting. But 'leisure' as you put it? That's just a waste of time.
You're currently single. Have you ever thought about starting a family of your own?
DING: I'm very content with my current work situation. I feel no need to start a family just because of societal expectations.

Many professionals say that family provides a strong motivation for their career. Would you care to comment on that perspective?
DING: That's a very normal attitude, but I know it doesn't apply to me. I have no time to enjoy whatever warmth a family might provide. And I'm afraid that if I did start a family now, I'd be forced to neglect them for the sake of my job.

Ms Mu read on and was stunned by how emotionless and robotic the professor appeared.

She was interrupted by Pei's return to the waiting room.

'A magazine interview?' he said with interest and quickly picked up another copy from the rack. He flipped through it and a gratified smile appeared on his face. 'You haven't gone anywhere, but it looks like you've already discovered quite a bit.'

'All I gleaned is that the professor has led a celibate life for the sake of his career,' she said with a careless shrug. 'I'm willing to bet you had more luck than I did. Let's hear it, Captain.'

Pei's attention, however, was still focused on the interview. He read it to himself until he came to a passage that seemed worth sharing.

'"I have no time to enjoy whatever warmth a family might provide",' he read out loud. '"And I'm afraid that if I did start a family now, I'd be forced to neglect them for the sake of my job." An obvious jab at his father,' he said.

'My thoughts as well.'

'There's more to this than you know,' Pei said. 'Captain Ding's dedication to his job alienated his wife. She eventually had an affair and the fallout tore their marriage apart. That was twenty years ago. Professor Ding was a teenager at the time.'

'To be a teenager, when you know everything and nothing

at the same time...' Ms Mu mused. 'The affair and subsequent divorce must have cast a dark shadow over the professor's early years – and had a massive impact on his adult life.'

'An outsider might assume that he ignores his emotional side because of his devotion to his work,' Pei said. 'But I think the reverse may be even more plausible – that it's because he's so emotionally damaged that he puts so much effort into his work. And come to think of it... What do you know about his relationship with Gao?'

'Nothing,' Ms Mu said. 'But I take it you do?'

'I've done some digging. You know, a man with Professor Ding's reputation and accomplishments – and he's not bad looking – would be one of Chengdu's most eligible bachelors. They say quite a few women have tried to woo him – including Gao. I don't know if you guessed, but she used to be one of his students. A number of students have fallen for him over the years, apparently, and the professor has always ignored them. But Gao was very persistent. After completing her postgraduate studies, she rejected an impressive offer from IBM and instead chose to work as a secretary in the department where she formerly studied. The reason? To stay close to Professor Ding. But despite that, he's remained all but oblivious. She's worked for him for three years and as far as I can tell they're nothing more than colleagues.'

Ms Mu felt a flash of pity for Gao. 'I can't believe she would let her emotions blind her like that.'

'Maybe she thought that things would change once they were working together,' Pei suggested. 'But Professor Ding is more than just emotionally unavailable – his life is positively Spartan.'

'Oh? What else did you find out so quickly?'

'He apparently stays cooped up in that office for weeks

at a time. He eats the same takeaway every single lunchtime. And he still lives in a cramped staff apartment provided by the college, despite having more than enough money to buy a villa downtown.'

'The man's an enigma. But how did you find out so much?'

'I had a pleasant chat with a talkative woman in the HR office,' Pei answered with a wry grin.

Ms Mu smiled mischievously. 'You should have taken me too!'

'I wanted it to be a natural conversation, gossipy, no filters. With two of us there, it might have felt more like an interrogation.'

'You wouldn't make a half-bad psychologist,' Ms Mu said. 'In case you're ever in the market for another job…'

Pei rolled his eyes playfully. 'In another life.'

'Well, we have a rough profile of Professor Ding's personality now. He's emotionally distant and focused on nothing but his work. I'm afraid the apple doesn't fall far from the tree. Thus it makes sense to conclude that father and son haven't communicated at all over the last decade. In other words, the professor was telling the truth.'

'Agreed.'

'Well, Captain, what's next?'

'There are the two major investigations to catch up on: the January 30th case and the Bagman case. In order to find out what happened to Captain Ding Ke, we'll need to look into both of them in considerable detail.'

10

STIRRING UP THE PAST

3:11 p.m.
Captain Pei's office

Two case folders lay on Pei's desk. Neither was as thick as he'd expected. In a hurry, the captain opened the first folder and scanned the file on top of the pile.

CHEN TIANQIAO [CT] ROBBERY: REPORT INTERVIEW
Please describe the events as you witnessed them.
CT: It was night-time and I was asleep when a sudden pain woke me up. When I came to my senses, I found that my hands had been bound. I couldn't move. My eyes were taped shut. Then someone whispered in my ear, demanding that I tell them the code to the safe in my house. I refused and... he tortured me. I was in so much pain, so I told him the code. Then I heard him open the safe. Once I heard my door shut, I tried to work my wrists free. I eventually got the ropes off and reported the burglary to the police.
What did this person take from your safe?
CT: Everything. 204,000 yuan in total.
Did you get a good look at him?
CT: Didn't you hear what I just said? I had tape over my eyes.

How did he torture you?

CT: He covered my mouth with a damp cloth so that I couldn't breathe. He did that at least seven times. Maybe eight. Each time he'd hold the cloth in place even longer than the last time. He threatened me, said if I didn't tell him the code he'd let me suffocate.

Can you describe this person's voice?

CT: He was male. I... I can't really describe him beyond that.

Could you identify his voice if you heard it again?

CT: Probably not. He didn't talk exactly – he just whispered to me. I couldn't hear what his real voice sounded like.

Besides asking for the code to your safe, what else did he say?

CT: He said he was helping someone collect a debt.

Who was he helping?

CT: I think he's one of Wen Hongbing's mates. When Wen kidnapped me two months ago, he extorted 10,000 yuan from me. Apparently that wasn't enough for him, so his accomplice came to get more.

Who do you think this person was?

CT: I don't know. Someone connected to Wen Hongbing.

The next document in the folder was an account provided by Chen's wife. The details in both reports lined up perfectly.

Pei looked over several more notes and reports from the scene of the crime. The more he read, the stranger the case appeared.

For a start, when the intruder entered Chen's home in the early hours of the morning, he did so without causing any damage to the door or windows. This already put him in a league above the average burglar. What was even more surprising was that all the rope and tape he used to restrain Chen came from the victim's home. The suspect was definitely experienced and knew how to cover his tracks.

Forensics indicated that the joint areas of the victim's arms and legs exhibited marks consistent with being bound. However, no other marks or wounds were found on his body.

The trace evidence report stated that all of the fingerprints and footprints taken from Chen's home (from the door, windows and safe) belonged to Chen and his wife. No trace of a third party was found.

In short, the crime scene contained not a single shred of evidence that could be used to identify the intruder.

The police records also showed that while Captain Ding Ke was in charge of the early stages of the investigation, Huang Jieyuan eventually took over. The implication was clear: Captain Ding quit while it was ongoing and his assistant took his place.

There were two soft knocks on Pei's door. Ms Mu entered before Pei could say a word.

'How's it going?' she asked, approaching the desk. 'Have you finished reading the case files?'

'One down, one to go,' Pei said, pushing a folder across the desk with one hand and gesturing at the empty chair with the other. 'The records don't say much. Have a look and then let's talk.'

Ms Mu began to leaf through the folder.

A few minutes later, she looked up. 'What do you think?' she asked.

'I think that the robbery is linked to the January 30th hostage case,' Pei said bluntly. 'It's very closely connected to Wen Hongbing, just like Chen Tianqiao thought.'

'What makes you so sure?'

'When we investigate violent crimes like armed robbery or assault, the first thing we do is ask the victim who they think the culprit was. Most crimes of that sort are perpetrated by someone known to the victim. Their testimonies often give us a lot of information we wouldn't uncover otherwise. Grudges, jealousy, that type of thing.'

Ms Mu nodded. 'So where do we look next?'

'Right before Captain Ding left the police, he was working on two different cases. One of them was that burglary. The other was the January 30th hostage case.'

'So you're saying that Captain Ding thought the two cases were connected.'

'Exactly. I don't see a reason to doubt his judgement.'

'But there's one thing I don't understand,' Ms Mu said. 'If the motive of Wen Hongbing's accomplice was to steal money to take revenge on Chen Tianqiao, he should have given it to Wen Hongbing's widow. But Mrs Wen died of an illness not long after that, and her son – Wen Chengyu – was sent to an orphanage.'

'I agree – it's definitely strange.' Pei shut his eyes and considered this for a moment. 'I think we should pay a visit to the doctor who treated Mrs Wen.'

Pei and Ms Mu quickly looked up the doctor's current status and learnt that he was now the director of the People's Hospital cancer centre. The captain called to request an immediate appointment and they made it to the hospital within the hour.

Dr Sun was a pudgy man with a tuft of white hair and rounded features that gave him a kindly appearance. Pei introduced himself and handed the doctor a folder containing documents and photographs pertaining to Wen Hongbing's family. Dr Sun glanced at the pictures for only a few seconds and then pointed his thick finger at the image of the wife.

'That's her. She was my patient.'

Pei let out a pent-up breath. 'That's some memory you have.'

'I can barely remember what I ate for breakfast today,' the doctor said, shaking his head self-effacingly, 'but this woman stood out. Her family ran into a lot of trouble – that I remember very distinctly. And there was another thing: she clearly had money, but she refused to let us go ahead with her treatment. Strange patient.'

Ms Mu lit up at the mention of the money. 'Tell us everything you remember about her,' she said.

'She had uterine cancer. Are you familiar with that type of cancer? It's actually not as frightening as it sounds. If the patient has surgery, the chances of remission are very high. To begin with, the family couldn't scrape together the money for surgery, so they opted for a very basic treatment. Later, her husband very shockingly kidnapped someone in order to get the money for her operation, and the police killed him. Unbelievable. And that was just the start of that family's problems…'

'But you said she obviously had a lot of money,' Pei said.

'Yes, but that was later. The initial treatment didn't work, and with the shock of her husband's death, her condition deteriorated. She needed to go under the knife quick or she'd be too far gone for us to be able to help. I remember I was so anxious about her condition that I actually had a hard time falling asleep most nights. I really felt for her, so I told her that if she got the necessary funds, the hospital would charge her the lowest possible amount for the operation. And then one day she said that she had finally got enough money and wanted to have the operation.'

'Did you ask her how she'd got the funds?'

'I did. I assumed that she'd scraped together all she could and borrowed the rest. But she said that her late husband had lent someone some money and that this person had finally paid the family back.'

'Did the police question you about that?'

'They did, in fact.' The doctor's eyes narrowed. 'Are you saying that... she came by the money illegally?'

'I can't say that for certain,' Pei replied as he considered the implications himself. The legal angle was one thing, but viewed from a different angle, the money was rightfully hers. He fought back the urge to shiver.

'I did smell something fishy when the police came,' Dr Sun said. 'They asked me whether or not Mrs Wen had suddenly come into money.'

'And did you tell them what she'd told you?'

'Naturally.'

Pei continued mulling this over. How did the police come by that lead? And, even more puzzling, why did they then ignore it? A sudden thought occurred to him. 'How many officers came to see you?' he asked.

'Just one.'

Nodding, Pei took out his wallet. He reached in deep and pulled out an old photograph. The image had yellowed, but the two young men in it were still clearly discernible. One was gaunt and had a piercing gaze. The other was dashing and shone with life. He pointed to one of them. 'Is this the man who came to see you?'

'No.' Dr Sun shook his head.

'Are you sure?' Pei asked, disappointed.

'It definitely wasn't him.' Dr Sun continued studying the photo. 'I do remember this young man though.'

Pei's eyebrows shot up. 'How do you know him?'

'That was the nice fellow who took care of the poor mother and son for quite some time. I just assumed he was a relative. The boy's uncle, maybe. You're telling me that he was a cop? He never mentioned that to me.'

'Do you happen to remember the name of the officer who came to question you?'

Dr Sun gave an awkward smile. 'I honestly can't recall. It's such a long time ago.'

Pei smiled apologetically in return. 'I understand. Now, am I correct in saying that Mrs Wen never had the operation?'

'Yes, that's right.' Dr Sun's expression soured. 'She died of complications not long after.'

'If she had the money, why didn't she go through with it?'

'She said she'd been carrying the cancer for so long that surgery would be pointless – "a waste of money". She said it would be more worthwhile to leave something for her son. But I don't think that was her only reason. If she'd had the operation, she would probably have survived. Forgive my lack of objectivity here, but what kind of a mother wouldn't grab even the tiniest chance to avoid leaving their child orphaned and all alone in the world?'

'What do you think her real reasons were?'

'I think it had to do with where that money came from. After that officer questioned me, he talked to Mrs Wen as well. I heard her tell him that she didn't have any money – which was the opposite of what she'd told me a few hours earlier. It was after the cop left that she decided not to go through with it. Which is why I think her decision had something to do with the money and its provenance.'

FATE

Ms Mu nodded silently as she listened to Dr Sun's explanation. His analysis made sense. But two mysteries still remained: the identity of the burglar who'd taken the money from Chen Tianqiao's safe, and the identity of the officer who'd questioned Mrs Wen and failed to report any concerns arising from that interview.

'It's all starting to make sense,' Pei murmured to himself. He extended his right hand to Dr Sun and the two shook hands. 'Thanks very much for your cooperation,' he said with an earnest nod.

An orange tinge lit the sky as the two investigators walked out of the hospital. Pei stopped at the edge of the walkway outside the entrance and stared off into the distance.

'What are you thinking?' Ms Mu asked.

'Exactly what role did Yuan Zhibang play in the investigation into this robbery?'

'You're thinking that even though he made it his business to look after Wen Chengyu and his mother, he might have also been the officer who spoke to Dr Sun?'

'Right. Otherwise it's hard to fathom how a clue as crucial as this one didn't make it into the official police record.'

'Let me see if I follow what you're saying,' Ms Mu said, rubbing her chin. 'Since Yuan was the one who killed Wen Hongbing, you think Yuan felt guilty about Wen Hongbing's son and widow. He helped them out, even going so far as to conceal any facts that might eventually cause them trouble. Also, as Dr Sun just told us, Yuan's relationship with the young Wen Chengyu and his mother was far from routine.'

Pei let out a long sigh. 'It might not be as simple as "helping" them, per se.'

Ms Mu froze in surprise. 'You think Yuan was behind the burglary?'

221

'A perfect crime – who else but the future Eumenides would be able to pull that off? I should have realised that earlier.'

'Yuan would have already visited the Chens during his investigations into the January 30th hostage case,' she said, thinking aloud now. 'Which would mean he was familiar with their house. And assuming he really did kill Wen Hongbing, his guilt would be motivation enough for him to want to help the widow. Psychologically speaking, this burglary may actually have been the prelude to the April 18th murders. It's possible that the Chen robbery – the first intentional taking of the law into his own hands – marked the creation of the vigilante that became Eumenides.'

Pei nodded as he reflected on what they had learnt about his former friend. Yuan had turned from being one of the police academy's top students into becoming a cold-blooded killer. They'd assumed that the murder of his ex-girlfriend Bai Feifei by her boss, Vice Commissioner Xue Dalin, had been the catalyst. Though that made sense in terms of a motive for Yuan, it did mean that Yuan's transformation from star student to serial killer had happened very fast. If, instead, Wen Hongbing's death and the robbery of Chen Tianqiao's home had been the start of it all, that would make Yuan's transformation more gradual.

Even so, two significant questions remained unanswered. There was the truth behind Wen Hongbing's death. If the situation in the apartment had been under control as Huang and the SPU marksman had both stated, what had gone wrong?

And then there was the robbery. Who had visited the hospital and decided to conceal their concerns about the provenance of Mrs Wen's money?

Ms Mu clicked her fingers. 'Actually, if we want to know who that officer was, all we have to do is ask—'

'—Huang Jieyuan!'

2 November, 12:13 p.m.
Private upstairs room, Black Magic Bar

'So tell me, what brings you two here today?' said Huang.

'We're searching for Captain Ding Ke,' Pei said, pausing to take a sip of tea. 'He's the one person alive who knows the whole truth behind Wen Hongbing's death. If we find him, we can untangle Wen Chengyu's history and perhaps even get closer to understanding Yuan Zhibang's rebirth as the first Eumenides. More importantly, we believe that the current Eumenides is also looking for Captain Ding. We need to stay one step ahead of him.'

Huang nodded in silent understanding as the thud-thud-thud of the heavy-metal music playing downstairs seeped up through the floor.

'Yesterday morning we met with Professor Ding Zhen, Captain Ding Ke's son,' Pei said. 'The professor told us about two particular cases that had stumped his father. One caused his father to retire and the other made him go into hiding. We've looked into them thoroughly, not only to test the veracity of the professor's story but also to try and glean some clues as to Captain Ding's current whereabouts.'

'I know which cases you're talking about,' Huang said. 'One of them has to be the April 7th robbery involving the hostage from the January 30th case earlier that year. The other is no doubt the infamous Bagman Killing from ten years ago. Those two cases changed my life as well.'

'You got it,' said Pei.

'As you know, the investigation into the robbery of Chen Tianqiao's home was what made Captain Ding decide to quit the force,' Huang said. 'I took over from him, so that was the first case I was in charge of. I was head of the criminal police for the next eight years, right up until the January 12th Bagman Killing. Eventually I was forced to resign as a result of how I handled that case.' Huang's eyes fluttered shut and he let out a long, barely audible exhalation. 'It's ironic that these two cases were such landmarks for both of us.'

'You shouldn't take it personally,' Pei said. 'After all, not even Captain Ding could solve them.'

'True enough. How could I hope to succeed where even *he* had failed?' Huang said, briefly animated, but a moment later his eyes crinkled with worry again. 'But doesn't that mean that all my work was for nothing?'

Pei shook his head gently. Huang may have retired a decade ago, but he was still absorbed in the past.

'Few things in life are cut and dried,' Pei said. 'Take the April 7th robbery. The reason it's still unsolved might not have anything to do with the skill of the perpetrator. It could very well be because of internal meddling.'

'Internal meddling? From within the police force?'

'All the information I have indicates that it shouldn't have been that hard to work out who committed the robbery. Mrs Wen came into a great deal of money immediately after the burglary and deliberately concealed that fact. I'm positive there would have been a breakthrough in the case had the police pursued that lead.'

'Are you sure about that?' Huang asked in a doubtful voice.

Pei nodded. 'Dead certain,' he said, and related what Dr Sun had told them.

Huang slowly shook his head in unwilling comprehension. 'I can't believe the money trail was missed. A clue that obvious? Come on, there's no chance we could have missed that.'

'That's the thing – you didn't. A police officer went to the hospital and spoke to the doctor about Mrs Wen's sudden windfall. Following the officer's visit, she decided not to have the operation. Presumably she changed her mind for fear of attracting police attention. She sacrificed her own life in order to protect the person who had committed the burglary.'

'That's impossible. Impossible!' The veins in Huang's neck bulged. 'I compiled our case files and they said nothing about this. I'd bet my life on it!'

Pei put his hand on Huang's shoulder. 'Don't you see? Your officer was aware of the lead, but he didn't report it. He covered it up. That's why the case went unsolved.'

Huang looked at Pei in bewilderment.

How could he still not understand, Pei wondered. It must be his pride. Huang was too damn arrogant to consider the possibility that one of his men had acted out of self-interest.

Pei gritted his teeth. 'So, can you tell me the name of the officer?'

Huang gave him a hard stare. 'Are you implying that he withheld evidence and shielded a criminal?'

'I'm not implying anything,' Pei growled. 'I'm stating a fact. There is substantial reason to believe that your officer did just that. If we track him down, we might be able to unravel the mysteries surrounding the April 7th robbery.'

Huang shut his eyes and took a deep breath. 'Captain Ding Ke.'

'It was Captain Ding?' Pei said, his jaw nearly dropping to the floor.

'Correct. It was obvious that the hospital was the best place to start our investigation. So of course Captain Ding went there.' Huang inhaled and regained some of his composure. His mouth contorted into a pained smile. 'Now you know why no one ever questioned it. And why I couldn't believe what you were saying. I've never had reason to doubt Captain Ding.' He threw up his hands and slumped onto the sofa.

Pei could understand Huang's confusion. How could he expect him to accept that his idol had betrayed the force eighteen years ago? Pei amended his earlier judgement: it wasn't pride that had kept Huang from seeing the truth, it was his blind admiration for Captain Ding.

Ms Mu was the youngest person in the room and the name 'Captain Ding Ke' meant far less to her than it did to her two seniors. But this did not dull her analysis of the situation. 'We've long been told that Captain Ding Ke retired because this particular case proved too challenging,' she said. 'But I would never have guessed that the greatest challenge actually came from within the man himself.'

Pei and Huang both looked at her in surprise, as though suddenly realising that she was right there next to them.

'Captain Ding obtained what might well be the most important clue in this investigation,' Ms Mu continued. 'An officer of his calibre could certainly have used this lead to solve the case. So why didn't he? Why did he quit instead?'

Pei's confusion vanished instantly. 'We underestimated Captain Ding,' he said. 'We believed that this case stumped him, when in reality he knew more about it than anyone else. He knew that Yuan Zhibang was behind the robbery!'

'Yuan Zhibang?' Huang asked, disbelief written all over his face. 'But how is that possible?'

'After Wen Hongbing's death, Yuan grew close to his widow and child. That gives him a motive. He was familiar with the layout of Chen's home, and also had the skills needed to carry out the robbery. That gives him the means.'

The truth was finally sinking in for Huang. 'Well, perhaps I shouldn't feel so bad about having been stumped on this case,' he said. 'But how could Captain Ding—'

'Captain Ding Ke had two choices,' Pei said. 'One option was to continue investigating. What do you think would have happened if he'd done that?'

'Hmm.' Huang cracked his knuckles. 'If your theory is correct, Yuan could have been arrested for burglary. Given the amount of money involved, he would have got a long jail sentence. The court would have returned the money to Chen Tianqiao and that would have left the widowed Mrs Wen and her son in a tight spot.'

'And not only that,' Pei added. 'Mrs Wen could have been accused of being an accessory to the crime or even an accomplice. Her statements indicated that she knew where the money had come from.'

'Isn't that rather excessive?' Ms Mu interjected. 'Chen Tianqiao owed Wen Hongbing that money. You seriously think that the courts would have returned Wen's money to the person who borrowed it from him and then prosecuted the widow?'

'The role of the courts is to uphold the law, not to be kind,' Pei said, trying his best to maintain a neutral tone.

Ms Mu fell silent.

'Captain Ding's second choice just so happened to be the opposite of the first,' Pei went on. 'Namely to ignore the lead and allow the investigation to go cold. If he did that, Mrs Wen and her son could keep the money. Justice would have been done in regards to Chen Tianqiao. And Captain Ding's star pupil would stay out of prison. If you were Captain Ding, which option would you choose?'

Ms Mu shook her head in frustration. 'What a choice! By "solving" the case, he would have sent Mrs Wen to her doom.'

'And,' Huang added, 'Captain Ding was grooming Yuan to be his successor in the criminal police. How could he bear to see his protégé's future ruined?'

Huang's words rang true. Pei remembered when Captain Ding had come to the academy to select a trainee. Every criminal-investigation student had been buzzing at the prospect. They all knew that whoever the legendary Captain Ding chose would one day take his place on the criminal police force. Pei himself had been a candidate before he began his tumultuous relationship with Meng Yun. Ultimately, it was Yuan who got chosen.

'However,' Huang continued, 'it's hard to be certain. Even though that first option would have pained Captain Ding greatly, that doesn't mean the other option would have felt liberating. I believe he would have been very averse to the second option. If he ignored Yuan's crime, he would have betrayed his duty as a police officer. I was Captain Ding's assistant. I knew him very well, and nothing mattered to him more than doing his duty. He sacrificed a lot for his career. Some of those sacrifices would have been too much for an ordinary person, but he was able to bear them all. He was the staunchest defender of the law I ever knew. That man would never have compromised his principles.'

'So he didn't choose either of those options,' Ms Mu said. 'Instead, he decided to run.'

The room fell briefly quiet. Pei leant forward in his seat. 'Our current thinking is that the April 7th robbery was the needle that broke the camel's back for Captain Ding. But wasn't Yuan under just as much stress when he committed the robbery?'

Ms Mu considered this then shook her head. 'It sounds like

you're saying that everyone was forced into their decisions and had no alternatives. Are we supposed to sympathise with every single person involved in this case?'

'Everything starts somewhere. Perhaps both Captain Ding and Yuan faced an impossible choice before the robbery was committed.'

'Are you talking about the January 30th hostage case?' Huang asked.

'We still don't know everything. If Yuan really did kill Wen Hongbing, perhaps we should reflect on the circumstances under which he did so,' Ms Mu said. 'His subsequent behaviour shows a level of concern for Wen Hongbing's wife and son that is far from normal. In fact, it's almost as if he was paying off a debt. Or felt very guilty.'

Anger flared in Pei's heart. 'He shot a man who was holding someone hostage and threatening to blow up an entire apartment building! Even if Wen Hongbing had good reasons for doing what he did, why would Yuan feel guilty?'

'While I don't know the specifics, I am sure that Yuan committed the robbery because of some emotional reaction after he killed Wen Hongbing,' Ms Mu said. 'The most likely scenario is that something unexpected happened inside the apartment. A mistake. And Yuan was the one who made that mistake.'

Pei avoided her gaze, but the gleam in his eyes grew brighter until he was practically trembling with excitement.

'What's on your mind?' Ms Mu asked.

Pei looked at her and then Huang. 'If my colleague is correct, we may very well have figured out a way to defeat Eumenides. A method that's less violent than what we originally intended but possibly far more effective.'

Huang blinked in confusion. Ms Mu, however, immediately

grasped Pei's meaning. 'That's right,' she said. 'We can seize Eumenides' emotional centre—'

'Stop speaking in code,' Huang said, scowling in frustration.

Ms Mu turned to him. 'We know that the orphaned Wen Chengyu became Eumenides and that he became a killer only after having undergone years of training from Yuan Zhibang. Eumenides sees Yuan as his mentor and the person who controlled his life's path. As far as we know, he's never had any reason to doubt Yuan. But how will he feel if he discovers that his path began with the death of his own father and that Yuan Zhibang was the one responsible for his father's death?'

Huang's face lit up. 'His faith in Yuan will be shaken to the core. He'll feel that Yuan was using him all along – that Yuan hurt him. Eumenides will feel like a pawn in Yuan's plans, like he's been really taken advantage of. He'll begin to detest everything about the man – including the very role of Eumenides that Yuan created.'

'And then we'll have defeated him without having struck a single blow,' Ms Mu said, curling a hand into a fist.

'It's a good idea. Damn good,' Huang said, his excitement rising. 'But there is one hole in it. We still don't know exactly what happened at Wen Hongbing's apartment.'

Ms Mu was undeterred. 'At the very least we have a lead. And it's the same lead that Eumenides is tracking. I'm confident that we will soon learn the truth behind Wen Hongbing's death. And so will Eumenides.'

11

THE BAGMAN

2:13 p.m.
Private upstairs room, Black Magic Bar

'It's time to talk about another case,' Huang said quietly. 'The January 12th case.'

Ms Mu shifted uncomfortably in her seat. The dim room seemed to grow even darker. 'The Bagman Killing,' she whispered.

'How much do you two know about that?' Huang asked.

'The files are in my office, but I haven't had much time to go through them,' Captain Pei said. 'I've spent most of my time today researching the April 7th robbery.'

'Hmmm.' Huang nodded. 'Ms Mu, you were born and raised in Chengdu. I assume you've heard a great deal about that case over the years.'

'There was a time when I heard a gruesome new rumour about the killer almost every day for months on end,' she said.

'Tell us what you know then. I'd like to hear how it felt from a civilian's perspective.' Making himself comfortable on the sofa, Huang pulled a cigarette from his pocket and prepared to listen.

Ms Mu clasped her cup of hot tea with both hands, as

though trying to gain all the extra warmth she could. 'The Bagman Killing... that was back in 1992, wasn't it? I was about to leave senior school. Actually, it happened right before my final exams. I always stayed late at school to study and one night our teacher wouldn't let any of us female students go home by ourselves. He insisted that our parents come and pick us up. My father eventually turned up. When I asked him what was going on, he told me that there was a very bad man on the loose in Chengdu and that I couldn't go out alone any more. He was going to accompany me to and from school from then on. I tried to ask more questions, but he clammed up. He just told me to focus on my studies and not to worry about anything else, but that only made me more curious.

'At school the next day, all of my classmates were discussing what had happened. That was when I found out just how terrifying the situation was. I still regret listening to all those rumours back then, but they were impossible to ignore. Everyone was talking about it, and I didn't get a good night's sleep for months.'

Huang took a long drag of his cigarette. 'What kind of rumours were floating around?'

Ms Mu took another sip from her cup to moisten her throat and dipped back into those decade-old memories. 'I heard that a girl had been killed. People said that the killer was a psychopath. They said that he chopped the girl up into little pieces and fried her. He *ate* pieces of her and scattered other bits around the city. Some even claimed that he'd boiled her brain and organs. We all thought that the killer's main desire was to eat human flesh.'

Ms Mu's voice faded and she shuddered. Even Pei grimaced at the grisly images her words conjured. Only Huang looked unperturbed. He'd been involved in the case from the very beginning and had long been numb to the details. What time could not erase, however, was his shame at the investigation's outcome.

Ms Mu took several deep breaths and the clamps around her chest began to loosen. 'Eventually, the police came to my school. They showed us pictures and asked us to identify the objects in them. The item that stands out most clearly in my memory is a red down jacket. It must have been what the victim was wearing when she was killed. I still remember the exact shade of red – it was as bright as fresh blood. I had nightmares about that jacket for days. It wasn't long before I heard rumours that the killer had made an announcement: he was going to devour a new victim every month. The next target would be a long-haired girl wearing a jacket like the one in the photo.'

'Pure fabrication,' Huang interrupted.

'I was just a teenager,' Ms Mu said, her hand grazing the edge of her bob. 'I didn't know rumour from truth. All I knew was that all the girls in my class cut their hair, including me, and none of us wore a single piece of red clothing for the next six months. That all-consuming fear didn't let up until I was at the police academy, in a safe environment.'

'Tell us what you know about the investigation, Huang – the bits you know to be true,' Pei said.

Huang sucked on the last of his cigarette and stubbed it out on the table. His voice took on a low, gravelly quality. 'You were right about the date, Ms Mu. The Bagman Killing came to light on the twelfth of January 1992 when a middle-aged street cleaner discovered a black rubbish bag by a public bin on Dongba Road. She was curious, so she prodded some holes in it with her broom, revealing several slices of what appeared to be fresh meat glistening in the early morning sun.

'She assumed it was a bag of fresh pork that a meat vendor

had dropped while rushing to the morning market. She took it home, thinking it would be impossible to trace its original owner – she thought she'd got lucky.' Huang attempted a smirk but couldn't quite manage it. 'It was only when she started going through the bag that she noticed something unusual. Three things, in fact. Three human fingers, to be precise.'

Pei glanced over at Ms Mu. Her face had gone pale.

'The woman ran shrieking out of her home. Her neighbours heard and called the police as soon as they learnt what she'd found. We received the call at exactly 7:23 a.m. Fifteen minutes later, I arrived on the scene with a team in tow. I knew from the start it was a major case.

'The sliced flesh was very fresh. As bizarre as it sounds, it really did look like pork from the market. The bag weighed four and a half kilograms and contained four hundred and thirty-six slices of flesh. It had been sliced with surgical precision and piled up very neatly. Very deliberately. Each slice was two to three millimetres thick. Forensics concluded that the slices had all come from the leg of an adult female and that the three digits were the index, middle and ring fingers of a woman's left hand.'

Huang paused to sigh and collect his thoughts.

'What we didn't realise,' he continued, 'was that this was only the beginning. Our dispatch centre received a second call at 9:37 a.m. Two construction workers had discovered an abandoned suitcase at a building site on Shita Road. We rushed over there as fast as we could. By the time I arrived, the local police had already set up a cordon and a crowd had gathered around it.

'I remember talking to the two workers who'd discovered the suitcase. They were frightened out of their wits. I didn't even have time to take notes. Nothing could have prepared me for what I saw inside that thing. It was the coldest day of the year, but my clothes were soaked with sweat.'

Huang stared at his hands in numb fear. He lit another cigarette.

Ms Mu suddenly found it hard to breathe, but it wasn't due to the smoke. 'What exactly was inside that case?' she asked.

'A human head and a complete set of human organs,' Huang said, digging his fingers into the palm of his hand. 'One of the rumours that you mentioned *was* true. The organs had been boiled.'

Ms Mu tried with all her might to suppress the nausea rising from her stomach.

'The head was a deep shade of red, all soft and bloated. The organs had been separated into five clear plastic bags, each placed neatly around the head. And the intestines were folded and stuffed inside the skull.'

The last detail alone sent a great shiver down Pei's spine. He pictured the killer calmly folding the victim's intestines, as composed and focused as an accountant preparing a client's tax return. Never in his entire career had he encountered a criminal that cold or detached. Not even Eumenides could be so disturbed.

Huang resumed his account. 'Everyone was shocked at the contents of the suitcase. I immediately reported the situation to my superior. Not long after, a task force was convened, led by the head of the public security bureau. Its first meeting was held at the construction site and marked the official start of the investigation into what we called the "January 12th Dissected Corpse Case". But everyone soon came to call it the "Bagman Killing".

'The task force came up with a three-part strategy. To locate the other bits of the body, the team would conduct a citywide search; to determine the identity of the victim, they would check Chengdu's missing persons records for women who'd recently gone AWOL; and to prevent the killer from striking again, they would step up patrols and increase the number of safety warnings issued to the public.'

Pei nodded steadily. 'They made the right choices. How did the investigation get on?'

'The search for the rest of body yielded results almost immediately. Some officers discovered another black plastic bag in a rubbish heap on Yanling Road. The bag contained five kilograms of human flesh, including two more fingers. Just before noon the same day, a member of the public discovered a bundle wrapped in an old bedsheet in some undergrowth beside the highway in east Chengdu. Inside the bundle was a third plastic bag, also containing fingers and slices of human flesh, as well as a complete set of women's underwear folded with machine-like precision. But that was the last thing we found. We never found any other remains.'

'So, to summarise, you found three bags of the victim's sliced-up flesh, along with a suitcase containing her head and internal organs,' Pei said.

'That's correct.'

'Those three plastic bags couldn't have weighed more than about fourteen kilograms, right? In other words, at least half of the victim went undiscovered, including the rest of her skeleton.'

'Yes,' Huang said, his face heavy with disappointment. 'We tried to analyse why that might have been. We concluded that the killer had probably used a more clandestine method to dispose of the other parts of the body: burial or incineration, or perhaps removal to a remote location outside Chengdu.

There were rumours too, of course – which, I should add, were unsubstantiated.'

'That the killer ate the rest of the body, you mean?' Pei said, recalling what Ms Mu had mentioned moments earlier. 'We can dismiss that possibility outright – why would a cannibal keep the bones but throw away so much meat?'

'What if it was a ritual killing?' Ms Mu asked.

Huang shook his head. 'We considered that as well. But there was nothing about the human remains or what had been done to them that indicated any correlation with known cult or ritualistic practices.'

He pulled out another cigarette, lit it and took several hungry drags. 'We didn't get any useful leads from the missing persons database, so I saw no option but to publish a notice in Chengdu's most widely read newspapers. We included a photo of a piece of the victim's red down jacket – the same picture you were shown in school, Ms Mu. On the fifteenth of January, three female students from a vocational college contacted the task force and told us that one of their roommates hadn't been seen for several days. And the down jacket in the papers looked exactly like the one she usually wore.

'The task force immediately brought the girls in to examine the jacket. All three were positive that it belonged to their roommate. At that point, I was 90 per cent sure that we'd identified the victim. The girls asked to see the body, but I didn't want them to. It was enough to turn the stomach of even the toughest cop. But they insisted, so eventually I gave in – after all, they shared the same room for an entire year.

'As soon as one of the girls saw the head, her eyes grew as wide as saucers. She yelled out "It's her!" and curled up like a shrimp, and everything started flying out of her – tears, mucus, spit. It was not a pleasant sight. But it was a massive breakthrough for the investigation. After the students left, we contacted the missing roommate's parents. They lived only two hours away from headquarters, so they arrived later that day.'

Ms Mu let out a long exhale through her nose. 'Was it their daughter?'

'By the time they left, we had officially confirmed the victim's identity: Feng Chunling, a second-year student of finance and accounting at Chengdu Vocational and Technical College.'

'What day did she go missing?' Pei asked.

'She was last seen leaving the college on the morning of the ninth of January.'

'The girl was missing for five whole days?' Ms Mu asked, stunned. 'And none of the other students noticed? How did the college explain that?'

'It was the end of the semester. Classes were over and the entire campus was busy preparing for final exams. No one at the college realised that Feng Chunling had gone missing. Most of her friends simply assumed that she was studying on her own. Her roommates noticed her absence of course, but they didn't think anything of it.'

'Her roommates didn't think anything of her having gone missing for several days?' Pei said.

'As I mentioned, Feng's home was relatively close to the school. They assumed she was studying at home. If it hadn't been for the notice we published in the papers, our search would probably have taken at least several days longer.'

'It doesn't sound like the victim was very close to her roommates.'

Huang nodded. 'Feng appeared to be a normal college student: average height and build, just shy of twenty. According to her classmates, however, she was introverted, bordering on antisocial at times. She rarely interacted with her roommates.

When she was in her room, she usually had her head in a book. She spent most of her spare time off campus, but we had little idea of where she went, what she did or who she associated with.'

'I take it you had a hard time coming up an accurate picture of her social life?'

'No kidding. If it had been now, it would have been so much easier – we could have just checked her mobile. But back then our officers had to do things the old-fashioned way – by interviewing people and hoping they'd give us useful answers. Since the victim kept to herself, it proved extremely difficult to get any leads.'

'And how did you conduct the search?'

'We had no option but to go for the simplest method: the old needle-in-a-haystack approach.'

Pei nodded approvingly. 'More often than not, the simplest approach is also the most effective. Provided you have the manpower.'

'Manpower wasn't an issue. Chengdu's public security bureau bowed to public pressure and pledged that they would solve the case within a year. That decision effectively mobilised the city's entire police force to assist with the investigation and we immediately launched a citywide manhunt. Our search radius covered two specific areas and targeted three types of individual. The vocational college was at the centre of the search radius, since that was where the victim was based. We investigated just about every student and faculty member at the college and conducted interviews at shops, restaurants and other public spaces in the vicinity of the college.'

'Did that produce any leads?'

'We didn't come up with any suspects. We did discover that Feng Chunling used to frequent a number of music stores and bookshops near the college's main entrance. And we were told that she hadn't been seen in any of them since the tenth of January. But the more we considered that information, the more irrelevant it seemed.'

'And how did you decide on the search radius?'

'The four locations in which the victim's remains were discovered happened to form the corners of a square. Given the logistical difficulty of lugging all four bundles at the same time, we concluded that the suspect would have made four separate trips to dispose of the remains. Our psychologist advised us that he would have avoided retracing his steps. So it followed that the murder had been committed somewhere within that square. We therefore concentrated our search on the large area formed by the square and on the college itself, including the music shops and bookstores near the entrance.'

'And was that productive?' Pei asked.

Huang shook his head.

Pei rubbed his palms together. 'You said you focused on three types of individual...?'

'Doctors, butchers and migrant workers. Judging by the amount of damage done to the body, the killer had a strong stomach and was skilled at dissection. Doctors and butchers were obvious matches. Migrant workers, as we know, come from the lower rungs of society and are responsible for a disproportionately high number of violent crimes.'

'Did that not throw up any leads?'

'Not one,' Huang said, lowering his head. His mouth twisted as he flicked some ash from his cigarette.

'This guy was good at what he did, that's for sure,' Pei murmured. In all fairness, the police force's strategy of one search radius, two areas and three types of suspect was a well-established one. But in this instance it hadn't netted a single result. Either the killer had stayed one step ahead of them or their approach was fundamentally flawed. 'It seems the needle-in-a-haystack method wasn't the best. What else did you find at the locations where the body parts were left?'

'It snowed in Chengdu on the twelfth of January,' Huang said softly, 'starting at midnight and only letting up at around nine in the morning. The snowfall destroyed any footprints, fingerprints or other traces that the suspect might have left when dumping the victim's remains. We deduced that the killer picked that day because of the weather conditions.'

'I agree with your conclusions. That guy calculated his every move.' Pei thought for a moment. 'Did you discover anything more about how he dissected and prepared the body? That could have given you a few leads.'

Huang shot him a sorrowful look. 'We thought the same thing, but it proved fruitless. The plastic bags the body parts were wrapped in were the sort that could have come from any market or department store. The suitcase containing the victim's head and entrails was unremarkable and its make and signs of wear and tear indicated that it was at least five years old. It would have been a wild goose chase to try to track down its whereabouts across the last half decade.'

Pei shook his head in sympathy. 'It's as if the killer planned for every eventuality.'

'The suspect seemed to be eerily familiar with our investigations procedures. No matter what approach we took, he'd already anticipated it. The task force and I worked on this case day and night for months, and all without a single tangible result. In the end I felt I had no choice but to swallow my pride and seek out Captain Ding Ke.'

'Captain Ding,' Pei muttered. 'He'd retired, what, eight years before the Bagman Killing? But he'd continued to lend you quite a bit of assistance, is that right?'

'Correct on both counts. He was essentially my mentor. Whenever I hit a stumbling block in an investigation, I'd ask for his help. He was hiding out in the suburbs at the time, tending to his birds and flowers. The simple life, so to speak. Even though he was already greying at the temples, he seemed much more energetic than he'd ever been as a cop. He never looked very happy to see me though. He used to say that each of my visits took days off his life.'

Pei understood that all too well. Police work wasn't a job everyone could handle. Once you began investigating a case, it took precedence over everything else.

'So what happened when you asked Captain Ding on this occasion?' Ms Mu asked impatiently.

'He complained, as usual. But once he'd finished his grumbling, he took a long close look at the case files. Then he told me to come back in a couple of weeks. A couple of weeks! He'd never spent so much time on a case before.'

'Was there a reason for that specific length of time?'

'It was the deadline he'd given himself to crack the case. On previous investigations he'd mostly told me to come back in a day or two. Five if he needed more time. Never more than a week. When I went back, he'd make a few comments and maybe ask a question or two. Barely a dozen words in all, but I could tell that he'd distilled long hours of thinking into each point. Every time I returned to an investigation after meeting Captain Ding, it was like my vision had cleared. Like answers were staring me in the face. Every single time.'

'And this time?' Pei asked.

Huang glanced at both officers and his face darkened. 'You already know what happened.'

'You never saw him again,' Ms Mu said.

'Having to wait a couple of weeks was hard enough. But then when I went back to his home, I was absolutely blindsided to find out that he'd already moved. No one knew where he'd gone or how to get in touch with him.'

Ms Mu's empathy did not dull her tongue. 'Seems to me he was intentionally avoiding you.'

'The case must have stumped him,' Pei said, changing the subject.

'I can't say for sure. All I know is that I never saw him again.'

Pei looked down at the table and shook his head. It was disappointing that someone of Captain Ding's calibre would run away rather than face his own inability to solve a case. The man had broken his word.

'Even Captain Ding gave up on it,' Ms Mu said, sighing. 'Was there any progress with the investigation after that?'

Huang gave them a pained smile. 'I won't lie to you. We were absolutely desperate when we lost touch with Captain Ding. But I was captain of the criminal police and however hopeless things seemed, I had to put on my bravest face and pretend that everything was going smoothly. Over the next few months, my officers and I went through the city with a fine-tooth comb. But, just as we'd anticipated, we never found so much as a trace of the suspect. To try and assuage the public outcry surrounding the investigation, I resigned as captain at the end of the year.'

Ms Mu's eyes softened as she looked at Huang.

Unexpectedly, he managed a slight grin. 'Believe it or not, leaving the police felt liberating. The case had turned me into a nervous wreck.'

'You and Captain Ding both chose to run away from the investigation,' Ms Mu said, 'but you responded differently. You may not be a police officer any more, but you haven't forgotten about the case. Even after it was officially classified as a cold case, you continued searching for the killer. You've never really given up on it – am I correct?'

Huang's eyes flashed. 'I'm going to make that killer pay. I don't care if it takes ten years. Hell, I don't care if it takes the rest of my life!' Having made his declaration, the rage faded from his face. 'Actually, the reason I opened this bar was to try and draw the killer out into the open,' he said. 'What did you think of the music you heard when you walked in earlier?'

'Suffocating,' Pei said.

'A fitting soundtrack for the bloody theatrics happening on the stage.' Ms Mu shuddered as she recalled the 'performance' downstairs, which had resembled a scene from a horror movie. The actor had invited a member of the audience to stab the half-naked actress on stage. Blood – fake blood, she presumed – had come spurting out of the woman's chest. 'That show surely came close to crossing any number of legal boundaries,' she said. 'And as for the boundaries of good taste…'

'It's all sleight of hand. No one's ever been injured in those performances – the blood is made by a little shop downtown.' Huang smiled politely at Ms Mu. 'Now, tell me more about how the music made the two of you feel when you walked in,' he said.

'There was fear in there, and desperation,' Pei said. 'It felt relentless – pounding away in your head, the shrieking and growling, the heavy guitar, the drums. In some people it could definitely stir up all sorts of unhealthy thoughts. Perhaps even violent fantasies.'

'Precisely. You mentioned "suffocating" just now. In fact, the track you heard when you came in was by a band called

Suffocation. The first time I heard it, I could barely believe that a group of people had actually rehearsed that and recorded it. But a week later, I couldn't drag myself away from it.'

After lighting yet another cigarette, Huang walked across the room and pulled a hefty evidence bag from the bedside table in the corner. Returning to Pei and Ms Mu, he held up the bag for them. 'Take a good look,' he said. 'All the music I play during the performances downstairs comes from these cassettes. I first listened to them late one night in the winter of 1993. Just me and my headphones. By the time I'd finished, I was sweating like a dog in August. I felt like the whole world was full of death and violence, totally desperate and with nowhere to run.'

Pei nodded slowly. He had felt the same way downstairs. He looked inside the transparent bag. The tapes were covered in English words and had holes punched through the sides.

The sight of the tapes brought a rush of memories. Although CDs were now popular, cassettes had flooded the Chinese music market back in the eighties and nineties. 'Are these tapes related to the January 12th case?' he asked curiously.

'They belonged to the victim. They're *da kou dai* purchased from one of the music stores near the university.'

'What's a *da kou dai*?' Pei asked, rolling the unfamiliar term around his tongue.

Ms Mu grinned in surprise. 'Guess you're too old for this one, Captain Pei. They're exactly as described – literally "hole-punched tapes". You see, when music stores abroad were overstocked with cassette tapes, they'd punch a small hole through the edge of each cassette and sell the excess stock to China as waste plastic. Generally speaking, the holes didn't pierce the tape itself, so the cassettes were still playable. These *da kou dai* tapes made their way into China's underground music market. All of my friends had them back in senior school and university.'

'The task force collected these tapes to dust them for prints,' Huang said. 'According to Feng's classmates, she was extremely fond of this particular set of tapes. If someone had got close to her, they might have left prints on them. Unfortunately, forensics weren't able to find anything of value. The tapes were never officially classified as evidence. Probably a slip-up, but eventually the task force forgot all about them. I stumbled across these the night I decided to retire. I don't know why I kept them, but I did.'

'And then one night you listened to them,' Ms Mu said.

'It wasn't an easy experience,' Huang said. 'Until that night, the heaviest music I'd ever listened to was probably Cui Jian' – Pei nodded imperceptibly at that name; even he was familiar with the so-called 'Father of Chinese rock' – 'or the Carpenters. But what I got out of it more than made up for any discomfort.' Huang's voice cracked and he sipped from his glass of tea. 'Listening to this music is what helped me truly understand Feng Chunling. It also gave me an insight into the sort of people she hung out with.

'When I was leading the task force, we used what we knew about Feng Chunling to create a rough psychological profile – lonely, introverted, emotionally uncomplicated. But as far as I was concerned, the feelings this music triggered in me completely subverted our original profile. Before I'd listened to it, I'd found it almost impossible to imagine what kind of monster could have committed the January 12th murder. What was such a person thinking when they killed Feng? I just couldn't understand the killer's thoughts or motivation... But that was before I heard the tapes. They're more than simple cassettes – they're letters left behind by the victim.'

Pei realised that he was still staring at the tapes inside the evidence bag.

'If you can read the English on those cases, you'll understand exactly what I mean,' Huang prompted.

Pei squinted at one of the tape cases for several seconds but wasn't able to make sense of what he was reading. He turned to Ms Mu. 'How's your English?'

'Decent enough.' She held out her hand.

Pei handed her the bag with a sheepish look. 'I haven't used a single English word since college.'

Ms Mu shrugged nonchalantly. She studied the J-card insert from one of the cassettes for a minute and then began to translate.

'It's a 1992 compilation by a record label called Roadrunner. The text on the insert reads something like: "The most prominent characteristic of heavy-metal lyrics is their fascination with death, violence and sexual desire... They are an exquisite expression of Nietzsche's musings on the abyss... Those who immerse themselves in this music will bear witness as death triumphs over good, the foundations of civilisation crumble, humankind's innate violence wins out and the world is consumed by lust... You can numb your senses with nihilism, but you will never be able to escape the shadow of death that shrouds everything... The only way to redemption is to savour the taste of death through metal."'

'You put my old English professor to shame,' Huang said approvingly. 'Unfortunately, we were so focused on getting fingerprints and other trace evidence from these tapes that we barely even noted what was printed on them. I had the text on the inserts translated after I listened to them, but by then our investigations window had long since closed. If we'd had someone like you on our task force, Ms Mu, things might have turned out quite differently!'

'"He who fights with monsters should look to it that he himself does not become a monster. If you gaze long into an abyss, the abyss also gazes into you",' Pei recited.

'We've already looked into the abyss,' Huang said in a tone as cold as ice. 'It's in these cassettes.'

Ms Mu's attention was distracted. She set the cassette gently on the coffee table. 'If that's true,' she murmured, 'then it would appear that Feng's emotional world was far deeper and more complex than that of the majority of her peers. Perhaps she found it impossible to relate to her fellow students. Why else would she have come across as so detached and solitary? If she had interests of her own, it would follow that she had a small group of likeminded friends. Those interactions must have taken place off campus. In a different circle, she might have shown a completely different side of herself. And judging from her alternative taste in music, she probably had some equally alternative life experiences.'

'Precisely!' Huang exclaimed. 'You've practically read my mind. But unlike you, I've got no psychology expertise so I have to rely on gut instinct. Here's my theory.' He straightened himself in his seat. 'The victim and the killer got to know one another through heavy metal. They may even have met at the music shop that sold those *da kou dai*. They became friends. The two of them talked about violence, sex, even death. For Feng Chunling, the lyrics were simply fantasies, as they are for most people. But for the killer, they were a way of exploring his twisted urges. Then one day, for whatever reason – perhaps following an unexpected argument or even a sexual rejection – the killer couldn't control his urges any longer. He took out all of those pent-up impulses on the victim. Rape, murder, mutilation – he enacted one horrific crime after another. And maybe, just maybe, this music was playing in his head the entire time.'

Huang watched Pei and Ms Mu as he spoke, eagerly anticipating their responses.

The clock on the wall ticked away the seconds in silence. Finally, Ms Mu responded.

'If it really was a psychopathic murder like you say, the killer's primary purpose would have been to extract a unique sense of pleasure through the transgressive act of murder. All our research into similar cases indicates that for a killer this kind of pleasure is hard to resist. It's addicting. They will carry on murdering until they're caught. We call them serial killers.'

'It sounds even more plausible when you put it like that,' Huang said, nodding thoughtfully. 'Now I'm even more confident that I can catch this prey of mine. It's been ten years since Feng's murder. The killer has to be itching to pull off another one. My bar just so happens to be the ideal place for the bastard to release his urges. He'll be able to unleash his violent and lustful compulsions, and all to his favourite music. So long as I continue running this bar, he'll come here sooner or later.'

Pei rose, his hands up, as if to call for time out. 'While I understand why you've laid this bait for him,' he said, 'your profile of the killer is based on conjecture and nothing more. Logically speaking, you still lack solid supporting evidence. These tapes have given you plenty to hypothesise about, but there could be many different possible profiles for the killer. I'm not convinced that this bar is a guaranteed way of enticing him into the open.'

Huang's eyebrows rose and fell as he appeared to consider this. Pei wondered if he'd got through to him. But Huang was not discouraged. His eyes lit up again.

'Even if there's a 1 per cent chance, I'm not giving up! I admit it, strictly speaking, the performances downstairs aren't exactly legal. But I can't afford to concern myself with things

ZHOU HAOHUI

like that. I need to satisfy my conscience. It's all because of
that bastard. When I do get my hands on him, I won't give a
damn what the law does with me!'

'*I won't give a damn what the law does with me!*' Captain
Pei stiffened as Huang's words sank in. Sitting across from him
was a man who was willing to break the law in order to punish
evil. It was a chillingly familiar MO.

Was this man his enemy or not?

And if not, then what did that say about Eumenides?

12

BLOOD IN THE OFFICE

11:25 p.m.
Downtown Chengdu

The Longyu Corporation was headquartered in a massive twenty-seven-storey edifice known simply as the Longyu Building. Although midnight was just half an hour away, the building's windows blazed with light. Security was extremely tight and the eighteenth floor was all but impenetrable. A guard was stationed at every corner of the hallway, and there were all manner of additional security measures in place between the lift doors and the security gate at the end of the corridor – everything from cutting-edge cameras to motion sensors and metal detectors.

The security hub was on the first floor. It was lined with banks of security monitors showing live feeds of the building's every entrance, exit, lift, corridor, hall and room. Anyone stationed inside the security hub could be aware of what was occurring in every single corner of the building. Tonight there were four men in there, all of them dressed in black. They stood in a line parallel to the screens, their eyes glued to their respective quadrant of monitors. Behind them were Brother Hua and Brother Long

Brother Hua and Brother Long were both staring at one particular image. At first glance it appeared to be twice the size of the other monitors, but it was actually formed of two adjacent screens. The image displayed was the interior of what had once been the eighteenth-floor office. Due to the room's large size, two cameras were needed to provide the panoramic image displayed. The tightly monitored room was formerly Mayor Deng's private office but had now been converted into a bedroom.

The bedroom was brightly lit. Mayor Deng's original desk, chairs and other furniture were still in place, but two beds had also been brought in. One was set against the eastern wall and the other was on the opposite side.

On one bed, a man as thin as a signpost was sleeping deeply. On the other, a comically plump man was snoring away.

Brother Long's eyes were tinged with red as he stood there watching. He let out a long yawn.

'Tired?' Brother Hua asked gently, keeping his eyes on the screen.

'I'm fine,' Long answered. He rubbed his face with both hands.

'There's no reason for you to push yourself so hard. I'm watching the monitors – it doesn't need two of us.'

'Even so, I feel responsible. I can't afford to cut myself any slack. We've already lost Mayor Deng – if we lose Vice President Lin as well, the Longyu Corporation is done for.' Long continued to watch the plump man on the screen, the Longyu Corporation's Vice President Lin.

Brother Hua chuckled. 'You don't trust me to handle this on my own, do you?'

Long smiled tightly. 'How can you say that? Lots of our colleagues were there when Mayor Deng was murdered – no one blames you for what happened. I'm not here because I doubt you, I'm here because I need to familiarise myself with this building's security system. How else will I be able to take some of the burden off you in the future?' He patted Hua's shoulder in a deliberate display of camaraderie.

Hua brushed his hand away. 'That's enough. Stay focused and just follow orders.'

'Of course.'

Hua glanced at the time in the corner of the screen. 'Less than half an hour left,' he muttered.

'I'm telling you, this guy is not going to win. How could he possibly sneak through security this tight? Only a ghost could make it into that room undetected.'

'We can't afford to be complacent,' Hua said, shaking his head. 'The closer we get to the deadline, the more vigilant we need to be. He could very well be waiting until the last moment to make his move.'

'I'm more worried about him not coming! If he so much as sets a foot in this building, I'll skin him alive and burn him as a funerary offering to Mayor Deng.'

Brother Hua made no response. He just kept his eyes fixed on the screens. The two men on the eighteenth floor were still fast asleep. Except for the time display flickering in the corner, everything inside the room was dead still.

Then, without warning, the screens went dark.

'What the hell just happened?' Brother Long shrieked.

'We lost power,' Brother Hua said.

They soon realised the extent of the power loss. The monitors hadn't just gone dark – the entire security hub had been plunged into blackness.

'Something's wrong!' Long yelled. He leapt out of his chair in the dark, only to realise that he had no idea where the exit was. 'What do we do now, Hua?'

Hua felt his way to the wall until his fingers closed around a thin chain. He yanked it, and the window blinds swept open. Artificial light streamed through the window, filling the room with a dim glow.

Brother Long could now see Hua's face, which only looked more grotesque in the light. 'The other buildings have power,' Long whispered. His heart sank. 'Zhao, Song, follow me!' He rushed to the door and two black-suited men followed close behind. Another two stood watching Hua, awaiting instruction.

'Nobody move!' Hua roared.

Long turned and stared numbly at him.

Hua's expression was utterly serious but completely calm. He took out a two-way radio. 'Jie?' he said into the radio.

'This is Jie,' replied the head monitor for the eighteenth floor.

'What's the situation like up there?'

'We've just lost all power.'

'I'm aware of that,' Hua said. 'I'm asking whether you've noticed anything else.'

'Nothing at the moment.'

A collective sigh resounded through the security hub.

'Do you have any light up there?' Hua asked.

'Two of us have emergency flashlights. We're all clear at the moment.'

'Excellent. No matter what happens, it's imperative that you keep guarding the door to the office. Don't let anyone inside. Do I make myself clear?'

'Crystal clear, sir!'

'Contact me if anything happens.' Brother Hua lowered the radio and looked over at the two men in black, who had still not moved from their positions in front of the darkened monitors. 'Do you know the location of the backup generator?'

'Yes, sir,' both men answered almost simultaneously.

Hua waved at them. 'Get moving, both of you! You have three minutes.'

Without saying another word, the two men strode off, their footsteps echoing down the hall.

Hua turned to Brother Long.

Although Long was older and taller than Hua, Hua's imposing presence made Long feel tiny. Summoning up his courage, he said, 'The situation has changed. Why are we staying here? We need to assist upstairs!'

'There's no power in this entire building,' Hua said. 'How long do you think it'll take to climb the stairs all the way to the eighteenth floor?'

'Well...' Long flushed, then ventured a guess. 'Thirty-five minutes, maybe.'

'Thirty-five minutes? Even if you did manage it, you'd be panting and wheezing by the end. And groping your way through the dark, you'd be a sitting duck for an ambush. What's the use of running up there? There are dozens of people already standing guard on the eighteenth floor. The office's iron double doors are sealed tight and we have the keys. Nobody can get in, so what's there to panic about? Don't you see, that's exactly what our adversary wants us to do. If we lose our heads, he'll have an opportunity.'

Cold sweat poured down Brother Long's back as he considered what could happen next. What if he did run up the stairway and came across the killer? He resisted the urge to shiver. 'So what do we do now?' he asked.

'We stick to our plan,' Brother Hua said firmly. 'The backup generator will kick in at any moment. Our job is to hold this position and make sure that no outside force interferes.'

He strode back to his chair and sat down. Seeing no better course of action, Long followed suit.

Behind them, the two remaining black-suited men waited in silence. Several minutes passed. Then with a dull hum, the building's lights flickered back to life.

The security monitors had begun to glow, but their screens

showed no more than grey blotches. Without uttering a word, the four men gazed at the displays until the images slowly began to sharpen into distinct shapes.

Brother Hua stared at the two monitors in the corner, his eyes so wide that Brother Long wondered if they might pop out of their sockets.

'How the hell did this happen?' Hua said, his voice barely louder than a whisper.

The footage on the monitor showed that the door was still shut and the lights were on. The occupants of the two beds were still fast asleep. Everything looked just as it had before the power had cut out, except for one detail. There was a third person standing in the room.

The new arrival approached the bed next to the western wall. He walked with a distinct swagger. His right hand stretched up towards the light and they saw a small, thin object glittering between his fingers.

'What should we do, Brother Hua?' Long asked. His knuckles were white as he gripped the arms of his chair.

Brother Hua had no answer. At that instant, the monitors went blank once more. For the second time that night, darkness swallowed the Longyu Building.

3 November, 12:45 a.m.

A chorus of sirens pierced the night air. Police vehicles circled the Longyu Building, which had already been cordoned off with yellow tape. Dozens of officers stood watch on both sides of the tape, making sure that the general public didn't cross it. Captain Pei and his second-in-command, Lieutenant Yin, along with a handful of the criminal police's finest, sprinted up to the building's eighteenth floor.

An assembly of men in black suits stood in the hall. Two figures emerged from the front of the group to greet the approaching officers.

'Hello again, Captain Pei,' Brother Hua said quietly.

'Are you the one who called this in?' Pei asked.

'I am,' Hua said, nodding. 'Neither of them were breathing. Rather than call for an ambulance, I thought it best to phone the police directly.'

Hua's face seemed oddly drawn, as though his features were still processing the deaths of the two men. His speech, however, was measured and assured.

'What makes you think that Eumenides is behind this?'

Without uttering a word, Hua handed Pei a sheet of white paper. Lieutenant Yin stepped forward and shone his flashlight onto the printed text.

Death Notice
THE ACCUSED: Vice President Lin Henggan, Vice President Meng Fangliang
CRIMES: Collusion with organised crime
DATE OF PUNISHMENT: 2 November
EXECUTIONER: Eumenides

Pei stared at the strip of paper, his lips tightening. Then he fixed his gaze on Brother Hua.

'When did you receive this death notice?'

'Two days ago,' Hua replied coolly.

'Why didn't you report it to the police?'

'The police?' Hua's nostrils flared in anger. 'Have you forgotten how Mayor Deng died?'

An image of the recent tragedy in the airport waiting room flashed into Pei's head. An enraged Hua charging towards the officer who had just killed not only his employer but his father figure.

'What are you police officers good for, exactly?' Hua spat.

Pei sighed uneasily. His former captain, Han Hao, had shot and killed Mayor Deng, the very man they'd been trying to protect. He could understand why Hua had been loath to involve the police this time. But Pei wasn't going to get tangled up in the past. He would concentrate on the crime at hand.

'Is anyone still in there?' he asked, peering past the open door of the office.

Hua's cheek twitched. 'All of our people have already vacated the office. I know the rules. We called you, so now it's your turn.'

In spite of Hua's initial spurning of police involvement, Pei appreciated the way he'd handled things since. 'Tell me exactly what happened, starting from when you received this death notice.'

Brother Hua clenched his jaw. The pain in his eyes melted away and was replaced by a steely expression. 'Two days ago I received this note along with an anonymous letter. This was shortly after Mayor Deng's death, which made me all the more wary. I immediately contacted Vice President Lin and Vice President Meng, at which point I discovered that they had also been trying to get in touch with me. Both of them had received death notices from Eumenides as well. The three of us met and discussed our next steps. They were both extremely anxious. Vice President Lin proposed alerting the police, but I rejected the idea out of hand.'

Pei held his tongue.

'To be frank, my distrust of the police wasn't the only reason I did that,' Hua said, squinting at Pei. 'Eumenides sent me that death notice as a blatant provocation and I accepted it.

Ever since he orchestrated Mayor Deng's death, I've dreamt of nothing else but squeezing his last breath out of him.'

Pei understood precisely what Brother Hua meant. Eumenides could strike fear into his enemies, but he was equally capable of inspiring obsessive thoughts of revenge. He'd felt it himself, many times during the investigation – the same temptation that now consumed former captain Han Hao.

'Vice President Lin and Vice President Meng eventually saw things my way. They decided not to call the police but to rely on the Longyu Corporation's own security for their protection. I summoned our best operatives and converted Mayor Deng's former office into the vice presidents' personal sanctuary.'

'How many of these guards were your own subordinates?'

'About half. The other half were Vice President Lin's people. Even though we all came under the umbrella of the Longyu Corporation, some departments were directly under Vice President Lin's control.' Hua gestured towards the well-built man standing behind him. 'This is Brother Long. He was Vice President Lin's most trusted man. The two of us were charged with protecting Vice President Lin and Vice President Meng.'

Brother Long seemed distracted. Brother Hua cleared his throat and Long then looked at Pei and attempted an awkward handshake. As their eyes met, Pei saw the grief in his face.

'Tell me exactly what happened,' Pei said.

Hua's face turned ashen. 'The date on the death notice was the second of November, as you saw. We brought the two vice presidents to Mayor Deng's old office at eight o'clock on the night of the first. The double doors were locked tight and Brother Long and I had the only keys. We set up layer after layer of protection in this hallway – especially here at the door, where we stationed more than a dozen guards. We also placed men at every entrance to the building. Brother Long and I each brought two of our most trusted colleagues with us and stood watch inside the security hub on the first floor. Our eyes didn't leave the monitors that were relaying the live feed from inside the office.'

Pei had already noticed the multiple security measures throughout the building. His instincts told him that it should have been all but impossible to get past them, even for someone like Eumenides. But the killer had somehow done exactly that. He had murdered both of his targets, and all without leaving any signs of a struggle. Was there another way in?

As though reading his thoughts, Brother Hua said, 'This office was designed according to Mayor Deng's exact specifications. The only access is via the lift. There are no hidden passages inside the office, just this door and a window set into the southern wall. On the outside, the window is surrounded by ten metres of smooth reflective glass that not even a rock climber could scale. Above that, there are rows of sharp metal blades jutting out every five metres. Anyone who tried to climb down from the roof would be sliced to pieces.'

Pei grunted in frustration. 'Then how did Eumenides get in?'

'Your guess is as good as mine,' Hua said. 'Brother Long and I have been watching the security monitors around the clock since the evening of the first. Everything was completely normal until around 11:35 p.m. when the building's power cut out.'

'Eumenides was trying to draw you out,' Pei said.

'Exactly. We didn't fall for it though. Every floor of this building is equipped with spare flashlights, so the guards didn't miss a beat. I sent two men to the basement to start the backup generator.'

Pei nodded approvingly. Had he been in Hua's shoes, he might well have made those same decisions. 'That was good thinking. But let me guess – the generator didn't work?'

'Someone must have tampered with it. It worked for no more than fifteen seconds and then shorted out.'

'So Eumenides entered the building in total darkness?'

'Well…' Hua's cool demeanour had been replaced by a rare look of vulnerability. 'We caught a brief glimpse of Eumenides when the generator kicked in. He was standing inside the office. But none of my men on this floor were injured and I honestly have no idea how he got in.'

Pei was equally stumped. 'And then?'

'The building went dark again and the security monitors shut off. Brother Long and I sprinted all the way up the stairs to this floor. Both the doors were locked. Neither of us saw any signs of tampering. We unlocked the doors and ran inside, but it was too late. Vice President Lin and Vice President Meng were lying there motionless. Their throats had been cut and Eumenides had vanished.'

'One thing's for certain – there has to be another way into this office,' Pei said.

Hua smiled bitterly. 'I can assure you there isn't. I've been in charge of Mayor Deng's security here ever since the building was finished. If there was another way into this room, don't you think I'd know about it?'

Pei peered into the office, which was now well lit, as the power had come back on. He saw a massive desk and behind it a window that was wide open. Bloody footprints tracked across the floor.

'How many of you went into the office?' he asked.

'Four of us. Brother Long and I went first, and we brought one man each.'

Pei quietly pictured the scene: the office would have been pitch black and Eumenides' location unknown as the four men entered the room. 'Lieutenant Yin,' he called out, 'tell the SPU to come in and perform a thorough search of every floor. I want them to scour every centimetre of this building.'

'Yes, sir!'

He turned back to Hua. 'Our search will proceed much more smoothly with the help of someone who's familiar with the building's layout.'

'Of course. I'll assist as needed,' Hua said.

'Brother Long, please take your people down to the lobby. Our officers would like to ask you all some questions.'

Long nodded. 'Of course,' he said, his deep voice cracking.

Finally Pei addressed the team of officers and forensic investigators who'd been waiting patiently behind him. 'Let's start by examining the office.'

As they stepped inside, Pei remembered how Ms Mu had described the office to him as a 'hall of mirrors'. That wasn't a metaphor: every centimetre of wall had been covered with reflective glass. But now the mirrors had been stripped away and the walls were bare.

As the team set to work, Pei studied the floor. Several thin trails of blood led to the window. But the new hypothesis that had been forming in his mind vanished as soon as he reached the window. Hua's earlier assertion was clearly correct – it was impossible for anyone to get in that way.

The building had been designed with extraordinary attention to detail. Despite its location in Chengdu's busy downtown area, its southern side faced away from the taller buildings surrounding it, giving the occupants an unobstructed view of the older, less congested surroundings near Wuhou Temple. That vast, open panorama must have made Mayor Deng feel like an emperor surveying his dominion, Pei mused.

Not only was the south side faced with smooth glass and windows that were widely spaced at intervals of up to ten metres, but it was also concave in its profile, so that its upper levels sloped inwards. As far as Pei could tell, it would be impossible to climb up to the windows from the lower levels.

Poking his head outside, Pei peered upwards. Rows of glittering metal tongues shone against the night sky. Though they appeared to be decorative, he could see that they were actually sharp blades, just as Hua had described.

Unless he'd sprouted wings, Eumenides couldn't have exited the Longyu Building from that window. But perhaps he had considered it, which would explain the bloody trail leading up to it. The largest splotches of blood were right in front of the window, as if Eumenides had paused there. But he must have decided to escape some other way.

As Pei considered this theory, he realised that it was completely out of character. Eumenides would have familiarised himself with the Longyu Building inside and out before even setting foot in it. Desperation wasn't his style.

There was another explanation for the blood below the window: Eumenides had planted it there in an attempt to mislead investigators. But that still left the question of his actual escape route. How had he done it?

Pei turned around and began studying the office's interior.

Most of the forensics team were crowded around the beds of the deceased, on the east and west sides of the room. The trail of blood from the bed on the west side quickly diverged. The sparser of the two trails, consisting mostly of round drops, led south to the window. Presumably the victims' blood had spurted over Eumenides and dripped onto the floor as he moved. The other trail consisted of a haphazard line of bloody footprints leading to the door. These had most likely been left by Brother Hua and his men after they'd inadvertently stepped in the blood from the two corpses.

Pei walked over to the bed on the west side. Lying on the

bloodstained mattress was the bloated corpse of Vice President Lin, the Longyu Corporation's second most powerful executive. A long, fierce gash across his throat gleamed dark red with congealed blood. The cut appeared to be deep and surgically precise. It was clearly the work of a sharp blade, a weapon that was no stranger to Eumenides.

The torso had rolled towards the edge of the bed and the left arm was dangling over it. The blood from the wound had travelled along the arm and dripped onto the floor, creating a pool beside the bed.

The lead forensic investigator looked up from the puddle of blood and noticed Pei. 'There are no signs of a struggle,' he said quietly. 'This man was probably dead as soon as the killer cut his throat. The guy was experienced, that's for sure.'

Pei studied the corpse again, then went over to the bed on the opposite side of the office.

The body lying on this bed was tall and slender – Vice President Meng, erstwhile holder of the top position in the Longyu Corporation. The wound across his throat was nearly identical to Vice President Lin's. But Meng was curled up and had presumably been lying in that position when the killer struck. As a result, the adjacent wall was spattered with blood while the floor was relatively unmarked.

Pei observed the shape of the spatter on the wall near the head of the bed. He reached out with his right hand and lightly punched the wall. Then he punched it again.

The investigator standing next to him glanced up from the blood samples she was collecting and gave him an incredulous look. 'What are you doing, Captain?' she asked.

Pei shook his head and said nothing. He took several steps parallel to the wall and struck it again. The wall issued a firm thud with each hit. Pei shook his head again and moved on.

The investigator nearly dropped the samples as she realised what he was doing. 'You think there's a hidden passageway built into the wall?'

'If there isn't, then we're dealing with a ghost,' Pei muttered.

But that hypothesis appeared more and more likely the longer Pei continued with his tests. Each section was just as solid as the last. Scowling in frustration, he crouched down and began to study the floor. No matter where he crawled, all he found was a smooth concrete surface and not so much as a single join.

He stood up at the centre of the room, his head spinning with questions. How had Eumenides done it? Pei even considered climbing up to inspect the ceiling but quickly dismissed the idea. Even disregarding the chandeliers, the ceiling's height, which was at least four metres, made a vertical escape impossible.

Pei left the office and rode the lift down to the security hub on the first floor. Lieutenant Yin and several officers from the criminal police were sitting in front of the monitors, gazing intently at the footage recorded earlier that night.

'Where's Brother Hua?' Pei asked.

Yin turned his head at the sound of the captain's voice. 'He's helping the SPU officers search the building.'

'What about Brother Long and his team?'

'The others are interviewing them in the lobby.'

Pei spoke into his radio. 'Bring Brother Long to the security hub.'

Pei met Brother Long at the entrance. 'Take a seat,' he said, moving one of the chairs towards him.

The man sat, but the distant look in his eyes told Pei that his thoughts were elsewhere.

'You're probably familiar with Mayor Deng's office, aren't you?' he asked, keeping his tone conversational.

Brother Long stiffened. 'No, not really,' he answered haltingly.

ZHOU HAOHUI

Pei grimaced. *Strike one*, he thought.

'But Brother Hua is,' Long blurted out, as if something had jogged his memory. 'I only visited the office occasionally with Vice President Lin.'

'The point is you've been inside. There used to be a red carpet on the floor, and the walls were covered with crystal glass, correct?'

'Yes.'

'Why are the carpet and glass gone now?'

'That was Brother Hua's decision. He had the carpet torn off the floor and the glass on the walls smashed.'

'Why did he do that?'

'Well, since Vice President Lin and Vice President Meng were both going to hide out there, Brother Hua said that the plainer the room, the better. The carpet could be used to camouflage a person or a weapon, and the mirrors would throw off anyone watching the security cameras. So we got rid of them and set up two beds in there.'

Pei nodded and a new thought came to him. *What if Brother Hua had actually been searching for a hidden passageway into the office?*

'Vice President Lin and Vice President Meng both moved into the office at eight o'clock on the evening of the first. Is that correct?'

Brother Long nodded.

'What made you choose that time?'

'It was Brother Hua's idea. The death notice was supposed to be carried out the next day, so he wanted to make sure that they were both settled in by then.'

Pei noticed that Long had intentionally attributed every decision to Hua. He could guess why. They had failed to alert the police, and two lives had been lost. Long might have been anxious and distracted, but he wasn't so stupid as to accidentally incriminate himself.

'How thoroughly did you search the office on the night of the first?'

'Very thoroughly. We even checked all the compartments inside the desk.'

Pei recalled the unusual size of Mayor Deng's desk. Some of the drawers were indeed large enough to conceal a person. 'Are you sure you checked every single one?'

Brother Long paused for a moment. 'Well, all except one. Only Mayor Deng had the key to that drawer. But it's small. Not even a child could fit inside.'

'And you locked the doors when you left?'

'That's right. There are two sets of doors at the entrance. Brother Hua and I split the keys, so that way only the two of us together could open them.'

'Did you open the doors again after you left?'

'Not until we saw the intruder on the monitor.'

'You didn't go back into the room at all before then?'

'No. We left food and water in the room, and we even put chamber pots under each bed. Brother Hua repeatedly stressed that no one was permitted to open the door under any circumstances. Unless, that is, the killer was actually in there.'

'So the two of you were watching the security monitors the entire time?'

'That's correct. We only left the room to go to the bathroom, and we did that in turns. There were also four of our most trusted men in the security hub with us.'

'Did anything unusual happen before the power cut out?'

'No. Nothing at all.'

That was not the answer Pei had been hoping for. 'Think about it for a minute,' he prompted.

Brother Long frowned and after a moment he shook his head. 'No, nothing out of the ordinary happened before the power shut off.'

Pei went over to the monitors displaying the footage recorded in the office. Lieutenant Yin was still watching it intently.

'Any luck finding anything?' he asked.

'Nothing yet,' Yin said, unable to hide his disappointment. 'This recording's just too long.'

Pei waved a hand dismissively. 'You don't need to watch the earlier footage. Just skip to 11:13 p.m. last night.'

Yin immediately slid the playback notch nearly all the way to the right until the timestamps in the corner read 23:13:00. The monitors showed Vice President Lin and Vice President Meng both fast asleep in their respective beds.

'Heavy sleepers, aren't they?' Pei said curiously.

'They both took sleeping medication that afternoon,' Brother Long said. 'It was—'

'— Brother Hua's idea?' Pei interrupted.

Long avoided his gaze for a moment. 'That's right,' he said. 'Brother Hua said that if they didn't take sleeping pills, there was no chance they'd be able to sleep. Even if nothing happened to them over the next twenty or thirty hours, the long wait would wreak havoc on their bodies.'

Pei could see the sense in that. He decided to focus on the recording. There was nothing was out of the ordinary in the image of the office displayed on the monitors, but everyone in the room held their breath as they watched. They all knew what was coming next.

The time in the upper-left corners advanced second by second. When the timestamp read 23:35:12 the image jerked slightly. Pei noticed another change. The timestamp now read 23:39:21.

'Pause it!' he yelled.

Lieutenant Yin tapped a key and the timestamp froze.

There was a clear explanation for the five-minute interval: the first power outage.

The current image differed from the previous image in several ways. Firstly, Vice President Lin and Vice President Meng had both changed their positions. This struck Pei as particularly odd. Even if Brother Hua had given them relatively small doses of sleep medication, why had both men shifted simultaneously, especially after having stayed relatively still for the past several hours?

He also spotted two other changes. The curtain over the window had been pulled wide open. And, more obviously, a tall male figure was now standing on the west side of the room.

'Eumenides!' Lieutenant Yin said.

With his back to the cameras, the man approached the bed, taking slow, deliberate steps. Vice President Lin's bed.

Pei recognised the figure instantly. He had studied it in security footage, surveillance footage and even in the videos that Eumenides himself had sent to the police. He was tall and athletic and wore tight-fitting clothes and a dark, wide-brimmed hat pulled low over his face. That silhouette, those precise, calculated steps – it certainly looked like the man who'd murdered businesswoman Ye Shaohong in front of the Deye Building.

Pei leant closer to the monitor. 'He's wearing gloves and shoe covers. We won't find any trace evidence from Eumenides inside the office. Keep playing the footage.'

Yin tapped the keyboard and the male figure crept closer to the bed near the western wall. He stood over Vice President Lin's sleeping figure like a tiger sizing up its prey. He was enjoying it.

Nausea roiled inside Pei's stomach.

As the lights flashed back to life, the figure waved at the cameras. The blade in his hand glinted in the air.

'He's taunting us!' Lieutenant Yin snarled.

The screen went dark. Clenching his teeth, Yin stabbed at the keyboard, but the recording had already reached its end. The timestamp was frozen at 23:39:32. Yin swivelled around in his seat and looked inquiringly at Pei.

'How the hell did he get inside that room? Through the window?'

Pei shook his head. 'He wants us to think that he came in via the window, but he didn't. I examined the crime scene myself. There's no way he could have got in through there.'

'Then how did he do it? Is there another way into the office?' Yin asked, scratching his head.

'No, there isn't.'

'This just doesn't make sense. The only way into the office was heavily guarded, and Brother Hua said that no one opened the doors. So how did he get in?'

'Logically speaking, he shouldn't have been able to get into the office,' Pei murmured. Suddenly, his eyes gleamed. 'Or maybe he didn't enter or exit the office at all!'

Lieutenant Yin mulled this over for a moment. 'You mean he was hiding inside the office all along? And then he slipped out into the dark… right when Brother Hua and Brother Long opened the doors?'

Pei stroked his chin. 'From what I saw of the room, it would be tricky to hide someone in there. I doubt that an intruder was hidden inside the office before the doors were locked.'

'But didn't you just say that he didn't go in or out of the room?'

'I didn't say that he was already inside. There's another possibility – that he wasn't inside the office at all.'

'But…' stuttered Yin, 'there's footage of him in there! He was there! We all just saw it.'

'What we saw might not be what actually happened. Video recordings can be faked.'

'You think someone doctored these recordings?' Yin looked amazed. 'Surely not. But then again, this is Eumenides we're talking about.'

'Indeed.'

'Captain, you think he recorded the footage of himself entering the room beforehand? And that he was somehow able to digitally splice in the footage during the first power outage? That way, Brother Hua and Brother Long would assume that he'd just entered the office. So they'd run up to the office and open the door, and only then would Eumenides have used the cover of darkness to creep inside and assassinate the two vice presidents.'

Pei nodded and snapped his fingers. 'We'll have to test a few parts of that theory, but I think you're on the right track.'

'But that's impossible!' Brother Long interjected.

Pei and Yin both looked over at him.

'When we entered the office, both Vice President Lin and Vice President Meng were dead,' Long said, sitting up straighter in his chair. 'There's no way he got in after we opened the doors. I was the first inside. When I ran over to Vice President Lin, I stepped in a pool of blood next to his bed. One of my men came over with a flashlight and I saw that his throat had been cut. The situation you just described could not have happened.'

Pei tapped his knuckles against the armrest. 'Play that last section of the recording again. Start from the first power outage.'

Lieutenant Yin started the video from 23:35:00.

Pei kept his eyes trained on the right-hand monitor, which displayed the western half of the room.

At 23:35:12 the image on the screen jumped to 23:39:21.

'I guess we were wrong after all. This video is real,' Pei muttered.

'How can you tell?'

'Look at the clock above the window.'

Lieutenant Yin did just that. There was an analogue clock above the window; it was displayed on the right-hand monitor, just like the intruder was. 'The time's correct!' he said.

According to the times displayed on the monitors, the electricity was cut at 23:35:12, and the backup generators started at 23:39:21. A close look at the clock showed that the time displayed before the outage was 11:34 and that the second hand was at the forty-five-second mark. The time displayed after the power returned was 11:38 and fifty-four seconds. Despite the difference between the times displayed on the clock and the monitor, the gaps were identical.

'Was there any delay between when Hua's men tried to activate the generator and when the generator actually came on?' Pei asked Brother Long.

'No. They told us that the generator started up right away. Keeping it running was the issue.'

That confirmed it, Pei thought. The video had to be authentic. Even if Eumenides had been able to control the timing of the power outage to the very second, he couldn't have known the exact time that Hua's people would turn the generator on. Eumenides was good, but he wasn't *that* good.

All the evidence pointed to one conclusion. A tall male had indeed entered the tightly guarded office at 23:39:21. He had a sharp blade with him, which he put to devastating use. But where had he come from, and how did he escape after committing the murders? These questions still perplexed Pei.

'Tell TSO Zeng and Ms Mu to come over,' he told Lieutenant Yin. 'The task force will hold a meeting here at four.'

13

INVESTIGATING THE CRIME SCENE

4 a.m.
The Longyu Building

With the exception of SPU Captain Liu, who was busy watching over the journalist Du Mingqiang, all the members of the task force were at the meeting in the first-floor security hub. They were seated around a small rectangular table strewn with printouts of security footage.

Lieutenant Yin was explaining to Ms Mu and TSO Zeng what they'd learnt since their initial inspection of the office.

'We've already determined the cause of the power outage. Someone planted a timed charge on the power line leading to the building's primary power supply. It was a weak explosive, but the detonation was hot enough to melt the insulation coating the line and short out the power. The backup generator was tampered with as well. Three of the four lines leaving the generator had been cut, forcing the intact line to carry four times its normal load. The generator overheated and shorted out mere seconds after it was activated.'

'That's intriguing,' Zeng said. 'If he wanted to sabotage the generator, why didn't he cut all four lines? Why leave one intact?'

'He wanted us to see what the cameras recorded during

those few seconds,' Ms Mu said. Her mind was starting to put the pieces together. 'But why? To show off? To provoke us?'

'Lieutenant Yin and I did some brainstorming before you two arrived. Our conclusions were shaky at best,' Captain Pei said. 'But seeing as almost everyone is here, it wouldn't hurt to do a recap. Our initial thoughts were that the video recorded after the first outage was a fake. In other words, that no one had entered the room after all. Eumenides' reason for doing this would have been to trick Brother Hua, Brother Long and the others into opening the doors to the office, at which point he could sneak in and kill the two vice presidents under the cover of darkness.'

TSO Zeng slapped the table. 'That would actually make a lot of sense!'

'How difficult would it be to fake that footage?' Pei asked him.

'A piece of cake,' Zeng said, waggling his eyebrows. 'Think about it. Everything you see on these screens consists of electronic signals transmitted from a terminal point. If the point in question is a security camera, then what we see here are the signals sent by that device. If Eumenides wanted to fake the security footage, all he had to do was disconnect the camera's transmission cable during the first power outage and connect it to a device of his own. When the power came back on, the security monitors would display the image he provided. Then, when the generator shorted out and the building went dark again, he'd simply have to reconnect the camera's output and the video feed would return to normal without anyone knowing that it had changed.'

Pei wasn't convinced. 'What about the time displayed on the video? How would he have pulled that off?'

'That's an easy one. The time on the footage is generated by the security system, regardless of the source of the video. In other words, Eumenides could have played any video through the system and the time would have matched up with when it was played.'

Pei pointed at the still image currently displayed on the monitor. 'But what about the time on that clock? It doesn't match up exactly with the time on the display, but the length of the gaps between the power outages is consistent.'

'Hmmm...' Zeng winced. 'Now *that's* impressive. I have no idea how he could have done that, other than with an extreme case of good luck.'

'We must have missed something.' Pei frowned. 'Some detail that's staring us right in the face.'

A phone rang and Yin jumped. He reached into his pocket and pulled out his mobile. 'This is Lieutenant Yin.' He listened to the other end for about fifteen seconds, nodding intermittently. 'I see,' he said finally, then ended the call and placed his phone on the table.

The other team members looked on expectantly, but Yin turned directly to Captain Pei.

'They've found Eumenides' clothes, Captain! They're covered in blood.'

Pei shot out of his chair. 'Take me there.'

The Longyu Building boasted a luxurious lobby on its ground floor, behind which was a terrace that protruded out beyond the swooping curve that made up the building's rear side. The terrace was planted with a lush garden, complete with hedges and trees, but despite its obvious attractions it was one of the building's least frequented areas.

It was at the edge of the terrace that one of the police officers found an athletic backpack.

As Pei approached the unzipped backpack, he donned a pair of nitrile gloves. A rolled-up bundle of clothes lay on the ground beside the backpack, where the other officers had placed it. On top of the bundle was a pair of white gauze gloves stained with blood.

Pei dropped the gloves into a plastic evidence bag and unrolled the bundle. It contained a bloody shirt, a black hat and a pair of plastic shoe covers. As he examined each item, he compared them to his mental image of the figure in the security footage. Everything matched. When he opened the bag's front pouch, he made an even more damning discovery: a razor blade smeared with partially congealed blood. The blade was sharp – it accidently sliced the index finger of his left glove as he placed it into an evidence bag.

'This must have been Eumenides' escape route,' Lieutenant Yin said. 'I'll bet he prepared a clean set of clothes beforehand and stashed them here. Once he'd pulled off the murders, he changed out of his bloody clothes, hid his weapon and made his escape.'

'It actually wouldn't have been that difficult to escape from here,' Ms Mu said, looking down from the edge of the terrace. 'It's only a few metres' drop to the ground from here. I doubt that would have been much of a challenge for Eumenides. What we should be asking ourselves is how he got to the terrace from the eighteenth floor. I'm assuming he didn't fly all the way down?'

Pei stood up and studied the trees that encircled the terrace. 'Do another thorough check in these trees,' he said, gesturing at them with a circular motion of his hand. Several officers obediently hurried into the greenery.

Just three minutes later, a cry came out from a clump of pine trees. 'There's a rope here!'

Pei and the other officers sprinted over. A long, messy coil of rope lay next to the tree. Bending over, Pei twisted a length of it between his fingers. The rope was barely as thick as his pinkie.

'Whoever used this knows his stuff,' one of the officers said. 'That's the kind of rope professional climbers use.'

'I can see that using that to climb down from the office is theoretically feasible – but to get all the way down to the terrace in that time?' Ms Mu muttered. 'To avoid being caught by the security cameras outside, he'd have had to start climbing as soon as the power was lost. Could he have made it down eighteen floors in four minutes? Where would he have anchored the rope and how would he have retrieved it once he landed?' She paced the scene, shaking her head as she pondered.

'Due to the building's steep concave curve, anyone climbing out of the eighteenth-floor window would almost immediately find themselves suspended in mid-air,' Pei said as he gazed straight up. 'It would be relatively easy to slide down, but to climb *up* from below would require extraordinary strength and endurance.'

'Now that we've found this rope, we can assume that he probably entered and exited via the window,' Lieutenant Yin concluded. 'And we have a fair idea as to Eumenides' skills. As for how he accomplished such a feat, I'd like to ask our friends in the SPU.'

At that moment, SPU Captain Liu emerged from the staircase and quickly jogged over to the others.

'What are you doing here?' Pei asked, concerned. 'You're supposed to be guarding Du Mingqiang.'

'I brought him with me. He's in the building right now, as

a matter of fact. My people are watching him. He couldn't be safer if we locked him inside a bank vault.'

'Fine.'

'What's the situation here?' Liu asked eagerly.

'You see the office window?' Lieutenant Yin said, pointing upwards.

Liu squinted up at the building. 'The one that's dark except for that single light?'

'That's the one.' Yin gestured down at his feet. 'Take a close look at this rope. Could it have been used to climb down from that window?'

'From that high? You'd have to hang in mid-air. I definitely wouldn't be able to pull that off.'

'Then how would someone have managed it?' Pei asked.

Liu registered the grim expressions on the faces of Captain Pei, Lieutenant Yin and the others on the terrace. They needed answers. 'Everyone in the SPU has to renew their climbing certification every year. That includes a vertical rope climb. The highest we attempt is about twenty metres. Any higher and the line starts to swing out of control. Not to mention the physical strain required to maintain your grip for that length of time.'

Rubbing his jaw, Pei ruminated on his colleague's words. Liu was one of the SPU's best officers; Pei was even willing to bet that he would stand a decent chance against Eumenides in a one-on-one fight. If even SPU Captain Liu thought such a task was difficult, would Eumenides have been able to manage it in only four minutes?

A voice from the greenery interrupted Pei's thoughts. 'Have a look over here, Captain! We've found something.'

Pei sprinted to the terrace's western side and the other officers followed. A white piece of styrofoam lay among the trees. Stray pieces of styrofoam were nothing unusual in Chengdu, but this one had a small patch of blood on it, which instantly drew Pei's interest. He picked it up with his gloved hands and examined it. Its thin, curved shape reminded him of the distinctive roof tiles found in traditional Chinese architecture.

Ms Mu edged to the front of the group. 'What's that doing here?' she asked, inclining her head at the chunk of styrofoam.

'No idea,' Yin said. 'Looks like it might have come from a box or something.'

An idea came to Pei and he eyeballed a couple of his officers. 'Go to the main entrance, step outside and continue walking west for about twenty metres. You should see an identical piece of styrofoam on the street. Bring it back here.'

The men immediately jogged to the entrance. Noting the confused expressions around him, Pei explained. 'I saw a piece of styrofoam out on the street when I first arrived, but I didn't think anything of it until I saw this one. There's something odd about the shape of these two pieces, but I'm not quite sure what yet.'

Lieutenant Yin inspected it closely. 'It looks like Eumenides grabbed this piece before he changed out of his clothes. When he did that, the blood on his gloves rubbed onto it.' He held his hand up against the styrofoam as if he was about to grab it. The shape between his thumb and forefinger was a close match for the stain.

'But why would he pick it up?' TSO Zeng asked.

Before anyone could answer, one of the officers came racing back, shouting, 'I found it, Captain!' Inside his large evidence bag was the other piece of styrofoam. It looked like an unremarkable piece of packaging, identical to the one found on the terrace except that it was slightly larger and had no bloodstains.

'Photograph it, pack it up and take it back to headquarters,' Pei instructed Lieutenant Yin. He turned to the group in charge of scouring the terrace. 'Keep up the good work,' he said. 'I want you to expand your search radius to one hundred metres and go over the ground with a fine-tooth comb. Focus your efforts on the south side of the building.'

The officers quickly went to work.

'Let's go back inside the building,' Pei told the rest of the task force.

The lobby was crowded with black-uniformed Longyu Corporation guards. Nearly the entire workforce was there and a group of officers from the criminal police were busy taking down their accounts.

Pei glanced over at the reception desk and was shocked to see two familiar faces sitting there – together. 'What's he doing?' he muttered irritably.

SPU Captain Liu looked up and scowled. The two individuals casually talking to each other as they sat in front of the reception desk made an odd pair – the Longyu Corporation's Brother Hua and the online reporter Du Mingqiang.

'I told you to wait inside the security room, Du,' Liu said, not bothering to hide his frustration. 'What are you doing out here?'

Du uncrossed his legs and said calmly, 'I was simply conducting an interview at the scene of the crime. As a reporter, how could I pass up an opportunity like this?'

Liu grabbed the journalist's arm in an attempt to haul him out of his chair. 'Get out of here! Are you trying to cause trouble?'

Brother Hua, however, grabbed Du's other arm. 'I don't think that's what he's doing at all, Officer. Since this man has himself been issued with one of Eumenides' death notices, he has the right to know what happened. And as a reporter, he has a duty to tell the public the truth.'

Newly confident now that he had Brother Hua's support, Du sat up tall in his seat. 'I'm a law-abiding citizen and we're on Longyu Corporation property. As long as I have Mr Hua's permission, you have no authority to stop me from speaking with him.'

SPU Captain Liu snarled but then restrained himself. He looked over at Captain Pei, as though waiting for him to make a decision.

'You shouldn't let him interview you,' Pei said to Brother Hua. 'He's just an online journalist specialising in sensationalist stories. If today's events start circulating online, it'll cause a public panic.'

'I know he's an online reporter. That's why I agreed to be interviewed by him. The traditional media is toothless. I would never waste my time with them. Just a few days ago, the television news reported that Eumenides was already dead and that the killer's reign of terror was over. Which is patently absurd.'

Pei grimaced. He had no great love for the media either, but he wasn't about to let Brother Hua get the upper hand in this conversation.

'I won't stand by and let Eumenides dominate the headlines,' Brother Hua said. 'I need to make my voice heard. People online are calling Eumenides a hero. Don't they realise that each of these bloody assassinations is a new act of evil? That the victims had friends and families of their own, people who loved them. Who will speak for the victims?'

The sincerity in Brother Hua's words caught Pei by surprise.

Puffing out his chest, Du said, 'I'm determined to record their experiences and show the public what kind of person

Eumenides truly is. He's no hero; he's simply a killer who murders in the name of justice.'

Pei eyed Du and began to consider how he might use the reporter to his advantage. Brother Hua was right about one thing: people were sympathetic to Eumenides. In fact, the police were having a difficult time bringing the public onside. Eumenides had received a lot of attention from the moment he'd first posted his manifesto online. And once he'd carried out his sentences against those individuals who were targets of online gossip and rage – the hit-and-run businesswoman Ye Shaohong; the Jade Garden owner Guo Meiran who'd bullied her lover's ex wife; the students who'd humiliated their teacher – public admiration for him grew. Just as Brother Hua said, Eumenides had become a hero.

People shared his manifesto on countless message boards and social media platforms. The internet-monitoring division of the Sichuan police was exhausted from the effort it took to combat these posts. Perhaps it was time for an opposing voice to emerge, for someone to expose the truth behind the killings. After all, China was changing. Citizens had more options for obtaining information and were more open-minded than ever. The best way to steer public opinion would be to provide people with more information and let them draw their own conclusions.

'How do you intend to approach this article?' Pei asked Du.

'I won't play up the gore, if that's what you're worried about,' Du said, with one eyebrow raised. 'I'm a journalist with a sense of social responsibility, not some tabloid reporter. What I'm concerned with is exploring the consequences behind the killings. For instance, the pain that these murders have caused in the victims' family and friends.'

'What about the crimes that Eumenides listed for each of his targets – how will you deal with those?'

Du snickered. 'That's going to be a major focus of the article.'

When Pei grunted in confusion, Du hurriedly explained. 'You see,' he said, 'Eumenides accused both Vice President Meng and Vice President Lin of colluding with organised crime. But what Eumenides didn't realise was that Meng went to jail for that over a decade ago. He was only released four years ago, in fact. So the law had already punished Meng. Eumenides' involvement was unnecessary, even by the twisted logic of his own manifesto. Meng cleaned up considerably after his release. He became a model citizen and even found religion. Taking all that into account, how could Eumenides possibly defend his decision to murder Vice President Meng?'

Pei scratched his chin as he thought about Du's perspective. Was he right? If so, Eumenides had just murdered an innocent man. If they revealed as much to the public, it might be enough to persuade the killer's supporters to switch their allegiances.

But Pei had no illusions about the true Du Mingqiang. He was flippant and impetuous, and even the mildest compliment would inflate his ego. Pei kept his expression deadpan as he pretended to mull over Du's words. He turned to SPU Captain Liu.

'Bring me Du's article once he's finished it. If it meets with my approval, we'll let him publish it. But if the final version differs in any way from what we discussed today, order TSO Zeng to strip all of his online accounts of publishing privileges.'

Liu let go of Du. 'Certainly, Captain.'

The journalist crossed his legs again and leant back in his seat. He drew his lips back in a wide, cocky smile.

Pei returned his attention to the investigation at hand. 'Brother Hua, tell Brother Long to come here. I'd like the two of you to accompany me upstairs in a moment.'

'Is there a problem?' Brother Hua asked cautiously.

'Brother Long mentioned a certain drawer in Mayor Deng's desk,' Pei said. 'One that wouldn't open.'

'That was his private drawer. I don't have a key and I don't know where Mayor Deng kept his, either.'

'I understand. However, it's important to our investigation that we open that drawer and I should warn you that I will do so with whatever means necessary. It would be helpful for all of us if you accompany me when I do this,' Pei said, staring Hua firmly in the eye.

'If you think it's important...' Hua said, nodding.

Several minutes later, Captain Pei, SPU Captain Liu, Brother Hua and Brother Long stepped out of the lift on the eighteenth floor.

Inside the office, the forensic investigators were still busy collecting samples from the bodies and photographing the room. Pei and the others steered clear of the bodies and walked straight to the imposing desk at the centre of the room.

'I'm confirming that I have your permission to open the drawer,' Pei said to Hua, his tone making it clear that this was not a question.

'Of course,' Hua answered.

'Go ahead and pick the lock,' Pei said to SPU Captain Liu.

Liu inserted a long thin tool into the lock. A few seconds later, a soft click resonated from inside the desk. Liu pulled, and the drawer slid open. Brother Hua and Brother Long both craned their necks to look inside.

The drawer was empty.

'That can't be right,' Pei said.

Liu ran his gloved hands over the smooth wood of the drawer's interior. 'Sorry, Captain, there's nothing in here.'

'Try pulling the drawer out of the desk,' Long offered.

Liu did exactly that. When he turned the drawer over, he saw something that made him suck his breath through his teeth. A plain white envelope was taped to the bottom of the drawer.

Pei felt just as tense. He put on his latex gloves and, using a thin knife, carefully cut the envelope free from the tape at its edges. Holding it up so that the others could see, he opened the envelope and pulled out the slip of paper inside.

The paper contained five neatly printed lines of text.

Death Notice
THE ACCUSED: Brother Hua
CRIME: Collusion with organised crime
DATE OF PUNISHMENT: 5 November
EXECUTIONER: Eumenides

In the uncomfortable silence that followed, all eyes turned to Brother Hua. He clenched his jaw and his eyes burnt. But if he was afraid, he didn't show it.

'That bastard. He's trying to kill us all, isn't he?'

To Pei's surprise, it was Brother Long who'd said that. He was trembling, but his teeth were set tight in an expression of raw defiance.

'Your name isn't on that paper,' Hua said, glaring at him. 'What do you have to be afraid of?'

'It'll be my turn soon enough,' Long insisted, his voice quivering. 'First it was Mayor Deng, then Sheng. Then he took out Vice President Lin and Vice President Meng, and now he's coming for you. I'm next!'

'Who's Sheng?' Pei asked.

'He was one of Mayor Deng's most trusted men. A few days ago he was killed in a so-called car accident. But Brother Hua and the others all guessed that Eumenides was behind it.'

Pei glanced at Liu and his expression hardened. Opening the drawer had complicated this investigation far more than he'd anticipated. After weighing up his options, he pulled Liu aside. 'I'm going to meet with the rest of the team at ten o'clock,' he said, keeping his voice low. 'Take Du back home. Keep an eye on him while he writes his article.'

6 a.m.
Sichuan Conservatory of Music

While the rest of the school was still asleep, one young woman walked alone through the dark campus. Dressed in a simple outfit of black and white, she looked like a lily floating through the morning fog.

Her steps were soft and graceful, and she moved at a slow pace. Her guide dog and companion, Niuniu, led the way. The two of them continued down the corridor until they arrived at a small practice studio.

For her, every day began at the studio. Because she was not currently enrolled at the conservatory, she needed to get there early, before any students or staff turned up. Once classes began at 8 a.m., she would sidle back out into the early-morning sun. She couldn't bear to go a single day without practising. If she didn't practise, her arms felt heavy and clumsy, as if the musical part of her had begun to atrophy. It was like losing another of her senses.

She removed her beloved instrument from its case and propped it against her shoulder. She pursed her lips together in a thin straight line, took a breath and drew the bow across the strings. An elegant, leisurely melody poured from her instrument, seeping out through the closed door and into the autumn air. With her eyes shut, the young woman revelled in this world of music. A world that was all her own.

The piece ended and silence engulfed the room. Niuniu, who'd been lying at her feet, sprang up and started barking at the door. The young woman set down her violin and cocked her head in curiosity. She concentrated, straining to detect any noises coming from outside.

There were three knocks on the door. 'Is anyone in here?' a male voice asked.

The door was unlocked, but she didn't hear any creaking of hinges, so she allowed herself to relax. 'Who's there?' she called out.

'Is that Ms Zheng Jia?' the man asked.

Her mouth fell open in surprise. She hesitated, unsure of what to say.

'I have a package that I'm supposed to deliver to someone named Zheng Jia at seven thirty this morning.'

'You can come in,' she finally said, lowering herself onto the stool beside her.

The deliveryman gently pushed the door open and she heard him walk in. 'It's your birthday today, isn't it? Someone ordered a cake for you online.'

She stiffened. Yes, it was her birthday. Since her father's death, she'd all but forgotten about it. But apparently someone else had not.

'Who's it from?'

'I don't know. They paid anonymously. I'm just the person making the delivery.' The man hesitated. 'Happy birthday,' he added in a forced tone.

'Thank you,' she said, smiling.

'Um, I'll put the cake on the bench then.'

'Wait. You're leaving already?'

'I have other deliveries to make.'

She bit her lip. 'Could you stay just one more minute? If you could, I'd like you to describe the cake for me. What does it look like? I can't see.'

The man stopped in his tracks. She heard the soft swish of cardboard against cardboard.

'It's a small cake but a gorgeous one. It's gold, with a thick layer of white icing on top. There's a violin made of chocolate in the middle, all black and glossy. There are bright red musical notes dancing all around the violin. They look like they're made of jam.'

She turned her left ear towards the man's voice as she listened. As his words painted a picture in her head, a smile crept across her face.

'Is there anything written on it?'

'Of course. It says, "Happy Twenty-First Birthday, Zheng Jia!"'

'Is it signed?' she asked, lifting her chin in anticipation.

'No. There's no other name on the cake.'

'Oh.' She bent over and gently petted Niuniu's head with her fingers. The dog sat down obediently at her feet.

'This is my guide dog. Her name is Niuniu,' she said.

The man chuckled. 'She looks like a good girl. Cute, too.'

'Niuniu is always very cautious around strangers,' she said, lowering her voice. 'But she hasn't barked once since you entered the room.'

There was no sound from the other side of the practice studio.

Her sightless eyes stared directly at the man across from her. She heard a floorboard creak as he shifted his stance.

Finally, she summoned the courage to ask him.

'Is it you?'

He let out a long breath, as though casting off a great burden. 'You might not be able to see, but I can't hide anything from you.'

'It really is you,' she said. But there was still some doubt in her mind. 'What happened to your voice?'

'I disguised it. But you still saw right through it. Oh, please excuse my turn of phrase.'

She heard a soft ripping sound. Tape being pulled off skin?

'That's more comfortable,' he said, the youthful energy returning to his voice.

It was the voice that she remembered. Smiling in genuine surprise, she stood up from the stool. But her excitement was short-lived. 'Why did you try to trick me?'

'I didn't want you to know I was here,' he said with sincerity.

'Were you afraid I'd be a burden?'

'No, not at all. It's just that I... I've got myself into a bit of hot water lately. There's no need to worry you. And I didn't want to drag you into it.'

He seemed genuine to her. Despite her suspicions, she felt a pang of concern for him. 'What sort of trouble are you talking about?'

'I can take care of it,' he said calmly.

She believed him. 'Do you want to sit down for a minute?' she asked, trying to keep her voice friendly. 'That is, if you're not in a hurry to leave.' She tried not to sound desperate, but she was truly very grateful for his company.

'Of course.' He moved to the bench across from her and sat down. 'I can't stay long, though.'

She nodded in understanding, felt her way over and took a seat next to him. 'You said you've been very busy lately. I didn't think I was going to see you for a while.'

'Today's a special day. I found the time, of course.'

She grinned. 'Just to give me a cake?'

'Everyone wants to get a cake on their birthday, don't they?'

If anyone else had said that to her, she would have burst into giggles. Coming from him, though, it wasn't sentimental or silly. His words felt solemn and sincere.

'Please cut me a slice,' she whispered. She almost thought she heard him smile, the slight noise of the crinkling of his cheeks. 'I guess today was a good day to skip breakfast,' she joked.

The bench creaked and she heard the rustling of plastic utensils and paper plates. Seconds later, a new aroma hit her nostrils. Sweet and rich.

She sniffed again. The icing must have been held right in front of her, but when she reached out for the cake she couldn't feel anything. She heard him trying to hold back a snicker and she grinned.

A hand gently took hold of her left wrist. 'Here,' he said, guiding it to the paper plate and placing a fork in her other hand.

'It must be so difficult being with someone like me,' she said. There was a fizzing in her stomach, as if she'd just gulped down a glass of soda water. It felt exciting.

'Not at all! I wouldn't mind if every day was like this.'

His hand left her arm, brushing against her as it passed. Her skin tingled where he'd touched it. Warmth spread across her cheeks. She lowered her head and took her first bite of the cake, hoping he hadn't noticed her blushing.

'How does it taste?'

'It's perfect.'

Bite by bite, she ate her slice in silence. The fork trembled between her fingers.

She felt his eyes on her. As the seconds passed, the silence grew heavy. She set the plate down on her lap and raised her head. 'What are you thinking about?' she asked.

'I remembered something. The first time I ate cake,' he said wistfully.

She laughed and covered her mouth with her hand. 'You must be dying of hunger, watching me eat this.'

At that moment, his mood changed. She was sure of it.

'It was my sixth birthday. What I wanted above all else was a cake, and my father bought me one.'

Something had sucked the energy out of his voice. It made her uncomfortable. Especially when he'd said 'father'.

'I'm sure your father loved you. He must have been a great dad, someone who never let you down.'

'No, actually. The person who eventually gave me the cake wasn't even my father at all.'

'What do you mean?'

'My father passed away that day.'

The air around her felt much colder now. 'I'm sorry. I had no idea,' she said. 'You were so young when you lost your father.'

He grasped her hand. 'No one understands what it feels like to lose a father more than I do,' he said. 'Since the first time I saw you, I've been filled with an irresistible urge to protect you, to take care of you...'

Her sadness and suspicions washed away. Only sweetness and tenderness remained. Before, she'd thought of him as a friend, albeit one she didn't quite understand. Now she felt a sudden closeness to him. It was unlike anything she had ever felt before.

The bench squeaked as he rose. 'I have to go. I've already stayed too long.'

Nodding, she slid her hand out of his palm. She was relieved that he was leaving; although she didn't want him gone, she needed time to process everything that had just happened.

'Can you promise me something?' he asked.

'What?'

'Some people might come and ask you about me. Don't let them know that we've ever met.'

'Of course,' she answered without hesitation.

'You don't want to ask me why?'

Smiling, she said, 'You don't want to tell me. Why should I ask? I don't think you're a bad person and I know you wouldn't hurt me. I trust you.'

She heard a quiet but strong exhalation. Had her response taken him by surprise? Perhaps. Still, she had no intention of taking it back.

'I'll come and see you as soon as I can.'

He left without saying anything more. She heard his footsteps outside the studio, soft but quick, like a sprinter wearing padded shoes.

14

LET YOURSELF BE HUGE

10:25 a.m.
Criminal police headquarters

A quick check of his watch told SPU Captain Liu that the task force's meeting had started nearly half an hour ago. He rushed to the conference room and found all the other team members already assembled there.

'What are you doing here?' Captain Pei asked him, making no attempt to conceal his surprise.

'Du's finished his article. My men are keeping an eye on him in the break room. I brought a copy with me. I assumed you'd want to see it as soon as possible.'

'Perfect timing,' Pei said and pointed at the conference table. 'Have a look at that and tell me what you think.'

The table was covered with a pile of white styrofoam. Liu counted at least ten separate pieces. Though the chunks were all different shapes and sizes, they had two things in common: they were thin and they were all curved to some degree.

'These were all found within the vicinity of the Longyu Building,' Lieutenant Yin explained. 'They're all extremely similar to the bloodstained packaging we found on the terrace and we believe they share the same origin.'

'Oh? You think these are connected to the case?' Liu scanned the objects on the table again.

'We've already analysed the styrofoam recovered from the terrace,' Lieutenant Yin explained. 'The blood on it came from Vice President Lin. So we now know for a fact that Eumenides came into contact with that piece of styrofoam after murdering Vice President Lin. From what we know of the killer's abilities, this cannot have been accidental. Although these pieces were all found on the south side of the building, some of them were as much as fifty metres apart. It's likely that they were thrown from somewhere high up. Taking into account the height of the eighteenth-floor office and last night's wind direction and speed, the scatter pattern proves that they were thrown from the office window.'

'But how would these have helped Eumenides commit the murders?' Liu asked.

Captain Pei shrugged. 'That's what we're trying to figure out right now. We don't have an answer yet.'

'Mind if I pick one up and have a look?'

'By all means. The guys in the lab have already examined them. It's okay to touch them now.'

Liu took a seat and picked up one of the smallest pieces. Except for the lack of blood, it was all but indistinguishable from the styrofoam they'd found on the terrace.

'Actually, there's another thing that's odd,' Ms Mu said.

'What's that?' Pei asked, his interest piqued.

'That we're examining these styrofoam pieces at all. If Eumenides used them at the scene of the crime, it would make sense for him to throw them out the window. They'd scatter over a large area and would look like ordinary pieces of litter. But he would definitely have noticed the bloodstain, however much of a hurry he was in. Why didn't he hold onto that piece? It's true that we got lucky with its discovery, but we only found it because of a choice Eumenides made. It would have been easier for him to have avoided any chance of that happening, and that is something we mustn't forget.'

'I've been wondering the same thing,' Pei said. 'And the bag we found on the terrace is just as suspicious. It isn't like Eumenides to leave behind evidence. Especially as blatant as that.'

'So why did he do it, then?' TSO Zeng asked, adjusting his glasses. 'To distract us?'

No one answered. Liu continued to examine the pieces of styrofoam, lazily clasping one piece under his forearm while using his other hand to pick up another bit.

Pei eyed him curiously. Suddenly, like a spark igniting a scrap of kindling, his curiosity transformed into excitement.

He sprang out of his chair, approached the table, reached out and grabbed the largest piece. After studying it for a moment, he set it down in an empty space at the far end of the tabletop. The piece was about half the size of a pillow, and it was similarly curved. Pei had placed it so that its convex side faced downwards. The styrofoam rocked gently on the table, not unlike an overturned turtle. He turned and picked up a similarly sized piece from the pile. This time he placed it on top of the first piece, convex side up, so that both sides faced one another. He grabbed one piece after another, placing each one into a specific position. Like a jigsaw puzzle being assembled, a unified shape began to form.

The team stared at what they were seeing. The pieces of styrofoam had become a human silhouette. It had a torso, a waist, legs and arms. All it was missing was a head. Its right forearm consisted of the small piece they'd found on the terrace. The blood was smeared precisely where its wrist would be.

'What the hell is that?' TSO Zeng blurted out.

Pei studied the emerging styrofoam mannequin. 'I'm not quite sure. But we can be sure about one thing. At one point it was wearing the bloody clothes that we found on the terrace.'

Understanding dawned on Lieutenant Yin's face. He rose from his seat and moved closer to the mannequin. 'You're right! The blood was on the shirt's right wrist too. Eumenides must have worn this inside his clothes when he committed the murders. That's how the blood got there.'

SPU Captain Liu looked at Lieutenant Yin with wide-eyed incredulity. 'You think Eumenides wore this styrofoam... like a suit of armour?'

'That does appear to be what it was intended for,' Pei said.

Ms Mu seemed equally dubious. 'But the man in the recording moved very naturally. He walked like a cat burglar, not a man wearing armour. Can you imagine how bulky this would be to wear?'

'Yet again, the lady has a point,' Zeng murmured.

Everyone quietly pondered the implications. But though Pei's initial theory had filled the team with a sudden rush of hope, their examination of the styrofoam lead had quickly come to a standstill.

'As we've nothing more to contribute at this point,' Pei said, 'I'm bringing this meeting to a close. Before any of you leave the building, I want you all to take some time to think about where we are in this investigation. We'll reconvene later and discuss our thoughts.'

As Lieutenant Yin, TSO Zeng and Ms Mu left for the cafeteria, SPU Captain Liu walked over to Pei and handed him Du's article.

'Take a look at this draft, Captain. Let me know if it's ready to publish.'

Pei whistled through his teeth as he flipped through the printout. 'The kid's a fast typist, I'll give him that. "Eumenides Takes Another Life. This Time He Slaughters the Innocent..."'

He read on.

Structurally speaking, the article was sound and meticulously organised. Rather than begin immediately with the scene of the previous night's murders, Du opened by describing Vice President Meng's early years.

Back when the Longyu Corporation was in its infancy, Meng was Mayor Deng's right-hand man. Before the company became one of Chengdu's most formidable businesses, Meng got his hands bloody on more than one occasion while defending it from external threats. Eventually he was arrested and found guilty of manslaughter during a drunken brawl at a dinner. He was sentenced to life imprisonment.

Du related this first part of Meng's story with plenty of pace and drama, in the style of a classic adventure story designed to keep readers on the edge of their seats. But once he started describing Meng's experiences post-sentencing, the article became a thoughtful character study. Apparently, Meng made a clean break with his past while in prison. Not only did he make an active effort to reform, he also became one of the prison's hardest-working labourers. After ten years inside, Meng was granted parole. He had won a second chance at life.

The section that followed was a stark contrast to Meng's trial-by-fire ordeal in prison. He converted to Catholicism and even became a community leader, frequently using his own life experiences to guide and educate young people. He had put his dark past behind him. Pei felt a tingle in the back of his throat as he read Du's depiction of the cheerful family reunion when Meng came home to his wife and daughter.

The final segment was succinct and quickly segued into the

main subject of the article: Vice President Meng's execution at
Eumenides' hand. After briefly outlining Eumenides' emergence
and the recent killings, Du described the vice president's reaction
to the death notice he received from Eumenides. Despite his
family's concerns, Meng responded to the death threat with a
light heart and a clear conscience. He proclaimed that he had
already been punished for his misdeeds and that as far as he
was concerned, he was a new man. If Eumenides knew what
he'd been through, Meng was sure he would rescind his threat.
So when he took sanctuary in the office on the eighteenth floor
he brought along his proof of sentencing, his certificates of
good behaviour from prison, his parole certification and the
journal he'd kept while in prison.

Everything in the article tallied with what Pei already knew
of Vice President Meng. He had pored over Meng's background
before going to the Longyu Building, and the police had indeed
found the journal and these other items beside his pillow. Pei
had seen the bloody documents himself. But reading the article
cast everything in a new light. Any reader would sympathise
with Vice President Meng and would be left with one burning
question: why would Eumenides carry out this sentence?

As the article reached its climax, Du described the hours
leading up to the previous night as if it were the script of a
Hollywood thriller. Pei even found himself holding his breath.
The conclusion, however, was inevitable.

Vice President Meng was found with his mouth slightly
open, as though attempting to speak to his killer. His
words, however, if he even managed to utter them, had
no effect. Blood spilt from the deep gash across his throat,
drenching the pages of the diary lying beside him. His

personal redemption, it seemed, counted for nothing. All of Vice President Meng's hopes for a better life with his family were left swimming in blood, just like his diary...

Letting out a quiet sigh, Pei set the printout down on the table. The article was essentially an accusation from the perspective of one of Eumenides' victims. Even Eumenides' most loyal supporters would find it hard to justify his behaviour after reading that.

'Let him publish it,' he told Liu. 'And tell him to do it as soon as possible. Hell, let him use one of our computers.'

'Yes, sir.'

Pei thought to himself for another moment, still processing what he'd read. 'And tell him that he shouldn't only publish this online,' he added. 'I want it sent to Chengdu's major media outlets as well. Run through our media contacts and tell them to use the article. The more outlets you get it featured in, the better. If we pull this off, we might be able to kill two birds with one stone.'

After they had eaten and rested, Lieutenant Yin and SPU Captain Liu went to meet Captain Pei in his office.

Pei had piled the styrofoam onto his desk. Next to it stood the athletic backpack that they had found on the terrace.

'Have you figured it out, Captain?' Lieutenant Yin asked.

'Oh?' Pei smiled through his exhaustion. 'How did you guess?'

'Because it looks like you've stopped thinking it over,' Yin said matter-of-factly. 'When you're thinking about something, you devote your full attention to it. Even if someone's talking to you, your eyes are somewhere else. You're not relaxed like you are now. Plus, if you hadn't made sense of it, you wouldn't have ended our meeting so early.'

Pei offered a noncommittal shrug. Then he looked Liu up and down, mumbled, 'Yes, you'll do,' and nodded to himself.

Liu and Yin glanced at one another in confusion.

Pei picked up the backpack, set it down near the front of his desk, unzipped it and pulled out its contents: a set of athletic clothing and a black hat.

'The forensics team have already examined this bag and everything inside it. They found next to nothing, save for blood from Vice President Lin and Vice President Meng.'

The two officers said nothing.

'SPU Captain Liu, put these clothes on,' Pei said.

Liu froze momentarily. But once he'd recovered from his surprise, he immediately stripped off his uniform shirt and put on the workout jacket that Pei had handed to him. Even though Liu was 1.8 metres tall, the jacket hung loose on his thin frame.

Liu stood still at first, aware that Eumenides had worn that jacket. He then noticed the large patches of blood on it and shifted uncomfortably, anxiously waiting for Pei to tell him that he could take it off.

But Pei was only just getting started. He picked up several pieces of styrofoam from the desk and handed them to Liu. 'Put these on inside the jacket.'

These were the pieces that had made up the styrofoam figure's torso, back and arms. Liu unzipped the jacket and placed each piece in its corresponding position, section by section. To his surprise, the pieces not only fitted his figure perfectly but filled the space between his body and the jacket so well that they almost seemed custom-made for him. When he zipped the jacket back up, he appeared much bulkier.

Pei put the hat on Liu's head, making sure to pull the brim low over his face. He nodded to himself, apparently satisfied at what he saw. Finally, he looked over at Lieutenant Yin and asked, 'What do you think?'

'I think,' Yin said, 'that he looks a lot like the person we saw in the recording.'

Liu had finally had enough. He tore off the hat and shot Pei a reproachful look. 'Captain, what on earth am I doing this for?'

Pei's expression became stern. 'I have a task for you,' he replied.

Liu straightened up and his eyes brightened. 'Yes, sir.'

'It's extremely important,' Pei said, enunciating his words carefully. 'Top secret.'

8:21 p.m.
The Green Spring

It was well known that Sheng had been a key figure within the Longyu Corporation, and his 'accidental' death was an obvious red flag for Captain Pei. Just as Brother Hua had done before him, Pei followed the trail of leads to the Green Spring restaurant, where he demanded to see all security footage of the dining area from the evening of the twenty-ninth of October.

The footage showed Vice President Lin and Vice President Meng leaving the restaurant after they'd finished their meal. Sheng, however, remained at the table, where he continued to eat and drink. Not long after, he appeared to lose his temper.

Unfortunately, the video came without an audio track, so Pei could only guess what he was saying. After berating a waiter, Sheng sprinted out of view of the camera as if in pursuit of someone.

'What's going on here?' Pei asked the restaurant's head of security.

'This particular customer had been drinking quite a bit. I believe his table got through three bottles of wine. He tried to go after our violinist. But our people kept the situation under control.'

About fifteen seconds later, several waiters carried Sheng back into the frame. Although he appeared to be muttering unhappily to himself, he was more or less docile.

Pei continued watching the monitor. Suddenly his eyes widened. 'Pause the recording!' he yelled.

The timestamp read: 21:37:15.

'Who's that man there?' Pei asked, pointing at the screen.

The security chief had to all but glue his nose to the monitor before he spotted the individual in question. The man was far away from the camera and he was walking towards the restaurant's exit. His head was turned slightly – he was watching Sheng.

'Just another customer,' the security chief said, shrugging. 'There was a commotion. Of course people were going to watch.'

Pei's heart was beating like a jackhammer. Even though the man was standing in a dimly lit area some distance from the camera, Pei was struck with an undeniable sense of déjà vu. From the way the figure carried himself, and from the brimmed hat he wore low over his face, he looked exactly like the person in the security footage of the Longyu office.

Unfortunately, he was too far away for the camera to get

a clear picture, and the darkness around him made it all but impossible to make out his features. 'I want to talk to the servers who were working that night,' Pei said.

The security chief sprinted out of the room and returned several minutes later with a young male and female employee in tow.

Pei pointed at the monitor. 'Look at this footage and tell me if you have any recollection of this customer,' he instructed.

After examining the image for a moment, the waitress slapped her forehead. 'Oh, that must be the customer who was sitting in the corner, right? I recognise the hat. He sent Zheng Jia flowers, but he didn't leave a name. I remember that very clearly. I'm totally sure that's him.'

'Who's Zheng Jia?' Pei asked.

'Our violinist,' said the security chief. 'The one that this customer chased after, earlier in the recording.'

'Oh?' Pei immediately began calculating what the connection between those three people might be. He turned to the waitress. 'Can you describe that customer's features to me?'

'Umm… I don't know. I didn't get a very good look at him.'

'You can spot him when he's just a speck on a screen, but you can't remember what his face looked like?' the security chief scolded.

'He was sitting in the couples' booth. It's tucked into the corner of the restaurant and the lighting is very low. You know, for the mood,' she said hastily, defending herself. 'And he wore a hat the entire time. I couldn't have got a good look at him even if I tried.'

This answer did not seem to satisfy her superior. 'If he was on his own, why did you have him sit in the couples' booth?'

'I'm sure the customer chose the seat intentionally. She had nothing to do with it.' Pei waved the security chief away, stood up and looked at the waitress. 'I'd like to take a look at that booth.'

She led him into the dining area. It was quite late now and the last diners of the evening were finishing their meals. A young woman in a white blouse and emerald dress was standing on the stage in the middle of the room, playing a piece on her violin. Her eyes were shut. Pei didn't recognise the piece – he knew hardly anything about classical music – but he did know good music when he heard it.

There was no doubt she had talent. Her violin-playing flowed like water and was as intoxicating as wine. He kept his eyes fixed on her.

'That's Zheng Jia,' the waitress whispered in his ear.

Pei nodded. 'I'd rather not interrupt her while she's playing. Show me the booth first.'

Just as the waitress had said, the booth was located in the dining area's most out-of-the-way corner. The lighting was dim and atmospheric, so that anyone passing would see only silhouettes sitting there. Pei sat down on one of its padded benches.

'He was sitting right here, wasn't he?'

'That's right,' the waitress said. 'How did you know?'

'This is the only seat in the place that gives you a view of the entire restaurant.' Noticing her puzzlement, Pei shook his head and shrugged. 'Don't worry about it. You can go back to your customers now.'

The young woman nodded graciously and hurried back to the maître d's desk.

Pei scanned the restaurant. With each second that passed, he grew more confident that Eumenides had been the customer in the security footage. Everything about this booth was perfect for someone who wished to observe his surroundings while remaining unnoticed. Plus it offered multiple potential routes out, should an escape become necessary. For someone like Eumenides, it would have been the best seat in the house.

Pei closed his eyes and attempted to reconstruct that night inside his head. Why had Eumenides come? What could have drawn him there?

Aromas of exquisitely cooked pork and fish floated into the booth. The violin's gentle melodies massaged Pei's ears. This restaurant was certainly a good place to unwind.

With his eyes still shut, an idea struck him. He recalled Ms Mu's earlier analysis of Eumenides.

'Eumenides may have fostered a love of music, the arts or perhaps fine cuisine. And notwithstanding his mentor's edicts, he may still have developed feelings for someone.'

His eyes flew open and immediately focused on the stage. Though it was a considerable distance from the booth, he had an unimpeded view of the woman performing. As the slender violinist played, her white and green outfit made her look like a frost-tipped blade of grass.

'Eumenides might look for a woman in a similarly frail state, subconsciously hoping that he will somehow be able to heal her. He may also be looking for someone who, like him, has just been bereaved. Someone he can empathise with.'

Pei needed to have a word with Zheng Jia.

Twenty minutes later, the final strains of the violinist's performance faded from the restaurant. She bowed to her audience, but rather than turn and set her instrument down, she remained rooted to the spot.

Within seconds, a waitress hurried to the stage. She took the bow from the young woman and reached for her left hand. Still holding her instrument in her right hand, the violinist slowly dismounted the stage, guided by the waitress.

Pei was genuinely pained to see a young woman with such skill at her instrument suddenly fumbling to walk. He rushed over to her.

'Let me hold your violin, Miss Zheng,' he said.

She turned her head.

As he registered her surprise, Pei noticed her clouded irises. 'My name is Captain Pei Tao,' he explained. 'I'm with the criminal police and I'd like to ask you some questions.'

'Captain Pei Tao,' the violinist repeated with a friendly smile. She handed him the violin. 'I'm sorry to have kept you waiting, Captain.'

Her voice reminded Pei of a feather falling to the ground.

'Your music was more than enough compensation,' he replied. He walked beside her, taking care not to stand too close, as if her fragile frame might tear at the slightest accidental bump.

The three of them walked over to the green room behind the stage. After helping Zheng Jia into a chair, the waitress politely exited.

The violinist gestured to an instrument case lying open in front of the opposite wall. Pei placed the violin inside it and pulled up a chair for himself.

Once he was seated, the young woman asked, 'You haven't been in Chengdu for very long, have you, Captain Pei?'

'I transferred here recently,' Pei said, frowning. 'How can you tell?'

'My dad used to tell me stories about what went on in the police department, so I've heard the names of basically everyone he worked with.' She looked down, her face clouded with sorrow.

Pei was taken aback. 'Your father was a police officer? Is he retired now?'

She raised her head, her expression one of genuine surprise. 'You don't know? You mean you're not here because of my father's death?'

Her question hit Pei like a smack in the face. And suddenly he understood.

'Your father – what was his name?' It was far from tactful, but he needed to know.

She shut her eyes and her dejection was obvious. 'Oh, I'm sorry. My mistake. I thought...'

'My apologies,' Pei said. 'It's my fault for not making myself clear.'

She forced a smile. When she spoke next, her voice was barely a whisper. 'His name was Zheng Haoming.'

Those three quiet syllables boomed in Pei's ears. He studied the young woman's face. While her features were certainly more delicate than her father's, there was a similar intensity in her eyes. Not even her blindness could take that away.

He had first met Sergeant Zheng Haoming eighteen years ago, when he was a young man and the sergeant had questioned him about his connection to the warehouse explosion that they thought had killed Yuan Zhibang and Pei's then girlfriend, Meng Yun. Sergeant Zheng had been the first person to investigate the Eumenides murders, and so many years later he'd been the first to realise that the serial killer had re-emerged. The last time Pei had seen the sergeant was at the scene of his murder.

Pei had had no idea that this blind young woman was Sergeant Zheng's daughter. But now that he'd identified the figure in the security footage, it made chilling sense that

Eumenides had been in the same restaurant as Zheng Jia. He had come here for her. But Pei still needed to find out why.

Although the young woman couldn't register any changes in Pei's expression, she did notice his silence. 'You didn't know my father, did you?' she asked with disappointment.

'Actually, I did. He was a legend. I heard countless stories about him while I was at the police academy. Not only that, but I first met him eighteen years ago. And… I know that your father died in the line of duty while investigating a case.'

Zheng Jia's lower lip trembled as she smiled. But Pei saw a new emotion break through her pain. It was pride.

'I should thank you,' she said, 'for having identified the killer so quickly. My father can rest in peace and I won't have to live with the torment of knowing that his murderer is on the loose.'

Pei took a deep breath. Zheng Jia had obviously been following the news reports too. She assumed that Yuan, who'd blown himself up at the Jade Garden restaurant, was her father's real killer. Her words, so heartfelt and full of gratitude, were like knives to Pei's ears. It was as if Eumenides himself were mocking him.

Eventually, Zheng Jia broke the silence once again. 'We don't have to talk about my father. I know your time is valuable. So what did you want to ask me?'

Pei wasn't sure how to broach the subject, so he decided not to reveal the whole truth just yet. 'I'm currently investigating a different case. There was a car crash. One that we believe was not an accident. The person killed in the crash had dined here earlier that evening. He caused something of a commotion, as I'm sure you recall.'

'The drunk customer?' Zheng Jia shivered. 'He scared me half to death.'

Pei nodded. 'That's the one.' He considered his next words

carefully. How could he avoid discussing the April 18th case while still asking about Eumenides?

'It's strange. You aren't the first person to ask me about that man,' she said. 'You know, my father used to come to the restaurant sometimes when I performed. If he'd been around that night, he would have taught that customer a lesson. But look at me' – she pointed to her eyes – 'do you really think I'm capable of taking revenge on anyone?'

'Oh, I didn't mean to imply that we suspect you,' Pei said hurriedly. Sensing an opening, he added, 'We're just interested in a friend of yours.'

'A friend of mine?' Her tone wavered, although her expression did not.

'That's right,' he said, in the most casual manner he could muster. 'He's around your age, maybe a few years older, and he enjoys your performances. He sent you flowers once. How well would you say you know him?'

She shook her head. 'Someone sent me flowers that night, but they did it anonymously. I don't know who he is.'

'Oh?' Pei sensed that he had to dig deeper. 'He hasn't attempted to contact you outside this restaurant?'

'No, he hasn't,' the young woman answered definitively. 'Why? Does he have something to do with the death of that drunken customer?'

Usually Pei could tell whether someone was lying by watching their eyes. With Zheng Jia, however, it wasn't so simple. But her last question had given him a hint, so he gambled with a lie. 'No, nothing that serious. He might have seen something though. We'd like to hear his testimony, in case there are any leads we've missed.'

'Oh,' she said indifferently. Her shoulders slumped slightly. 'But I don't know him.'

Pei shut his eyes and shook his head. 'If that's the case, then it looks like I've done all I can here. If you do happen to hear from him, could you please let me know? The security chief has my card. He can put you in touch with me.'

She nodded and Pei left.

Zheng Jia listened as Captain Pei's footsteps grew fainter. She thought about his request.

'*If you do happen to hear from him, could you please let me know?*'

The world seemed to fall away from her. Like she was standing on a stage but without an audience. If only she knew when her friend would visit her next.

15

BEHIND THE MURDER

5 November, 8:35 p.m.
Jin River Stadium

The stadium was packed and buzzing. It was the first football game of the season for the Chinese Super League and the Chengdu Peppers had just taken the kick-off. Brother Hua was sitting in the middle of the front row watching the match with a permanent scowl. He wore a pair of dark glasses, and a flesh-coloured listening device was embedded in his ear.

It was the date of his death notice. That the day coincided with this opening game, an event that Brother Hua was scheduled to attend, seemed quite intentional. But despite the threat to his life, he'd refused to back out.

The Longyu Corporation had purchased the Peppers two years prior. They'd invested millions in the team and had finally turned a struggling side into one of the most prominent rising stars of Chinese football. Today's match was their debut in the elite national league and the game had attracted attention from across the country. There were even some international scouts and journalists in the stands.

Months before his death, Mayor Deng had announced that he would attend this match in person. But the tragedies that had struck the Longyu Corporation in recent days had changed many things. Mayor Deng, Vice President Lin and Vice President Meng had been murdered one after the other and the once-towering corporation now teetered on the brink of collapse. Brother Hua had taken it upon himself to come to the match as the Longyu Corporation's official representative.

The Jin River Stadium could seat 54,000 and it was full. Such a crowded, noisy environment would provide excellent cover for Eumenides, and Brother Hua had taken this into account. A decade as Mayor Deng's bodyguard had honed his mind into a finely tuned instrument and he had already assessed Eumenides' possible entry points along with several potential methods for an attempted assassination.

Captain Pei had implored him to stay at police headquarters, but Brother Hua had insisted on going to the game.

'I won't retreat into my shell like a turtle. This is a moment of crisis for the company and our competitors are frothing at the mouth at the thought of the Longyu Corporation's collapse. They're already lining up to take our place. By attending this game, I'll be sending them a message that we're still standing and will not be cowed. I'm going to sit right there in front of everyone and I'm going to watch our team win. At the same time, I'm going to wait for Eumenides to show his face, and then the two of us will finish this once and for all.'

On hearing Hua's impassioned speech, Pei stopped insisting that he remain at police headquarters and instead dispatched a team of plainclothes officers to protect him at the stadium. Sending out bait for Eumenides was an impossible paradox, as Pei's predecessor, former captain Han Hao, had discovered to his cost. But there was no other way to bring Eumenides out into the open. In any case, this was ultimately Brother Hua's decision.

Twenty members of the criminal police force were dressed

as football fans and stadium employees and dispersed around the stands, their sharp eyes monitoring their surroundings for any unusual activity. Brother Hua himself was flanked by six men that he had handpicked from the company's best bodyguards.

The journalist Du Mingqiang stood near them, looking out of place beside such hulking figures. His gaze roved from seat to seat and then back to Brother Hua, his features registering first excitement and then fear, seemingly flitting between the two emotions every few seconds.

It was now two days since Du had published his article about the murders in the Longyu Building. It had swept the internet like a raging fire. Innumerable readers had posted comments online, questioning Eumenides' motives, wondering whether he'd abandoned his quest for justice or whether he'd never truly believed in his supposedly honourable mission.

Thrilled by the article's success, Captain Pei had encouraged Du to strike while the iron was hot and write a follow-up piece. So Du interviewed Vice President Meng's widow and daughter, and the public's opinion of Eumenides finally began to shift. The image of the noble vigilante crumbled, revealing a heartless killer. The second article concluded with the most shocking revelation of all: that Eumenides had issued Brother Hua with a death notice. Du followed this bombshell with a public plea for Eumenides to stop his killings and find a peaceful resolution.

Brother Hua was pleased with Du's work and immediately hired the reporter as his official mouthpiece for all communications with Eumenides. Du had become his personal biographer. He had specifically requested that Du accompany him today as he made his last stand against the serial killer. If Eumenides were to carry out his threat, then Du would chronicle the day's events and report on them in another article that would publicly attack the killer.

As far as Captain Pei was concerned, the stands were the best place for Du to be. By putting Eumenides' two targets together, the police could focus all their efforts on protecting both of them simultaneously. But the reverse scenario was also a concern. If he and his officers failed, they'd be serving Eumenides his victims on a silver platter.

From his seat, Brother Hua could see the Golden Sea Hotel looming over the opposite side of the stadium. A single street separated the five-star hotel from the stadium, and any guest staying on its upper floors would have a full view of the game and most of the stadium's seats. Brother Hua was alert to its strategic importance and had stationed several men inside a room on the hotel's twentieth floor.

The police had also taken advantage of the hotel's useful location. For the past two hours, Captain Pei, Lieutenant Yin and Ms Mu had been standing in front of the window of Room 2237. The curtains were drawn shut and the room was pitch black. Anyone peering in from outside would only see the curtains. The three of them, however, had a perfect view of the seats and were in constant radio contact with the officers on the ground.

Ms Mu glanced up from her binoculars. 'Where's SPU Captain Liu? I don't see him among the other plainclothes officers.'

'You wouldn't recognise him even if he was standing right next to you just now,' Pei said.

'I doubt that,' Ms Mu replied with a chuckle. She brought her binoculars back up to her eyes and, as if challenged, continued to look for Liu.

'Echo Two, this is Echo One.' Pei spoke into the microphone attached to his headset. 'Please respond.'

'Echo Two here.'

Ms Mu's forehead creased. It was SPU Captain Liu's voice. 'What's your status?'

'Still in position. Nothing appears to be out of the ordinary.'

In position? Ms Mu squinted into her binoculars, trying to figure out where exactly he was.

'Stay alert,' Pei said, his voice solemn.

'Understood.'

From inside Room 2107 a man watched the stadium. He was tall, with a sturdy, athletic body. He wore a loose set of exercise clothes and a tight-fitting cap. His face was hidden behind a beard and he had sunglasses on despite being indoors.

As soon as the match began, he stood in front of his window and did not move. He observed the stadium through a small portable telescope, dividing his attention between the pitch and the rest of the stadium.

At the same time, the man was also being observed.

A camera had been hidden inside the central ceiling light and was pointed directly at the window. As soon as the man walked over to the window, all of his actions were filmed. A wire ran from the camera and through the ceiling, transmitting these images to a small surveillance monitor the size of a paperback novel.

Another man in his mid-thirties was watching the monitor. He was dressed in the uniform of a hotel employee, but his calculating expression did not resemble that of a member of staff. Hatred smouldered in his eyes as he stared at the screen.

This was not the only screen in the tight space. In fact, the room was packed with hundreds of surveillance monitors.

One of them showed Captain Pei, Ms Mu and Lieutenant Yin huddled in front of the window of Room 2237.

Another screen showed a live broadcast of the football match. The referee whistled three times, two short blasts and one long, and the game was over. A low roar emanated from the stadium, clearly audible from inside the hotel. On the screen, the members of the Chengdu Peppers pumped their fists and high-fived one another in celebration of their victory.

The spectators' cheers were deafening. The man dressed in the hotel uniform watched as Brother Hua and others in the crowd leapt out of their seats and added their applause to the mix. Down on the pitch, the players were ecstatic. They lined up, grabbed each other's hands and bowed to the spectators. An even greater roar filled the stadium and the crowd surged towards the field. A handful of rowdy youths leapt onto the pitch, their eyes glinting eagerly as they got closer and closer to their heroes.

The man picked up a microphone.

'Move!' he shouted.

The police had kept most of the unruly spectators at bay, but a few fans had managed to get around them and onto the pitch. The team was high on adrenaline and several players tore off their jerseys and tossed them at the fans that had got closest. This only encouraged the other spectators, and within seconds they began leaping down from the stands at an alarming rate and stampeding towards the players.

The Chengdu Peppers looked nervous. Two more players hastily tossed their jerseys into the crowd and the team sprinted towards the dressing rooms. The police were pushed to their limits to contain the rabid fans, but even their best efforts barely managed to slow the surging human tide. People fought over the thrown shirts, clawing and kicking one another.

The Jin River Stadium was in chaos.

Eight figures broke away from the throng of spectators and ran towards the stands. Their muscular legs pumped as they sprinted across the pitch.

Across the street, Captain Pei was gripping the curtain so tightly as he watched the unfolding riot that his knuckles turned white.

'Echo Two, defence level one!'

No answer came through his earpiece. Pei had not expected one.

The man in the hotel uniform glanced at the image of Pei on the screen but quickly turned away to focus on the one monitoring Room 2107.

The athletic man was gazing intently through his telescope, searching for a specific target.

The man in the hotel uniform curled his lips into a sneer as he watched his displays. He was ready.

He stood up, walked over to the door and draped a large white towel over his shoulder. His disguise was complete.

He stepped out of the room and into the dimly lit hotel basement. He navigated the dark hallways with ease, slipped into a lift and pressed the button for the twenty-first floor.

The athletic man in Room 2107 was keenly observing the commotion in the stadium below. He moved his telescope slightly to the left, following the individuals racing towards the stands. Once they were about twenty metres away, they were blocked by a dozen fans and stadium staff. He nodded in understanding. *Cops.*

The running men halted at once, and the plainclothes officers subdued them in seconds.

With that, the athletic man in Room 2107 put down his telescope. He turned his head slightly to one side and heard a quiet beep behind him.

Recognising the sound of the door's electronic lock, he whirled around. The light from the hallway illuminated the silhouette at the door. He saw a hotel uniform and the long towel draped over one shoulder, but other details were too dark to make out.

'Who's there?' he yelled.

The microphone hidden in his collar picked up his voice, transporting it away…

'*Who's there?*' the voice squawked into Pei's ear.

Pei spun around and sprinted towards the door. 'Move!' he yelled into his microphone. Lieutenant Yin was right behind him.

At the sound of Pei's order, fifteen plainclothes officers stationed on the street outside the Golden Sea Hotel began running to the hotel entrance.

In Room 2107, the man in the hotel uniform stood motionless in the doorway. Scowling at the athletic man inside, he pulled the trigger of the gun hidden beneath his towel.

A loud echo reverberated through the room and the bullet struck the athletic man in the chest. After letting out a long wheeze, he dropped to the floor.

The shooter shrugged off the towel and trained his pistol on the man. He approached the window. His victim was lying on the floor, breathing in shallow gasps, with both hands covering his chest and his face contorted in pain.

Crouching down, the shooter pressed the gun's long silencer against the man's temple. With his free hand he tore off the man's sunglasses and false beard. Despite the darkness of the room, a stream of light coming through the doorway was enough for him to make out the man's features. 'It's you!' he bellowed.

The man stared back at his attacker with bloodshot eyes. Recognition came to him quickly. Beneath the hotel uniform, it was definitely him. 'Captain Han Hao!' he shouted, each syllable causing him sharp pain.

Han recognised the face of the man he'd shot all too clearly. Without the sunglasses and beard, there was no doubting that this was the SPU officer who had handcuffed him at the airport when they'd last met.

SPU Captain Liu glared at Han with a look that could only be described as pure hatred.

Another thought suddenly came to Han and he unbuttoned SPU Captain Liu's collar. A microphone was taped to the other side of the fabric. Shock turned to panic and Han stood up straight away, pulled the curtain open and stared down at the street below. More than a dozen men were swarming into the building.

Gritting his teeth, he pivoted around. Pain shot up his right leg – Liu had grabbed his ankle. Han levelled his pistol at the SPU officer's forehead. 'Let go of me!'

Liu's grip did not loosen. He met Han's eyes with a ferocity that struck the former task-force leader like a fist to the gut. Han lowered his gun and kicked Liu in the temple with his other foot. The SPU officer went limp.

Han had wasted enough time. He ran out of the room. As soon as he emerged into the hallway he heard the clatter of approaching footsteps from the nearby staircase. They were coming from upstairs. He immediately knew who it was. Sweat beaded on his forehead.

He had only seconds to act before he'd be seen. Reaching into his pocket, he pulled out his universal key card and swiped it over the lock for Room 2108. He disappeared inside, slammed the door and locked it. With his heart pounding in his ears, he pressed his eye against the peephole.

Captain Pei and Lieutenant Yin raced out from the stairwell with their guns drawn and quickly kicked in the door to Room 2107. SPU Captain Liu was lying on the floor, bleeding and unconscious. Han was gone.

'Where did he go?' Lieutenant Yin asked in a strained voice. He searched the room anxiously, checking the bathroom, the cupboard and the window.

Pei crouched down and examined Liu's wounds. 'Seal all exits from this building,' he said into his microphone. 'Send two men to the hotel's security centre.'

Another set of footsteps approached and Ms Mu entered. When she saw the body on the floor, her mouth fell open. 'What on earth is SPU Captain Liu doing here? What the hell happened?' she asked.

Pei had no time to explain. He held his fingers near Liu's mouth and nostrils, checking for breath. Then he pressed hard against the pressure point located between the base of his nose and his upper lip. After almost five seconds, Liu finally stirred.

'Captain,' Liu murmured weakly. His eyes fluttered open and his voice became tense and urgent. 'Have you arrested Han?'

Pei shook his head. 'He was gone by the time we got here.'

'He couldn't have gone far,' Liu said, trying to prop himself up. He fell back, grimacing in pain, and held his hand over the wound in his chest.

Pei moved Liu's hand away, slid his own hand beneath the officer's shirt and felt the bulletproof jacket beneath it. The bullet hadn't pierced the Kevlar. He sighed in quiet relief.

'Damn it,' Liu said. 'I got careless. I didn't expect him to shoot me as soon as he opened the door.'

Pei placed a reassuring hand on his shoulder. 'Stay where you are. You might have a broken rib.'

Ms Mu came over. Despite her concern for Liu, her mind was still on the operation. She couldn't hold back her questions any longer. 'What was Han doing here in the hotel? What the hell were you people up to?'

'Captain Pei put this together,' Liu said between gasps. 'His analysis was spot on. Unfortunately I just wasn't up to the challenge.'

They quickly filled Ms Mu in.

Two days earlier
Captain Pei's office

Pei called Lieutenant Yin and SPU Captain Liu into his office for an impromptu meeting. 'We know two things,' he said. 'One: no one was able to enter or exit Mayor Deng's office when the murders happened. Two: the recording of the killer between the blackouts is real. These two things sound contradictory. But if we untangle this paradox, we must reach a new conclusion: the killer was in the office the whole time.'

'But I thought we already agreed that there was no one

in the office besides Vice President Meng and Vice President Lin,' Lieutenant Yin said. 'The cameras started recording when the two victims entered the office, and they kept recording uninterrupted until the first power outage. No tampering could have occurred between those two points. There were clearly two people in the room when the power went out. So where did the third person come from?'

Pei raised his head. 'Another paradox. But we shouldn't fear these contradictions. We should welcome them. You see, most paradoxes have a single explanation. We can find the answer.'

Lieutenant Yin brightened slightly as he attempted to put the pieces together. 'There were only two people in the room when the power went out. No one was able to enter the office once everything went dark, but the killer was there. The only explanation for what happened—'

He was about to continue with his hypothesis, but he stopped himself. It was too absurd for him to say out loud.

'—the only explanation,' SPU Captain Liu said, picking up Yin's thread and giving him a knowing nod, 'is that the killer was one of the two men in the office.'

Lieutenant Yin looked at Captain Pei, his eyes alert. Pei nodded silently, but Yin shook his head. 'But how is that possible? Vice President Meng and Vice President Lin were the two people inside the office. They were both Eumenides' targets. Don't forget the recording from after the first blackout. When the killer appeared, both men were still in their beds.'

'You're thinking yourself into a corner,' Pei said, raising his eyebrows. 'I don't blame you, though – it took me a long time before I figured it out. Our adversary did a lot of careful planning and if that piece of styrofoam hadn't got stained with blood and fallen onto the terrace downstairs, I honestly don't think I would have come up with the answer.'

Lieutenant Yin looked over at SPU Captain Liu, who was trying on the styrofoam and bloodstained clothes.

'Do you remember what you said about Liu earlier?' Pei asked.

'I said that he looked a lot like the person in the security footage,' Yin answered, before clicking his fingers in realisation. 'That's it! Someone else wore this styrofoam. It wasn't Eumenides!'

'You've sidestepped the first trap,' Pei said approvingly. 'The "killer" in the recording wasn't Eumenides at all. It was someone who was the same height as Eumenides but much thinner.'

Yin and Liu exchanged glances.

'Vice President Meng!' Liu blurted out. 'But how do you explain the fact that the recording shows three people in the office?'

'That's the second trap,' Pei said. 'It had me completely baffled at first. But once I realised that the figure I thought was Eumenides was actually Vice President Meng, that dead end disappeared. Remember, there were two separate recordings that night, made by two separate cameras.'

Lieutenant Yin slapped his hand against Pei's desk. 'The recording of Vice President Meng's bed was fake!'

'It all adds up,' Pei said. 'The clock was on Lin's side of the office, which was the same side on which the supposed killer appeared. Until now, we haven't had any reason to doubt the recording of Meng's bed.'

'That recording must have been looped,' Liu said.

Lieutenant Yin paused for a moment as the pieces fell together in his mind. 'The first power outage lasted five minutes. During that time Vice President Meng must have changed out of his clothes and put on the styrofoam to pad out his figure and make himself look more like Eumenides. He must have planned for the emergency generator to kick in as well, because he needed to show his back to the camera so that the police would suspect Eumenides. When the power cut out again, he went to work.'

Yin started to pace around the room, continuing with his train of thought. 'Vice President Lin had taken sleeping medication, so he wouldn't have put up much of a struggle when Meng slit his throat. Once he'd killed Lin, Meng took off his clothes, stuffed them into the backpack and threw it down onto the terrace. And the rope we eventually found? He hid that on the terrace beforehand. Meng did all of these things to make us believe that someone broke into the office and killed Vice President Lin. The styrofoam pieces, however, would have given him away, so he tossed them out of the window, figuring that they'd be light enough to scatter across a broad area and so avoid attracting anyone's attention. He didn't realise that a single piece of styrofoam, the one stained with Lin's blood, would land on the terrace.'

'So after all that, Meng got back into bed and slit his own throat?' Liu asked incredulously.

Lieutenant Yin shook his head insistently. 'Of course not. Whatever happened to Vice President Meng, it wasn't suicide. I think we can safely assume that he didn't cut his own throat, put the knife in the backpack and throw it down to the terrace before climbing back onto his bed and choking on his own blood. And anyway, based on the angle of the cut to his throat if nothing else, it had to have been made by someone else.'

'Who killed him then?'

Yin had already asked himself this question and now he had an answer. 'Meng wouldn't have been able to pull off a scheme that complicated on his own,' he said. 'He must have had an accomplice. That's who killed him.'

Pei was impressed. 'And do you have any idea who this accomplice could have been?'

'Brother Hua,' Yin said without hesitation. 'If it was impossible for anyone to get in or out through the window, then there was only one way to kill Vice President Meng – by sneaking into the office and taking him out when the power was down. Four people went in there before anyone else – Brother Long, Brother Hua and their two trusted subordinates. Brother Long ran over to Vice President Lin, the man he worked for, while Brother Hua went over to Vice President Meng with his subordinate in tow. Meng would have been pretending to be asleep and he certainly wouldn't have expected Brother Hua to cross him.'

'All of that could have conceivably happened, given the evidence, but what about a motive?' Liu pursed his lips. 'Why would Vice President Meng want to kill Vice President Lin? Why would he agree to work with Brother Hua? And why would Brother Hua want both of them dead?'

'I can't say for certain right now,' Pei said cautiously, 'but I do know that Mayor Deng's sudden death created a power vacuum inside the Longyu Corporation. It's inevitable that there'd be a struggle for control of the company. And bearing in mind that many of the high-ups in the Longyu Corporation have criminal backgrounds, we should expect their methods to be somewhat... extreme.'

Liu's face fell. 'So the death notices were fake. It was all an internal power struggle masquerading as a double murder by Eumenides. In other words, we've been wasting our time here.'

Pei narrowed his eyes. 'Not necessarily. Remember the death

notice we found taped to the locked drawer in Mayor Deng's desk? The one with Brother Hua's name on it?'

Lieutenant Yin took his time before answering. 'Perhaps Brother Hua was just being thorough.'

'How so?' Pei said.

'Vice President Meng must have hidden the styrofoam and the extra clothes inside the office. But before the two vice presidents were isolated there, Brother Long and Brother Hua must have done a complete sweep of the room. In that case, Meng's only option would have been to stuff the clothes and styrofoam into the backpack and then put everything in the locked drawer. The desk belonged to Mayor Deng, so Brother Long wouldn't have had a key. But Brother Hua did. He must have given Meng the key after having told Brother Long that he didn't have one.'

'I see.'

'Brother Hua had to think ahead. He knew we'd open the drawer during our investigation and that we'd be suspicious when we saw it was empty. If we suspected that the drawer had been used to store something and that this had been removed, then we might see through this plot to impersonate Eumenides. That's why Brother Hua placed an additional death notice inside the drawer, so that we would assume that it was Eumenides who'd cleaned out the drawer and left a note behind.'

'Hmm. That does make sense.' Pei nodded. 'But how would Brother Hua follow through with the death notice? If the execution date passed without any actions from Eumenides, wouldn't Brother Hua just be incriminating himself?'

Lieutenant Yin was silent.

'Actually, I think the internal struggle at Longyu is just a part of this,' Pei continued. 'Brother Hua wants to use this opportunity to accomplish another goal of his. He wants to draw out Eumenides. Do you really believe that Brother Hua asked Du to write that article just so people would change their minds about Eumenides? He even told me that he wants to include a copy of his death notice in the follow-up piece. Who do you think he's really doing that for?'

Yin paused. 'He wanted to provoke Eumenides!'

'Exactly. He accused Eumenides of killing an innocent man and he turned the public against him. Eumenides thinks of himself as the embodiment of justice. He won't let these slights go unnoticed. I'm absolutely certain that he's plotting a way to get back at this imposter.'

'So when the date on the death notice arrives, so will Eumenides,' Yin said. 'He'll be watching and waiting to see who this imposter really is. He might have his suspicions, but he won't know for certain who's behind it all. Brother Hua, of course, will use it to set a trap. He'll wait for Eumenides to take the bait, and then he'll avenge Mayor Deng.'

'What should we do if Eumenides really does come?' Liu asked, his fingers now twitching with excitement.

'That's the assignment I'm giving you now,' Pei said, fixing his gaze on the SPU captain. 'I want you to wear this styrofoam disguise, dress up like Eumenides and appear with Brother Hua on the day of his supposed execution.'

'You want me to be bait for Eumenides,' Liu said. There was no questioning tone in his voice at all. On the contrary, he felt honoured to have been given this task. He looked down, examining the layer of styrofoam encasing his body. His earlier disgust was gone, replaced by pride.

'It's going to be extremely dangerous,' Pei warned. 'Eumenides won't be the only person you'll need to watch for. You might have to deal with Brother Hua as well.'

Despite Pei's seriousness, Liu grinned. 'Now I know what

you meant when you said we could kill two birds with one stone!'

Pei didn't look quite as optimistic as Liu. He paced behind his desk. 'There's another person who might show up. Someone I know you're dying to see.'

'Who?' Liu asked, his heart beating faster.

'Han Hao.'

A shudder went through the room. Lieutenant Yin's expression in particular grew tense at the mention of his former superior's name. After all, he was the one who'd helped Han escape, albeit unwittingly. 'How do you know that?' he asked.

'I believe that Han has already allied himself with Brother Hua,' Pei said bluntly. 'In order for Brother Hua to have produced perfect replicas of Eumenides' death notices, transformed Vice President Meng into Eumenides for the security cameras, and even cut his colleagues' throats, he'll have needed someone on the inside. Someone who's extremely familiar with Eumenides' methods. No matter how many times I've tried to come up with a name, the only person I've been able to think of is Han Hao. I suspect that Han himself may have killed Vice President Meng; he could very well have been the guard who followed Brother Hua into the office. It takes a certain kind of training to kill someone in complete darkness without making a sound.'

Lieutenant Yin nodded numbly, trying to accept Captain Pei's theory but at the same time finding it almost impossible to do so. 'How could the two of them end up working together? Han shot Mayor Deng. Brother Hua should hate him even more than he hates Eumenides.'

'I'm sure Brother Hua still harbours a grudge against him, but an alliance isn't necessarily so unlikely. After all, Han was also tricked by Eumenides. They share that common enemy, and they can be valuable assets to each other.'

Realisation and acceptance slowly crept across Lieutenant Yin's face. 'You know, I was wondering why we haven't been able to find Han. So Brother Hua's been hiding him this whole time and working to eliminate his enemies. Up to and including Eumenides.'

'This just keeps getting more interesting by the minute,' SPU Captain Liu said. His gaze hardened into an icy stare. 'Let them come. I'll be waiting.'

5 November, 9:55 p.m.
Golden Sea Hotel

Lieutenant Yin sprinted back into Room 2107.

'I've just checked, Captain Pei. There's no sign of him.'

Pei ran into the hall and looked left and right. He'd chosen that room because it was midway along the corridor, a good distance from the stairwells at either end. The room that he, Yin and Ms Mu had used as their base had been right next to a stairwell. When he'd heard Liu say Han's name over the radio, he'd rushed straight for the stairs.

'There's no way Han is that fast,' Pei said. He turned to Yin. 'Get two master key cards and have a pair of officers go right and left, checking every door as they go.'

Their reinforcements reached the twenty-first floor moments later. A discovery followed almost immediately. 'Sir!' an officer cried out. 'The ventilation grille on the ceiling of the bathroom in Room 2108 has been prised open.'

Several minutes later, Pei was looking at a map of the hotel's ventilation system. They quickly checked all the openings that were large enough to accommodate a person and blocked them off.

He was already too late.

Two minutes earlier

Han climbed out of the ventilation shaft of one of the hotel's fireproof emergency rooms. As he emerged, he saw a pair of figures standing in front of him.

The two men in black suits bowed respectfully and walked over to him.

He froze.

'Brother Hua sent us here to wait for you, Captain.'

16

FALLEN SOLDIER

10 p.m.
Golden Sea Hotel

'How do we get out of here?' Han immediately asked.

The black-suited man on the left pointed to the service lift behind him. 'We take this lift down to the car park. Brother Hua has a car waiting for us. There's a secret tunnel from there to the car park under the stadium. The police won't have had time to seal off the entire stadium, so you'll be able to slip out of there unseen among the crowds.'

Han grunted approvingly. The plan was sound.

'There's no time to lose,' the man on the right said, stepping aside. 'Get in the lift.'

'After you,' Han said calmly.

The two men looked at one another. The man on the left pressed the button to summon the lift. Taking out his gun, Han entered and slid into a corner with his back against the wall.

Thirty seconds later, the doors opened onto the underground car park. Han waited for the two men to exit before following them. Their footsteps echoed across the empty space like the clatter of falling hailstones.

'The car's parked up ahead, past this bend,' one of the men said as he rounded a corner. Suddenly, he shrank back.

'What is it?' Han whispered.

'Cops. Put your gun away.'

Han melted into the wall. Slowly, he extended his left hand along the wall and used the reflection in his watch face to peer around the corner.

He saw several cars and a blue minivan, but no police. There was no one up ahead.

Glancing rapidly behind him, he saw that the man closest to him had just pulled a knife.

'Shit!' he hissed. The knife was centimetres from his back. He ducked and it plunged between two of his upper ribs. Wheezing, he spun round, the knife still stuck between his ribs, jabbed an elbow at his attacker and yanked the man's arm away.

The other man in black also pulled a knife and rushed towards them. Before he could reach them, Han raised his right hand. A crack echoed through the car park and the man fell to the ground with a bullet between his eyes.

The other man struggled to free himself and aimed a kick at Han's face. Dodging the foot, Han straddled the man's leg and used his left hand to pull him near until their faces were so close he could smell his breath. He knelt and delivered a swift knee to his crotch. The man moaned in pain and curled up on the ground.

Holstering his firearm, Han gritted his teeth and pulled the knife from his ribs. In some corner of his mind he knew that it hurt like hell, but the adrenaline rush kept him from fully feeling it. He stabbed the bloodied knife into the centre of the man's chest, plunging it through muscle and bone until the blade was buried all the way to the handle.

As the man slumped to the ground, Han turned away and headed deeper into the underground garage. Blood streamed from the wound in his back. As he walked, he used the hem of his jacket to tie a makeshift tourniquet around his ribs.

Five minutes later

'The black suits are a giveaway,' Captain Pei said. 'These are Brother Hua's men.'

Lieutenant Yin inspected the bullet hole in the larger man's forehead as Ms Mu surveyed the car park. 'It looks identical to the one in SPU Captain Liu's vest,' Yin said. 'I'm sorry to say it, but Han did this.'

'He's got to be hiding somewhere in here,' Ms Mu said. 'We've had all the hotel's exits and entrances sealed off and that includes the ones in and out of this car park. Han can't have got out.'

Pei took several steps away from the bodies and crouched down to get a closer look at some glistening patches on the ground. At first they were hard to distinguish against the dark surface, but once he knew what he was looking at, they formed an obvious trail.

Yin, Ms Mu and the others followed the direction of his gaze. 'He's wounded!' one of the officers said.

Pei turned to his men. 'Fan out in every direction. Open the boot of every vehicle you see. If you find more blood, let me know immediately.'

The officers dispersed and began searching in pairs.

'Captain, there's another exit here,' came a shout from the southeast corner of the car park.

Pei raced over. An opening of about one and a half metres

was set into the wall. It appeared to be a tunnel, but its interior was too dark to be able to see where it led. He turned to Lieutenant Yin. 'Why didn't we know about this exit?' he demanded.

Yin shifted uncomfortably. He'd been in charge of sealing off all of the hotel's entrances and exits. 'This tunnel… it wasn't in the building's blueprints.'

'Are you sure?' Pei asked angrily.

Yin met his boss's gaze. 'I'd bet my life on it.'

'I want the two of you to search this tunnel,' Pei said to the officers who'd discovered it. 'Stay alert and radio in as soon as you find something.'

'Understood, sir.'

He turned back to Lieutenant Yin. 'Talk to the hotel staff and find out why the hell this tunnel is here!'

Yin hurried away to the hotel lobby, where he demanded to speak with the hotel manager. Several minutes later, he radioed his answer back to Captain Pei.

'The tunnel wasn't in the original design for the hotel, apparently. It was only built after the stadium's underground car park was constructed. The idea was to connect the two car parks, but that never happened. These days the tunnel is only ever opened up during major events at the stadium, as access to overflow parking.'

'Damn it!' Pei screamed.

'There's a good chance that Han's in the stadium now,' Lieutenant Yin said. 'We don't have enough people in there to search for him. He'll blend into the crowd and get out without anyone noticing.'

'Send officers to the stadium car park,' Pei shouted. 'I want the footage from every security camera there over the last twenty minutes. Take down the number plates of every vehicle that left the car park during that time and track them all down. Post an alert to all other law-enforcement agencies in the city. Check small hotels, pharmacies and clinics for anyone matching Han's description. Monitor the radio frequencies used by taxis. And add a new detail to the description of Han: a knife wound to his torso.'

It was soon reported that the eight men who'd charged the stands all claimed to be Brother Hua's men. They insisted to the police officers who apprehended them that they'd been stationed in the stands for their employer's security. When the pitch descended into chaos, they rushed to protect Hua. They hadn't expected the police to misunderstand their actions.

Brother Hua had left his seat to calmly walk down the VIP passage behind the stands, with Du hurrying close behind. A circle of plainclothes officers and bodyguards formed around them and the group made its way to the hotel's underground car park, where the police had already set up a cordon. As soon as Brother Hua spotted Pei there, he stepped over the police tape and approached him. 'What's going on, Captain?'

'Han is here,' Pei said emotionlessly. 'He's already killed two of your men. We're searching for him right now.'

'Han?' Brother Hua asked, his mouth open in apparent shock.

'We'll get him. You can be sure of that,' Pei said, watching him closely.

'If I were you, I'd just shoot him. Save yourself the trouble of chasing him down the next time he escapes,' Hua said. 'Well, I won't delay you any longer, Captain. My team won today – I'm off to find somewhere to celebrate.' He turned and strode off towards his car.

The head of the plainclothes officers assigned to Brother Hua approached Pei. 'Should we stay with him, Captain?'

'Yes,' Pei replied instantly. 'But not to protect him. No one's going to try to kill him. Your mission now is to keep an eye on him. He's actually connected to the murders from two days ago. Once we've found Han, Brother Hua will be our next target.'

The officer nodded, though he was surprised. 'Yes, sir,' he said obediently, then pointed to Du. 'But what about him?'

Pei considered the journalist for a nanosecond. 'Keep him here,' he said.

Brother Hua, meanwhile, had passed the group of police officers and reached his car. Since he'd been the driver for his late boss, he was still in the habit of driving himself. He fished out his keys and slid into the driver's seat. As he pressed his key into the ignition, he paused. Something didn't feel right. The rearview mirror had been moved.

'Shit!' he muttered.

The driver's seat collapsed backwards. Caught off guard, Brother Hua fell back with it. By the time he'd tried to right himself, it was already too late. An arm was hooked firmly around his neck and the cold steel barrel of a gun was resting against his head.

'Captain Han,' he said without looking at his captor. 'Funny we should meet here. I'd assumed you were long gone.'

Han made a sound halfway between a laugh and a cough. 'I've been stabbed. Even if I ran, I wouldn't make it far. I'd rather finish things with you before I'm taken in again.' He took a deep, wheezing breath and screamed at the top of his lungs, 'If anyone comes within five metres of this car, I'll blow Brother Hua's brains all over the upholstery!'

★

Brother Hua's odd behaviour had already attracted the attention of the officers and bodyguards in the car park and they'd formed a loose semicircle around the vehicle. Han scanned their surprised faces through the side and rearview mirrors. He smirked, taking comfort in the knowledge that they couldn't see him through the car's tinted windows.

'Don't come any closer! I'm being held hostage! Han is in here and he has a gun!' Brother Hua reached for the window control and the driver's-side window rolled down slightly. 'Everyone, stay five metres back!' he yelled.

Pei hurried over and he and his officers surrounded the car while keeping their distance. Despite their shock, they all had their weapons carefully drawn.

'Very good,' Han said darkly. 'If you'd had that much tact to start with, things would never have gone this far.'

Pei's voice boomed into the car. 'Han, put down your weapon and get out of the vehicle with your hands up! This is your only option. As a former police officer, you know we won't listen to your demands, no matter how many hostages you take.'

Han twisted in his seat. The movement aggravated the wound between his ribs, causing him to gasp involuntarily.

'Seems like more than a flesh wound,' Brother Hua said, snickering. 'I guess my men weren't as useless as I thought.'

'You double-crossed me,' Han spat. 'Anyone who betrays me has to pay the price.'

'Feeling all superior now, are we? I'm sure you could teach me a thing or two about botched double-crosses. You murdered Mayor Deng and that's more than enough reason for me to kill you. I just haven't got round to it yet.'

'So don't blame me for showing you no mercy. I've plenty of reasons for wanting to kill you too.' Han pressed the icy barrel more firmly against Hua's head.

Hua was undaunted. 'You haven't shot me yet, which means you want to negotiate. So go ahead and tell me your conditions.'

'You call this is a negotiation?' Han sneered. 'You must think I'm an idiot. I haven't shot you yet because I want your death to be as drawn out and painful as possible. I'm going to give you some time to remember your family, to remember the things you treasure. I'll only let you leave this world once you're begging me to let you stay.'

His words stopped Brother Hua cold. 'That's your goal? You've given up trying to run, and now that the police have you surrounded, you just want to make me suffer before I die?'

'That's right,' Han said through his teeth. 'That's what you get for fucking with me.'

Brother Hua grimaced. 'We're not the same at all. I've killed people, but only as a way of solving problems. I've never revelled in it.'

'Too bad. This is my style.' Han sneered again. He was almost giddy.

Brother Hua sighed and fell silent.

They both saw flickers of movement in the mirrors. The police were dispersing the crowd that had gathered around the car.

Han knew he didn't have much time. He extended his index finger along the side of the gun. 'I hope you're finished reminiscing,' he growled.

'And have you?' Brother Hua asked quietly.

Han scowled. 'What do you mean?'

'It seems to me that you've forgotten all about your wife and son. But I haven't. I've been looking out for them these last few days.'

Hua's tone was neutral, even gentle, but Captain Han's blood boiled at his hostage's words. He jabbed the gun barrel into Hua's temple. 'You'd better be lying to me, you son of a bitch.'

Brother Hua's smirk sent shivers down Han's spine.

'Dongdong's a smart kid. It's too bad he isn't old enough to look after himself. I've had a few of my men keeping an eye on him – from a distance, of course.' An audible chill came into Hua's voice. 'But if I die, there won't be anyone to tell them to hold back. I can't guarantee they'll continue to have your son's best interests at heart.'

Han felt a sudden tightening in his chest, as if a fist had struck him directly in the heart. His hand began to tremble. With a deep breath, he swallowed his pain. 'What's your game here?' he said.

'As I told you, I don't enjoy hurting people. Personally speaking, I have no desire for your son to come to harm. But sometimes measures need to be taken in order to achieve the required outcome. Here's my game: I want you to make a choice. It's like flipping a coin, except you're completely responsible for the results.'

All colour drained from Han's face. A moment later, he thumbed the window control. With the window fully open, he yelled out, 'I want to discuss my conditions!'

Outside the vehicle, Pei stepped closer to his disgraced former colleague. 'I'm here. Let's hear what you're thinking, Han.'

'No,' came the answer. 'Lieutenant Yin's the only person I'll talk to. Tell him to get in the car.'

Pei scowled, but before he could think of a response, Lieutenant Yin approached.

'Let me do this, Captain.'

Pei hesitated. Was it a trap? Something about the look in Yin's eyes told him otherwise. Yin and Han had worked closely together for years. They had a connection. But there was something there – a will to fight.

'Go ahead,' he finally said. He patted the younger officer on the shoulder and lowered his voice. 'Be ready to use your firearm. I'm authorising you to use whatever methods are necessary to resolve the situation.'

Lieutenant Yin's face paled as he registered his captain's meaning. 'Yes, sir,' he replied solemnly. He walked to the car, and the ring of officers looked on.

Lieutenant Yin leant in through the open window.

Han nodded towards the passenger seat in front of him. 'Get in,' he said.

The door handle clicked and Yin lowered himself onto the seat. His right arm was bent away from his chest at an odd angle.

Han tutted impatiently. 'Take your gun out, Lieutenant. No need to be coy.'

Yin pressed his lips together. He raised his gun and aimed it at his former superior's head. 'I'm sorry, Captain. Your best option is to put down your weapon and leave the car with me. Don't make things difficult.'

Han glared at him. 'This is your job. What's there to be sorry about? I should be the one apologising. You do what you have to do.'

Yin's mouth froze in surprise.

'I know I must have made things difficult for all of you after my last escape. Today I'll make things easy. Go ahead and shoot me.'

'No,' Yin said. 'I don't want to do that. I just want to bring you in.'

'What's the use of that?' Han said. 'Only by shooting me now can you make up for your mistakes from last time. I'm the one who made you what you are today. Try to show a little respect!'

Yin shook his head. 'Put down the gun. Don't make me do this.'

Brother Hua let out a long, melodramatic sigh. 'Looks like your old buddy's having second thoughts, Han.'

Han huffed angrily through his nose. 'A cop needs to be resolute, Lieutenant Yin. It's the only way you'll ever succeed. If I hadn't—'

His words caught in his throat like a fishbone. He was about to mention the incident at Mount Twin Deer Park all those years ago. If he hadn't been so resolute about covering up his accidental murder of his police partner, Zhou Ming, back then, he wouldn't have been promoted to captain. But if he *had* come clean, Eumenides never would have been able to blackmail him into accidentally killing Mayor Deng.

The seeds of that cursed day had been planted long ago. He shuddered, as if trying to tear himself free of his memories, then leant forward and looked at Lieutenant Yin with pleading eyes.

'When you were my assistant, did I ever fail to follow through after saying I would do something?'

'No.'

'Then listen to me. In a moment, I'm going to count to three. If you don't pull the trigger by then, I'm going to shoot Brother Hua, open this door and run. I'll be shot dead and Hua's men will go after my son.'

'No! You can't do that!'

'As long as you understand...' Han said, glaring one last time at Lieutenant Yin. 'One...'

'No!' Lieutenant Yin roared.

Han ignored him. 'Two...'

A thick blue vein bulged along Lieutenant Yin's jaw. His gun trembled.

'Three.'

A deafening blast filled the car.

Every available officer sprinted towards the vehicle. Pei led the way and immediately pressed himself against the rear right door so he could peer through the open window.

Brother Hua sat up in the driver's seat and used his right sleeve to wipe some of the blood from his face. Lieutenant Yin was sitting next to him, still frozen in his shooter's pose, his face emotionless. His eyes were focused on Han, who lay slumped across the back seat, blood pooling from the wound in his forehead.

'That was his final lesson for you,' Brother Hua said softly.

Several seconds passed before Lieutenant Yin reacted. He turned to Hua, dazed. 'What did you say?'

'You listen to your emotions too much. In this regard, at least, you have a lot to learn from your late mentor.'

Hua stepped out of the car. The air in the garage was smoky, but to him it felt fresh and life-enhancing. He took a deep breath.

6 November, 1:13 a.m.
Interrogation room, criminal police headquarters

'I've already told you everything I'm required to. Can I go now?' Brother Hua asked, glancing at his watch.

Pei sat across from him in silence, fixing the former bodyguard with a razor-sharp stare.

Brother Hua wasn't intimidated. He leant back in his chair and yawned. He may have been physically exhausted, but mentally he seemed more relaxed than ever.

Pei tossed a copy of Hua's testimony down in front of him. He pointed to the dotted line at the bottom. 'Sign here, please.'

Brother Hua smiled. 'I'm not a cultured man. My handwriting's too sloppy. A fingerprint will do just as well.' He opened the inkpad at the corner of the table and pressed his left thumb against it, rolling it against the pad with practised ease. Exhaling calmly, he pressed his thumb over the dotted line, leaving behind a bright red print.

Without another word, Brother Hua got up and walked out of the room. Two bodyguards were waiting for him at the door and they handed him a padded coat. He seemed to come to life as he put it on, full of new confidence; he even seemed taller.

To Pei, Brother Hua suddenly looked quite unlike the loyal bodyguard he'd first met just days earlier, when the investigation had begun. From behind, he was actually indistinguishable from Mayor Deng. And why not? The man had just seized complete control of the Longyu Corporation.

17

A PACT

Lieutenant Yin sprinted into the meeting with the energy of an exploding bomb.

'Vice President Meng's widow just called our switchboard! She said she has a tape that proves Brother Hua was behind the conspiracy to kill her husband and Vice President Lin!'

'Oh?' Pei stirred in his seat. 'Tell her to wait for an officer to come and collect the evidence. On no account is she to leave the house. Notify the nearest police station and have them send someone over. Let's go!'

'Yes, Captain.'

Within minutes, Captain Pei and Ms Mu were in the police SUV with Lieutenant Yin at the wheel. Five minutes into the drive, Yin's mobile phone rang a second time. He kept one hand on the wheel as he answered it.

'The emergency response team from the Eastern Suburbs station are already at the scene,' he said, handing the phone to Pei. 'I'll let you talk to them.'

Pei pressed the phone to his ear. 'This is Captain Pei from the criminal police.'

'Where are you now, Captain Pei?'

344

'We're on our way. We should be there in twenty minutes.'

'Have you sent anyone else over?'

'There's no one else to send,' Pei said. He frowned. 'Why? What's wrong?'

'Mrs Meng tells us that the police have already been to her home. She says they took the tape with them.'

Pei inhaled sharply. 'They weren't our officers – they're fraudsters! You need to track them down immediately!'

Lieutenant Yin leant on the accelerator and the engine roared. Thirteen minutes later they screeched into Jingan Gardens Villas and Vice President Meng's home loomed into view.

Having spoken with the officers outside the house, they were even more confused. The officers had arrested the two men who'd posed as policemen, but, after some prodding, the imposters claimed that someone else had stolen the tape from them immediately afterwards.

'I need to see the security footage,' Pei said.

The housing development's security office was lit with blinding fluorescent bulbs. The smell of damp, day-old tea leaves filled the room. As Pei watched the footage, hope fluttered in his chest when he saw that the two fraudsters had been caught on camera.

At 9:35 a.m., two people wearing police uniforms stepped out of a white Volkswagen parked about thirty metres from Vice President Meng's home. They walked over to the house and knocked. Mrs Meng opened the door and after a brief conversation allowed them inside. At 9:40 a.m. the men left in a hurry. One of them was hastily stuffing something into his pocket. As they walked towards their car, they were followed by a third male figure.

'Is that him?' Lieutenant Yin muttered. Although the man's hat and clothing obscured his features, his gait was hauntingly familiar.

In the footage, the third man swiftly knocked out the other two. He searched their pockets, extracted a single item and strode off.

'Should we go after him?' one of the officers asked Pei.

'We can forget about retrieving the tape,' Pei replied glumly. 'We'll have more luck talking to Mrs Meng. Maybe she made a copy.'

His instincts, however, told him that she almost certainly wouldn't have had the presence of mind to make a backup. His thoughts had anyway already turned to other matters. Eumenides must have known that his actions would be caught on camera. So why had he intentionally provoked both Brother Hua and the police?

11 a.m.
Mount Tianzi Villas

Mayor Deng's family home was located in the middle of Chengdu's most luxurious private housing development. The complex had four swimming pools and twelve tennis courts. On the third floor of the house, the spirit of its deceased owner lingered still. A woman dressed in plain clothing was sitting on the sofa with a young boy next to her. The two of them were staring at the man on the end of the sofa in great confusion.

Brother Hua was perched on the edge of his seat and sitting up very straight. No matter how much power and prestige he gained, he would always remember his place within the household. He owed Mayor Deng that much.

'You look tired. Have you been getting enough sleep?'

Mrs Deng said. She sounded genuinely concerned, as though addressing a beloved family member.

'I've been busy, Mrs Deng. But it's all done now, finally,' Hua replied respectfully. Using both hands, he politely set down several printed documents on the coffee table in front of her.

'What are these?' she asked, flipping through the papers.

'Documents for the transfer of share ownership. I've purchased all of Vice President Lin's and Vice President Meng's shares. All of the assets of the Longyu Corporation are now in the names of you and your son.'

Mrs Deng smiled graciously, but her forehead remained furrowed. 'I have no idea how to run a business, much less one as large as my husband's. And Deng Jian is so young. These assets could be put to much better use elsewhere.'

'There's no need for you to worry about that. I'll hire the very best people to look after the company's day-to-day operations. All you have to do is make sure your son pays attention in school. Once he's completed his education, he'll be ready to take his place at Longyu.' Seeing that she still looked concerned, he added, 'And don't worry. I'll take care of those people. As long as I have breath in my body, the Longyu Corporation will always be run by a Deng!'

Mrs Deng inhaled deeply, then turned and patted her son on the shoulder. 'You'd better go upstairs and start studying,' she said gently. 'I'm going to talk to Brother Hua for a few more minutes. I'll be up soon.'

The boy nodded and obediently headed off. Brother Hua stood up and bowed slightly as he watched him leave.

'Please sit down,' Mrs Deng said. 'You're family. There's no need for such formalities.'

'Of course,' Hua replied, but he only sat down again once the boy had left his sight.

Mrs Deng leafed through the documents again, this time reading them line by line. Several minutes later, she set the stack of papers back down on the table and looked at Brother Hua for a moment.

'Tell me the truth. How did Vice President Lin and Vice President Meng die?'

Hua stared at his feet in silence. He had no right to lie to his employer. An appropriate explanation was necessary. Finally, he looked up at her. His voice was low and solemn. 'They wanted to take something that didn't belong to them. They died for that reason.'

She sighed. 'There are probably some questions I'm safer off not asking. Mayor Deng had a saying: "It's better for a sheep not to know the ways of the wolf." I put my trust in him, and I didn't need to know any more. But over time I've learnt that every action has its consequences…'

Her voice cracked. She turned and stared at a portrait of Mayor Deng on the mantelpiece. Tears welled in her eyes.

'Mayor Deng once held my life in his hands,' Brother Hua said with quiet sincerity. 'For his family, I'm willing to live with the consequences, whatever they may be.'

As she looked into his eyes, he realised that she understood. She wiped her tears away and said, 'Give me your hand.'

Brother Hua stiffened but then yielded and extended his right hand.

She removed the Buddhist prayer beads she wore around her wrist and gently slid the bracelet over Hua's hand until it came to rest on his own wrist.

'Remember what I said.'

7 November, 1:37 a.m.
Brother Hua's personal suite

Brother Hua was taking a shower in his en-suite bathroom. He needed to wash the grime from his body and his soul. But though the water rinsed the dirt from his skin, it would not wash away the memories that continued to flood his mind.

When Mayor Deng's widow had given him those prayer beads, he'd completely understood her pain and desperation. But it could not change the resolve in his heart. In this business, he told himself, one seldom acted of one's own volition.

As the water streamed, his thoughts whirred.

As soon as Lin and Meng's plan to embezzle the Longyu Corporation's assets had come to his attention, Brother Hua knew there was no looking back. The two vice presidents had already begun plotting their fatal blow against the company. Measures had to be taken.

But Hua had been stunned to learn that Meng also had his own selfish interests in mind. He'd approached Hua one morning and talked disparagingly about Lin, whom he believed was overstepping his authority. Meng hinted very clearly that he wished to work with Hua in order to get rid of his rival. 'If only something were to happen to him...' he said.

Hua agreed and had gone on to share his own plan with Meng. He would prepare two replicas of Eumenides' infamous death notices – one for Vice President Lin and one for Vice President Meng. It would give them the perfect excuse to confine the two men within Mayor Deng's former office. They would put on a show for the security cameras, and with the help of some props, Meng could pretend to be Eumenides and kill Lin.

Meng was very interested in Hua's plan. But there were

349

details that he was unsure about. 'I'm not young any more. If Lin fights back, I might not be able to kill him.'

'I'll make sure that you're both given sleeping medication. Yours will be a placebo, of course. By the time you get out of bed, Lin will be sleeping like a dead man. And better still, you won't need to worry about the police questioning you – you can just say, "I was asleep."'

'But if both Lin and I receive death notices and only Lin is found dead, how will we explain that?'

'You've already been to jail. You reformed. Eumenides shouldn't have put your name on the notice to begin with. Before you go back to bed, put those things we talked about next to you. That way, when Eumenides sees them, he'll decide to spare you. At least, that's what everyone will assume.'

Brother Hua had his doubts about Vice President Meng before that fateful night. Namely, whether he was planning to double-cross him. As a safeguard, he installed listening devices inside Meng's villa and assigned two subordinates to keep watch outside. If anything happened, they'd be able to take appropriate action before the police arrived.

Something did happen, but much later than Hua had expected. Yesterday morning, Vice President Meng's widow received a special delivery. Inside was a tape, which held a recording of the incriminating conversation between Brother Hua and Vice President Meng.

When Hua heard about that, he knew that Han Hao was behind it. Han must have set another plan of his own in motion, so that if he died as a result of Hua's scheme at the stadium, this evidence would arrive at Vice President Meng's home the next day.

That tape had then been stolen. Hua had an idea as to the identity of the thief, but he couldn't work out what his motive was. Regardless, knowing that the tape was out there was like sleeping on pins and needles.

Brother Hua emerged from his bathroom fifteen minutes later, put on a dressing gown and decided to make himself a mug of tea in the living room. As he stepped out of the bedroom, his muscles tensed. Someone was sitting on his couch.

The figure turned and looked at him. 'Tea's ready. Sit down and have a cup.'

'What are you doing here?' Hua shrank back instinctively.

The man smiled. 'Haven't you been looking for me?'

Hua gasped. 'It's you!'

Even when seated, the man looked tall, with broad shoulders and a sturdy frame. Brother Hua was very familiar with his physique, having studied it over countless hours of stolen security footage while preparing Vice President Meng's styrofoam disguise. Now he was finally seeing the man in the flesh.

His eyes blazed. He raised his fists ready to fight. 'I must be an idiot not to have—'

'There's no need to get all worked up,' the man interrupted. He sipped placidly from a mug of steaming tea.

Hua took several long breaths to steady his nerves. He lowered his fists. As his hammering heartbeat gradually slowed, he stepped into the living room and took a seat on the chair opposite the couch. The two men studied one another.

'Why are you here?'

'I want to make a deal.'

'A deal?' Brother Hua clenched his jaw. 'How about this deal – I'll kill you right here in this room.'

'I thought death threats were my domain,' the man said, offering a friendly smile. He pulled an object from his pocket and set it on the table. 'This is my bargaining chip.'

Hua's pupils contracted as he gazed at the cassette tape. 'Name your price,' he growled.

'I want you to look after someone for me,' the man said. He turned his hand over to reveal a photograph resting in his palm. It was of a beautiful, delicate young woman.

Hua thought she looked familiar, but it took him a moment to place the face. He'd seen her at the restaurant when he'd been investigating Sheng's death.

'Why do you want me to look after her?'

'Because you're a bodyguard by trade. And because I believe that no other bodyguard in the world is more dedicated to his work than you.'

Brother Hua was, to say the least, conflicted. On the one hand he hated this man with every fibre of his being. On the other hand he couldn't argue with a compliment like that. He spread his lips in a weary smile. 'You can't look after her yourself?'

'I've lost control of my fate.' The man set the photo on the table and his gaze lingered on it for another moment. His voice grew distant. 'I have no choice but to provoke a fearsome foe and I can't guarantee what the outcome will be. For that reason I need to make sure that proper arrangements are in place.'

Brother Hua nodded cautiously. He reached out and picked up the photograph. 'How exactly do you want me to take care of her?'

'She's blind. I want you to send her to America for an operation. That won't be too difficult for you, will it?'

'It's a reasonable demand, considering your bargaining chip,' Hua said as he picked up the cassette. 'Is there a copy of this tape?'

The man chuckled. 'All transactions should be based on trust, shouldn't they?'

After a moment, Brother Hua nodded decisively. 'It's a deal.'

'Thank you.'

'We're even now,' Hua said with finality.

'I know.' The man was no longer smiling. 'The next time we meet, only one of us will walk away.'

'I'm pleased to hear that.' Hua lifted the mug to take a sip of tea. 'Out of interest, who is this foe you mentioned?'

'Why do you ask?'

'You owe me a life. I don't want you to die too early.'

The man calmly licked his lips. He appeared to be mentally preparing himself to say the name. After what felt like minutes, he finally spoke it.

'Captain Ding Ke.'

18

PORTRAIT OF A SUSPECT

7:36 a.m.
Conference room, criminal police headquarters

The April 18th Task Force was once again assembled around the conference table. But this time the fifth seat was occupied not by SPU Captain Liu but by Huang Jieyuan, former officer of the Chengdu criminal police and current owner of the Black Magic Bar.

'My apologies for calling you all here so early,' Captain Pei said by way of a polite introduction before quickly switching to a sterner tone, 'but this is extremely urgent. Lieutenant Yin, you can begin.'

Lieutenant Yin turned on the projector next to him. Familiar-looking lines of text gradually took form on the screen.

Death Notice
THE ACCUSED: The Bagman
CRIME: Homicide
DATE OF PUNISHMENT: 7 November
EXECUTIONER: Eumenides

'This notice appeared in the mailbox of the reception office just one hour ago,' he explained. 'Captain Pei immediately contacted me and told me to put this meeting together so that we can discuss our strategy.'

'That's today's date,' TSO Zeng said. 'Did Eumenides forget to set his alarm yesterday?'

Ms Mu scowled. 'Given that the Bagman Killer was never found, what exactly does Eumenides expect us to do about this?'

'That's the first question we need to answer. And we have less than seventeen hours to do so.'

'So we have seventeen hours – or not even that – to solve a cold case from a decade ago, find the Bagman Killer and come up with a plan to stop Eumenides.' TSO Zeng forced a tired grin. 'Well, this task force has had a good run, huh?'

'Eumenides has issued his challenge. We have no choice but to put every effort into meeting it,' Pei said.

'Captain Pei is right,' Yin said. 'If Eumenides can find the Bagman, what's stopping us from finding him too? We have at least as much information as he has, don't we?'

'Eumenides...' Huang said, looking down and shaking his head. 'Are you really so sure he'll be able to find the Bagman?'

Pei understood why Huang was dubious. He decided to be as diplomatic as possible. 'Eumenides has followed through with every one of his death notices. Each of you in this room knows that. Eumenides isn't one to make idle threats.'

Huang scanned the faces around the table. Everyone nodded in quiet agreement. He slumped back in his chair.

'That bastard,' Zeng said, rubbing his forehead. 'I've been wondering why he's been silent for the last few days. And now we find out that he's been busy investigating the Bagman Killing. But why's he interested in that old case all of a sudden? Is he trying to distract us or is he trying to show off and make the police look useless?'

'Eumenides is only interested in one thing right now,'

Ms Mu said, 'and that's finding out where he came from. If he's searching for the Bagman Killer, that must have something to do with learning the truth about his father's death. I think there can only one be reason – he wants to find Captain Ding Ke.'

Pei cleared his throat. 'We have one task. We need to find the Bagman Killer as soon as possible. I've made copies of the files for the January 12th Bagman Killing investigation, one for each of you. You have thirty minutes to read through these documents, after which we'll continue our discussion.'

A tense hush fell over the room, punctuated only by the rustling of paper on paper.

Thirty minutes later

'Huang, since you're the one who's most familiar with this case, I'd like you to speak first,' Captain Pei said.

The former police lieutenant nodded. Taking a deep breath, he organised his thoughts. As the rest of the team listened, he began to tell them about the investigations conducted by his original January 12th Task Force, its failures, his thwarted attempts at contacting Captain Ding Ke and his motivation for establishing the Black Magic Bar as bait for the killer.

'So our killer is the kind of guy who likes to pour himself a glass of red wine and chill out to some Celtic Frost?' TSO Zeng asked, waggling his eyebrows.

Ms Mu, who was sitting next to Zeng, shot him a sharp look. His grin faded.

'And in all these years,' Zeng said, 'you still haven't found a single match for the Bagman Killer's profile?'

Huang exhaled, the breath whooshing out of him like the air from a deflating balloon. 'Not one. For a start, the way the murder was carried out – chopping the body into a hundred pieces – isn't exactly something that the average person is capable of. That's why I've included a secret knife-skills test inside my bar, to narrow down the pool of suspects. Only a few people have successfully completed that test, and those who did…' Huang's voice trailed off and he shrugged. 'They were either too young, weren't living in Chengdu at the time, or weren't—'

'Wait a second,' Zeng interrupted. 'There's something fishy here. Why are you looking for a knife expert? Couldn't they have just used a machine to get cuts that precise?'

'Using a meat slicer wouldn't fit the killer's psychological profile,' Ms Mu said. 'All the evidence suggests that he savours killing. He wouldn't have used a machine – he'd definitely want to cut up the body by hand.'

Zeng slapped the table. 'Come on! Isn't it enough to chop up a body? What difference would it make if he did it by hand or machine?'

'Actually, we don't need to use psychological data to eliminate the possibility of a meat slicer,' Huang said. 'If the killer had used a machine, all the pieces would have been of equal size. That's not what we found. Some are wafer-thin and others are several centimetres thick. It's obvious just from looking at them that they were cut by hand.'

'Is that so?' Zeng muttered. He flipped through the documents until he came to a photograph showing a pile of chunks of human flesh. He held it up close until his nose was nearly touching it. Ms Mu, who was watching him intently, suddenly looked away.

'I guess you're right,' he said, setting the photo back on top of the pile. 'But what if he used a machine to cut up part of the body and then cut the rest by hand? If he mixed the pieces together, they'd appear to be different sizes.'

Huang's heavy eyebrows dipped low. 'But why would he do that? Everything about this case indicates that the killer was focused. If he wanted to be efficient, he'd use a machine to cut up the body. If he wanted to savour the process, he'd cut it by hand. Combining the two methods just doesn't make sense.'

'Are you sure about that?' Pei asked, scrutinising his own copy of the photograph. 'If you look closely, you'll see that only a small portion of the flesh is thinly sliced. The rest is in thick chunks. They look machine-cut to me.'

'You're right that most of the chunks are thick.' Unlike the other members of the task force, Huang did not need to look at the pictures. The details came to his mind readily enough. 'But I think you're underestimating our killer here. Hell, even my own mother could cut pieces of pork that size.'

'The size of those smaller pieces could have been intentional, to make the police think that the killer was skilled with a knife, thus falsely skewing our profile of the suspect,' Pei said. 'We can't eliminate the possibility that after an initial venting of his suppressed urges, the killer used a meat slicer on the rest of the body in order to mislead the police.'

Huang stayed silent for nearly half a minute. Finally he asked the question that had been dogging him for years. 'Could I have been wrong all along?'

'I can't say for certain. But for the time being we need to expand our profile of the suspect. We need to look at people other than just doctors, butchers, chefs or those with good knife skills.' Pei paused and glanced at the others around the table. 'Does anyone have any suggestions regarding the killer's profile?'

Ms Mu, who'd stayed quiet while the gruesome details were being discussed, pondered this for a moment before responding. 'I agree with Huang's decision to use underground metal music to narrow his search for the suspect. Non-mainstream music could very well be the thing that tied the killer to the victim. And given the genre's preoccupation with death and violence, what could be more fitting?

'By combining this observation with the accounts we have of the victim, we can sketch a rough portrait of the victim before she was killed. She was probably a sensitive girl with a mind more developed than those of her peers. That would have put her at odds with her fellow students. She'd have felt that she had little, if anything, in common with them. So her social life would have happened off campus, which was how she came into contact with the killer.'

'Hold on, Ms Mu.' Zeng interrupted again. 'Are you sure you're not reading a bit too much into this? What if this twisted killer met the victim by chance? In which case, this theory about a "heavy metal bond" between them is not simply wild speculation but an impediment to our investigation.'

'They couldn't have met by chance. The precise, meticulous way in which the killer dissected the victim's body could only have been done in a confined, private space. A shy, introverted girl like the victim wouldn't go into that kind of place with a stranger. Before the murder occurred, the killer must have got into the girl's head and somehow gained her trust.'

'I agree,' Pei said. 'And if you're right, it means that the killer had a home equipped with everything he used to carry out the murder. Lieutenant Yin, write that down.'

Lieutenant Yin scrawled a couple of lines onto his notepad:

Bagman Profile:
1. Lived alone in an isolated place. Home equipped with everything he needed to dissect the body.

'You can go on, Ms Mu,' Captain Pei said.

Ms Mu looked at the other team members. 'We can try analysing the killer by imagining ourselves as the victim. Like I said earlier, she was emotionally sensitive and more mature than other young women her age. It would have been difficult for her to find someone to confide in. I believe that the killer would need to have been at least five years older than her to meet with her acceptance.'

'She was just shy of twenty when she was murdered. So the killer would have been at least twenty-five. Should I write that down?' Lieutenant Yin asked.

'In that case, write "twenty-eight". I was talking about psychological maturity. Generally speaking, women in their twenties and thirties tend to be around three years ahead of their male peers in that regard. Taking that into account, the killer would have been at least eight years older than the victim.'

'You don't think it's possible the killer was female?' Zeng asked. 'Equal opportunities extend to murderers too.'

'But with a female victim? A mutilated corpse? Nearly every murder of that sort that we know of was done by a man. It's not sexist to presume that the killer was male. It's Occam's razor,' Ms Mu said.

'Who's shaving what now?' Zeng asked, bewildered.

'Occam's razor,' Lieutenant Yin said. 'In other words, you shouldn't make things any more complicated than necessary when the simplest explanation is most likely to be true.' He turned his attention to his notepad, where he jotted down another detail.

2. *Male, at least 28 at the time of the murder.*

'The victim was a university student,' Ms Mu continued. 'Sensitive, introverted and with quite a high opinion of herself. For someone to get close to her and gain her trust, he would have to impress her with his knowledge and character, among other things. That's why I recommend that we narrow down the profile of this killer even further: he was good-looking, well educated and of relatively high social standing.'

'Are you sure about that?' Yin asked, setting down his pen. 'The victim was at a vocational university. Her grades were unremarkable. And to be quite blunt, she seems average-looking to me. Why would she have such inflated expectations for someone else?'

Ms Mu smiled sympathetically. 'People like her tend to hold others to higher standards than they expect of themselves. She may have been emotionally mature, but she was average in most other respects. People like that tend to have an inferiority complex that's linked to their vanity. So she would have looked down on the people around her who were otherwise her equals and focused instead on mixing with those of a higher standing – her way of raising her own status and compensating for her sense of inferiority. By contrast, someone who's already in a socially superior position can be pretty indifferent to the things around them, because they don't need to prove themselves.'

Yin considered this argument and added a third point to his notes.

3. *Educated, high social status, attractive.*

'Anything else?' he asked.

'That's all I can think of from the victim's perspective,' Ms Mu said. 'Next we should look at things from the killer's perspective. As I already mentioned, the killer would have been superior to the victim in many regards. But given that he was willing to associate with the victim, I believe he himself suffered from what's known as a hidden inferiority complex.'

'Meaning?' Pei asked.

'Some people with superior external conditions actually harbour feelings of inferiority that they find hard to express to others. In psychology this is known as a hidden inferiority complex. For example, if you observe the people around you, you'll notice some individuals whose personal strengths far surpass the humble environment they find themselves in. By "environment" I'm referring to things such as their spouses, careers or social circles. Most people assume that these individuals lack goals or ambition, but they're often victims of a hidden inferiority complex. They feel flawed, but the people around them don't see their flaws. The way that other people treat them makes them afraid to expose their flaws. So they conceal them. And they feel compelled to operate at a lower level, in environments that are beneath their potential. It's how they feel safe.'

'The killer was just looking for someone to murder, not someone to make friends with,' Huang said, making a fist.

'It doesn't matter whether the killer wanted to get close to the victim. You can't change someone's instincts,' Ms Mu said. 'Murders like this are often sexually motivated. Even if the killer did intend to harm his victim, he would have chosen a woman who excited him sexually. Hurting and killing her would give him a much bigger thrill. But he chose someone who appeared average to most people, which means he lacked self-confidence, do you see? He thought he could only control a girl from much lower down the social scale. Otherwise he'd feel insecure.'

This last point piqued Pei's interest. 'What kind of factors might cause these feelings of inferiority?'

'He might have grown up in a broken home or he may have been abused by a family member during his childhood. Those factors are pertinent in up to 90 per cent of people with hidden inferiority complexes.'

Huang rubbed his temples and let out an exasperated sigh. 'Ms Mu, I appreciate your attempt to reduce all of our questions to percentages and textbook definitions, but—'

'Why haven't you considered the possibility that the Bagman Killer was just, you know, crazy?' Zeng asked.

Ms Mu took a deep breath. She had encountered scepticism like this before. 'Psychology is the science of analysing a person's future, past and present based on their history. It's evolved out of countless investigations which prove the reliability of these sorts of discussions. I'll say it as clearly as I can: there's a 95 per cent chance that the Bagman Killer had a traumatic childhood.'

'How much research has really been done on killers like the Bagman?' Zeng asked dismissively.

'As a matter of fact, I can think of one right off the top off my head,' Ms Mu answered quickly. 'The American FBI recorded a very similar case in the state of Ohio in 1989. The victim was a woman cut up into nearly a hundred pieces. The ensuing investigation confirmed that the killer had been sexually abused by his father as a boy and that this abuse had caused him to be sexually impotent. In his mind, he could only achieve sexual stimulation by killing a woman and cutting her up.'

'Geez, who signed us up for the psych seminar?' Zeng mumbled under his breath.

Lieutenant Yin added another point to the growing list on his notepad.

4. Suffers from a 'hidden inferiority complex'. Traumatic childhood, frustrated sexuality in adulthood.

Pei glanced at Yin's notes and passed the pad to Ms Mu. 'Have a look,' he said. 'Is this an accurate summary or is there anything we should change or add?'

Ms Mu pointed to the second item on the list. 'We can narrow the age down a little further. The killer would have been around thirty.'

'What makes you say that?'

'Another statistic. Research shows that most killers with these sorts of mental illnesses commit their first act of homicide at the age of thirty. They may begin by torturing animals at a younger age then work their way up. It's usually when they're around thirty that they reach the point when their urge to kill can only be sated with a human victim.'

Pei handed the notepad back to Lieutenant Yin. 'We'll amend the age then. And we'll add a fifth detail: he's a registered resident of Chengdu.'

'Why?' Huang asked in surprise. 'We specifically focused our investigation on people who weren't local residents.'

'If a thirty-year-old came to Chengdu, he'd most likely have to rent an apartment. You must have searched the records of rented apartments as part of your investigation, right? The fact that you didn't find any traces of this person shows that he's a local who's been able to stay hidden.'

A flicker of movement caught Pei's eye. Ms Mu was gently shaking her head. 'You object, Ms Mu?'

'There's a problem with the logic of that assumption. If the killer is local, it's possible he'd have a better chance of evading the police. But on the other hand his neighbours, family or acquaintances would likely have been aware of his previous criminal record.'

'How can you be sure that he had a criminal record?'

'Psychological disorders don't just take hold overnight. Before he chopped up Feng Chunling, the Bagman Killer would have satisfied his criminal urges in a variety of more minor ways – with violence, theft or, as I mentioned, by harming small animals. The FBI studies can testify to all that. The killer would have appeared warm and kind to most people, but he would have found it much harder to conceal his abnormal behaviour from those closer to him. So if he is from Chengdu, the police would have come across reports of that sort of behaviour during their extensive investigations.'

Pei grimaced. 'On second thoughts,' he said to Lieutenant Yin, 'leave that last part out for the time being.'

'Actually, what worries me more,' Ms Mu said, her eyes narrowing, 'is that the killer might have left Chengdu after the murder and never come back.'

'What makes you think he might have done that?'

'Chiefly because it's been ten years since the murder and we've not seen a second one like it.'

'That's right,' Pei said. 'From what you've said, the Bagman exhibits all the signs of a serial killer. But he's only killed once.'

'Exactly. Which makes me suspect that he's no longer in Chengdu and hasn't been here for quite some time.'

Something about this explanation didn't quite ring true to Pei. 'But then he'd have committed a similar murder somewhere else – and news of a crime that appalling would definitely have made it back to the Chengdu police. As far as I know, nothing like that has happened anywhere over the past decade. How do you explain that?'

'Are you sure you would have heard about it?' Ms Mu asked sceptically. 'China's a big place.'

Before Pei could respond, TSO Zeng spoke up. 'I don't know about the captain, but I'm positive. I help sift through and reorganise the country's criminal files every single year when we perform our annual systems update. The Bagman case is the only murder of its kind that's happened in all of China over the last decade.'

Ms Mu shut her eyes and tapped her temples, like someone trying to fix a faulty appliance by hitting it. 'I don't understand it,' she said, her features locked in a deep scowl.

'How likely is it that this killer would have become addicted to murder? What if one was enough?' Lieutenant Yin asked.

Ms Mu looked up. 'It's almost a certainty,' she said. 'This is a psychological disorder we're talking about. Murder is like a drug to these people. They can't get that kind of thrill from anything else. The urge sets in deeper with each life they take, like a vicious circle.'

'So where is he then? Dead? Overseas? In jail for a different crime?' TSO Zeng shrugged. 'In which case, what's the point of this discussion?'

Pei felt as if Zeng had just taken a swing at him. 'He hasn't gone anywhere,' the captain said angrily. 'He's here in Chengdu! We know that because Eumenides has already tracked him down.'

The others around the table glanced wordlessly at one another. Pei noted several sceptical looks.

'One of us has to be wrong. Either us or Eumenides,' Huang said. He frowned and stared down at his files, as if the answer was hidden somewhere on the paper.

'Let's keep going,' Pei ordered. 'Huang, the victim's skeleton was never found, right?'

Huang looked at the captain, surprised at the question. 'Never,' he said glumly.

'How did you explain that at the time?'

'We concluded that he'd either hidden the body extremely well or he'd kept it inside his own home.' Huang avoided Pei's gaze and began leafing through his copies of the files.

Ms Mu perked up at the mention of the latter hypothesis.

'It's unlikely that he kept the body at home. While it's true that many psychopathic killers are in the habit of preserving cadavers, they typically choose to keep a symbolic part of the body, like the head, an internal organ or even the genitalia. There's no documented case of a killer keeping only the skeleton and not the skull or any other parts. Holding onto a body part of that size would be more than just logistically inconvenient for the killer – it wouldn't have any special significance either.'

Huang flapped his hands despairingly. 'My team searched the whole city top to bottom. We practically dug up all of Chengdu. I have no idea where he could have hidden the rest of the body.'

'What if he hid it inside his home – under the floorboards, say?' Zeng asked, shifting anxiously in his seat. 'It isn't exactly easy to move a corpse. He could have hidden it at the murder scene – wouldn't be the first time a killer has made that choice.'

Pei looked at him. 'Two things about that theory don't make sense. First, burying a body inside your home would be extremely risky in a metropolis like Chengdu. People would hear you. Sure, they might assume you were refurbishing, but if anyone got suspicious, you'd have nowhere to run. The body would be indisputable evidence.'

Lieutenant Yin grunted in agreement. 'Last year we arrested a man who used bricks and cement to build a wall around his wife's body out on the balcony of their home. It was the most idiotic way to hide a body I've ever heard of. If our killer was that stupid, he wouldn't have made it ten days, let alone ten years.'

'And secondly,' Pei continued, 'if he did manage to hide the body inside his home, why did he dispose of the victim's head, organs, clothing and flesh?'

'He was showing off, wasn't he? It was a challenge to the authorities, just like what Eumenides does,' Zeng insisted.

'If that was his intention,' Ms Mu said, 'he wouldn't have stopped after the first murder. I can say that with 100 per cent certainty.'

Pei rubbed the stubble on his chin. 'If he was challenging the police, wouldn't a single bag of chopped-up flesh be enough? Why did he send out three bags, plus the suitcase with the victim's skull and organs? And her clothes as well. What would be the point of going through all that if he never intended to do it again?'

Zeng propped his elbows on the table and rested his head in his hands. 'Knowing that won't do jack squat for us if we can't figure out where he hid the body,' he muttered.

'He hid it in a very particular place,' Pei mused. 'And what made that place so particular was that it had room for the victim's torso but not her head, organs, flesh or clothing. That's why the killer had to get rid of them.'

Ms Mu's mouth widened in realisation. 'We've been thinking of him as a serial killer this whole time. But what if that was merely what he wanted us to think?'

A hint of a smile came to Pei's lips. He nodded encouragingly at Ms Mu.

After giving herself a moment to collect her thoughts, the psychologist continued. 'The killer got rid of the victim's skull and clothing, but he made no effort to conceal her identity. That means he wasn't worried about the police investigating the victim's background or social connections. From this we can conclude that the killer and the victim met by chance. No one else knew about it.'

'Given the victim's personality,' Pei added eagerly, 'anyone who wanted to get close to her within a short period of time would have to have been pretty charismatic. Which is why I agree with the rest of Ms Mu's deductions about the killer's age, personality type and so forth.'

'Since we're certain that the killer and his victim met by chance, we can focus on two possible theories,' Ms Mu said. 'The first of these is that the killer was a psychopath and his murder of Feng Chunling was premeditated. The Bagman's goal in finding Feng was to kill her and to enjoy the process of killing her. Since it was premeditated, he prepared for each stage, including how to lure the victim to his home, how to kill her and how to dispose of the body. His plan was extremely thorough and he executed it perfectly, which is why we've failed to find him for the past ten years.

'However, there are several things about this hypothesis that are impossible to explain. For instance, why didn't he continue killing? And why did he dispose of the victim's skull, organs, flesh and clothing in different places? Which leads us to the other possibility – that the killer never intended to murder the victim at all. He simply wanted to befriend her. But once she'd got to his home, something unexpected happened, and it was this that made him kill her.'

'Even if he didn't plan to kill her, it's pretty hard to "accidentally" murder and dismember someone who comes to your home,' Zeng said in disbelief. 'He's still a psycho, regardless of what his intentions might have been.'

Lieutenant Yin turned to Ms Mu. 'So was it because of some kind of abuse he suffered when he was younger?'

'I don't think that's very likely. About a year ago I participated in a study focusing on the psychological traits of rapists as well as victims of rape. Neither the killer nor the victim in this case fits those profiles. The circumstances of this case suggest that the male killer's external conditions surpassed those of the female victim. That the victim felt able to accompany the killer home indicates that she identified with the killer a great deal. Of course we can't eliminate the possibility that the two misunderstood one another's intentions. The killer may even have faced strong resistance from the victim. Often a man stops in that situation because in his view the woman is not worth the effort. And as someone who saw himself as superior to the woman in nearly all regards, he wouldn't have wanted to stoop to the level of a violent rapist.'

'The girl's undergarments were completely intact when they were discovered,' Huang pointed out. 'Which suggests she was not violently raped.'

'So what was the killer's motive for suddenly killing her?' Lieutenant Yin asked, clicking the top of his retractable pen. 'He didn't have a grudge against her and he certainly wasn't after her money. After all, you said that he was basically rich.'

'That's the key. Since the killer surpassed the victim in terms of looks and social status, we don't need to figure out what he wanted from her. I believe that if the murder was sudden and unplanned, it's likely the victim did something to enrage him.'

'Any thoughts as to what that might have been?' Pei asked, his curiosity growing.

'The girl was sensitive and introverted, but she also suffered from an inferiority complex. People like that aren't exactly skilled when it comes to social interactions. It's easy for them to say something that unintentionally hurts someone else.'

'And that's how you think she provoked the killer?'

Ms Mu answered with another question. 'What sort of comments do people find most hurtful?'

Pei pursed his lips. Her question had caught him off guard.

'That reminds me of something. TSO Zeng,' Ms Mu said, turning to the computer expert, her tone suddenly stern. 'I've been reporting on your recent performance to the captain over the last two weeks.'

'That's, um, very thoughtful of you,' Zeng said, the confusion clear on his face.

Ms Mu's expression hardened. 'Firstly, I think you greatly overestimate your skills as a computer expert. Secondly, and more importantly, Captain Pei and I have serious questions about the strategies you've implemented in our investigation so far. I'm going to recommend you be dismissed from the task force.'

Zeng's jaw dropped. He looked at Pei with pleading eyes.

To the surprise of both Pei and Zeng, Lieutenant Yin slowly began to grin. A muffled chuckle escaped his lips. 'Of course,' he said. 'Yes, that would do it.'

'What?' Zeng slammed his hands against the table. 'What the hell's going on?'

Ms Mu smiled apologetically at him and let out a small laugh. 'Forgive me! It was an experiment. I just wanted to see how you'd respond when I said those things – to prove my point about the killer's reaction.'

'Oh,' Zeng said, his cheeks flushing.

'How did you feel when I said that you overestimated your computer skills?'

'Not angry, that's for sure. You don't know the first thing about computers, so why should I listen to you?'

'What about when I criticised your investigative abilities?'

'That's different,' Zeng said. 'You and Captain Pei know far more about investigating a case than I ever will. But you'd never attack someone like that. That's why I couldn't believe what I was hearing.'

'Again, it was just an experiment. Please don't take it to heart.' Ms Mu squeezed his shoulder sympathetically and Zeng grinned like a child who'd just been given an extra sweet.

'Could you explain the point of this "experiment" to everyone else?' Pei said impatiently.

'It's only natural to get angry when someone attacks your vulnerable points or scratches you where you're most sensitive. These are known as "psychological wounds" and, just like physical wounds, when they're prodded, intense pain follows.'

'You mean that the girl did or said something to trigger the killer's psychological wound?'

'Exactly. A wound right at the heart of his hidden inferiority complex. It could have been this wound that caused the killer to seek out someone he could feel superior to. But somehow she still managed to hit the spot that set him off. That's my hypothesis.'

'So what exactly might this wound be?' Pei asked, squinting at her. This was *it*, he sensed – the detail that would allow them to pinpoint the killer.

Ms Mu, however, just shrugged. 'Hard to say. Perhaps some lingering childhood trauma or memories of a dysfunctional family. Or maybe it's a physical flaw or defect. Either way, it's something he doesn't want other people to see. And given that he's actively tried to hide it from the world, it would be extremely difficult to identify and search for. Impossible, even.'

Pei responded with a resigned nod. He didn't doubt the accuracy of her analysis.

'Assuming the killer wasn't totally psychotic and that the victim did trigger him by making some kind of personal jibe,' TSO Zeng said, eager to prove himself in the discussion, 'who here can explain why this individual mutilated the girl's body?'

'To answer that, we need to put ourselves in the killer's shoes,' Pei said. 'As he stood inside his home staring at the body of the girl he had just killed, what was the most pressing issue on his mind?'

'Getting rid of the body, of course,' Huang answered immediately.

'And what clues did he need to conceal while disposing of the body?' Pei asked.

Huang muttered to himself for a moment. Tapping his knuckles against the table, he said, 'Besides leaving trace evidence? More than anything else, he'd need to prevent the police from pinpointing his location.'

'Now I understand,' Ms Mu said. 'If the killer met the victim by chance, it wouldn't matter to him that the police could identify her. But the fact that the murder took place inside his own home was definitely something to worry about. When he disposed of the body, his priority would have been to prevent the police from discovering where the murder happened.'

'Obviously, the safest thing would be to dispose of it as far away from his home as possible,' Pei said, nodding. 'But the killer was on his own and he hadn't prepared for that. How was he able to get rid of an adult body a sufficient distance from his house?'

'First he'd need to find something to put the body in,' Ms Mu said. 'A large suitcase or a cardboard box, for example. Then he'd have to use some kind of vehicle, like a car or something that could carry cargo. He'd have to set out at night, using the cover of darkness.'

'Given all that, the only option would have been to divide up the body and scatter its parts around the city,' Lieutenant Yin said. 'But that wouldn't have been easy. He'd have to have accessed a vehicle and the containers right away.'

'The way he eventually disposed of the evidence tells us that he used the simplest and most effective methods available to him, all while minimising the risk of being discovered,' Pei said.

Huang snapped his fingers. 'What if he threw the torso into some water? The Jin River, for instance? We dredged the rivers back then, but if he'd only disposed of part of the body, we could have missed it.'

'Good point!' Lieutenant Yin exclaimed. 'If the killer lived near a river, that would be the easiest way to get rid of the rest of the body. It could be lying right on the bottom.'

'He hacked off the girl's head, scooped out her organs and cut off her skin and muscles,' Huang said, thinking aloud. 'He was trying to prevent the body from floating, wasn't he?'

'Precisely,' Pei said. 'For the moment, let's assume he lived by a river. He was completely unprepared when he killed her, so he began wracking his brains for a way to get rid of the body. The river near his home was the first place that came to mind. But he was smart enough to know that the corpse would bloat and float to the surface if he tossed it in, thus drawing the police closer to where he lived. So he stripped the girl's clothes off, chopped off her limbs, carved off her flesh and sliced her chest open, ensuring that she wouldn't float to the surface.'

Ms Mu clutched her stomach. She regretted having had breakfast before the meeting.

Pei, however, showed no sign of stopping. 'Thus leaving a bloody, unidentifiable torso, which he wrapped in something that would soak up water and sink with it. Maybe a bedsheet. He tossed it into the river while it was still dark. With that out of the way, he dealt with the remaining pieces of the cadaver. That was much easier; he simply collected some plastic bags for the flesh and a suitcase for the head and organs. After packing everything up, he drove or took some sort of transport away from his home, dropping the grotesque parcels along the way.'

'Causing the police to assume that they were dealing with a serial killer in the making,' Lieutenant Yin murmured. 'And thereby barking up the wrong tree.'

'Does that explain why he cooked the organs and the skull – to misdirect the police?' TSO Zeng rasped.

'That must have been one reason,' Pei answered. 'But the primary reason would have been convenience. If he hadn't boiled those body parts, the suitcase would have got soaked with blood and who knows what else. It would have leaked all over the place.'

Pei now had a clear idea of how the killer had disposed of the body. He paused to give the rest of the team time to process the new information. 'What does everyone think?' he asked.

'It makes sense,' Ms Mu said. 'We now have answers to the questions that previously stumped us. We thought we were dealing with a psychopath, but it seems we've been looking at this case all wrong.'

Lieutenant Yin and TSO Zeng both nodded approvingly. Huang was the only person in the room who still appeared hesitant. He shut his eyes and mumbled something under his breath. After letting out a long sigh, he finally opened his eyes again.

'Okay, I admit it. Things do make more sense if we're to believe this theory of yours.'

'Excellent,' Pei said, smiling. He felt proud. Not only had he made headway in this investigation, he'd also won the approval of a former police investigator. He turned to the two junior officers in the room. 'Lieutenant Yin. TSO Zeng.'

'Yes, sir!' they said in unison.

'Start looking for an individual who fits this description: male, around forty years of age, relatively handsome, of notable social status, unmarried, lives alone. Focus your search on people who live near a river. Use whatever means necessary to find them. Report back to this room when you're finished. We'll be here discussing the case.'

'Yes, sir!' the two officers repeated.

What with Lieutenant Yin's contacts throughout Chengdu and TSO Zeng's access to police databases, Pei was hopeful that between them they would have a broad reach. With luck, they might find a suspect soon.

1:09 p.m.

'Finished already?' Captain Pei asked as Lieutenant Yin returned to the conference room. 'Incredible.'

'We aren't 100 per cent done with our searches,' Yin hastened to say, 'but we have identified a prime suspect. You need to see this.'

Pei's brow creased. 'If you haven't finished analysing everyone, how can you have come up with a main suspect?'

'Let me explain. We haven't had time to organise all of our results, but as soon as we saw this person's file, we both knew we had to tell you. His name...' Lieutenant Yin gulped, choking on his own excitement. 'It's Professor Ding Zhen!'

Huang gaped at Lieutenant Yin, seemingly unable to believe his ears.

Only Ms Mu remained unfazed. As she reflected on the meeting she'd had with Professor Ding several days earlier, she was struck by how closely he fitted the suspect's profile. He was good-looking, a respected professor, had experienced an unhappy childhood and was a confirmed bachelor. Nodding thoughtfully, she said, 'Good work. Professor Ding does fit the description all right.'

'He lives in Jinjiang District, beside the Jin River. The university provided him with the apartment when he began working there. He's been living there for over a decade now,' Lieutenant Yin said.

As Pei recovered from his surprise, he realised why Yin had come to him before he'd completed the full search. This revelation alone answered so many questions.

He now knew why Captain Ding Ke had gone into hiding and why Eumenides had chosen to pursue this decade-old case. The answers were now staring them in the face.

Captain Ding Ke's son was the Bagman Killer.

19

DEATH OF THE SON

1:21 p.m.
College of Environmental Engineering, Sichuan University

Every morning at eleven o'clock, Gao ordered Professor Ding's lunch. She then took it into his office. The professor always read as he ate, typically from a scientific journal. Gao would return to her desk and when her phone rang she'd know that he had finished eating. She then retrieved the detritus from his office while he used the rest of his break to take a brief nap.

Today was different though. Gao had taken his lunch in at eleven thirty, but by the time she looked up from the stack of applications she had just finished reviewing, she realised that nearly two hours had passed without the professor's usual phone call.

She walked over and tapped twice on his door. There was no sound from inside.

Was he sleeping? While it was unlike the professor to take a two-hour nap, that seemed to be the most likely explanation.

Another thought suddenly occurred to her – if the professor had forgotten to put on his jacket, he might catch cold. Worried, she gently pushed the door open and slipped inside the room.

To her surprise, Professor Ding wasn't sleeping. He wasn't

377

working either. The middle-aged man was sitting ramrod straight at his desk, his gaze seemingly fixed on a point at the opposite end of the office.

Gao took several cautious steps towards him. She noted the unopened carton of spicy tofu and steamed vegetables on the desk. The disposable chopsticks were still in their wrapper.

'You haven't eaten, Professor,' she said, her tone a mix of concern and mild rebuke.

The professor slowly turned his eyes on his secretary, as though just noticing her presence. He appeared somewhat dazed and preoccupied.

'I know how busy you are, but surely you can spare a little bit of time to eat your lunch!' Gao reached for the carton. It was cold to the touch. 'I'll go and find a microwave.'

'That won't be necessary,' Professor Ding said in a low voice. He attempted to wave her out of the office, but he could barely lift his arm above his desk before it flopped back down.

'Is something wrong? Are you feeling all right, Professor?'

Gao set down the container and hurriedly stepped around the desk. Professor Ding raised his arm again. 'I'm fine,' he rasped, his voice as gritty as sandpaper. 'You can go back to the other room.'

Now even more concerned, she placed the back of her hand against his forehead. 'Do you have a fever?'

Professor Ding trembled slightly at Gao's soft touch. He looked up at his secretary, taking in her young, attractive face. She was so close, he could smell her perfume. A primal urge crept through him, but he flinched and recoiled.

Sadness washed over Gao's face. She turned for the door but then stopped and looked back. Her eyes locked onto his. As the afternoon sun streamed across his face, something glistened in his eyes. Her heart leapt. It wasn't like him to show such naked emotion. For years she'd thought he was incapable of feeling strongly about anything except his work. During the long hours she spent at her desk, she'd begun to imagine that a mechanical heart ticked away inside his body, one that prohibited him from feeling any emotion or affection. But now she knew that he could cry.

She hesitated before summoning up the courage to speak. 'Zhen, what's wrong?'

She had never addressed him by his first name before, but the sight of his tears had dispelled her inhibitions.

'Go back to the other room,' he said, managing a pained smile. Tears still glittered in his eyes. 'There's nothing here you can help me with.'

She came closer. As she wiped the tears from his face, she whispered, 'I may not be able to help you, but at least let me stay here with you. Even though you never say it, I know you need me.'

The professor closed his eyes but could not stop the tears from coming. They ran over Gao's fingers, gleaming in the light. She leant in and kissed the corner of his right eye. His tears were bitter on her tongue, but the feeling rising in her heart was sweeter than anything she'd ever experienced.

Professor Ding did not reject her advances. Instead, he bent his head towards her, savouring her perfume. It smelt like lilies and honey. Suddenly, an overwhelming desire surged through him.

It was a pure, animalistic impulse, one that he had not allowed himself to feel for years. He had dulled himself to its siren call with an ever-increasing workload, erecting an icy wall between himself and such lustful thoughts. Deep down, he had feelings and even wished that someday he might find love. But he never dared indulge that line of thinking. The same fear always lingered: that he would destroy himself, and that he would destroy someone else, again.

Now, however, he no longer had to consider the consequences. His life would soon be consequence-free.

Gao sensed this change in his mood. She moved her lips to his cheek and then to his mouth. His skin was wet from his tears and cool in the autumn air, but that did not dampen the passion smouldering between them.

At some point his own tears stopped and he found he was tasting Gao's tears instead. He didn't know why she was crying.

'You like me. It's as clear as day,' she said as she wept. 'So why do you treat me like this?'

Professor Ding couldn't answer but just pulled her closer. Gao knelt on the floor and as she buried her head in his arms she began to sob uncontrollably.

He pressed his nose into the nape of her neck. For far too long he'd dreamt of embracing someone like this. The woman in front of him now had appeared in his dreams more than any other. He had held her tight in so many of those fantasies.

This was no dream. For a fleeting moment he wondered if the reality would really be better.

Her shapely back trembled and her breasts pressed against his leg through her tight-fitting top. There was a new sensation between his legs. Gao's sobs immediately stopped and she looked up at him through misty eyes.

The professor's breathing quickened. He squeezed her harder and began kissing her neck; his other hand reached inside her sweater to explore the supple curves beneath.

A quiet moan escaped Gao's lips. She responded eagerly, placing her hand between his legs. His hand cupped a breast and her fingers moved to his belt buckle. Seconds later the belt fell to the floor. Her hands slid inside his trousers and he groaned with pleasure.

'Do you like me?' she whispered gently in his ear.

He had no energy to speak; he simply nodded.

'Then take me,' she said, drunk with desire. She tore off her sweater. 'I'm yours.'

She felt for the clasp of her bra and let it drop to the floor. Professor Ding took in the sight of his secretary's naked body. Her skin was as pale as flawless jade. He inhaled sharply. Old memories began rushing in, too fast for him to control. Painful memories.

It was sometime during middle school. He'd come home early because of a nosebleed. As he'd opened the front door, he'd seen that same shade of white. A pale female torso pressed beneath the swarthy body of a man, the two entwined with each other. The image burnt into his consciousness.

The woman was his mother, but the man was not his father. It was too early for his father to be home.

His memory jumped forward, as if it were a film with a missing reel. The next thing he remembered was his mother's panicked scream: 'Get out! Get out of here!' It rang in his ears, replacing the carnal excitement with painful humiliation.

Gao felt the professor go limp. She looked at him in shock and disappointment. 'What's wrong?' she asked.

Professor Ding said nothing. Years of hard-won dignity fell away in an instant. In his view, a man's dignity was everything. He would sacrifice anything to protect his, even if it meant spending ten long years without a woman's touch.

'I guess you're not a real man after all.'

He would never forget those words, nor the smug, condescending expression on the young woman's face as she'd said them to him on that icy winter's night ten years ago. That expression had pierced his heart like a dagger, shattering his proud self-image into a hundred jagged pieces. Then the rage had come. He detested that snow-white body. It was the embodiment of all the world's evil and ugliness, mocking him with the memories of his own humiliation.

He'd pounced upon that body and wrapped his hands around her throat until his anger bled out. When he finally returned to his senses, his fingers were soaked in tears and mucus. The putrid scent of human excrement filled the room. By the time he'd realised what he'd done, it was too late. As the minutes passed, the warmth drained from her body. He had to wrack his brains to try and work out how to cover up what he'd just done.

Professor Ding had never trusted a woman since, not even an infatuated admirer like Gao. He built an impervious shell around himself to protect his dignity – and his bloody, ten-year-old secret.

But fate had other plans for him. The shell had crumbled today, when he realised that his secret had been uncovered. His passion, which he had suppressed for so many years, had finally been reignited. But the shadows of his past lingered still.

What could he say now? He shut his eyes, hoping vainly that he had wandered into a nightmare.

Tears welled in Gao's once eyes again, and now they were tears of indescribable torment. 'You don't like me?' she asked, her voice quivering.

'No,' Professor Ding said coldly. 'I despise you. Get out of here. I can't stand the sight of you!'

The colour drained from Gao's face. She fixed her eyes on the professor as though trying to peer through to his very soul. He immediately dropped his gaze to the floor.

'I don't believe you,' she said. She moved closer, taking slow, deliberate steps. 'You do care for me. So why are you lying? What's there to hide from?'

Before he could answer, she bent forward, opened her mouth and put her lips around the soft flesh between his legs.

Heat swept through the professor's body once more, this time with an unstoppable force. His mind went blank. All of his past sins and humiliation were forgotten. He was like a newborn, wrapped tight in naked lust. No one could hurt him again.

Gao breathed excitedly as she felt him swell inside her mouth. She controlled him now. She even dared to believe that he would never leave her.

Professor Ding and Gao lay on the office sofa, entangled in each other's arms. The sound of the ringing phone in the outside room gradually brought them back to reality.

Gao gingerly rose and covered herself. 'I should answer that,' she said, shy once more.

The professor nodded and watched her walk to the door. Her clothes were still lying on the floor and her pale body glowed, pure and beautiful.

A moment later she was back in the office.

'Who was it?' It took all of Professor Ding's energy to squeeze those words out.

'Campus security,' she said casually. 'They wanted to know if you were here in your office. I asked them what it was concerning, but they wouldn't tell me.'

Sorrow, pain and desperation flashed across the professor's face, wiping out any last traces of happiness. Gao, who was hurriedly putting her clothes back on, didn't notice.

'Could you please heat up my lunch?' he said. 'I'm hungry.'

'Sure,' Gao said with a teasing smile. 'You know, I used to think that you could survive for months without food. Or emotion.'

He didn't answer. His eyes were fixed on her and they were

filled with longing and greed. It had been so long since he'd allowed himself to feel these things.

She blushed, picked up his lunch and paused for a moment. 'I'll go to the kitchen in the cafeteria. I'll be back in a minute,' she said and walked out of the office.

Those were the last words she ever said to him.

Fifteen minutes later

After leaving the cafeteria, Gao headed back to the environmental engineering building. As she turned the corner, the familiar grey structure came into view, but that wasn't all she saw. She froze, and the plastic carton of food nearly slid from her fingers. The building was surrounded by police cars and all the entrances were blocked by groups of uniformed officers.

'What's going on?' she asked a pair of students watching the commotion.

'I'm not sure. It looks like they've come to arrest someone, but that guy's also about to jump off the building,' the taller of the two said. He pointed at the building's upper floors. 'See him? Up on the eighth floor?'

Gao looked and saw a figure standing on a window ledge eight floors up, so close to the edge that a strong gust of wind could blow him off.

She gasped, and Professor Ding's lunch tumbled to the pavement. Scrambling her way through the crowd, she sprinted for the building's entrance.

'Let me in! I'm his secretary! I'm that man's secretary!' she shouted to the police outside the door.

★

Professor Ding watched Gao rushing towards the building. A hint of a smile cracked the blank veneer of his expression. Maybe she was the reason he'd been standing out there for so long. Even though he could make out little more than her silhouette, it was comforting to know she was there.

Upon reflection, he realised that she was one of the major regrets in his life. Why had he ignored her all these years? What would things have been like if he hadn't?

He looked up at the shimmering sun. The blinding light painted brilliant designs on his irises, as if he was looking at the gateway to another world.

'Goodbye,' he whispered – to himself and everyone else. He stepped off the ledge with a small hop.

His senses shut off one by one, except for his hearing. An instant before his body met the ground, the pained cry of a woman broke through the roar of rushing air.

'No!'

That moment seemed to fill an eternity. He wished that he could remain on earth just a moment longer, if only to keep hearing that voice.

Professor Ding's body thudded against the cement, and Gao collapsed. A couple of police officers rushed over and carried her to the edge of the crowd. As one of them radioed for an ambulance, another felt her wrist for a pulse.

Another group of officers had gathered around the corpse, led by Captain Pei. He crouched next to the body, studying the bloodied face, half crushed into the pavement. Despite the damage done to the body in the eight-storey fall, the man's features were still recognisable.

'It's him,' he said. 'Lieutenant Yin, make sure all the exits and entrances to the building remain sealed. I want this building searched inside and out.'

'Yes, sir!' Lieutenant Yin replied. He set off towards the building with a handful of officers.

A middle-aged man had knelt in front of the body and, with a glazed expression, was studying the deceased's smashed face. After a moment, he reached out and pinched the pressure point between the corpse's nose and upper lip.

'What are you doing, Huang?' Pei hissed. He'd sensed from Huang's expression that something was wrong, but he hadn't expected *this*.

Oblivious to Pei's question, the retired police officer grabbed Professor Ding's collar. 'Wake up!' he rasped. 'Wake up, you bastard!'

Pei glanced at a nearby officer. 'Get him away from the body!' he shouted. 'Now!'

Two younger officers grabbed Huang's arms and pulled him away. Huang twisted and struggled against their grip. 'What the hell are you doing? Let me go!'

'Get a hold of yourself, Huang!' Pei barked.

The captain's sharp reprimand appeared to bring Huang to his senses. He stopped struggling and his manic expression slowly relaxed. Tears streamed down his face. 'I waited ten damn years to find him,' he finally said. 'Why couldn't he have waited just one more day? Why couldn't he talk to me face to face?'

Pei sighed and silently placed a hand on Huang's shoulder. There were no words to say.

Over the next several hours the police thoroughly searched every floor of the environmental engineering building. They also examined its security footage, but even after repeated viewings they uncovered no trace of Eumenides. Hours later, however, TSO Zeng made an unexpected discovery while scrolling through the chat records on Professor Ding's laptop. The professor had been chatting with a user named Eumenides.

The timestamp for Eumenides' first message was 11:35:32 – a few minutes into the professor's regular lunch break. The conversation opened with a digital death notice. It was nearly identical to the notice that the police had received earlier that day but with one important difference.

Death Notice
THE ACCUSED: Professor Ding Zhen
CRIME: Homicide
DATE OF PUNISHMENT: 7 November
EXECUTIONER: Eumenides

His heart racing, TSO Zeng read the rest of the conversation.

11:36
Professor Ding: Eumenides?! WHO ARE YOU?
Eumenides: The important thing isn't who I am. It's what you've done.

11:39
Professor Ding: Are you trying to threaten me? I'll call the police.
Eumenides: That won't be necessary. They'll be there soon enough.
Professor Ding: What do you mean?

11:40
Eumenides: If I can find you, so can the police.

11:41
Professor Ding: I have no idea what you mean.

11:43
Eumenides: Ten years ago, on 12 January, you murdered a university student. You cut up her body and threw the largest piece into the Jin River, behind your apartment. Then you dumped the rest of her sliced-up body parts across the city.

11:44
Eumenides: Does that ring a bell?

11:47
Professor Ding: Are you going to kill me?
Eumenides: Yes. But perhaps you'll be smart and beat me to it.
Professor Ding: That's absurd!

11:50
Eumenides: The police will be there very soon. They're investigating the Bagman case again and you will be of particular interest to them. Funny name, isn't it – 'Bagman'.

11:53
Eumenides: When the accusations begin, the media will flock to you like flies to rotting meat. Your crimes will win you far more fame than your academic achievements ever could. You'll have to look at the remains of the girl you killed. Her skull, and the bones that the police will dredge from the river, will lie before you as evidence of your guilt. I promise that you will regret everything when

that time comes. And, more than anything, you will regret not having taken the easy way out when you had the chance.

11:56

Eumenides: Later today, the police will perform a full search of your home. Your fate will be sealed if they find so much as a speck of that girl's blood on your wall or your floorboards. And then there's the suitcase and the plastic bags you used for transporting her body parts during your wild ride around Chengdu. Her clothes as well. The police have been holding onto them like precious antiques for the past ten years, in the hope of finding some bit of evidence they missed before.

11:58

Eumenides: It could be a DNA test: a flake of dandruff from your scalp or perhaps a fibre that matches something in your home. Regardless of what the piece of evidence is, the police will spare no effort in using the most cutting-edge technology to trace it back to you. And of course they won't hesitate to use all sorts of interrogation techniques that you can't even imagine.

12:01

Eumenides: If you happen to be gifted with an extraordinary amount of luck and are a lot stronger-willed than I think you are, you might actually make it out of this ordeal as a free man. But you won't escape justice. You don't know who I really am, but I'm sure you've heard of Eumenides. The promise written on that death notice will be fulfilled eventually. It's just a matter of time.

12:03
Eumenides: I realise that this is not an easy choice, but you don't have much time left. Once the police take you in, you won't even have the power to choose.

Professor Ding didn't respond to Eumenides' last message, and the conversation ended. The latter half of the conversation was essentially a monologue from Eumenides, Zeng noted. Professor Ding had barely typed anything at all.

Zeng anxiously presented the laptop's logs to Captain Pei, who read them closely.

'So that's it?' Pei remarked when he'd finished. 'I suppose it's not surprising the professor wasn't very talkative. There'd have been too much going on inside his head.'

The security footage confirmed the timing of Professor Ding's final decision. When the first police vehicle pulled up outside the building, he was already standing out on the ledge.

'Can we track his IP address to a physical location?' Pei asked, pointing to Eumenides' username.

'That's easy.'

Zeng's fingers clacked across the keyboard. A few seconds later a command window appeared on the screen.

'That's the location of his IP address,' he said, shrugging. 'But tracking it won't do us any good.'

'I don't care. Try anyway. We can't let a single opportunity slip through our fingers, no matter how unlikely it may seem.'

Zeng stood up from his chair. 'Sure thing, boss,' he said and walked out of the room.

Zeng had left the laptop on the desk and Pei now turned his attention to its screen. The laptop was still online, so he clicked on the chat window, typed a quick message and sent it.

Are you still there?

Barely ten seconds later a new message flashed up.

Who is this?

Inhaling quickly, the captain typed his reply.

Pei Tao.

There was a longer pause before the next message appeared.

Eumenides: You work fast. It took me three days to figure out it was him.
Pei: Professor Ding is dead. This one didn't really fit your usual style.
Eumenides: ???
Pei: He killed himself. He didn't die by your hand. Which means your name shouldn't have been on that death notice.
Eumenides: Which name matters more – the person who physically ended Professor Ding's life or the one who pushed him to do it? My goal is to make sure that these criminals receive their just desserts. Nothing more, nothing less. If anything, it was a boon that I didn't have to resort to violence. If you police were better at your job, I wouldn't have to send out these death notices in the first place.
Pei: If you don't like violence, why don't you try finding another way to resolve these problems?
Eumenides: In many cases violence is the only option.
Pei: Violence is a double-edged sword. As you know from personal experience.

Half a minute went by without a response from Eumenides and Pei began to get worried. He needed to continue the conversation if he was to get any useful information out of him. What could he do to needle him further? Pei leant forward in his chair and grasped at the first idea that came to him.

Pei: I've already met the girl.
Eumenides: …
Pei: You know who I mean, don't you? If I were you, I'd give up now.
Eumenides: Things have already been set in motion. What difference would stopping make?
Pei: You can't change what's been done, but you still have a chance to redeem yourself.
Eumenides: Why are you telling me this?
Pei: Because I can see that you want to be redeemed.
Eumenides: What exactly do you mean? What about the girl?
Pei: You're watching her. Protecting her. She's a window inside you. If you could go back to the beginning of all this, you wouldn't kill Sergeant Zheng Haoming, would you?
Eumenides: You're wrong.
Pei: Why? Why would you kill someone who'd done nothing wrong?
Eumenides: We stand on opposing sides. Only one of us can live. I needed to kill an enemy in order to keep my faith strong. That way, I wouldn't hesitate the next time I came up against the police. There's a saying that Yuan liked to repeat – I'm sure you're familiar with it too: 'Being merciful to one's enemies is being cruel to oneself.'
Pei: I have one more question for you and I want an honest answer.

Eumenides: Ask the question first.

Pei: Did killing Sergeant Zheng really make you more determined to kill a police officer, your so-called enemies, the next time one got in your way?

Eumenides: ...

Pei: Well?

Eumenides: ...

Pei: It's been two minutes. What's the hold-up?

Eumenides: ...

Pei: Yuan's theory was wrong, wasn't it? Killing Sergeant Zheng didn't strengthen your resolve at all; rather it plunged you into a deep mire of guilt and procrastination. Why else would you seek out that girl? Admit it – you're motivated by guilt.

Eumenides: Amusing. You're imposing your own ideas on me.

Pei: Yuan's the one who imposed his ideas on you. He's the one who made you kill Sergeant Zheng. He brainwashed you into believing that the police are your enemy. He even gave you that infamous moniker you still use. Have you never wondered why Yuan expected you to accept all those things without question? Have you never wondered why you had to become Eumenides? Deep down, you know you're only living out someone else's twisted desires.

Eumenides: He gave me a second chance at life. After all he did for me, what right did I have to refuse him?

Pei: Do you really think Yuan was just being generous, that he didn't have an ulterior motive?

Eumenides: I've heard enough from you.

Pei: You know that it was Yuan who killed your father. The situation in your father's apartment was already under

393

control, but Yuan still opened fire. Why did he do that? Have you never asked yourself that question?

Eumenides: Enough! I don't need your lies. I can find out the truth on my own, without your help.

Pei: Fine. Perhaps the truth will change you more than you expect.

Eumenides: What could it change? I'm already a killer.

Pei: What you already are isn't what matters. What matters is that everyone has a future.

Eumenides: You're the leader of the April 18th Task Force. I'm a wanted murderer. Do we really need to talk about the future?

Pei: My role as head of the April 18th Task Force is only temporary. If enough time passes without there being another murder, I'll go back to Longzhou.

Eumenides: You'll give up on your mission?

Pei: My mission is not to seek revenge, it's to prevent crimes from happening. I have two options. If you continue with these murders, I'll find you and arrest you. If you vanish and are never heard from again, then it's over.

To be honest, I'd choose the second option in a heartbeat. If you try to seek redemption for your past crimes, my choices become a little more interesting.

Eumenides: As long as I keep killing, you won't stop looking for me – am I right?

Pei: Yes. Right now you still have a choice, but the moment you commit another murder, everything else is off the table. I'll give you until the end of the month.

Pei hadn't chosen that deadline arbitrarily, of course. It was the deadline Eumenides had written on his death notice for the journalist Du Mingqiang.

He waited for Eumenides' reply. None came.

Three days later: 10 November, 9:27 a.m.
Funeral parlour

It was still early in the day and the road in front of the funeral parlour was wide and flat. Even so, few drivers went that way. Most gave the funeral home a wide berth and chose instead to take the long way round.

About a dozen vendors had set up their stalls outside the building. They were selling flowers, ghost money for burning with the corpse on its journey into the afterlife, and candles – all traditional products associated with death and mourning in China.

'Sir, would you like to buy some flowers before you go inside?'

'Ghost money! Cheap, very cheap!'

An older man stepped out from the crowd of newly arrived mourners. He was gaunt, his hair and beard flecked with grey; he appeared to be in his seventies. After scanning the vendors for a few seconds, he approached a flower stall.

The vendor was short and young. Neither his cheap clothes nor his greasy hair appeared to have been washed in at least a week. At the sight of his approaching customer, the man straightened up.

'How can I help you, sir?'

Ignoring the vendor's wares, the older man said, 'Where's your captain?'

The vendor blinked in confusion. He glanced at the other vendors then looked back at the man. 'What do you mean? We're just a bunch of vendors. We don't have a captain.'

'Drop the act,' the man said with a disapproving shake of his head. 'You're with the criminal police. So is the young man who got off the bus with me. The one with the green jacket.'

The vendor's eyes darted left then right. He forced a smile. 'I'm sorry, sir. You must have confused me with someone else.'

After letting out a long, frustrated sigh, the man reached out with his right hand and grabbed the greasy hair at the vendor's right temple. The vendor jerked his head back, but the grizzled man held on tight. Something flashed in front of the younger man's eyes and he felt a gust of air against his face. When his vision focused again, he saw that the other man was holding a wireless microphone between his fingers.

The vendor looked at the microphone and then at the face of the man holding it. *This wasn't covered in the briefing,* he thought.

'Call your captain over. I'd like to speak to him.' He placed the microphone on the stall counter and walked away.

The younger man hastily snatched the device from the counter. He could sense the intense gazes of the other vendors on him.

The older man walked into the funeral home and headed directly for the mourning hall in the building's west wing. Several funeral parlour employees were milling around inside, seemingly absorbed in their work. He stopped at the entrance and quickly singled out one of the employees, a well-built man in his twenties dressed in a shirt bearing the funeral home's logo; he was doing a better job of blending in than the 'vendor' outside, but the stiffness in his gait was a dead giveaway. There was a distinct difference between being genuinely comfortable in your surroundings and simply pretending to be.

In the centre of the hall was a glass coffin. An elderly woman was standing beside it, weeping silently. The older man walked over, gently placed his hand on the glass lid and lowered his head to look at the body lying inside.

The woman turned. When she saw him, the grief on her face quickly turned to hate. 'So you've come,' she said, her voice hoarse. 'I was hoping I'd never see you again.'

He slowly swept his hand along the top of the coffin, as though he could feel the face of the man inside. 'He's my son. Of course I'm going to come and see him.'

'Enough with the false charity. When have you ever cared about him? If you'd been a true father, we wouldn't be burying him.'

The man's face froze. 'You think our son has only just left us? His heart's been dead for years already.'

'Are you still blaming me? You honestly think this is my fault?' the woman spat.

He lowered his head and his eyes slid shut.

Ignoring him, the woman gazed down at the body of her son. Then she leant forward and embraced the coffin. She burst into long, heaving sobs.

The man's eyes watered, but no tears fell. Suddenly, he sensed something. In a flash, he turned around to face the room's entrance.

A man and a woman were standing at the double doors. Judging from their expressions, they regretted having to be there. Although the man was silent, his eyes spoke volumes. The woman appeared to be a decade his junior.

'Are these your people?' the older man asked as they came up to him.

'They are. I'm the new captain of the criminal police. Pei Tao. I meant no disrespect in assigning my people here. I did it for your security.'

'Captain Pei?' Recognition flashed in the older man's eyes. He looked down at the corpse inside the coffin. 'You're the one who found him, aren't you?'

'I was too late. Someone else got to him first.'

'What do you mean?'

'It was Eumenides. The serial killer. You've heard of him, I presume?'

The man frowned. 'Yuan Zhibang? The news reports said he died in an explosion.'

'Yuan is dead, but Eumenides is still out there. Long ago, Yuan chose a successor to bear that name.' Pei kept his eyes on the man as he spoke, watching for any signs of surprise or confusion.

'A successor.' The man blinked silently for a moment. He shook his head gently. 'It makes sense, considering what kind of person Yuan was.'

'Are you aware of who it is that Yuan chose?' Pei probed.

The man stared deep into Pei's eyes. Comprehension slowly spread across his wrinkled features. 'I am now,' he said softly. 'But only because you just told me.'

Pei shifted uncomfortably. Behind him, Ms Mu looked on silently. Pei had been anxious about meeting this man and now she understood why. He was reading the captain like an open book.

'He's looking for the truth behind his father's death, isn't he? That's why you were looking for my son.' He exhaled slowly. 'What father wouldn't want to say one last farewell to his recently departed son?'

Pei nodded in silent sympathy. He had planned for this day when he'd instructed all of Chengdu's major newspapers to publish Du's article about Professor Ding's death, but he hadn't been sure what to expect when he actually met the man.

'Eumenides contacted your son online and threatened to expose his crimes. His threats manipulated your son into taking his life. That's the real reason he jumped.'

'You don't need to explain yourself. I'm not looking to

blame anyone for his death. In truth, I'm the one that should be held accountable.' Captain Ding Ke shut his eyes again and rested both his hands on the coffin.

Pei and Ms Mu look at each other in discomfort. Pei turned back to Captain Ding.

'It wasn't my intention to disturb you today, sir. I had to send these officers as protection because the killer is looking for you with greater urgency than ever and we need to make sure you're safe.'

'I can take care of myself – a few extra officers watching my back won't make any difference. Today is the day I say my final goodbyes to my son and I don't want to be interrupted.'

'I understand,' Pei said.

'How about this?' Ms Mu suggested a moment later. 'We'll leave just one person in this room and the rest will be stationed outside. The individual in question will be someone you're already very familiar with. He shouldn't be a distraction.'

'I suppose you mean Huang Jieyuan,' Captain Ding said dryly.

Ms Mu nodded.

'Fine.'

Captain Ding looked down at the pale, expressionless face of his son, the professor. The funeral parlour's make-up artist had done a fine job of covering up the evidence of his eight-storey fall. To an untrained eye he would appear flawless.

'Once I've said goodbye to my son, I'll tell you what you want to know.'

20

CAPTAIN DING KE

11 November, 4 p.m.
Captain Ding Ke's home

The members of the April 18th Task Force – with the exception of SPU Captain Liu, who was still watching over Du Mingqiang – were sitting outdoors around a table with Captain Ding Ke. Huang Jieyuan, the task force's newest provisional member, was there too. The meeting was being held in the courtyard of a single-family country house just outside the city. It was Captain Ding's home.

'Have you noticed anything out of the ordinary today, Captain Ding?' Ms Mu asked.

'You're referring to that killer? He won't come after me. Why would he, with you watching me so closely. Huang told me your thoughts on the Bagman case, Ms Mu. I admire your psychological approach. Your analysis of my son was spot on.'

Ms Mu nodded awkwardly. Inside, she was beaming with pride, but given the circumstances, she was trying to keep her expression neutral.

'My wife left me more than twenty years ago. I don't resent her for it. I always had my nose deep in a case back then, and I barely contributed anything to my family's wellbeing. What woman wouldn't leave a husband like that? Unfortunately, my son – Ding Zhen – walked in on my wife in flagrante when he was very young. She sent him to a series of counsellors and psychologists, but there was no helping him. He was traumatised by what he saw that day. When he got older, he abstained from having any relationships. That aspect of his life was taken away forever, because of that day.'

Ms Mu nodded glumly at this revelation. *So that was the source of Professor Ding's hidden inferiority complex,* she thought.

'I didn't know any of this until yesterday,' Captain Ding said despondently. 'I always did think it was strange – my son was smart, successful, good-looking, so why couldn't he get a girlfriend? I started getting anxious; he was my only child, after all. So I began pushing him to find a wife and start a family. But ten years ago, he couldn't take it any more. He—'

'It's okay, Captain Ding,' Ms Mu said gently. 'You don't need to say any more.'

'Don't you see?' he said, hanging his head. 'I'm the one who's truly responsible for that disgusting murder. That's why I disappeared ten years ago.'

There was an air of intense sorrow about him, and Ms Mu looked away. Even with her background in psychology, she could barely imagine the weight of his guilt.

'But you don't need to hear my lamentations about my failings as a father,' Captain Ding finally said. 'Captain Pei, tell me why you're all here. Is it because of the January 30th hostage case?'

Pei nodded solemnly. 'I'd like to know if we still have a chance to stop Wen Chengyu.'

Captain Ding gazed up at the cloudless sky. 'Yesterday, when you told me that Yuan had found someone to succeed him as Eumenides, Wen Chengyu was the first person

I thought of. To tell you the truth, I could have stopped this from happening a long time ago, but I ignored Yuan. I certainly didn't expect him to go into hiding for eighteen years and train a new Eumenides.'

'Do you mean that eighteen years ago,' Pei said, arching an eyebrow, 'you knew that Eumenides was Yuan Zhibang?'

Captain Ding nodded. 'I retired before the warehouse explosion, but I couldn't exactly ignore a case like that, could I? I went to your dorm to investigate, and I also read the statement you gave to the police. That two-minute discrepancy you mentioned – it stuck with me. It was what helped me figure out how Yuan had done it. Once I knew that, I knew who Eumenides was. But the explosion had already crippled Yuan, so I assumed that his crazy plans had come to an end right there. As for his sudden transformation into a killer, I couldn't bear to look into that any further. The two of us were connected, you see...'

Pei's eyes widened.

'Cause and effect,' Captain Ding said. 'It's the one principle that connects everything in this world. When I started to think about retiring, I began searching for someone to take my place on the force. Can you guess who my first choice was?'

Pei had a name in mind, but he was hesitant to voice it.

'One of the best students the academy has ever produced. Pei Tao.'

'What?' Pei said, taken aback.

Captain Ding eyed him intently. 'Steady, quick-thinking and with superb attention to detail. Exactly the kind of student who would make an excellent officer of the criminal police.'

'If he was your first pick, why didn't you choose him?' TSO Zeng asked.

'Unfortunately, I soon discovered some blemishes on Pei's

record. Specifically, he created the character known as Eumenides.'
He kept his gaze locked on Pei.

The head of the April 18th Task Force shut his eyes and
breathed out slowly.

'But that was just for a competition between him and his
girlfriend, Meng Yun,' Ms Mu insisted. 'At the worst, it was
only a bit of good-natured mischief. I wouldn't consider it a
"blemish" on his record by any means.'

'The individual I chose would become the backbone of
Chengdu's police force for years to come. I couldn't afford
to overlook even the smallest infraction,' Captain Ding said,
adopting the sort of tone that a professor would use when
lecturing a student. 'As it happens, I had someone else in mind.
That student was also exceptional in all regards. In fact, I'd
had quite some difficulty deciding between them. Thanks to
Pei's pranks, I was able to make that final decision fairly easily.'

'Yuan Zhibang,' Ms Mu said. 'I can't imagine how much
you regret that now.'

Captain Ding immediately shook his head. 'I don't consider
it a mistake. Yuan and Pei were both more than qualified for
the role, and they were both unique in their own ways. Pei was
introverted, calm and persistent. Had I chosen him, he would
have developed at a steady rate, performing capably every step
of the way. Yuan, on the other hand, would have been quite
different. He was an extrovert and impulsive to a startling
degree. I was more interested in short-term developmental
prospects.' He looked closely at Pei and then Ms Mu. 'If I had
to trace Yuan's transformation back to its source, I would
summarise it with a single word.'

'I presume you're going to tell us what that is?' TSO Zeng
asked sarcastically.

Captain Ding's brow wrinkled. 'Fate.'

Pei gawped at him in dumb shock.

'Fate,' Captain Ding repeated, staring back at Pei. 'You, me, Wen Hongbing, even Wen Hongbing's son – all of us are connected. It's hard to say which mistakes were made by whom, but all of these factors somehow combined and became the catalyst for Yuan's transformation. Everything that happened may have simply been Yuan's fate, the result of a series of inevitable events beyond any one individual's control.'

'How could Wen Hongbing's son have influenced Yuan?' Zeng asked. 'Yuan's the one who influenced the rest of that boy's entire life.'

Captain Ding paused. 'During the hostage situation at the apartment, we had things under control. But then the boy said something. Something that, well, *triggered* his father.'

'What did he say?' Ms Mu asked anxiously.

'I heard it through my earpiece. He said, "Daddy, did you buy me a birthday cake yet?"'

Pei waited for Captain Ding to continue, but that was it. 'That's all he said?' he asked in astonishment.

'That's it.' Captain Ding nodded. 'The thirtieth of January happened to be Wen Chengyu's birthday and his father had promised to buy him an extravagant cake. But Mrs Wen's illness had left the family dirt poor. By the time his son's birthday came, Wen Hongbing was truly at the end of his rope. He didn't have two coins to rub together. Which was what forced him to kidnap Chen Tianqiao – a desperate attempt to get his own hard-earned cash back from the man.'

'So Yuan used Wen Hongbing's love for his son to encourage him to think about his son's future,' said Ms Mu. 'But as soon as his son spoke those words, Wen Hongbing found himself pulled back into his own desperate reality. He couldn't even provide his son with the birthday he'd promised him. That sudden realisation must have been soul-destroying.'

Captain Ding let out a slow, rustling sigh. At the same time, Pei felt a strange constriction in his throat.

Captain Ding's voice was softer now. 'Wen Hongbing lost control when he heard his son speak. He screamed at Chen Tianqiao, demanding his money, but Chen insisted that he had no money to give. Wen was furious. He started beating him up. Remember that Wen was wearing a bomb, so every sudden movement put all of us at risk. The situation was critical and Yuan was forced to do the only thing he could. He pulled the trigger and shot Wen Hongbing in the head.'

'Considering the circumstances, Yuan's actions were perfectly defensible. However...' Pei exhaled loudly. He suddenly found it difficult to speak.

'The results are hard to accept, aren't they?' Captain Ding laughed bitterly. 'You weren't there and yet you're still moved by it, even now. Yuan was the one who pulled the trigger, and he already felt a connection to the boy – can you imagine what that must have felt like?'

Pei shut his eyes again. He remembered what Huang had told him. *The suspect had a bullet in his forehead. He was on the ground, motionless. The hostage, however, was safe and sound. Yuan held the boy close, cradling the child's head against his chest. He didn't let him see the bloody scene at all.'*

'It was his first time taking part in a real police operation,' Captain Ding continued, 'and that was the result. I was worried that he wouldn't be able to handle the psychological stress, so I ordered the marksman at the scene to claim responsibility for Yuan's actions. Unfortunately, things didn't go as well as I'd hoped. I saw Yuan later that night. He just sat there, stiff as a dead man. I knew that hundreds of thoughts must be going through his head. He looked at me with bloodshot eyes and said, "Captain, I regret everything. Why didn't I miss? Wouldn't it have been so much better if that bullet had struck Chen instead?"'

Ms Mu put a comforting hand on Pei's shoulder. 'Had we been in Yuan's shoes, we might have had the same thoughts. When it comes down to it, it's our respect for the law that keeps us knowing what's right.'

'Therein lies the rub,' Captain Ding said gravely. 'Those of us around this table all have clear views on what's right and wrong, but we're also restricted by societal rules and regulations. None of *us* would overstep those boundaries. Yuan, on the other hand, was hot-tempered. He couldn't control his emotions – if anything, they controlled *him*. When he told me that he wished he'd shot Chen instead, he'd lost sight of what it meant to be a police officer.'

'Yuan originally channelled all his natural intensity into his desire to become a police officer and defender of justice,' Ms Mu said. 'But on his first mission out in the field, he watched helplessly as his own firearm distorted his definition of justice. Captain Pei would have reacted differently in that situation. Think of the two of them as sprinters encountering a large boulder in their path. Captain Pei would have slowed down and stepped around it. Yuan, however, was running too fast. He was too highly strung and impetuous to stop. He collided with the boulder and when he regained his footing, he began running in a different direction.'

Captain Ding nodded. 'Two months after that, someone broke into Chen's home and stole money from his safe.'

'The April 7th burglary,' Pei said. 'We've researched that case. We already guessed that Yuan was the culprit, in fact.'

'You must have figured that out fairly quickly, Captain Ding,' Ms Mu said. 'But then you concealed the truth again.'

'That's correct.'

'If you hadn't shielded Yuan like that, none of this would have happened,' TSO Zeng grumbled.

'Not necessarily.' Ms Mu shook her head. 'Even if Yuan had been prosecuted for the break-in, he might still have gone through with his plan to become Eumenides. It would have just delayed his transformation into a killer.'

'Cause and effect,' Captain Ding murmured. 'It was bound to happen sooner or later. I only protected Yuan because I had no other choice.'

'You felt sorry for him,' Ms Mu said. 'You couldn't bear to blame him, and you couldn't bear to take away the money that Mrs Wen would use for her operation. So you decided to end your career as a police officer there and then.'

Captain Ding grinned bitterly. 'To be fair, I'd been wanting to retire for a while, but I'd put it off because I hadn't yet found a successor. The change in Yuan disheartened me. It left me cold to the world of law enforcement. I officially resigned soon after. But never in my worst nightmares did I imagine he could have been planning something so terrible.'

'Of course not,' Pei said, keeping his eyes on the retired captain. 'Because something else happened before the April 18th warehouse explosion. Something that you might not even be aware of.'

'What's that?'

'You must have been involved with the March 16th drug-trafficking case, right?'

'Barely. Vice Commissioner Xue was in charge of the investigation,' Captain Ding said with a distant look on his face. 'As I recall, one of Xue's most trusted informants was pivotal to the success of that drugs bust.'

'Yes,' Pei said. 'Deng Yulong. Who later became the powerful Mayor Deng. Deng stole half of the drugs and cash that the police confiscated during the raid. Vice Commissioner Xue found out about it but decided to cover it up. However, Xue's secretary accidentally recorded that crucial conversation between Deng and the vice commissioner. The secretary, Bai Feifei, also happened to be Yuan's ex-girlfriend. Deng killed Bai Feifei to stop her from leaking the recording, disguising her death as suicide. Yuan became Eumenides in order to avenge Bai Feifei. That was when he truly passed the point of no return.'

'Oh, so that's what happened!' Captain Ding said in surprise as he processed this new information. 'That makes Yuan's transformation a lot clearer.'

'The January 30th hostage case was a psychological turning point for Yuan,' Ms Mu concluded. 'He was unable to get over the stress of Wen Hongbing's death and he began to question what it meant to be a police officer. But Bai Feifei's murder on the twentieth of March was what made him finally turn his back on a future with the police. He became convinced that only he was truly capable of meting out justice, and Captain Pei's creation, Eumenides, served as a guiding light for him in that regard. All of these factors ultimately combined to turn Yuan into a single-minded killer.'

'Now do you understand why I used the word "fate" to describe Yuan's transformation?' Captain Ding asked. 'So many unanticipated events converged around him. If Pei and his girlfriend Meng hadn't created Eumenides, I wouldn't have chosen Yuan. If that boy hadn't taken a liking to Yuan, I wouldn't have ordered Yuan to be on the scene during the hostage situation. If the boy hadn't suddenly mentioned a birthday cake, the hostage situation might have ended peacefully. If the marksman had chosen a better position, Yuan wouldn't have needed to use his gun. If Bai Feifei hadn't died, Yuan might not have resorted to such drastic measures to get revenge. Given all that, how can you explain it as anything other than *fate*?'

Captain Pei took his time before responding. 'Even if it was fate, there's one thing I'll never forgive him for,' he whispered, fixing the old man with a look of deep pain.

'Meng Yun's death,' Captain Ding said, nodding. 'I understand.'

Pei stared up at the blue sky. Taking a deep breath, he pushed his feelings down inside himself, as far down as they could go.

'There's an important reason why he killed Meng. One that wasn't part of his plan,' Captain Ding said.

Pei's bloodshot eyes blinked. 'What was the reason?'

'You, Pei, were both his closest friend and the adversary for whom he had the greatest respect.'

Pei said nothing.

'Yuan's emotions were so intense that not even he could control them. He was fully aware of that. As he prepared to embark on his new life as Eumenides, you were the one huge obstacle he dreaded. He was unable to give up the close friendship you two shared, but he also knew two things. Firstly, the two of you were destined to become irreconcilable enemies. And secondly, he must never underestimate your abilities. He needed to sever the bonds of friendship between you for those two reasons. For he knew that when the two of you eventually came to face off against each other, that friendship would prove to be his fatal weakness.'

Pei clenched his fists at the thought of Yuan and Meng and all his memories.

'After the two of you became enemies, did your emotions

ever make you forsake your own principles?' Captain Ding asked.

'No,' Pei answered with a resolute shake of his head.

'You can control your emotions. Yuan could not. If the two of you got into a life-or-death struggle, Yuan's emotions would put him on the losing side.'

'And that's why he killed Meng?'

'That's a key reason, yes. Yuan's cautiousness and eye for detail were just as good as yours. He recognised his own weaknesses. That was why he needed to sever any remaining emotional connections between the two of you. At the same time, his plan also required an innocent victim whom he could use to verify his own "death". He chose Meng. If she died in the explosion and you then discovered that he had survived it, the two of you would become mortal enemies. Your friendship would be irreparable. And so his erstwhile weakness would have evaporated.' Captain Ding stopped to catch his breath. 'You could even say that Meng's involvement was what made his plan perfect.'

'No!' Pei snapped, looking up at Captain Ding in defiance. 'Meng exposed the flaws in his plan. She sacrificed herself! As a result of which, Yuan's so-called perfect plan fell apart and he was crippled for the rest of his life. If Yuan had been just a bit slower, he would have ended up a pile of ashes on the floor of that warehouse.'

Captain Ding froze. He considered Pei's rebuttal. Yuan, Pei and Meng had been some of the police academy's best students. Somehow the three of them had become embroiled in the same struggle. Each of them had suffered, to vastly different degrees. None of them had emerged unscathed.

It was fate.

The sun was in the west now. Captain Ding looked up at the

deepening blue of the sky and decided to change the subject. 'It's nearly sunset. As this is such an unusual occasion, I'd like to invite you all to stay for dinner and a chat. There's a garden behind the house with a good range of fruit and vegetables. My crops have done well this season. Pick whatever you like and I'll have a meal ready in no time.'

'Is that so?' Ms Mu's interest was piqued. 'You don't seem like the gardening type.'

'You sound like my wife,' Captain Ding said with a good-natured smile. 'Huang, why don't you take Ms Mu round the back and help her choose some fruit and vegetables for dinner?'

Ms Mu was startled as the chair behind her creaked and Huang lumbered forward. He'd been so quiet over the last few hours that she'd all but forgotten he was there.

'You coming?' he asked, looking back at her.

She nodded and stood up. TSO Zeng followed them.

'Let's go and lend them a hand, Lieutenant Yin,' Pei said. But as he made to stand up, he felt a foot under the table being pressed firmly against his. Yin headed off with the others, unaware that Pei wasn't behind him.

Once everyone else had disappeared, Captain Ding turned to Pei and said, 'I want to give you something.'

Reaching into his jacket pocket, he pulled out a small rectangular object and placed it on the table. Pei recognised it at once. It was a microcassette. Before computers had come into widespread use, microcassettes had been the usual choice for police surveillance recordings.

'Yuan wore a recording device during the January 30th hostage situation. This tape is a recording of what happened that night. In order to protect Yuan, I kept many secrets from the rest of the police force, but I saved this because

I didn't want the truth to be buried. Take this with you and listen to it. Everything that transpired immediately before and after Wen Hongbing's death is on it.'

Pei picked up the tape. 'Why didn't you show this to us earlier?'

'I don't want anyone else to listen to it. There are things on that tape that Wen Hongbing's son must never hear,' Captain Ding said, his eyes narrowing.

A shiver ran down Pei's back. 'You have your doubts about someone on the team?' he whispered.

'As far as I know, there's only one set of files on the January 12th Bagman case and they're the ones in the PSB archives. There's nothing on any computer database. How else would Eumenides have found out where the files were kept?'

The more Pei considered this, the more anxious he became. He was shocked to realise that his forehead was now slick with sweat.

'Don't get too worked up,' Captain Ding said in a reassuring voice. 'I'm just putting it out there. But if you really do intend to stop that young man from continuing his crime spree, I recommend extreme caution. For the time being, you're the only person who can know about the contents of this tape.'

Pei frowned. 'Do you mean that what you just told us wasn't the truth?'

'I told you the facts. Just not all of them.' Captain Ding smirked humourlessly at Pei. 'To put a stop to these murders, we don't necessarily need to pursue the source – we just need to halt the vicious cycle of cause and effect.'

Pei gripped the cassette tightly and wondered what he meant. What secrets did that small chunk of plastic hold?

21

RITE OF THE DEAD

12 November, 8:07 a.m.
Conference room, criminal police headquarters

The entire task force was seated around the conference room table and this time they'd been joined by the journalist Du Mingqiang.

Du yawned loudly. Wiping his nose, he said, 'My sleep patterns are nothing like yours. The next time you want me to wake up this early, you might as well just kill me.'

'The early bird gets the worm,' TSO Zeng chirped.

Captain Pei stood up and everyone took this as a sign that the meeting had begun. 'Lieutenant Yin,' he said to his assistant, 'give it to him.'

Lieutenant Yin placed a large envelope in front of Du.

'Oh, what have we here?' Du opened it and pulled out a slim folder and a miniature MP3 player.

'The scoop you wanted. Take a look at the documents inside the folder first.'

Du perked up and immediately began to read the folder's contents in earnest. They comprised an extremely detailed account of an eighteen-year-old hostage case, including background on the people involved as well as the events surrounding the perpetrator's eventual standoff with the police.

'This case has a nice strong conflict. It also raises some interesting ethical questions,' Du said once he'd finished reading. 'But it's ancient history. Unless I can find a way to link this article to something current, I doubt it'll get many clicks, no matter how well written it is.'

'The boy in the case is the man we now know as Eumenides. The police officer who shot his father was Yuan Zhibang, the man who trained him,' Pei said, emotionless and serious.

'Is that so?' An eager smile spread across Du's face. 'Well, that changes everything! I can use these files to document the psychological journeys of two generations of killers. The public will eat this up!'

Nodding slowly, Pei turned to Lieutenant Yin. 'Play the recording for him.'

Yin pushed a button on the MP3 player. As everyone in the room listened, the sounds from the hostage scene eighteen years ago began to play.

The first thing they heard was Yuan's voice calling out to Wen Hongbing, trying to persuade him to give up his hostage and surrender. As Yuan continued his impassioned appeal to Wen Hongbing's emotions, Wen Hongbing began to talk less about Chen Tianqiao and the debt. The hostility seemed to have melted away.

'I just want to hold my son,' Wen Hongbing said.

'I'll give you your son if you deactivate the bomb and release your hostage,' Yuan replied, his voice calm and conciliatory. *'There's nothing for you to worry about. All of this will be over soon and everything can go be back to normal.'*

'My son,' Wen Hongbing repeated.

When Yuan spoke again, his tone was slightly more urgent. *'Do you not understand? Think about what really matters*

414

to you. *If you continue down this road, what will it mean for your wife and son?'*

'*My son, my son...*' Wen Hongbing mumbled, like a mystic reciting a mantra. His resolve was crumbling.

'*Turn around, Chengyu. Call out to your dad,*' Yuan said to the young boy he was holding in his arms.

'*Did you get me a birthday cake, Daddy?*' a young voice called out.

An anguished cry came through the MP3 player. '*Give me back my money! I want my money!*'

'*I keep telling you – I don't have it,*' a new voice protested. Chen Tianqiao.

'*Stop right there and stay calm!*' Yuan yelled, his own voice anything but.

'*You bastard! Liar! I'm going to kill you!*' Wen Hongbing shrieked like a wild animal roaring at its prey. Suddenly he began panting. The sounds of a scuffle came through the speaker.

'*Let him go!*' Yuan yelled.

Next came the unmistakeable crack of a gunshot.

The recording ended. No one in the conference room spoke. After nearly half a minute, Pei broke the stifling silence. 'What are your thoughts?' he said to Du.

The journalist's usual nonchalant expression was nowhere to be seen. Du shook his head. He was still visibly shocked by what he'd just heard. 'That boy... It was all because of just one sentence.'

'That's right. That one sentence changed everything. It's heartbreaking, but there's nothing that could have been done.' In a softer voice, Pei added, 'I sincerely hope that you can include that in your article.'

'Hmm?' Du studied Pei closely, as if trying to work out what he meant.

'I don't want you to just write about this. Take that MP3 player and upload the audio file online as well.'

Du's mouth slowly twisted into a sly grin. 'You're using me, aren't you?'

'If you're not up to the task, you can always say no,' Ms Mu said icily. 'You aren't the only journalist we've been in touch with.'

Du looked over at her and raised his hands in mock surrender. 'I'll do it, of course. Given a scoop like this, what kind of reporter worth his salt wouldn't? But I hope you'll tell me how you really intend to use my article. Then I'll be able to properly consider how I write it.'

That sounds reasonable enough, Ms Mu thought. She shot Pei an inquiring look. When he nodded, she focused back on Du. 'Wen Chengyu, the man now better known as Eumenides, has no memory of that day. He was too young. We're hoping that you can write an article that will be seen by him. The details within it may very well cause him to abandon his murderous ways.'

'You want me to write a letter exhorting Eumenides to give up?' Du asked, grinning.

'You could say that.' Ms Mu shrugged. 'Wen Hongbing's death is what turned Yuan into a killer. In a sense, the young Wen Chengyu was the catalyst for Yuan's transformation. Our goal in telling Wen Chengyu about this part of his past is to make him reflect on those events. To make him realise that continuing as Eumenides is not his only option and that the things Yuan taught him aren't as absolute as they might seem. All of this was simply a matter of chance – the result of something he said as a child. The facts surrounding that bloody tragedy can now be used to bring this to an end.'

Du stroked his chin thoughtfully. 'I see exactly what you mean.'

'So how will you approach the article?' Ms Mu asked, arms folded.

Before Du could answer, Pei decided to raise the stakes. 'I want you to write this article as if your life depended on it. Because, in truth, it does. You understand what I'm saying?'

'Of course.' Du snickered. 'If this article has the impact you're hoping for, I'll become the first person to receive a death notice from Eumenides and live.'

'Good to see you still have your wits about you,' Pei said. 'SPU Captain Liu, take him home. I want to see the article as soon as it's ready.'

'Yes, sir!' Liu stood up and snapped a quick salute.

Du rose lazily from his seat and picked up the envelope. 'What if this is simply my fate?'

'Move it!' Liu grabbed the reporter's arm and dragged him out of the conference room.

Once the doors had shut, Pei turned to Ms Mu. 'How good do you think our chances are?'

'Hard to say,' she mumbled noncommittally. 'But regardless of what else happens, the article will certainly shake Eumenides' belief system. He's likely to be very frustrated by now after such a long and tireless search for the truth about who he is, and that frustration may have worn him down and dented the strength of his feelings. Whether those are feelings of love or hate, he has no reason to persist with them. If an external stimulus were to come along at this point, it's extremely likely it would have a massive impact on his current path.'

Pei's heart speeded up. *It's already happening*, he thought.

13 November, 10:16 a.m.
Captain Pei's office

Captain Pei was sitting silently at his desk, looking at a copy of the morning paper spread out in front of him. The paper was dated the first of November and he was reading a news story printed in one of the sections inside:

Jinjiang District
The body of a young man was discovered floating in the Jin River early this morning. Forensics tests confirmed that the individual drowned. His blood alcohol level was recorded at 213 milligrams per litre, indicating that he was intoxicated at the time of his death. The police suspect that the man slipped and accidentally fell into the river while attempting to urinate sometime after midnight. Chengdu's law enforcement authorities have also issued a reminder to all city residents, urging them to consume alcohol with caution.

Pei stared at the story for several minutes and tapped absently at his desk with his right index finger.

There were three knocks on the door, which finally brought him out of his trance. 'Come in,' he called out. He folded up the paper and placed it in a drawer.

Lieutenant Yin entered the room smiling. 'Captain, it's your birthday today, isn't it?'

'My birthday?' Pei unconsciously glanced at the calendar at the edge of his desk. The thirteenth of November. Yin was right. He grinned sheepishly. 'Slipped my mind completely. How did you know?'

'Someone's here with a gift for you,' Yin said, still smiling.

'Who?'

'No idea. Why don't you ask him?' Yin turned back towards the hallway. 'You can come in,' he said.

A man in a sky-blue uniform came in carrying a small box. 'You're Captain Pei, head of the April 18th Task Force?'

'Yes, I am,' he said and looked at the envelope on top of the box. He had no idea who'd sent it.

'A friend of yours ordered you a cake for your birthday. He specified that I must give it to you in person.' The man stepped forward and placed the cake on Pei's desk. 'Happy birthday!' he exclaimed at a volume that made Pei's eardrums flinch.

Pei looked at the envelope, but it was blank. 'Who sent the cake?' he asked, a smile playing on his lips. Although he was suspicious, it was hard to fight the almost boyish sense of surprise at receiving a present.

'He didn't give a name, but I'm sure you'll recognise him from the description,' the man said, his face twisting slightly. 'He looked pretty ragged, if you know what I mean.'

Pei stiffened and his smile vanished. 'Was he covered in burns?' he asked hesitantly.

'He was. All over his body. His whole face was scarred. To be honest, he looked like something out of a horror film.'

'Yuan?' Lieutenant Yin whispered.

Pei waved to silence him. 'When did he place this order?'

'About three weeks ago.'

Pei's eyes widened in understanding. Three weeks ago, Yuan Zhibang had strapped a bomb to himself and gone into the Jade Garden restaurant. Someone as thorough and meticulous as Yuan wouldn't have done that without having made all the necessary arrangements beforehand, but Pei never would have expected those arrangements to have included the birthday present currently in front of him. Was it a final farewell from a former friend or something more sinister?

'Captain Pei, if everything's all right with the cake, I'll need you to sign here.'

'Oh,' Pei said, returning to reality. He took the clipboard and signed the paper. 'That'll be all.'

'Got it!' the young man exclaimed and promptly turned around to leave the office.

Lieutenant Yin shut the door behind him. He looked tense. 'Should I have the lab test this cake first, Captain?'

Pei understood his meaning well enough, but he knew that Yuan would never resort to something as base as poisoning a cake. 'That won't be necessary,' he said softly.

He untied the string from around the box and picked up the envelope. Inside he found a birthday card, a slip of paper and several photographs. Each picture showed the same scrawny man. Pei didn't recognise him. He frowned as he searched his memory for a corresponding face. When nothing came to mind, he opened the card.

To Pei Tao, my closest friend and my greatest adversary.
Happy Birthday.
I've sent this person to you as a gift – I know you're all looking for him.

Yuan was clearly referring to the man in the photos, but who was he? More confused than ever, he finally looked at the slip of paper. His entire face turned pale.

Chen Tianqiao
Apartment 609, Building 18, Southern Coast Forest Community, Haikou, Hainan Island

17 November, 9:41 p.m.
Conference room, criminal police headquarters

Captain Pei and Lieutenant Yin looked at one another and saw that they were both equally exhausted. Just an hour earlier, their flight from Haikou on Hainan Island had touched down at Chengdu's Shuangliu Airport. Along with their meagre luggage, they had also brought something else back with them – Chen Tianqiao.

The three-day trip to Haikou had been no vacation, but Pei had found his target without much trouble. The police there had been very cooperative and with their help they'd cornered Chen in his apartment and arrested him in almost no time at all. Chen had been living under an assumed name for quite some time, but his fake ID hadn't deceived Pei for a second.

Chen looked exactly as he had in the photographs: thin and swarthy. He spoke with a silver tongue and his small eyes emitted a crafty gleam. Although he was pushing seventy, he had none of the trustworthiness that Pei typically associated with people of that age. Pei had an innate antipathy for people who made a living out of being deceitful. It was a struggle even to make eye contact with him when they spoke.

Once they were back at police headquarters in Chengdu, Pei took Chen to the holding cells and assigned an officer to guard him. He then called Ms Mu and TSO Zeng to the conference room, and together with Lieutenant Yin they began to discuss what to do next.

'We need to understand one thing first: why did Yuan do this?' Zeng asked. He kneaded his temples as he spoke. 'Right when we were worrying that we'd never be able to find Chen, Yuan basically delivered him to our doorstep. And if that wasn't enough, he arranged it three weeks ago,

421

before he died. Are we seriously supposed to believe that all this was simply intended as a generous birthday gift for you, Captain Pei?'

'I've been asking myself that same question for the last few days,' Pei said. 'I believe the most likely answer is that Yuan was attempting to fight with us for psychological control over Wen Chengyu. Three weeks ago, Yuan knew that his true identity was about to be exposed, which is why he killed himself at the Jade Garden restaurant. The new Eumenides already possessed all the technical skills he needed, but Yuan was still uncertain as to his apprentice's commitment to his mission.'

'You're absolutely right,' Ms Mu said. 'Wen Chengyu never had an opportunity to establish an independent worldview. Once his mentor left him, his faith in the Eumenides project would be tested. Yuan would have been shrewd enough to foresee that.'

Pei nodded approvingly. 'Yuan guessed that we would focus on Wen Chengyu's psychological weak points to try and make him give up being Eumenides. Before he died, Yuan made one last move. He gave us Chen, thus creating a new conflict between us and Wen Chengyu.'

Zeng shook his head in amazement. 'Yuan knew that his true identity would be revealed after the Jade Garden explosion. He also knew that Wen Chengyu would begin looking into his own history as soon as he found out who his mentor really was. Once Wen started delving into the January 30th hostage case, he'd see Chen Tianqiao as the person who caused his father's death. Which means that now, if Wen Chengyu wants vengeance, he'll have to kill a man in police custody. Thus sending him deeper into his role as Eumenides.'

'He left no possibility unaccounted for,' Lieutenant Yin said with grudging admiration. 'Even in death, this guy's controlling his apprentice like a damn puppet. He's a monster, through and through.'

'It's official, then. Our plan to convert Eumenides has failed,' TSO Zeng said.

Ms Mu shook her head. 'Not necessarily.'

Pei's tiredness suddenly lifted and he looked at the psychologist with newfound hope. Ms Mu had surprised him before and he was hoping that she was now about to do so again.

'Yuan knew that Wen Chengyu would begin investigating his background, but he may not have expected that he'd go so deep. Yuan killed Wen Hongbing, and the six-year-old Wen Chengyu was inadvertently responsible for putting Yuan in that position. I don't think Yuan would have anticipated his apprentice uncovering those particular details.'

Pei grunted in agreement. 'What kind of psychological impact will this knowledge have on Wen Chengyu?'

'A major one,' Ms Mu said. 'Were it not for that, Wen Chengyu would blame Chen for his father's death. But now that he has more information – and especially after he listens to the recording that Du's going to put online – things will get much more complicated. He'll see Yuan Zhibang, and even his own father, as ultimately responsible for what happened that day. More importantly, he'll know that the situation in that room was calming down before he made his birthday cake comment. That's going to make him feel guilty. He'll ask himself how differently things might have turned out if he hadn't asked his father that one question. That guilt will even overshadow his animosity towards Chen.'

'Yes! That's perfect!' TSO Zeng exclaimed, clapping his hands together. 'All we have to do is release Du's article and that audio recording to the public and we can finally say a long-overdue goodbye to Yuan Zhibang.'

Zeng's grin was infectious. Even Captain Pei felt the corners of his lips being tugged into a smile. He had no doubts about the success of Du's article.

Earlier, Pei had read Du's account of the hostage crisis with his heart in his mouth, almost forgetting that he already knew the outcome. He couldn't have hoped for a better piece of writing from the journalist. How could Wen Chengyu's anger and violent faith possibly remain intact after reading the piece?

'We can't allow ourselves to be too optimistic, though,' Ms Mu said. 'Nothing in the world is harder to understand than the human brain. Psychological research is extremely accurate when it comes to collecting and analysing data, but it becomes a much trickier science when trying to predict an individual's future thoughts or actions. Which path will Wen Chengyu choose? I'm afraid that's not something we can determine just by sitting around this table and talking.'

Pei looked at each team member around the table. 'And that means that regardless of what Wen Chengyu's decision is, we need to prepare for two possible outcomes,' he said.

'In that case, sir, I recommend that we consider using Chen as bait to catch Eumenides,' Lieutenant Yin said. 'Frankly, we don't have a choice. Even if Eumenides assassinates Chen and is then caught by the police, at least in a way that would be killing two birds with one stone.'

Pei waved his hand dismissively. 'Not so fast. First we need to hold Chen for suspected fraud. That way he'll be much more agreeable to anything we suggest. Right now we need to focus all of our attention on Du Mingqiang. If we have too much bait, we'll only get distracted.'

Lieutenant Yin nodded, but he didn't appear entirely convinced.

'It won't be easy to find hard evidence to support fraud charges against Chen. We won't be able to hold him for very long.'

'We just need to hold him until the end of the month,' Pei said. 'If by that time Du has actually been killed and we still haven't caught Eumenides, then we can concentrate our efforts on protecting Chen. Whatever happens, we'll get more opportunities to catch this guy. For now, we can wait.'

30 November, 11:59 p.m.
Du Mingqiang's apartment

The clock in the living room ticked away the seconds. A young man was sitting on the couch, staring at it. His face was red and coated in sweat. A row of empty beer bottles stood on the floor at his feet.

After so many days of being locked away, his moment had finally come.

He watched as the hands on the clock slowly aligned at the twelve.

It was time. He began to chuckle. He lurched up from the sofa and pumped his fists in the air.

The crash of shattering glass ended his impromptu victory dance. He froze, only to realise that he had kicked one of the bottles over and broken it. A moment later he resumed his laughing, even more wildly than before.

But laughter alone didn't seem quite enough. He picked up a second bottle and threw it against the wall. Then another. And another. The sound of breaking glass, almost musical to his ears, filled the room.

Once all of the empty beer bottles lay shattered across

the floor, the man looked at the clock again. It was five past midnight. The excitement of the past five minutes finally wore off. He raised his hand towards the chandelier, making a V-sign with his index and middle fingers.

Concealed inside the chandelier was a small camera. Identical cameras had been in place throughout his home for many weeks.

It was finally over.

He opened his apartment's heavy security door and looked out into the dark hallway. He coughed twice and the hallway lights flashed on.

A shadow dashed out of the darkness and suddenly there was someone standing by his door.

'Mission accomplished, SPU Captain Liu!' he exclaimed. 'It's all over!'

SPU Captain Liu looked closely at the man in the doorway. No one had ever survived beyond the date printed on a death notice from Eumenides – no one, that was, except Du Mingqiang. 'So it would seem,' he replied, and then directed Du to stay still while he checked for cuts or other injuries. He found none. Except for his drunken slouch, the journalist was in fine shape.

Liu took out his radio. After adjusting it to the correct frequency, he raised it to his mouth and said, 'Delta One, Delta One. This is Delta Three.'

'Go ahead, Delta Three,' Captain Pei replied.

'We've passed the deadline. Situation normal.'

The line was silent for a moment. Finally Liu heard the words he'd been waiting for.

'Return to headquarters.'

'Yes, sir!' he replied.

'Wait – let me say something!' Du exclaimed, reaching for the radio.

Liu hesitated, but he presumed that Du merely wanted to thank the police, so he controlled his temper and handed over the radio.

'Hey, is this Captain Pei?' Du asked, giggling excitedly. 'I'm still alive! Eumenides didn't even show up!'

'That does seem to be the case,' Pei said happily. 'You go ahead and get a good night's rest.'

Du wasn't ready to end the conversation just yet. 'Do you know why he didn't come?'

'Why's that?' Pei asked, humouring him.

'Because of my article. It was a masterpiece! I made one of the country's most infamous serial killers lay down his weapon. Name another journalist with that kind of talent! You can't, can you?'

Du didn't hear Pei's response because Liu had already snatched the radio away from him. Liu glared at Du and suddenly the night air felt much chillier.

'I'd drink to your health,' Liu said, 'but I can see that you've already done that.'

Du blinked and before he knew it the SPU officer was gone. Moments later, the stairway lights flashed off and the hallway was in darkness.

Alone, Du returned to his home of broken glass.

1 December, 8:07 a.m.
Criminal police headquarters

With his hands clasped behind his back, Captain Pei watched the guard open the iron door to the holding cell. Seconds later, the guard dragged out a dark, skinny man with a sour look on his face.

After two weeks in lockup, it was Chen Tianqiao's first taste of freedom. He squinted as he peered at the room's wide window, savouring the sight of the morning sky. 'It's almost winter, but the sun still feels good on these old bones,' he said.

'Chen Tianqiao,' Pei said, drawing closer to the man, 'having arrested you on suspicion of fraud, we've found that we have insufficient evidence with which to charge you. We can't detain you any longer.'

Chen's raspy snicker sounded like nails dragged against sandpaper. 'Like I said, no matter what you brought me in for, you were always gonna have to let me out sooner or later.'

Pei waved his hand to get the guard's attention. 'Bring him his things.'

Chen chuckled as he came closer to Pei. 'I'll never see the inside of an actual prison, no matter what you think I've been up to. You know why?'

Pei glared silently at him.

'Because I've never broken the law. I know what I'm doing, and I know the legal system better than any of you!'

The guard handed Chen a plastic bag containing his possessions. Chen set it down on a nearby table and rooted through the contents. Seconds later, he swaggered off speedily in the direction of the exit.

'You're letting him go just like that?' Lieutenant Yin asked, visibly disgusted.

'What would happen if we kept him here – would you punish him, like Eumenides?' Pei put his hand on his assistant's shoulder. 'Try not to dwell on it too much. The rest of the team is waiting for us.'

Ten minutes later, Pei and Lieutenant Yin joined Ms Mu, TSO Zeng, SPU Captain Liu and Huang in the conference room. It was there that the captain made an unexpected announcement to the task force.

'As of now, I'm temporarily dissolving the April 18th Task Force.'

'What?' SPU Captain Liu gasped in astonishment. 'But we haven't caught Eumenides yet!'

'And how are we supposed to catch him?' Pei replied equitably. 'The past two weeks haven't exactly been productive. We're at a standstill.'

Liu threw up his hands, while TSO Zeng simply shrugged. Ms Mu watched Captain Pei carefully, displaying no visible reaction.

'As far as we know, he's already given up,' Pei said. 'We have no usable leads. We have no idea what his public identity is, and besides his general height, weight and some grainy footage, we have no clear idea what he looks like. Now that Du Mingqiang's deadline is past, it's time we cut our losses.'

'But what about Chen Tianqiao?' Liu asked. 'Why haven't we assigned someone to keep an eye on him?'

'There's no need. Wen Chengyu has already let Du live. He won't go after Chen. He isn't Eumenides any more.'

'So that's it? This investigation is over, just like that?' Lieutenant Yin's face was long with disbelief.

Pei shrugged again. 'All we can do now is put the investigation on hold indefinitely. At least until another death notice appears.'

'I don't think we'll see another one of those,' Ms Mu said, shaking her head. 'It seems he's already given up the Eumenides role, so why would he return to it?'

'So the band's breaking up?' TSO Zeng asked, stretching lazily in his seat. 'I'm not heartbroken, to be honest. These last few weeks have been exhausting. It's time we all got some rest.'

The team members exchanged silent glances as they thought about all the work they'd put into this investigation. Eumenides, it seemed, was finished. While their collective efforts hadn't resulted in failure exactly, after six weeks of sweat and tears they couldn't help but feel short-changed by such an abrupt and unsatisfying ending.

Could it truly be over?

22

FATE

9:37 p.m.
The Green Spring

After she'd finished the violin piece, Zheng Jia slowly stood up and bowed to her audience. Although she couldn't see, she instinctively angled her body towards a certain table. It was where a certain man used to sit, but she didn't know when or if he would ever return.

She was greeted by the refined aroma of fresh lilies. Her heart pounded and she straightened up. She heard incoming footsteps – the heavy clack of hard-toed shoes – and felt a waiter press a bouquet into her hands.

'Where's the customer who sent these?' she asked, unable to restrain her excitement.

'He didn't come in.'

'Oh,' she said, her shoulders drooping slightly.

'But he said you'd know where to find him,' the waiter added cheerily.

One hour later

Zheng Jia opened the café's glass door and the familiar smell of freshly ground Arabica coffee and sandalwood incense wafted over her. She took a seat at the same table as the last time.

'Are you all finished?' she asked, unconsciously adopting a quiet, affectionate tone.

'I believe so,' the man answered a moment later, his voice as gentle as hers.

When they'd first met, she'd deflected his advances with polite, guarded smiles. Over time, that had changed. Today, she hid nothing and beamed openly at him.

'I've already contacted a doctor in America. I'll take you there and you will have that operation.'

'Really?' Her voice cracked. *Stay composed*, she thought. 'Why are you doing all this for me?'

As she waited for him to answer, she listened to the sounds around her. Clinking ceramic, the hiss of an espresso machine.

'Maybe it's fate.'

She frowned. 'Do you really believe in that?'

'In fate?'

'You don't strike me as the superstitious type. Although it is strange, come to think of it...' She tilted her head slightly to the right.

'Hmm?'

'Just over a month ago, before we met, I was standing beside my father's grave as his coffin was being lowered into it and I met someone – someone... *strange*. He gave me a gift.'

'What do you mean by "strange"?' the man asked suspiciously.

'He had a very raspy voice that was almost painful to listen to, but there was a weird charisma about him. With every word he said, I found myself oddly drawn to him. I didn't want to walk away. He must have looked very special, too. It's too bad I can't really describe him to you. I've never met anyone with that kind of power before.'

She heard a sharp but suppressed intake of breath from across the table.

'What did he give you?' His question came out unexpectedly choked.

'I don't know,' she said with a teasing smile. 'He wouldn't let me open it. He told me I had to give it to you.'

'To me? But you didn't even know me back then.'

'That's what's so strange. He told me that I might one day come across a certain man who would get very close to me but that it would be hard for me to get close to him. Sounds a lot like you, doesn't it?'

'What else did he say?' he asked with trepidation.

'He said that if the man really wanted to be with me, I should give him this.' She took a small box out of her handbag. 'I've been bringing this with me to the restaurant for the last few days, but I was starting to worry that I'd never actually get the chance to give it to you.'

He took the box from her and she heard him open it.

'He also told me to tell you something. Come to think of it, it's really similar to what you just told me,' she exclaimed enthusiastically.

'What did he say?'

'He said that it's your fate.'

He looked down. Inside was a microcassette tape. As he pondered what it could be, the memory of a raspy voice echoed in his ears. *'It's your fate – it was set in motion eighteen years ago.'*

10 December, 7:21 p.m.
Haikou, Hainan Island

The city of Haikou, located at the northern tip of Hainan Island, was well known as the premier place to retire in China. Chen Tianqiao had always loved its breathtaking views and balmy weather and was very pleased to be back after two weeks spent locked up in Chengdu.

He was at his favourite outdoor beachside restaurant for another evening of celebration, savouring his freedom and relishing each scallop and every mouthful of fresh crab as he sat there in the warm sea breeze. He liked to treat himself. Chen's philosophy of life revolved around eating, drinking and women. Everything should be enjoyed to the fullest, he thought. Personal pleasure was paramount, far more important than morals or friendship.

He'd already gone through most of his life that way, with no friends or family to speak of. That didn't bother him. The only thing that mattered was wealth, not sentiment. Money had allowed Chen to live out his final years in a seaside paradise and he was happy.

When those police officers had come to his home, they'd given him a fright. For a while he'd wondered if they'd somehow got hold of some incriminating evidence. In the end, though, they'd been unable to pin anything substantial on him. When he'd walked out of the police headquarters in Chengdu, it had taken all of his willpower not to throw his head back and laugh at the sky. He knew he'd won; he had triumphed over every single person he'd ever done business with, and in the end he'd even triumphed over the law.

Chen no longer had any worries.

Content, he polished off the last piece of crab on his plate.

As he dabbed at his mouth with his napkin, he raised a hand and called out, 'The bill!'

A tall waiter strode over to his table. Chen glanced at him and saw a beard and a mane of dark hair. It was hard to judge the man's age. 'New here?' he asked, and belched. 'Haven't seen you before.'

Smiling politely, the waiter respectfully used both hands to give his customer a small leather folder. Chen put on his reading glasses and scanned the piece of paper inside. His hands began to shake.

Death Notice
THE ACCUSED: Chen Tianqiao
CRIME: Homicide
DATE OF PUNISHMENT: 10 December
EXECUTIONER: Eumenides

'Is this some kind of joke?' he asked incredulously. He crumpled the paper into a ball and threw it at the waiter.

The balled-up death notice struck the waiter's face, but the man barely seemed to notice.

'It's time for you to pay,' the waiter said coldly. His right hand lunged at Chen and swept across his face.

Chen felt something cool running down his neck. Panicking, he tried to yell. No sound came out.

The waiter watched as blood poured from Chen's throat.

Chen gurgled and clutched at his neck. He pulled his hands away and gaped dumbly at the blood covering his fingers.

'This is a debt you've owed me for eighteen years,' the waiter said emotionlessly.

Eighteen years? Chen tried to remember where he'd been eighteen years ago.

As the blood continued to spurt from the gash in his throat, his senses gradually shut down. He fell forward onto the table, and one last thought filled his head before everything finally went black.

That was 1984, wasn't it?

The other diners noticed Chen's bloodied, lifeless body almost immediately. In seconds, the entire restaurant was in chaos. The waiter made his way out to the road with quick, bounding steps, removing his gauze gloves as he went. The streets were full of commuters on their way home and the traffic would provide him with plentiful cover.

As the waiter dashed into the street, the driver of a black Nissan looked up from his mobile phone in time to see him only a metre in front of him. In a panic, he slammed on the brakes. But he was already too close.

The waiter dove away from the car, but the middle finger of his left hand touched the side of the bonnet just before he tucked his head in and rolled across the tarmac. Ignoring the startled glances of several pedestrians, he quickly jumped up from the kerb and disappeared into the crowd.

Shrieks echoed down the street as more people spotted the dead man at one of the tables. Their piercing screams carried on the cool sea breeze.

10:40 p.m.
Haikou seaside bathhouse

He immersed himself in the steaming water, leaving only his head above the surface. The water scalded his skin, but he enjoyed the sensation.

The pool was almost completely silent; there were only two

other bathers. He let his limbs float freely, suspended in the hot water. The rising steam clouded his vision and his thoughts grew hazy.

In his mind he could hear music – a sweet violin melody. At one time he'd been fascinated by that music. It was the closest he'd ever come to experiencing heaven. But another sound quickly overpowered those luxurious strains. This was the sound of an eighteen-year-old recording. A recording that told an ugly story and which had forced him onto a path that he would pursue for the rest of his life. His ears ached at the memory of those hissing words and the untold anguish they'd caused.

There were some things he wished he could forget. But no matter how painful the path, he could not turn back. It was his fate.

The initial scalding sensation had passed, giving way to a mellow numbness that now suffused his entire body. He propped himself up on the seat that ran along the inside edge of the pool. 'Come and dry my back!' he called out, waving his hand high.

'Coming!' replied the attendant from his bench outside the bathing room. But the attendant didn't get up; instead, he turned to the older man sitting behind him, who was wearing a large towel around his waist. The second man smiled and gave the attendant a thumbs-up, then walked into the bathing room.

The attendant thought the older man was odd. Earlier, the man had handed him a hundred-yuan note and requested that when the young man in the bathing room asked to be towelled off, he should let the stranger do it. The attendant was thrilled. To have someone else both pay him and do his job – what could be better than that? He was surprised, but he happily agreed.

He didn't judge, but he did watch curiously as the strange man pulled a hot towel from the shelf and approached the young man in the water. Clouds of steam drifted across the room, casting a ghostly haze over them both. Once he was behind the bather in the pool, the older man used his left hand to towel down the young man's back; with his other hand, he held the man's right arm.

The attendant on the bench shook his head. *Amateur*, he thought. The protocol was to dry a bather with the right hand and hold his left arm with the left hand. This man had it all backwards.

In the pool, the younger man sensed that something was wrong. He turned his head to the side and felt a sudden chill on his right wrist. He tried to move his hand away, but something heavy was pinning it down.

Click.

The man spun around and through the fog he saw a familiar figure. A pair of handcuffs gleamed in the moist air, linking their hands together.

'Captain Pei?' he said in shock.

Pei snapped the towel over their hands, covering the handcuffs. 'If you try anything, you'll attract the attention of the local police,' he said, glancing over at the attendant on the bench. He removed the towel from his waist and joined his captive in the water. 'Let's have a chat.'

The young man's shock had already faded. He grinned at the police officer. 'You're vacationing here as well, Captain Pei? What a coincidence.'

Pei returned his smile. He sat down beside the young man and lowered his left hand, submerging the handcuffs well below the surface. 'So what should I call you – Wen Chengyu or Du Mingqiang?'

'What do you mean?' he asked, giving Pei a blank look.

Pei narrowed his eyes at the feigned confusion that the young man wore like a mask. With a bitter smile, he said, 'I have to give you credit for one thing. You put on an extremely convincing act. Even after I realised who you really were, it was still hard to believe you were the same person who'd been terrorising us for the last two months.'

'I don't understand,' he said.

'I've been watching you for the past ten days, since December the first, when the April 18th Task Force was disbanded. Do you really want to keep this charade going?' Pei sighed. 'We're having an honest, naked discussion. There's no one else around. You can stop pretending.'

An intense silence followed. The man stared out into the swirling vapour. When he finally looked back at Pei, the captain felt like he was seeing a different person. The mask had dropped. He was no longer Du Mingqiang. The arrogant, narcissistic reporter was gone and in his place was a cold, calculating killer. He stared into Pei's eyes as if he was boring deep into his mind.

Pei had never met anyone who could juggle two identities so skilfully. Not even Yuan.

'What gave me away?'

'Our breakthrough in the January 12th Bagman Killing,' Pei said. 'You hadn't stolen the archive files for that case, but you still analysed it very accurately. So I knew that you had a source inside the police. Once I realised that, I began to suspect you. I was sure that no one in the task force was a mole. Maybe they were being used by someone else without their knowledge, but that was unlikely. And at that point there was only one outsider the task force was in frequent contact with. You.'

'I was impatient,' Wen Chengyu said, his voice tinged with regret. 'I should have played it cool.'

'Since I couldn't figure out exactly how you were getting this information, my only option was to dissolve the task force. Doing that would cut off your inside access and would also avoid arousing your suspicions.'

'The day you took me in, I used Ms Mu's phone. When I switched out the SIM card, I installed a listening device inside her phone casing.'

Pei couldn't help but smile at the terrible irony. Ms Mu had been present at all of the task force's discussions on the January 12th Bagman case. Eumenides had listened in on every meeting, like a fly on the wall.

'I didn't have any other options,' he explained. 'I was anxious to find out the truth behind my father's death and your team was keeping a tight grip on every potential lead. That's why I decided to piggyback off your efforts for my own investigation.'

'When we brought Huang to the internet café,' Pei said, 'I intentionally mentioned the reporter "Zhen Rufeng". But you killed that reporter and took his place. When we tried to bring Zhen Rufeng in, we actually gave you an opportunity to infiltrate our headquarters.'

'Oh?' Wen Chengyu raised his eyebrows. 'You know I killed the reporter?'

'The way "Zhen Rufeng" questioned Teacher Wu was nothing like your usual style. You couldn't have been the one who made that recording. Also, Eumenides would never issue a death notice that he couldn't carry out. After I realised those things, I spent a lot of time thinking about the ink blotting out the date on Du's death notice. It was meant to be November the first, wasn't it? You played mind games with us in order to conceal the truth. When we found the notice, we immediately stepped up our safeguarding efforts for the rest of the month. But we failed to realise that you had already made good on your notice several hours before we found it.'

Wen Chengyu gave Pei an approving look. 'Spot on.'

'No murders were recorded on November the first,' Pei went on, 'so I checked the police records for any accidental deaths that day. I discovered that a man named Tong Mulin had been found in the Jin River early that morning. According to the report, he was intoxicated and fell in by accident. After digging into his financial records, I was positive that he was the unscrupulous online reporter who called himself Zhen Rufeng. I made sure to carry out that investigation through a separate branch of the criminal police. Not even your listening device would have helped you there.'

'You're so careful, Captain. I was sloppy when I killed Tong Mulin. You were doing all you could to track him down, so I needed to take his place as quickly as I could. I didn't have time to take care of all the details surrounding Tong, so I just took a few key pieces of information and used them to disguise myself.'

'And then you were right in the heart of enemy territory. You even wrote about the fake Eumenides killings at the Longyu Building, knowing all along that they were a setup! You have guts – that's for sure. Did you even consider the possibility that we might see through your ruse? It could have been all over the second we found Tong.'

'Yes,' Wen Chengyu said calmly, 'but I knew you wouldn't try to find him. If I hadn't got anxious when I was forcing Captain Ding to reveal himself, you wouldn't have suspected me at all, would you?'

Pei made no attempt to refute that. 'You had me fooled. I wouldn't have seen the complete picture if it hadn't been for someone else's input.'

'Whose?' His face lit up with sudden comprehension. 'Ah. It was Captain Ding, wasn't it?'

Pei nodded.

Wen Chengyu chuckled. 'Provoking him was far from wise, but what other choice did I have? There were things I needed to clear up.' He somehow sounded both resigned and relieved at the same time.

'There are still two things I don't entirely understand,' Pei said.

Wen Chengyu stared at him in silence.

'Firstly, why did you voluntarily restrict your own movements? When you turned yourself over to the police, you knew we'd be obligated to watch you around the clock. Were you prepared to stay cooped up for an entire month?'

'My situation wasn't as absolute as you think. I made sure to leave myself a way out if I needed one. You'd understand what I mean if you'd checked the bedroom.'

'A hidden passageway?'

He nodded. 'I rented the adjacent apartment as well. There's a ventilation shaft in the bedroom that connects to the other apartment. Whenever I needed to leave, I just waited until SPU Captain Liu was fast asleep, then disguised myself and slipped out for a while.'

'I suppose I should have thought of that,' Pei said. 'But there's something else I haven't been able to work out – how did you fake your identity? We both know that your real name isn't Du Mingqiang, but no matter how many times I checked your credentials, I couldn't find a single problem. How did you pull that off?'

Wen Chengyu was silent for a moment. 'I didn't fake those credentials,' he finally said. 'They're real.'

'But your name is Wen Chengyu,' Pei said, giving him a suspicious look.

FATE

'My name is Wen Chengyu, and it's also Du Mingqiang. I have a lot of names,' he said with a hint of pride. 'Legally speaking, every one of my IDs is completely valid.'

Every nerve in Pei's body tensed.

'It began when I was fourteen years old. My mentor took me to every province in the country. We scoured the streets for young men of around eighteen years of age who'd run away from home. If we found someone who fitted our requirements, we discreetly took care of them. Once I had their ID, I went to their home and stole their residence book. I then had a new ID card made with my photograph. That's how I started accumulating new identities, all of them technically legal. I've got more than a dozen in all. They originate from all over China, from the countryside and from major cities, and they're for a range of ages in the twenties and thirties. I have identities ready to deploy in every conceivable situation.'

Despite the scalding water he was immersed in, Pei shivered. Yuan Zhibang and Wen Chengyu had killed those young men. They'd killed more than a dozen people simply to further their own criminal ends.

'What do you mean when you say they fitted your requirements?' he asked in a near whisper.

'They had to have no criminal record, and the more estranged they were from their family, the better. Ideally, they were orphans. Take Du Mingqiang, for instance. Even if you knew that I wasn't really him, you'd have no way to prove it.' Wen Chengyu seemed to notice Pei's horrified expression and he turned away slightly. 'They might have been young, but every one of them had committed a lot of despicable acts. If we'd let them live, they would only have wreaked more havoc on society.'

Pei took a deep breath. Wen Chengyu had gone too far. Pei

443

realised there was a truly unbridgeable gulf between them. Another thought came to him. 'So that explains why we never found any records of your training. You have so many different legal identities.'

'That's right. I trained in different places, using different identities. You'll never be able to track down someone who matches my background. In a way, I'm made up of almost twenty different selves. Individually, there's nothing special about any one of them.'

'You spent eighteen years preparing,' Pei whispered.

'Yuan made sure we were ready for anything – financially, logistically and psychologically.'

'I'm still curious as to how you and Yuan managed to accumulate enough funds to carry out this plan.'

'Isn't it obvious?' Wen Chengyu said with a dark smirk. 'Let me give you an example. If you hadn't handcuffed me after I killed Chen Tianqiao, tomorrow I would have poured millions of yuan into one of my various bank accounts.'

Of course, Pei thought. By Eumenides' skewed logic, the property of any one of his victims was fair game.

'I've already answered enough of your questions.' Wen Chengyu looked Pei in the eye. 'Now I'd like you to give me some honest answers.'

Pei met his gaze and nodded.

'If you'd already figured out who I was after Professor Ding killed himself, why didn't you arrest me then?'

'I didn't have enough evidence. Like I said, I couldn't find a way to discredit your ID. Interrogating you wouldn't work either.'

'So everything you did after that point was done to gather the evidence you wanted?'

Pei hesitated. 'What are you referring to?'

'During our final meeting, you gave me that tape as well as the files for the January 30th hostage case. You also told your task force that you hoped to stop Eumenides from killing by using psychological methods, even if that meant forfeiting the chance to catch him.'

'I was telling the truth. I did hope that those things would make you cast off the mantle of Eumenides,' Pei said. 'But I knew, of course, that the outcome of Du Mingqiang's death notice wouldn't tell me anything. I had to wait and see what happened to Chen Tianqiao. Our long wait through the rest of November was indeed a diversion. The real battle began on the first of December, when I started following you.'

Wen Chengyu snickered dryly. 'You'd make a good killer, you know. I had no idea that someone was following me.'

Pei grinned. 'So, if I may ask, what's going on between you and that young woman?'

'I like her music, nothing more,' he answered sourly, staring up at the ceiling.

'Oh, I know it's much more than that. I saw the two of you together the other night, just hours after I began following you. She's very fond of you and I'm sure you like more than just her music.'

Wen Chengyu remained silent. He'd either been rendered speechless by that observation, Pei thought, or he simply couldn't bring himself to deny it.

'I honestly believed that you'd given up on being Eumenides,' Pei said. 'You'd found someone you wanted to be with.'

Wen Chengyu shut his eyes.

'The next day, I discovered that you'd begun to discreetly follow Chen. As you pursued him from Chengdu all the way here, to Haikou, I stayed right on your tail. It's hard to say exactly how I felt while I was following you. I knew I was finally close to arresting Eumenides, but that wasn't the result I truly wanted.' Pei sighed. 'Why? Why, after all this, did you still make the same choice?'

Wen Chengyu didn't open his eyes. 'Why did you wipe the end of the recording from the tape?'

'You've heard the end of that recording?' Pei asked in surprise.

'My mentor anticipated every eventuality,' Wen Chengyu said with a sardonic grin. 'When he realised that I'd fallen for the young woman, he knew what path I'd eventually take. Before he died, he entrusted her with a tape. She gave it to me on the night you saw us together.'

Pei began to feel like he was suffocating. With all his planning, how could he have overlooked something so obvious? Eighteen years ago, Yuan had taken the tape and copied it. All these years later, he'd anticipated Pei's ploy and he'd pre-empted it by divulging the tape's entire contents to Wen Chengyu.

Wen Chengyu finally opened his eyes and looked directly at Pei. 'There's no need for you to ask me why I've made the choice I have,' he said softly. 'The fact that you were faced with the truth but erased the end of the recording already tells me enough.'

Pei pressed his lips together. Perhaps Wen Chengyu was right. He'd wiped the end of the recording, just as Captain Ding had recommended, for one simple reason: he thought the truth would be too much for Wen Chengyu to bear.

'Did you get me a birthday cake, Daddy?' a young voice had called out.

A brief silence passed before Wen Hongbing answered. *'I... I'll buy it for you soon.'*

'Your dad's lying to you, kid! He doesn't have any money. He can't afford to get you a cake,' a shrill voice interrupted. *'You'll never get a cake for your birthday.'*

The child began to sob.

'Give me back my money! I want my money!'

'I keep telling you – I don't have it.'

'Stop right there and stay calm!'

'You bastard! Liar! I'm going to kill you!'

'Let him go!

There were the sounds of a scuffle, and the shrill voice yelled out in pain. Then came the deafening crack of a gunshot.

'Are you insane?' Yuan shouted. *'Why the hell did you provoke him? Did you not see the bomb he was wearing?'*

'What's there to be afraid of?' the shrill-voiced man asked slyly. *'It's not like it was going to go off!'*

'What do you mean?'

'The bomb was a fake!' shrieked Chen Tianqiao gleefully.

The noise of approaching voices had swelled as the police swarmed in, and the recording had ended.

'It isn't some complex web of cause and effect,' Wen Chengyu said. 'There's no helplessness, no confusion. Everything is as clear as it could be. So clear that the thought of what happened still makes me shudder. I felt only one emotion after listening to that recording. Hatred. A hatred so pure that it forced me to take certain actions.'

Pei shook his head disconsolately. He tried to think of a way he could have been more resourceful, but his mind was empty. How could he tell him that he was wrong? Perhaps Captain Ding's theory of cause and effect really did have nothing to do with it. Yuan Zhibang, Wen Hongbing, even the young Wen Chengyu, who had simply wanted a birthday cake – none of them bore any responsibility for that day's tragic outcome. All the facts pointed to a single catalyst: Chen Tianqiao.

On that day, Chen had been victorious. His creditor was shot dead right in front of him, leaving him free to abscond with Wen Hongbing's cash. Yuan had known the truth from the start but was unable to take any action against Chen. In the eyes of the law, Chen wasn't guilty.

A police officer's firearm was supposed to be an adjunct in the administration of justice. But the bullet fired from Yuan's gun had become part of something sinister. This shattered his faith in the institution of law enforcement. Never again would he trust in the law; he would trust only in himself. Pei understood why at that moment his old friend had vowed to use his abilities to rid the world of evil.

'After I finished listening to that tape, I had a revelation,' Wen Chengyu said in the measured tone of a teacher instructing a student. 'I no longer had any doubts. The tape was a guiding light leading me to the truth. I thank my mentor, for in the end he gave me Chen.'

A feeling of utter helplessness pressed down on Pei. He'd once believed that he could win Wen Chengyu over to his side, but that was no longer a possibility. Pei had said all that he could. He stared down into the water. 'Perhaps I should notify the local police.'

'You didn't bring your own people with you?'

Pei shook his head. 'Like I said, I dissolved the task force. I came here on my own. I feel more comfortable dealing with you myself, anyway.'

'That was a wise move. If you'd joined forces with anyone else, I'd have noticed. But I'm still surprised you came on your own.'

'We police may have a lot of resources at our disposal, but you've always had an advantage over us. You work in the shadows, whereas we work in the light. But once I found out who you really were, our roles were reversed, and that's how I was able to catch you off guard.'

Wen Chengyu gave a slight nod. 'But you're just one person. No wonder you didn't try to confront me back at the restaurant.'

'Exactly. I had to work alone in order to stay off your radar, but catching you wasn't easy. I had to wait for the right opportunity. Like this one.' Pei gestured at the bathing room with his free hand. 'We're naked and handcuffed together. It's not exactly easy for you to try anything in a situation like this.'

Wen Chengyu smirked sheepishly.

On a whim, Pei decided to say one more thing. 'Actually, there's another reason why I acted alone.'

'Oh?'

'Something occurred to me after I listened to that tape. I understood how difficult it would be for Chen's accused crime of homicide to stand up in court.'

'Do you mean that you think it was right that he died? You actually agree with me?' The corners of Wen Chengyu's eyes crinkled.

'Perhaps Yuan was right about some things,' Pei said. 'We stand on opposing sides, but we can have similar goals.'

Wen Chengyu flashed a large smile. 'Well, since you didn't apprehend me at the scene of the crime, what evidence do you plan to use to bring me in? After all, my credentials will stand up to scrutiny. You've already admitted that.'

'It's been difficult, trying to get evidence on you. I didn't want to be on the same flight to Haikou as you and risk being discovered. As soon as I got off the plane, though, I followed Chen Tianqiao. I knew that you'd turn up eventually. When he got to the restaurant earlier this evening, I finally spotted you. Even though you were dressed as a waiter and wore a fake beard, I could tell from the way you moved that it was you. I watched you kill Chen, and I watched as you merged into the crowd and crossed the street. You were so fast that I actually lost you for half a minute. When I spotted you again, you'd already discarded your disguise.'

Wen Chengyu looked pleased. 'My question remains: where's your evidence?'

'I wouldn't have handcuffed you without evidence,' Pei said confidently. 'Specifically, a photo that I took.'

'Of me killing Chen? How are you going to prove that the man with long hair and a beard covering half his face is actually me?'

'Remember when you were ripping off your disguise? When you crossed the road, a black Nissan nearly hit you. You dodged it, but you also touched its bonnet as you got out of the way.'

'That's right,' he said, sighing. 'My middle finger touched the bonnet.'

'I took a picture when that happened. I was several storeys up. High enough to get a full shot of the vehicle's licence plate.'

Wen Chengyu's eyes widened in realisation. 'You've already got my fingerprint, haven't you?' Though he sounded unruffled, Pei noticed that his chest had begun to rise and fall more quickly.

'With this fingerprint, the photograph of you touching the car, and the testimonies of the driver and the witnesses in the photograph, I'm sure I'll have enough evidence.'

Surprisingly, Wen Chengyu smiled again. 'Captain, do you remember which of my hands touched the car?' he asked.

Pei frowned. He wasn't sure where Wen Chengyu was going with this, and there was something unsettling about his question. 'Your left hand. I remember that very clearly.'

'Then you shouldn't have handcuffed my right.'

Wen Chengyu raised his left hand. As Pei watched, he stuck the first joint of his middle finger into his mouth and bit down.

'What the hell are you doing?' Pei yelled. His heart raced as he tried to think of a way to stop Wen Chengyu. Was he already too late?

Blood flowed from Wen Chengyu's lips and dripped down his chin. When he took his finger out of his mouth, the first joint was missing.

Pei watched, stunned. Wen Chengyu's blood spattered into the pool like raindrops, quickly staining the water a sickeningly bright shade of red.

Wen Chengyu showed not even the slightest hint that he was in pain through any of this. With an expression as serene as a monk's, he swallowed.

'My name is Du Mingqiang. I'm an online journalist. Tong Mulin and I worked together. We both used the same pseudonym: Zhen Rufeng. It's true that I infiltrated your task force and even installed a listening device in your colleague's phone. But I had a reason for doing all of that. You see, a journalist needs to seek out the truth.' His lips spread into a smug, familiar grin. 'My mission is to become the world's greatest journalist!'

EPILOGUE

11 February 2003, 4:07 p.m.
Chengdu Intermediate People's Court

The members of the court stood as the judge prepared to deliver the sentence.

'The People's Procuratorate of the city of Chengdu has charged the defendant, Du Mingqiang, with falsifying identification credentials, illegally obtaining national secrets, the illegal use of audio recording equipment, and multiple counts of homicide. After accepting this case and assembling a full court in accordance with the law, we have called this court to order and held a hearing. A verdict has been reached.

'This hearing has ascertained that during November 2002 the defendant misused the police protection afforded him and used electronic listening equipment to monitor an ongoing police investigation for his own purposes. These actions satisfy the charges of illegally obtaining national secrets and the illegal use of audio recording equipment.

'Due to the plaintiff's failure to provide the necessary evidence of falsified identification, this court finds no basis for this charge. Due to the inconclusive evidence submitted regarding the murders of Tong Mulin and Chen Tianqiao, this court finds no basis for this charge.

'According to the stipulations as detailed in Clause 282 and Clause 284 of the Criminal Law of the People's Republic of China, the court's decision is as follows. The defendant is sentenced to three years' imprisonment for the crime of illegally obtaining national secrets. The defendant is also sentenced to two years' imprisonment for the illegal use of audio recording equipment. In total, the defendant is sentenced to five years' imprisonment.'

The members of the April 18th Task Force shook their heads. Just as they had expected, their most important charges had failed to hold up under the scrutiny of the court.

Out of all of them, Captain Pei took this news the hardest. It was his negligence that had allowed Wen Chengyu to bite off and swallow the tip of his finger, thus erasing conclusive evidence that would have finally linked him to murder. Even though this action had raised no small amount of suspicion in court, it wasn't found to be sufficient for a guilty verdict.

Nevertheless, Wen Chengyu was going to prison. And his missing fingertip would help them identify him when they went looking for him after his release. A distinguishing feature like that would be hard to overlook.

As Pei thought about how he would still be able to track Eumenides in the future, his guilt lessened. He even felt slightly relieved. Somewhere deep in his heart the captain didn't wish to send Wen Chengyu to his end just yet.

Wen Chengyu concealed a faint smile beneath his expressionless face. He was still alive and that was the most important thing.

His survival was partly down to luck, to be sure, but it was also thanks to his own meticulous planning.

Caution had guided his every action during the month he'd spent with the April 18th Task Force and he'd made sure that they'd not obtained so much as a single fingerprint from him. Before he'd gone to the bathhouse, he'd wiped down every surface in his apartment. He'd actually felt conflicted at the time, wondering whether that was really necessary, but his training had kicked in. Yuan had saved him once again.

Although the remaining evidence had allowed the court to sentence him to several years in jail, he was not afraid of prison. At Yuan's prompting, he'd once spent an entire year in prison. He knew all too well how those places operated and how to deal with the people inside.

'Du Mingqiang' now had a criminal record. But Wen Chengyu still had more than a dozen identities that had never been linked to a single crime. He also knew that Pei would never be able to discover them. When he walked out of prison a free man, he would easily be able to vanish into the shadows once more.

He had lost part of his left hand, but he had not lost everything. The path of Eumenides was still his, and he knew that he was fated to follow it to the end.

END OF PART TWO

ABOUT THE AUTHOR

ZHOU HAOHUI was born in 1977 and lives in Yangzhou City, Jiangsu Province. His *Death Notice* trilogy is China's bestselling crime series. An online TV drama based on the novels has received more than 2.4 billion views, making it one of China's most popular online shows ever.